In a rush, Landon remembered last night.

The way she'd climbed on him, claimed him. Kimber thought about it, too. He could tell by the way she tipped her chin… And he was kissing her again. With no more invitation than that. He moved his lips slowly, gently over hers, his fingers stilling on her neck, her hand covering one of his. Then it was over and he was pulling his head back to train his eyes on hers.

"I want you," he told her. "Badly."

She watched him, motionless and silent instead of fidgety and flabbergasted.

A good sign. "Say something."

"This is the part where I'm supposed to say this is a bad idea, right? That we should be responsible and not get involved."

"Probably," he admitted.

Her eyes turned up to his. "But I don't want to say that."

His hopes levitated. Despite his reasoning not to encourage her, he did. "Then say what you want."

"I want you," she whispered.

"Honey," he rasped, tightening his hold on her arms. "You can have me."

ACCLAIM FOR
TEMPTING THE BILLIONAIRE

"A smashing debut! Charming, sexy, and brimming with wit—you'll be adding Jessica Lemmon to your bookshelves for years to come!"
    —Heidi Betts, *USA Today* bestselling author

"Lemmon's characters are believable and flawed. Her writing is engaging and witty. If I had been reading this book out in public, everyone would have seen the *huge* grin on my face. I had so much fun reading this and adore it immensely."
    —LiteraryEtc.wordpress.com

"If you are interested in a loveable romance about two troubled souls who overcome the odds to find their own happily ever after, I would certainly recommend that you give *Tempting the Billionaire* a try. It was definitely a great Valentine's Day read, for sure!"
    —ChrissyMcBookNerd.blogspot.com

"The awesome cover opened to even more awesome things inside. It was realistic! Funny! Charming! Sweet!"
    —AbigailMumford.com

The

MILLIONAIRE
AFFAIR

The

MILLIONAIRE
AFFAIR

JESSICA LEMMON

FOREVER

NEW YORK   BOSTON

Copyright © 2014 by Jessica Lemmon
Excerpt from *Tempting the Billionaire* copyright © 2013 by Jessica Lemmon
Excerpt from *Hard to Handle* copyright © 2013 by Jessica Lemmon
All rights reserved. In accordance with the U.S. Copyright Act of 1976, the scanning, uploading, and electronic sharing of any part of this book without the permission of the publisher constitute unlawful piracy and theft of the author's intellectual property. If you would like to use material from the book (other than for review purposes), prior written permission must be obtained by contacting the publisher at permissions@hbgusa.com. Thank you for your support of the author's rights.

Forever
Hachette Book Group
237 Park Avenue
New York, NY 10017

www.HachetteBookGroup.com

Printed in the United States of America

First Edition: June 2014

10 9 8 7 6 5 4 3 2 1

OPM

Forever is an imprint of Grand Central Publishing.
The Forever name and logo are trademarks of Hachette Book Group, Inc.

The Hachette Speakers Bureau provides a wide range of authors for speaking events. To find out more, go to www.hachettespeakersbureau.com or call (866) 376-6591.

The publisher is not responsible for websites (or their content) that are not owned by the publisher.

*For Mom & Dad, and all the sacrifices
you made (and continue to make) for me.*

Love you guys.

ACKNOWLEDGMENTS

Oh, Landon Downey. To understand this hero's motivations, I had to first figure out one very important component: Why would a man voluntarily choose emotionless, controlled relationships when he's from a close, loving family? The answer took me on a deeper, more emotional journey than I'd anticipated. And was *so* worth it. But, I didn't find the answer alone.

Thanks to plotting partners-in-crime Teri Anne Stanley, Charissa Weaks, and Maisey Yates for helping me wrestle with the initial ideas for this book. Some I used, some I didn't, but this book was a journey, and you all are a valid part of it. To my agency sib (and fellow extrovert) Tonya Kuper for beta reading and for loving this book. You're encouraging and genuine—I'm blessed to know you.

My agent, Nicole Resciniti, who gushed over this story and made me feel as much a millionaire as Landon. My editor, Lauren, whose comments always cause me to smile. I love working with you both—you push me to mine for gold and when we find it, I'm reminded of the value of a team.

To my publicist, editing team, cover artists, and all the other hardworking people behind the scenes at Forever, thank you for all your hard work.

And to you, reader, for sharing this journey with me. Don't tell Aiden or Shane, but I think Landon may have won my heart. If anyone deserves a happily ever after, it's Landon Downey and Kimber Reynolds. I hope you enjoy reading their story as much as I enjoyed writing it.

~Jess

The

MILLIONAIRE
AFFAIR

$\mathscr{P}$ROLOGUE

$\mathscr{L}$andon Downey clutched the baby name book *From Abba to Zed* to his chest and knocked on his girlfriend's dorm room door. While he was certain he didn't want to name their child Abba or Zed, he was also certain he couldn't show up empty-handed. Not after the ugly way they'd parted last week. He should have shown up with something nicer than a book with a bent corner and a bouquet of half-dead flowers, but the twenty-four-hour convenience store on campus hadn't offered many options.

He'd been an asshole. Rachel had come to him in full-on panic mode. Rightly so, considering the stick with two blue lines she'd carried in her hand. Landon had been severely hungover courtesy of a late party at Cliff's house. At the moment she had burst into his apartment sobbing, he'd had two things on his mind: *Where is the Tylenol?* and *I'm running late.* Finals week had started with a bang.

While he'd hustled around the house looking for his books and swallowing a couple of pain relievers, Rachel had followed, irate by this bit of inconvenient news, angry because birth control was *"supposed to work, dammit!"*, and generally pitching a fit about how she had neither the time nor the patience to deal with a baby. "I won't sacrifice my law career for a child I didn't plan to have!" she'd said.

He'd hastily agreed while gathering his things—admittedly not the best thing to do—but he simply couldn't focus on the huge, life-changing news she'd laid at his feet. Especially when he was running on only three hours of sweaty, post-drunken sleep *and* before he'd had a single drop of coffee.

Hindsight being what it was, he now knew what he *should have* done. He should have ditched class entirely. He should have stopped rushing and given Rachel his full attention. He should have reminded her they loved each other and they could work out whatever sharp curve life had thrown their way.

But he hadn't done either of those things. Instead he'd agreed with her that *yes*, the timing was bad and *yes*, the birth control should have worked, and then he'd told her he'd see her after class. But he hadn't seen her that night. Or the next. She'd managed to avoid him the entire week.

He knocked again.

Finally, the door opened and her roommate, Tina, blocked the doorway, her expression a mix of fury and protectiveness. "What do you want?"

Ignoring her tone, he held up the bouquet of flowers. "I need to talk to Rachel."

"Maybe she doesn't want to talk to you."

"Yes," came a small, tired voice from behind Tina. "She does." Rachel patted her friend-slash-bodyguard's shoulder and Tina stepped aside, shooting a final, wary look over her shoulder at him. He studied his girlfriend—probably now his *ex*-girlfriend given the way things were going tonight. Rachel was pale, her face splotchy, and looked like she had the flu. No, not the flu. Probably morning sickness.

His heart lurched in a not entirely uncomfortable way. *A baby*. He clutched the book to his chest, still hidden behind the sad bouquet of dyed purple and pink and royal blue daisies, and forced the words out of his throat. "Can I come in?"

She pushed a lock of long, brown hair away from her face and shook her head.

Okay. She was angry. But he could get past angry. He'd thought a lot about their predicament, about the unexpectedness of raising a child while they were in college—of getting married way, *way* sooner than he'd planned. She'd have to drop some classes as her pregnancy advanced, though he knew she'd insist on working after. Meanwhile, he'd hustle to finish his degree. He'd landed an internship at an ad agency in Chicago that sounded promising. The two-hour train ride from campus would be inconvenient, but he was willing to commute. When the internship turned into a career, she could finish out her degree and he could balance the rest. They'd make it work.

Rachel, like him, was far too logical and pragmatic to allow her future to be compromised. Besides, people dealt with unexpected pregnancies all over the world, all the time.

We'll make it work, he told himself again.

"Come on, Rachel. Let me in. It's one in the morning and I'm standing out here getting eaten by mosquitoes." When she didn't smile, he said, "We need to talk."

"There's nothing to talk about."

Was she joking? There were fifteen things to talk about. He knew because he had a typed list in his back pocket. "Yes. There is," he told her. "Plans need to be made. Plans for us."

"There is no *us*," she said, her face a placid mask.

He blinked, taking in her puffy, red eyes and curled upper lip. She was...leaving him? What was she going to do? Raise his child without him? No, no. He wouldn't allow it. She was angry; saying things she didn't mean. First, he'd talk his way into her room, give her the name book, then pull out the list he'd made and *they would work this out*.

"If not for us"—he swallowed thickly and tried again—"then for the baby."

She lifted her chin, her eyes filling with tears. "There is no baby." She shot him the coldest, hardest glare he'd ever seen. Landon's heart dropped into his stomach, the air snagging in his lungs.

Then she slammed the door in his face.

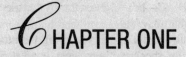HAPTER ONE

16 years later.

*A*nother shout sounded from beyond the bathroom door and Landon reached out and silently flicked the lock. He didn't know how long he could remain in here undetected, but it was worth a shot.

"Hang on," he said into the phone.

His sister, Angel, chuckled. "Where are you, anyway? You sound all echoey."

He pressed his cell phone to his cheek and lowered his voice. "Echoey is not a word. I'm hiding in the bathroom."

She barked a laugh. "From our nephew? Landon, really."

"I think I bit off more than I can chew," he mumbled, pacing the tiled floor. On his second pass between shower and sink, he noticed the ruckus that had driven him in here had stopped. *Suspicious.* He shushed Angel and held his breath, pressed his ear to the door to listen. Nothing. He unlocked it and poked his head out.

"Hello?" she whispered.

"He's gone into stealth mode," he said quietly. She erupted into another fit of laughter. "Send reinforcements."

Tiptoeing in his socks through his bedroom, he sidled along the wall and around the dresser. Back pressed against the bedroom door, he peeked into the hallway.

"*Rawr!*"

A blur that may well have been his life flashing before his eyes nearly took Landon's head off. He stilled the object with one palm—a plastic light saber—and Lyon grinned up at him, a gap where one of his front teeth should be. Thankfully, the tooth had been missing when he got here.

"You're dead!" Lyon shouted.

"Not in the hall." His voice held a comical tremor. "You're going to break something." *Like my nose.*

"Okay!" With that, Lyon turned on a heel and went tearing down the hallway, swinging the light saber with renewed vigor.

"Do you want Auntie Angel to talk to him?"

Landon stepped into the hallway and, with one more cautious look over his shoulder, made a break for the kitchen. "I can't get anything done with him here," he said as he neared the end of the hall. "How did you keep him for *two weeks*?"

The way he'd said it made two weeks sound like *two years*. May as well be. Lyon had thwarted both attempts at getting on his company's conference call and several other attempts to check his e-mail from his phone. "Seriously, did you drug him or something?" he asked, only half kidding.

"Maybe I'm more maternal than you think," she quipped. He thought of Angel's struggle to get pregnant and felt the pang of loss for his only sister. She would make an excellent mother, and they all knew it. Never one to welcome pity, she shifted subjects before he could respond. "First of all, I took off work the first week he was here. After that, he had a routine and I was able to work some in between."

"And you had Richie." Her husband. Landon had himself,

and the team of designers he'd assigned to the account, who were having a conference call without him with their client and the owner of Windy City potato chips, Otto Williams, this very minute. "I can't take off this week."

"Yeah, well our billionaire cousin used to say the same thing. Funny how after Shane found Crickitt, he found time for a vacation."

At the mention of his cousin, he thought back to Shane and Crickitt's summer wedding last year. Shane was a lucky bastard. He'd managed to meet Crickitt, who was not only considerate and kind, but also understood him. Landon had yet to find a woman who possessed one of those qualities, let alone all three.

That thought brought forth one involving his ex-girlfriend—technically ex-fiancée—Lissa, and his eyebrows scrunched together. They were better off apart, especially since their relationship had been an empty husk for years—way before she'd locked lips with actor Carson Robbins on the temporarily-famous YouTube video that had gone viral. Carson Robbins, Landon thought with a chuff, his pride stinging despite his efforts to keep from it. Why she had left him for that no-talent ass clown, he had no idea. The mind boggled.

A remote-controlled monster truck sped down the hall, narrowly missing Landon's toes before crashing into the baseboard. The *recently installed, special-order, Macassar Ebony* baseboards. He pulled in a deep breath. The slapping sound of tennis shoes on the wooden floor followed the path of the car as Lyon blew past. "Careful, buddy!" he called to his nephew. Then to Angel he repeated, a little desperately, "I can't take off this week."

The truck slammed into his ankle and he bit back a curse. "Lyon!" His nephew's eyes grew wide and Landon promptly slapped a patient smile on his face despite the pain in his foot. "Not in the house, okay, buddy?"

"Okay, Uncle Landon," he said, lifting the car and stamping in the other direction again.

Landon limped into the sanctuary of the carpeted living room. "Help me, Angel, you're my only hope."

She laughed, at his expense, but he was beyond caring. The mighty Lyon Downey had defeated him. "Well, you can't ask Evan to leave his immersion workshop."

"Give me a little credit." He knew what this workshop meant to his youngest brother. Evan hadn't done much for himself since his wife died and he'd become a single dad. His MO up until six months ago had been caring for Lyon and making as much money as possible at his tattoo shop. Then he'd started painting on the side, for fun, or so he'd told everyone. But it wasn't Evan's dark, broody cartoon-style works that had captured Landon's attention. It was the light back in his brother's eyes. Evan had finally started living again instead of just surviving.

Next thing he knew, Evan was calling to let him know a friend of Angel's had a friend in the children's book publishing industry.

"He needs to create five more paintings this week for his agent," Angel said, still arguing her point.

"I know that."

"He could be a *real* illustrator, Landon. You have to find another way. Ever since Rae died, he's been marginalizing the things he wants. It's about time—"

"Angel." She stopped speaking. "I'm not going to ask Evan to bail me out."

"Okay. I'm sorry. I just . . . I want him to succeed."

He smiled. Although a few years younger than him, Angel had always acted the part of mother hen to her brothers—Landon included. She'd gotten worse since Mom died. But Angel wasn't the only one who wanted the best for Ev. Landon wanted him to succeed, too. His brother's tattoo shop was profitable, successful, and, until the artwork of his heart had gotten attention in the literary world, all he'd wanted to do. Now his paintings were all he could talk about. Landon wouldn't deny him this opportunity. No way.

"Can you delegate a portion of your work and lessen the load?" she asked, back on task. "You'll still be able to get things done...just maybe not as much as you're used to."

This account was too important to take his hands off it. But he wouldn't miss an opportunity to tease her. What were big brothers for? "Sure. You want to set a project aside and take the lead on Windy City? Maybe today while you're in town?" She was scheduled to fly in this morning to handle a pitch for Holstein Electronics. A pitch he needed her, as the head of his art department, to nail. A pitch he'd never in a million years ask her to skip.

Predictably, she took him at his word. "You can't be serious!" Her voice went an octave higher. "You asked me to bump up the Holstein account so we can get the billboard design done by next Tuesday! I'll barely have time to breathe between flights from Tennessee to Chicago and back."

"Exactly. And like you, the rest of my staff is buried. The delegation thing? Not going to happen."

Angel heaved a sigh, then blew out the word "okay" before falling silent while she thought. A moment later, he heard her snap her fingers, a sign she'd landed on an idea. "What about the day care in your building?"

"What? No." He wouldn't abandon his nephew in a strange place, not even the day care at work, which he knew was staffed with well-trained professionals. Last night, Lyon had a nightmare because of the change of scenery. Evan had warned Landon it might happen, but nothing had prepared him for the helplessness of holding his nephew and being unable to comfort him. He remembered Lyon's eyes, wide with terror and filled with tears, his little heart racing against Landon's chest.

"No," he repeated firmly.

"Okay ... Well, what about a nanny?"

A plump, proper woman with a British accent popped into his mind and he made a face. "You can't be serious."

Angel's voice dipped conspiratorially. "What if she was someone you knew? Someone *we all* knew?"

He crossed an arm over his chest and narrowed his eyes at the lake view outside. She was up to something. Plotting and scheming as per her usual. "Spit it out, Angel."

"You remember my friend, Kimber Reynolds? She came down to visit me last month and I mentioned she owns a vintage clothing store in Chicago."

"The girl who stayed at Mom and Dad's house one summer when we were kids." The same summer his college girlfriend had given him the worst news of his life.

"Yes!" Angel said with game-show-host enthusiasm. She sounded proud he recalled who Kimber was. "While she was here she'd mentioned she could use some extra money. And since she lives not all that far from you ..."

Kimber. He remembered bits and pieces about the girl who'd lingered in his peripheral for an entire summer. He remembered she had red hair, liked to read, and drank Mountain Dew. She'd offered to help him with his creative writing paper, the makeup assignment to save him from failing his college class after Rachel's pregnancy time bomb. He recalled balking at first—what help could a sophomore be to a college senior?—but Kimber had insisted, and then surprised him. She was smart. Turned out she'd had some helpful advice.

"... sure she would be willing to help you out," Angel was saying.

He blinked out of his daze and tuned his sister back in.

"Want me to use my three and a half minutes between stops to pay her a visit while I'm in town?"

He started to ask about Kimber's credentials, then some-thing Angel said earlier crawled out of his subconscious. "Wait, did you say 'live-in'?"

"Of course." He pictured her shrugging. "You'll need someone to bathe Lyon and feed him dinner at night in case you need to work late at the office. And in the morning, you won't want to wait for her to arrive. What if she catches a late train? Then your progress will be impeded."

She was being a smartass, but she had a point. If Kimber were here with Lyon taking care of the day-to-day, Landon could focus on work and be home in time to play with Lyon or tuck him in. But a woman *living* in his penthouse? Not that his place was small. At six thousand square feet, it'd easily hold the three of them. Before Lissa had moved out following the video debacle, she and Landon could go hours without so much as running into one another. But living with a stranger?

"I don't know, Ang. Has Kimber . . . done this sort of thing before?" *Cared for the nephew of a bachelor workaholic millionaire whose fiancée dumped him for a D-list actor?*

"Of course!"

He recalled Kimber's unruly hair, braces, her affinity for Stephen King. Surely living with her wouldn't be the same as living with Lissa. Kimber wasn't his girlfriend, wasn't his lover, wasn't his anything. He'd pay her to do a job, she'd show up to do it, and then they could part ways and live their separate lives. *Without* exposing him to humiliating YouTube videos popping up online and on his employees' smartphones.

"Admit it. I'm brilliant," Angel said.

He smiled. "Never."

"Admit it and I'll ask her," she sang.

"I could always give it one more day." He was kidding, but he wouldn't give in right away. Where was the fun in that?

A sound, suspiciously resembling a toy monster truck

crashing through the new sixty-inch LED television, came from the direction of the bedroom. Followed by a penetrating silence and a quiet, *Oops.*

He trekked down the hall, mentally preparing himself for the electronic carnage he would likely encounter. Lyon poked his head out of the bedroom, shoulders down, eyes wide, a sickly expression on his face.

Landon managed a small, if not pained, smile for his rambunctious nephew, who looked everywhere but at him.

"Fine," Landon told Angel as he put a supportive hand on Lyon's little shoulder. "You're brilliant."

"Really?" she cooed.

"Really," he admitted. He held his breath, peeked in the room, and confirmed that, yes, the LED had indeed met its demise. God rest its electronic soul.

On a heavy exhale, Landon said, "Ask her."

CHAPTER TWO

*M*e? Babysit?" Kimber couldn't say the word without laughing. But seriously. *Her with a child?* It was ridiculous.

Angel lifted a turquoise silk shirt and held it up to her chest. "Does this bring out my eyes?" She'd come into town for a meeting at Landon's behest, and somewhere between the plane ride and a cab, managed to convince herself that Kimber—who had no experience with children whatsoever—should be in charge of her nephew.

Kimber took the top out of Angel's hands and hung it back up. "You know it does."

Angel rolled her eyes. "Anyway, it's not *babysitting*. It's a nanny position."

"Oh, that's so different." She turned to walk away.

"It is!" Angel followed. "Nannies are sophisticated."

And now her friend was reaching. Kimber plopped down onto the goldenrod, button-top ottoman at the rear of the store. Angel stood over her, hands on her narrow hips, the Downey look of determination lighting her blue eyes.

Kimber would have to give her a reason. Angel was terrier-with-a-chew-toy tenacious. And a little rabid when challenged. "I can't leave Hobo Chic for an entire week." Which was *so* not the issue. The issue was her...with a kid. A kid she didn't know. *That's not the issue, either.* It wasn't. Not by a long shot.

Her friend elevated her arms and did a neat little turn. "You're telling me none of your employees can handle this place while you're gone? What do they do when you have a day off? What did they do when you came to visit me in Tennessee last month?"

"That was different."

"How?"

Kimber shook her head rather than fib again. Neil or Ginny, even Mick, could handle this ghost town in her stead. Right now, across the street, Jilly's bakery and the restaurant next door teemed with customers. While she sat here in an empty shop and tried to use her powers of telekinesis to move customers from the food shops to her store. Maybe she should start offering a free pastry with every purchase.

"He'll pay you whatever you want." Angel knelt in front of Kimber, her eyes doughy.

"I don't need the money." Angel had mentioned a dollar amount right after she suggested the position. An amount that had caused Kimber's knees to buckle. True, Kimber may not *need* the money, but she sure could use it. To fund Operation "Get My Ex-Boyfriend and Co-owner of My Store Out of My Life For Good."

Removing Mick's name from the lease was a huge, huge motivator. But she also had her pride. "I'm an only child," she said. "I have had zero experience with siblings or babies or children of my own. Do you want to entrust your only nephew with someone who has never changed a diaper?"

Angel laughed the next two words. "He's six. And well out of diapers."

"See?" She stood and paced to the other side of the store

where she straightened a rack that didn't need straightening. "I should have known that." She slid a hanger into another with a *shink* sound. "More proof I'm unqualified."

"You knew that!" Angel stopped the next hanger with her palm, her eyes boring into Kimber's skull. A human lie detector, her friend.

"I know." Kimber crossed her arms. "I just...feel uncomfortable."

She waved her off. "My nephew is a doll face. Like me." Angel batted her eyelashes.

"You know I know you're not *really* an angel, right?"

A loud, awkward cough sounded from the other side of the store. Angel's eyes flicked over her shoulder where her husband Richie stood, arms braced around his body, looking decidedly uncomfortable. At his side was Mick, who was texting and doing his level best to completely ignore him. Mick. What a jackass.

"They seem to be hitting it off," Angel said dryly. "Need I remind you *why* you'd like to speed up the process of getting Mick out of here?"

She didn't. Every day got harder than the last. But that didn't change the other potentially bigger issue Kimber was worried about. "I'm not opposed to being Lyon's babysit—" At Angel's stern glare, she corrected herself, "*Nanny*."

Kimber could get through her discomfort, figure out how to handle a six-year-old. The main problem with this whole scenario was that Angel had said this was a "live-in" situation. And Kimber couldn't fathom a world where she might live under the same roof as Landon "Sexy Pants" Downey. Unless it was a fantasy world of her making.

Granted, she was a far cry from the teenager who had a mouth full of metal and a nervous hyena laugh, but Landon was awfully...GQ. She picked a piece of lint off her secondhand capris and avoided Angel's scrutinizing gaze. Kimber wouldn't even know how to behave around him.

Angel lowered her voice, though there was no need. Mick was paying no one any attention, not even Richie who was supposed to be running interference for this elusive talk. "I know you had a crush on Evan way back then," she started.

It was a wrong assumption Kimber had never corrected when she was a teenager. Or since.

Angel smiled supportively before continuing. "But Evan won't be there, so you don't have to be nervous about seeing him." A twinkle lit her light eyes. "Unless you'd like to see him. He is single, and if you and Lyon get along—"

"No." She halted her friend's speech, snuffing the hope that had begun blooming in Angel's eyes. "I don't want to date Evan. The crush I had on him"—*Landon*—"was over a decade and a half ago."

Angel blew out a defeated breath. "Fine. Sorry. Well, if you're worried about Landon, don't."

She nearly swallowed her tongue at the mention of his name. If Angel had any idea about the debilitating crush Kimber had harbored for him way back when…

"Would it make you feel more comfortable if I told you that Landon isn't suffering any weird rebound or depression from Lissa leaving him for Carson Whatshisname?"

Would it? A little. She liked to think he was over Lissa instead of pining for that awful woman.

"Landon and Lissa's relationship wasn't"—Angel scrunched up her face like she'd tasted spoiled milk—"normal."

Whatever that meant. Kimber wondered if he'd had some strange sex fetish she didn't know about. Some weird room rigged up with chains and—

Ew. No.

"And his penthouse is about three times the size of my

house, so it's not like you won't have any privacy. Plus, it overlooks Lake Michigan." She smiled.

Right. Because the view would seal the deal.

Angel lifted her purse off the counter and slipped it over her arm. Richie picked up on her cue and started for the door. Mick may be able to charm the ladies, but his bromance skills needed work. She lifted a finger to let her long-suffering husband know she'd be another second. "Landon is going to provide your meals and incidentals for the week."

"I can feed myself, Angel. He doesn't have to—"

"So don't argue with him when he calls."

Kimber felt her heart sink to her stomach. Or maybe her kneecaps. "What did you just say?" Because it sounded like Angel said he'd be calling.

"It's a formality. He just wants to square away the details. He likes details."

"When?" she asked numbly.

"After lunch."

It may have been a long time since Kimber had seen Landon in person, but she'd seen a picture of him six months ago in the Arts & Entertainment section of the *Chicago Tribune*. In the photo, he and Lissa were leaving the charity dinner after the infamous YouTube video of Lissa making out with another man had gone viral.

The millionaire advertising guru and CEO of Downey Design had worn an immaculate black tuxedo and a frown that brought out the angle of his sexy, squared jaw and enviable cheekbones. Lissa had worn a practiced look of remorse, her hand hung limply over his arm, her body candy-coated in a clingy red Gucci dress, her gazelle-like legs long and graceful. Unfortunately for the supermodel, she had zero percent self-respect to go along with her zero percent body fat. Who cheated on someone as hot as *Landon Downey*, anyway?

He'd been perfect all those years ago before Kimber had

lost her virginity, and having tested the waters a few times, she could see he was even more perfect now. She let out a sigh, and Angel leaned forward and kissed her on the cheek. "Richie and I have to catch our flight home. Thank you for doing this. It means the world to Landon. And Evan," she added with a lift of her manicured eyebrows.

"You knew I'd say yes, didn't you?" Kimber asked, defeated.

Angel grinned, the expression lighting her whole face. "I knew if I stopped by in person you'd fold like a cheap suit." She stole a glance over at Mick, who was pecking something into his phone. "Have fun breaking it to Romeo."

But breaking it to Mick wasn't what had her stomach in knots. It was that Landon was going to call her. *Her.* And she had no idea what she'd say when he did.

* * *

She spent the remainder of the afternoon with one eye on the telephone wondering what "after lunch" meant to a millionaire. What time did he eat lunch? Most people ate at noon, but sometimes she got caught up in a task and forgot to eat until two. Which is what time it was nearing now.

She sort of hated how money had been the factor that clenched the deal. But the plain truth was the amount Landon offered for the weeklong gig was tempting. As tempting as opening her mouth under one of those cascading, melted-chocolate fountains at a wedding. She'd done that once. For far less than what Landon offered.

Her eyes went to Mick, who'd abandoned his cell to touch up the daisy-yellow window paint that read *Hobo Chic* on the front window. He was the real reason she'd said yes; why she'd sold her soul for quick cash. Never underestimate the power of needing disentanglement from a bad relationship.

When she'd met Mick at a nightclub two years ago, her best friend Gloria in tow, Kimber hadn't expected to have so much in common with him. But they had. Aside from being sexy in a rascally way, Mick, like Kimber, loved all things vintage.

Eleven months ago she and Mick caught the entrepreneur bug and went into business, opening Hobo Chic together. She hadn't stopped to think what would happen if they split—which they had, three months later—or what a colossally bad idea it was to tie her professional life to a guy she was sleeping with who refused to call himself her "boyfriend."

Now here they were, stuck together like *The Odd Couple* except neither of them was particularly neat. Mick had been haranguing her to sell Hobo Chic for a few months now. He wanted to split the profit from the sale and go his separate way. She agreed with the separate-way part, but not the selling part. She'd put him off each time he asked.

Hobo Chic was her dream, her baby. She wasn't willing to let it go. Not yet, anyway. She had a plan to buy Mick's half of the store as soon as she saved enough. Landon's money— and a gig she was woefully underqualified for—would be a good start to doing just that. In the meantime, she and Mick would just have to endure one another.

She fed a hanger through the shirt she'd ironed and shook her head. She'd thought prematurely partnering with Mick—both in her personal life and her professional one— had marked the end of her lapse in sanity. Clearly not, considering she'd agreed to become a live-in nanny for a man on whom she'd once harbored a knee-weakening crush.

Bats, meet belfry.

The cordless phone rang on the counter next to her, and she nearly jumped out of her lightly freckled skin. As she'd expected, the caller ID read: *Downey Landon*. She stared at the ten digits on the display, her only disjointed thought being, *Ohmygawd, I have his phone number.*

At the third ring, Mick turned and raised his eyebrows at her, paintbrush elevated in one hand. "You gonna get that?"

"Cover the floor for me?" She snatched up the phone without waiting for his answer. By the fourth ring, she'd shuffled her ballet flats along the battered wooden floor to the curtain-covered stock room. Once the curtain swished shut, she answered with a breathy, "Hello?"

"Kimber Reynolds, please."

Oh, his voice. She had been too young to know what the sound of Landon's deep, hypnotic voice had been doing to her. The nights she'd lain awake in Angel's top bunk and listened to the melody of his words float up from the porch. She remembered how goose bumps lit her skin whenever he'd spoken. Now a woman, she knew exactly what that sensually deep voice had been doing. Making sweet love to her ear canal.

"Hello?" he asked when she'd gone silent.

"Speaking," she said on a near moan.

"Landon Downey, Angel's brother."

Like he needed any introduction.

"Thank you for agreeing to stay with Lyon this week. I appreciate your willingness to step in at the last minute."

Wow. Official. His tone made her stand straighter. "Oh, um. Sure." She stepped behind a clothing rack and skirted another, distancing herself from the doorway. She didn't need Mick overhearing her side of the conversation.

"I wanted to go over a few items with you if you don't mind."

"Oh. Sure." Could she sound like more of an idiot? *Say something besides "oh" and "sure." And probably stop thinking of his voice and your pending orgasm.*

If her stern self-talking-to wouldn't jolt her out of her thoughts, Landon's next question did.

"Do you have any food allergies or special requests for meals while you're here?"

Last thing on the planet she'd expected him to ask. She'd been pretty sure he'd ask for her credentials; qualifications for being entrusted with Lyon. She'd spent the last few hours trying to decide if she should make up a story or be as vague as possible. She'd opted to wing it, though now it appeared she had nothing to worry about. Angel must have convinced him if his first question revolved around provisions.

"Whatever you have is fine," she answered.

"What I *have* is Kona coffee and PowerBars," he said in the same official tone. "I'm sure you'd prefer something else."

Kimber tittered out a ridiculous little laugh and slapped a hand over her mouth. She did *not* just do that. She hadn't nervous-laughed since she was a simpering teen. She cleared her throat.

"Do you eat organic?" he continued. "Require a certain brand of creamer for your coffee? I want to make sure you have what you need."

Aw. That was kind of nice. And detailed. Kimber tried to think if she was brand loyal about anything she ate. Her cabinets were full of uninspiring foodstuffs like Hamburger Helper, macaroni and cheese, and cans of tuna. She couldn't request *that*. Feeling like she should say something, she finally blurted, "I like potato chips."

And I'm a moron.

He did chuckle this time, and she may have emulsified into a puddle of humiliation if it hadn't been for how sexy he'd sounded. It was the way he laughed, deep in his throat, the sound short but powerful. Like a punch to the gut. How, again, was she supposed to live with this man for an entire week?

"Potato chips," Landon repeated. "Perfect." She had no

idea what he meant by that, and he didn't offer an explanation. She heard a scratching sound like he'd put pen to paper
to write it down. He went through a list of questions, reiterating how he would provide all her expenses for the week she
stayed with Lyon, and ignoring her when she insisted that
wasn't necessary. "There's additional garage parking for
your car, if you have one."

She did. But she wouldn't be taking her rust-filled rattle-
trap to his six-million-dollar penthouse on Lake Shore
Drive. No, thank you very much. "I'll take a cab if we need
to go anywhere."

"On me," he said, writing again.

"No, that's not—"

"Kimber." His soft annunciation of her name mingled
with his commanding tone stalled her brain cells like her
head had flooded. "Thank you again for doing this. I believe
that's all I have from my end."

She heard the shuffling of papers, the collapse of a stapler. The man was organized. She frowned at the random
cardboard boxes filled with clothing in her storeroom. One
had the word *Mend* written on it, another read *Sell*, and the
other wasn't marked at all, overflowing with sleeves and pant
legs and belts. No way was she qualified to live in Landon
Downey's white-glove-tested, immaculate home.

"Do you have any questions for me?" he asked, wrapping
up the call.

Just one. Where was her bedroom in relation to his?
Because if they were side by side, she didn't think she'd survive the week listening to his shower turn on without dis-
solving into a lust-puddle.

"None," she said solidly. Then, to her horror, she blurted,
"I'm sorry to hear about you and Lissa."

Silence.

Why had she said that? Not only was it inappropriate, it

was a lie. She wasn't the least bit sorry Lissa and Landon were split.

Mick picked that moment to poke his nose through the curtain. "Who are you talking to?"

She peeked her head around the clothing rack she was half-hiding behind and waved him away frantically. "Thanks, Landon. I'll see you tomorrow. Bye." Only it had come out more like: *ThanksLandonIllseeyoutomorrowBye* because she'd said it in one hurried exhalation. She gaped at the phone in her hand, at her thumb covering the Talk button. She didn't recall him saying good-bye. She'd hung up on him?

You hung up on a millionaire. Extra idiot points for you.

She stepped out from behind the rack, still staring down at the phone in her hand. "I . . . need to go over the schedule with you for this week," she told Mick.

"Who was that?" He gestured to the phone with the arm covered in tattoos. She'd found them sexy when she'd first met him. God only knew why. Or maybe she was just being petty. She'd been petty about a lot of things lately where he was concerned.

She weaved her way around the racks and boxes in the storeroom. "Neil is working my shifts in addition to his own, so he'll be pulling some overtime this week. But Ginny's coming in for extra hours to help him," she said, ignoring his question.

Mick took the store phone from her hand and pressed a button. "Who's Landon Downey?"

"A friend." Sort of.

"A boyfriend?" His lips curved up in one corner, making his dark eyes sparkle. From his full mouth to mile-long eyelashes and thick, overgrown curls, it wasn't any wonder she'd picked him up in that nightclub two years ago. The mistake she'd made was not recognizing a fling when she saw one.

Mick wasn't exactly permanent material. Definitely not the right person to own a business with, she thought, regret poking her.

"He's not a boyfriend. He's Angel's brother. And he needs a babysitter this week."

Mick laughed. It was sharp and didn't send a flock of butterflies fluttering in her stomach like Landon's rich chuckle had. "You? Babysit?"

She crossed her arms over her breasts, hoping to cause some cleavage in her V-necked blouse. Not that he'd notice. He liked large breasts and hers were B cups on their best day. *What are you thinking?* She didn't care if he noticed her cleavage or not. She dropped her arms. It was none of his business what she and Landon were to one another. She refused to engage Mick in this up-and-coming argument. Plus, the truth was far more disappointing than the reality.

"Do you think you can come in on Saturday?" she asked. "It's the only day Neil will need backup."

"You know I hate to work the floor," he said, his shoulders slumping. He reminded her of a put-upon fifteen-year-old.

Sometimes she thought he hated work, *period.* She had taken care of the schedule since the store's inception. And the special orders, stock, mending, financials, the floor plan... He had taken on the tasks of painting the front window and flirting with the female customers.

"Unless Ginny is here." He waggled his brows.

Her ire rose and she took a deep breath. She shouldn't fight with him, but it'd become the norm. The last two months, Hobo Chic's sales had plummeted and they'd managed to needle each other not only about work issues but every grievance they'd had as a couple. It was like she couldn't help being catty. Which was probably why she couldn't muzzle herself now. "Can you have the decency not to flirt with other women while I'm around? We did used to date, you know."

"Oh, I know." His smile oozed into the come-hither tilt he'd used to get her into bed the night they'd met. When he reached for her, she stepped away from him. His charm hadn't worked on her for a while now. He licked his lips and chewed on the ring in his bottom lip in frustration.

She wasn't going to get anything done if they stood here sniping at each other much longer. "Please?"

He ran a hand through his too-long hair and pretended to think about it. "Yeah. Okay."

She smiled, and because she really did care about him as a friend, squeezed his hand as she walked by. But not before she took the phone out of it.

* * *

"I'll cover her expenses," Landon told Evan over the phone moments after hanging up with Kimber. Or, more accurately, moments after she'd *hung up on him.* He was still obsessing over that fact. He didn't like being hung up on. It was rude. But he was trying not to overreact, and it wasn't as if he'd had a list of available options for this situation.

"Fine by me, brother," Evan said over the din of voices in the background. "Have you seen her recently? Because I ran into her after the funeral."

Their mother's funeral was nearly two years ago. Landon had flown to Ohio and out again, allowing as little downtime in between as possible. He'd told himself it was because he couldn't leave work for long, but if he were being honest, he hadn't wanted to marinate in the sadness that had overtaken his father's house. Anyway, Aiden had been there. He was better for Dad than Landon in this situation. In *any* relationship situation as it was turning out.

"The last time I saw her was when she lived at our house that one summer."

Evan let out a sharp laugh. "When she was in the tenth grade? Dude. You should see her now."

He frowned. "Don't be a jerk, Ev. She's a family friend."

"Trust me. I'm not." Laughter edged his voice. "Just... be prepared. For the hot."

He recalibrated. He'd thought Evan may have been revving up to tell him about an unattractive attribute of hers.

"I mean, not my type," Evan added. "Redhead. But still hot."

She sounded hot, came the out-of-left-field thought. Her voice had been a smoky, mid-range tone as opposed to Lissa's childlike soprano. Kimber had a sultry laugh, too, even though he could tell it was borne of nervousness. He supposed that was understandable. How odd to go and live with someone she'd never met. Clearly, he hadn't put her at ease. He was unable to pull off the charm both Evan and Aiden had when it came to the opposite sex. For some reason.

For some reason? You know why. Because he wouldn't allow himself to, that's why. Charm led to emotions, which led to attachment, which led to... disaster.

"It doesn't matter how 'hot' she is," Landon stated more harshly than he'd intended. "I hired her to take care of Lyon."

"Sure. Whatever you say, Master of Your Domain. Look, I have to get back to my immersion class," Evan said.

"What's up next? Trust falls?" It was a jab. And Evan knew it.

"Not funny," Evan said, followed by a creative curse word.

Ah, being the oldest had its perks. Landon had gotten every one of his siblings with that trick. He'd held out his arms, promised to catch them, then step back and let them hit the dirt. He chuckled.

"None of us will take care of you when you're old," Evan growled.

"I am old." Thirty-seven and single. He'd crafted a plan to avoid this situation. Lissa had dismantled it.

"I gotta go," Evan said abruptly. "Good luck reining it in when you see her, dude." He let out a low whistle. "Gooooood luck."

The line went silent and Landon shook his head.

He'd been hung up on again.

* * *

Since he'd given the security desk Kimber's full name and let them know it was okay to bring her up to the penthouse floor when she arrived, the knock on his door the next morning didn't take him by surprise. She was a few minutes early, which surprised and impressed him. He prided himself on being punctual. Her prompt arrival almost made up for the hanging-up-on-him part.

Almost.

Landon smoothed his tie and opened the door to greet—

He froze, blinking at the redhead gracing his doorway, the blood rushing from his head and straight to his groin.

Hot.

It was the only coherent word pounding in his skull. A sexual awareness he hadn't felt in years hit him mercilessly… and kept hitting. For a moment, all he could do was stare at Kimber Reynolds, his jaw slack.

Soft-looking, cream-colored skin was draped in a delicate vintage dress in a pale hue of pink with tiny black polka dots. Black lace sleeves rested over slight, feminine shoulders, revealing more of her flesh through the peek-a-boo holes in the material.

Lord in heaven. *She looks like a 1940s wet dream.*

And he was still staring.

He snapped his mouth shut and stepped aside, recalibrating

his thoughts onto something less distracting than the way the dress floated over her frame. "Kim—ah, Ms. Reynolds, good to see you again."

She slid her hair behind her ear, a delicate gold charm bracelet slinking along her wrist and the barely visible freckles on her arm. "Been a while," she said, her mouth tipping into a shy smile.

His gaze slid from her arm, to the curve of her hips, and down her legs. Before he became wrapped up in a fantasy involving the pair of high-heeled saddle shoes she wore, he averted his eyes to her luggage. "May I?"

"Oh. Sure." She winced but it looked to be a reaction to herself rather than him.

When he reached for the suitcase, she pulled her hand away frenetically. He took the handle from her, as careful not to touch her as she was him. Her soft scent captured his attention briefly before he stood and distanced himself. Evan was right. She did *not* resemble the sixteen-year-old in his memories.

No longer a mushroom cloud atop her head, her hair fell in coppery, shoulder-length waves beautifully offset by porcelain skin and a full cherry-red mouth. A simple gold chain with a tiny key pendant dipped into the hollow of her throat when she inhaled as her bright green eyes swept the room with interest.

"Nice place," she muttered in that sensual voice of hers.

He blinked a few times in succession to test if the woman in his living room was *really* as beautiful as he'd first thought. But closing his eyes didn't make her any less attractive. The smattering of freckles dotting her nose begged to be touched.

He squeezed the handle on her luggage to keep from the ill-advised impulse. "Thank you."

She sent him a tight smile. It, and the death grip she had on her purse straps, hinted that she was uncomfortable.

Of course she's uncomfortable. You're staring at her like a serial killer.

He gave her a tour of his place while she made comments about the curtains or the furniture, guessing at brand or style or the year it was made. He had no idea about any of it. When Lissa left, he'd had the furniture she'd decorated the place with donated and had hired a team of designers to redecorate for him. He didn't know if the new furnishings reflected his taste, but it didn't reflect hers, and that was good enough for him.

He shouldn't compare Kimber to Lissa as he showed her down the hall, but found himself doing just that. There was something about Kimber's style—a uniqueness, as if each item she wore had a sentiment attached. Lissa's wardrobe had been more generic, trendy, and brand-name laden. His eyes moved to Kimber's breasts, a tad smaller than his ex's—but natural, he'd guess—to her shoes with a low heel. She was taller than Lissa by a few inches. Kimber's hips were lush and round, the epitome of gentle, feminine beauty; whereas Lissa—with her spray tan, pointy hip bones, and silicone C-cups—more represented the industry that had perverted it.

They turned left off the main hall. Kimber's accommodations were at the very end, his bedroom at the end of the opposite hallway. Lyon's room sat cattycorner to Landon's bedroom, which was one of the reasons he'd purchased a high-tech video baby monitor. The gadget was top of the line, outfitted with infrared night vision and a room temperature indicator. One could never be too safe, and he wanted to make sure she'd be able to keep an eye on Lyon from anywhere in the house. Both eyes, technically. He knew from experience she'd need all the help watching Lyon she could get.

She took a look around her bedroom. He followed her

scrutinizing gaze from the thick cream rug to the gold and green flowered bedding, to the striped curtains parted over a window view of the city, and finally to the attached bath with a fluffy robe hanging in welcome.

His housekeeper had stocked extra toiletries and left a vase of fresh flowers by the window as well as some women's magazines. He hoped the setup didn't make Kimber feel like she was staying in a hotel. Landon had ordered a basket of body wash and chocolates from a local boutique. It'd arrived yesterday. He'd agonized over choosing a scent, but the woman on the phone assured him cucumber mint was their best-selling product.

Kimber went to the bed and touched the basket, smiling over at him as she did. "Is this for me?"

No telling if she was impressed or being polite. "Yes."

She flattened the plastic covering her gift and leaned in to study the contents. He felt a surge of something foreign wash through him. *Doubt.*

How . . . disconcerting. He frowned.

"Fair trade chocolate." Her grin had widened, parting her red lips over straight, white teeth. *Braces, remember?* Worth it, he thought automatically. She tilted her head, which sent her fiery hair over one shoulder, and regarded him through eyes that complemented the colors in the room. "A girl could get used to this kind of treatment, you know."

Okay. He was definitely attracted to her. On a basic, carnal level. *Ask her to leave. This won't end well.* But he couldn't. For one, Lyon needed a nanny and Landon needed to go to work.

The other reason was far more selfish. Far more discriminate. He was genuinely attracted to her. And damn if it didn't feel a hundred times more amazing than he'd imagined it might.

His attraction to Lissa had been the real thing when he'd

met her six years ago. But since their mutual agreement, the initial buzz had worn off. His attraction to her turned out to be more about sticking to their arrangement than a genuine reaction to the model. Everything about their relationship since then had been planned, expected. *A duty*.

The terms had been simple: sex, companionship, a partnership, designed to keep them both out of the messiness of entangled hearts. Until Lissa met Carson backstage at one of her lingerie shows. Then she'd tossed her and Landon's arrangement into the incinerator and sent him back to square one.

But Kimber... While he wouldn't act on the volatile mix of attraction and desire he felt for her now, she *did* fill a need in this pocket of his life. She'd agreed to one week. A week to watch over his nephew, live in his home. With the stress of Lissa's adventure just now wearing off, the pressure of nailing the Windy City potato chips account, and the added challenge of having a six-year-old in tow, Landon considered that having her here was, in many ways, a gift to himself as well.

Selfish? Maybe. But it'd been a while since he'd been selfish. Eons. He'd respect her space. Keep his hands to himself. Keep his borderline-erotic thoughts and his heated gazes to a minimum. He'd be at work most of the time. It wasn't as if he'd have to suffer under the scrutiny of those guileless eyes of hers for most of the day.

And since women were as unpredictable as lit bottle rockets, rarely firing in a straight, even line, he'd be smart to stay away. The women in his life veered and circled, then exploded too near for comfort.

"You should meet Lyon," he said abruptly.

"Will I need an appointment to get in?" She toyed with the bow on the basket with fingernails coated in a sheen of pale polish. "Is there an elevator leading up to his floor?"

His lips twitched. She was sassy. Smart. Feisty.

Intriguing.

Forcing his mouth into a neutral line, he refused to give her the smile trying to come forth. Flirting with this woman would be all sorts of bad news. She was Angel's friend. She was Lyon's nanny. She'd be sharing his house for the remainder of the week.

He gave her a curt nod toward the door, and himself a final stern reminder to ignore the instant attraction. It was the only thing about this entire situation he couldn't afford.

CHAPTER THREE

Kimber needed to shut up. But her default nervous reaction was the stupid laugh that kept bubbling from her throat and a smart-aleck remark or two. Or three.

Bad enough she'd marched around here babbling about décor like he'd any interest in brands, fashion, or style. Mick had been interested, but he was an exception to the rule...and the last thing she needed was another guy like him. She needed to remember that. Landon was *not* Mick. And she was here to watch Landon's nephew, not ogle his... everything.

But she'd never been in a six-thousand-square-foot penthouse with a drool-worthy view of Lake Michigan before. And she'd never been gifted gourmet chocolates by a man who smelled like a waterfall on a spring morning. Who wouldn't be distracted?

When she'd met his stormy eyes through the lenses of his stylish black glasses, she'd made it her goal to crack that buttoned-up façade. At the moment, she thought as she watched him march down the hall and adjust his cuff links, he was not amused.

What he *was*, was out-of-this-world, F-I-N-E *fine*. He looked every bit the clichéd successful millionaire. His razor-sharp black pants fell over a pair of shining black shoes, his long legs eating up the corridor as he walked. The freshly pressed gunmetal gray shirt stretched over his back, and she watched the muscles there shift as he swung his arms at his sides. Earlier, she'd caught the way his sleek black-and-charcoal tie made his eyes appear a matching shade of gray. She'd forgotten about his hazel eyes that changed color to complement his wardrobe. What a fashion accessory.

Landon stopped short in the hall and, lost in her thoughts, Kimber nearly plowed into him. His hands landed on her shoulders and she halted inches from his toes, narrowly avoiding scuffing shoes that had cost as much as her entire outfit. Jewelry included.

His lips pursed and he dropped his hands, leaving the imprint of his heated palms on her bare skin and her thoughts tangled in a knot of attraction and longing.

"My room is there"—he pointed to the end of this corridor—"and Lyon's is right here." He gestured to the door before them.

She fervently ignored the part of her brain squealing, *Landon's bedroom!* and focused on the panel in front of her instead. No sound came from behind Lyon's door.

"Is he always this quiet?" she asked.

Landon let out a loose laugh before tucking it behind his schooled expression once again. A rush of heat coiled in her belly. Oh yes. She'd have to see about getting him to laugh some more while she was here.

"He's *never* this quiet. He had trouble falling asleep last night and I didn't want to wake him." He slid his sleeve forward and studied a shiny, large-faced watch. "But," he said with a sigh, "looks like I'll have to wake him after all. My apologies if he's grouchy today."

He popped open the door to reveal a room the same size as hers, decorated with neutral bedding and curtains. Lyon's dark mass of curls laid on top of a red and blue pillowcase, and a comforter with the likeness of Superman on it was tucked under his round, mocha-colored cheeks. He opened a pair of dark eyes rimmed with impossibly long lashes when Landon pulled a cord and opened the blinds.

"Kimber is here to meet you, buddy." Landon's official tone had been replaced with a soft, deep tenor. Meant to soothe. She had no idea if it was soothing Lyon or not, but it was working on her. She was already feeling swoony.

He sat on the edge of the bed and placed a palm over his nephew's small shoulder. The scene tugged at her heart, surprising her. She'd never considered herself to be particularly enamored with kids.

"Kim?" Lyon asked, his voice groggy.

"Kimber," Landon corrected. "Do you want to meet her?"

The boy yawned and blinked at her like a sleepy puppy. "Yeah." He slid out of the bed and she bit back a smile at his Superman pajamas, complete with a red "S" emblazoned over his chest. He rubbed his eyes and inspected her, yawning again.

All of a sudden, Lyon's eyes lost their haze. His limbs struck out to grab the nearest toy on the floor and, with a shout, he shot over to her like a bolt of lightning. The blur came to a stop at her feet, sword drawn, and she was nearly downed by his cuteness. From his mussed curls to his wide eyes, to the look of sheer determination drawn across his chubby face, Lyon Downey was *a-freaking-dorable*.

"Hi," she said on an exhale of laughter.

His expression grew severe, and he thrust the weapon and growled, "You gonna make me breakfast?"

"Lionel," Landon said with enough authority that Lyon dropped his elbows slightly. "That's not how we greet a guest. Especially a lady."

Lyon lowered the sword and squinted up at her. Kimber wasn't sure if he was wondering what a lady was, or wondering if she qualified. She gave him her best demure eye-blink in order to allow Landon to dispense a valuable life lesson.

"Especially one this pretty." Landon had spoken so low, she thought for a moment she'd imagined the compliment. Her heart fluttered. Seriously. *Fluttered.* Once again she was sixteen, peeking out of Angel's bedroom window and watching Landon do push-ups on the dock outside their rented lake house. She'd longed for him so much back then. Even when he wore a sweat-soaked white T-shirt and navy gym shorts. She glanced at him but, like back then, he didn't notice her now, either. She still longed for him. That would make this, the choice to come here and stay the week, her latest entry in a diary of bad decisions.

"What am I s'posed to do?" Lyon asked his uncle, sounding inconvenienced that he couldn't charge her, then demand sustenance.

"First," Landon said, taking the toy from Lyon's grip and tossing it onto the bed. "You don't challenge her to battle."

She bit her lip to stifle a laugh.

"You say hello. Introduce yourself." Landon faced Kimber to demonstrate, offering his palm, not in handshake mode, but like he might kiss her hand. She slid her palm into his warmer one and he wrapped his fingers around hers gently, but with enough strength that her every body part recognized him as a man. "Landon Downey," he said, his voice like velvet and as warm as the sunshine streaming in from the window behind him. He tipped his chin, and a shadow dipped into a small cleft there. Had she never noticed it until now? Or, like his eyes, had she simply forgotten the detail over the years?

"Kimber Reynolds," she said on a sigh. He lifted her hand and her breath caught expectantly.

But rather than his firm lips grazing her knuckles, instead he turned her hand to the side and gave her arm two short, professional pumps. The warmth in her palm receded the instant he pulled his hand away. "Nice to meet you."

Before she had a chance to realign her frittering hormones, Lyon clasped on to her and gave her arm a vigorous shake. "I'm Lyon Downey."

She stiffened her muscles and managed to regain control of her arm. Barely. "Nice to meet you, Lyon."

"Now will you make me breakfast?"

Kimber spent the next half hour getting acquainted with Lyon, which basically involved him showing her every toy he had, which was *a lot of toys*. She wondered if Landon bought them especially for this visit, or if he kept them here for whenever Lyon came over. After Lyon had tired of show-and-tell, and Landon was satisfied that Kimber would not cook up his nephew and have him for dinner, Landon stood from the bed, pulled his phone from a pocket, and motioned for her to follow him out.

She smoothed her dress as she stood from the pile of superhero figures Lyon had dragged from the closet.

Landon didn't look up from his phone. "You're good, then?"

Lyon threw a toy in the air and nearly put his own eye out. She forced a steady smile. "Yep. We're good."

"Great. Lyon, I'll see you after dinner, okay? Be good for Kimber."

"Okay," he answered in a sweet little-boy voice that warmed her heart. Goodness. The kid had more personalities than Dr. Jekyll.

"Walk with me," Landon murmured to her as he strode by, still fervently avoiding her eyes. She followed him into a den or office of some sort where he gathered his briefcase, head down. "You know about Lyon's mother?"

She nodded, then answered aloud since he still wasn't looking at her. "Yes. Angel told me." Rae Lynn Downey had died when Lyon was three. Poor Rae. Poor Evan. Poor Lyon. Tragedy struck everyone in one form or another, never granting immunity even to those most deserving.

"Just wanted to be sure you knew," he said quietly. "Sometimes he talks about her." Then he added in a harder voice that was all business, "I will be home at eight. Lyon's bedtime is eight thirty. I'll say good night to him when I get in." He stopped at the doorway where she lingered. She took in his stubble-free face. The crisp, clean smell that wafted off of him. Aftershave, maybe? "Any questions?"

She licked her bottom lip, the only questions entering her consciousness a string of highly inappropriate requests. He lifted a sandy-colored eyebrow, his eyes flickering to her mouth.

"Actually, yes," she said, pausing to clear her throat. "Do you have a map of the penthouse so I can find my room?"

His lips twitched and smile lines bracketing his mouth appeared before disappearing just as quickly. Her eyes lowered to the shallow dent in his chin, and she could swear her breasts grew heavy. She definitely did not remember that cleft. *Meow.*

"Trust me," he said, his low voice ticking down her vertebrae. "Lyon is as good as a bloodhound."

Even sexier when he teases back.

Landon walked for the front door and she turned the opposite direction, impressed that she'd avoided ogling his backside as he walked away. She'd noticed earlier he looked as good coming as going…which made her have a brief, dirty thought she had to force from her mind as she neared Lyon's room.

At the threshold, it appeared a rogue cyclone had struck the six-year-old's bedroom in the time it took for her to wind her way through the maze of corridors and hallways. She blinked at the mess.

"Ready to play?" Lyon asked, a huge toothy grin on his face. Well, toothy save for the one missing from the front.

Kimber took in her dress and black and white spectator pumps, then glanced over at the pile of uncapped magic markers on the carpet. She'd dressed to impress Landon, but it was apparent that she needed to change her clothes...*and* her expectations.

As fun as it was to flirt with her charge's uncle, as much as she wanted to coax a smile to Landon's lips and the knee-weakening laugh from his chest, she was *not* here for him. Her focus, her priority, was the little boy in front of her.

Not Landon, she reminded herself as a pang of loss shook through her chest. Not even if he sprouted a pair of dimples to go with that sexy divot in his chin.

* * *

Landon parked in his private garage, lifted his briefcase from the floorboard of his BMW, and stepped out. If not for the cardboard box stuffed with Windy City potato chips he'd brought home for Kimber, today might be like any other weekday. A day where his only plans would be a glass of scotch and a long night of work ahead of him. Hell, it'd been a long night already.

Picturing Kimber caused a smile, albeit a tired one, to inch across half his mouth. He juggled the box, the briefcase, and his keys, and walked to the elevator. Once inside, he nodded at Tony, the security guy, and inserted a key for the private penthouse on the thirtieth floor.

He met his haggard reflection in the steel doors of the lift as it carried him up. He looked like hell. Tie offset, jacket crumpled over one arm, five-o'clock shadow decorating his jaw. When he'd gotten into advertising, he'd imagined gliding around pristine offices and efficiently checking items off his to-do list. What he ended up doing most of the time was working from dawn well into the middle of the night, hammering away at an idea contented to stay underdeveloped.

He'd always had a precise, specific style when it came to design. Clean, crisp organization on a page. Blame it on his perfectionist streak, or on the control-freak-first-born characteristic alive and well within him. The style suited him. It also suited high-end products in the industry, part of the reason for Downey Design's success in a short period of time. He'd experienced further success since having paired with his successful cousin. Shane's business had shooed in several accounts and they hadn't yet celebrated their first year together.

Not that Landon hadn't done well on his own. Downey Design had created advertising packages for private airlines, liquor companies, and fancy electronics. But, as profitable as ads were for companies like Bose and Apple, he'd coveted a chunk of the ever-profitable food industry. Windy City had landed in his lap, whetting his appetite further.

Food was the commonality between all classes. Food owned the highest percentage of all aired commercials, and not just during big football games, but during every hour of every day. Windy City was his opportunity to break into the industry. The elevator doors opened on his private floor. He intended not only to succeed in that endeavor, but knock the potato chip company's ad design right out of the park.

Regardless of how many nights I come home after ten o'clock, he thought with a weary sigh.

He walked through the open, empty foyer to his front door and unlocked the deadbolt. His penthouse didn't appear much different from most nights he returned from work. The small dining room table gleamed, a pile of mail neatly stacked in one corner. The contemporary lighting fixtures over the kitchen island were on, casting a soft glow onto the cabinets and reflecting off their glass doors. He dropped his briefcase and jacket onto the chair and edged the box of snacks onto the table.

The house was silent as he pocketed his keys. No apparent sign of either of its inhabitants. Then, a flash of copper waves and skin appeared in his peripheral vision.

A lot of skin.

Kimber entered from the hallway, head down as she punched what was likely a text into her phone. She wore short cotton shorts, the cuffs tickling two of the most delicious-looking thighs he'd ever laid eyes on. His mouth went dry.

There it is again.

The jolt that shot down his spine and made his pants grow tighter. Awareness, pheromones, or maybe good old-fashioned attraction sizzled in the air between them. She looked up, her green eyes widening before she slid the phone into the minuscule pocket of those tight shorts. With Herculean effort, he dragged his eyes to her face.

Well. Sort of. He was distracted on the way up by her shirt: a faded image of the robot from the movie *Short Circuit*, the word "Input" silk-screened over her left breast.

"You're home." Her eyes strayed to the clock on the wall. "Late."

He palmed his neck. "I know." A shimmer of regret wafted over him. He'd wanted to tuck his nephew in tonight. "How did things go today?"

She moved to the fridge, looking comfortable opening the appliance and poking around inside. "Good." She came out with a bottle of water. "Lyon is a bottomless pit of energy, but after I figured out your fancy espresso machine, I was able to cope. Probably why I'm still awake." She cracked

the top off the bottle and took a drink. He watched her delicate throat work as she swallowed, feeling another surge of
awareness zip through his bloodstream. "He finally went
down after I read him *Green Eggs and Ham* three times."

Landon's features pulled into a tired smile. At least he
hoped it was a smile. After the long day, he may be grimac-
ing at her for all he knew. "Three times? That's too bad."

"Not really. It's my favorite book, too." Her eyes strayed
to the box of potato chip bags on the table. "What's that?"

He lifted a random bag of chips by the corner and pulled
out the jalapeño ranch flavor. "You said you liked potato
chips."

A smile spread her luscious lips. "For me?" She no longer
wore the red lipstick or the retro dress, but damn, she looked
good enough to...

*But you're not "going to" anything, so don't bother fin-
ishing that sentence.*

"I assumed we'd share them," he joked, gesturing to the
twelve bags he'd brought home from the office. Windy City
had delivered fifty cases of chips to Downey Design today.
One would think his employees had won the lottery for
how happy they were to get free potato chips. A spark of a
thought for their campaign snapped, then fizzled, his brain
too tired to lock on to another idea.

He dropped the bag back into the box. "I happen to be in
the middle of reimaging the best potato chip brand on the
planet." He sat heavily in one of the kitchen chairs, and she
came around the island to stand at the table in front of him.

"You look exhausted."

"I am."

"Having branding issues?" She rifled through the box,
inspecting the different flavors. Either because she was hungry or checking out the artwork, he couldn't tell.

Thrown by a woman's apparent interest in anything he

did from nine to five...or ten, he hedged. "It's a process." Not that he'd launch into it if she pressed. He preferred to chase problems around in his head until he found the answer. It was in there. Somewhere. Hopefully it'd surface before tomorrow's team meeting.

"I made spaghetti. Are you hungry?"

The air shifted, no longer crackling with just sexual energy, but with something else. Something familiar and foreign at the same time. She leaned casually on the table, waiting on his answer to her offer of leftovers. If he said yes, would she microwave him a plate? Bring him a fork? Sit with him while he ate and make idle conversation about his day?

The domesticity of the moment hit him front and center, nearly causing him to clutch on to the table to ground himself. Not only about the dinner and casual way Kimber watched him now, but also the discussion about Lyon, almost as if they were a couple and were discussing a child of their own.

Hi, honey. How was your day?

Good, thanks. How was the kiddo? Get anything good in the mail?

Man. It was weird. Weird and sort of wonderful. Landon was suddenly dizzy...and concerned he was far more tired than he'd realized.

Scrunching his eyes closed, he shook his head. "No, thanks. I'm not hungry."

"Oh. Okay." She fiddled with the water bottle, her fingers intimately stroking the condensing water that had settled in its plastic ridges.

His voice taut with attraction, his next sentence came out harsh. "I don't expect you to cook my dinner."

She blinked at him, her lips parting slightly.

Dammit. He had to get a hold of himself. "That's not what I'm paying you for," he added, wincing at his tone. Now he sounded mean. A visual of him in a hole, digging for China, popped into his weary skull.

"I'm…um, I'm going to go to bed." Her lips lifted into an unsure smile, making him feel like a grade-A jackass.

"Kimber, wait."

She stopped short of walking down the hallway, wrapping her fingers around the wall and leaning back into the open doorway. Her teeth stabbed her bottom lip, her eyes were wide and innocent, her cinnamon-colored brows raised in curiosity.

Every last cell in his body wanted to rush across the room and fold her against him, sample her lips, and bury this… this *bizarre*, but unmistakable need in her fiery hair and plush mouth. He blinked, stunned and overwhelmed by his thoughts.

"Chips." He snatched a bag out of the box and held it up.

Kimber came into the room and accepted it, a look of confusion on her face as if she'd been expecting him to say—or do—something else. But no matter how much he'd wanted to say or do that something else, he wouldn't.

Seducing Kimber wouldn't be productive. Not for either of them.

$\mathcal{C}$HAPTER FOUR

$\mathcal{L}$andon leaned into the back of the conference room chair, now permanently molded to his body. He flipped his Mont Blanc pen end-over-end on the legal pad in front of him, listening with half an ear to his team rounding the long, oval boardroom table.

He'd climbed into the shower this morning almost amused by the direction of his thoughts last night. He supposed the combination of fatigue and stress could cause the borderline mania he'd experienced. When he'd entered the kitchen to find Kimber making coffee and Lyon kicked back on the living room sofa watching cartoons, he'd felt none of the strange longing he had hours prior. Yes, she was still undeniably attractive, but that . . . *need* he'd felt for her was gone.

He hadn't been able to ignore her beauty but, thank God, he was able to have a normal conversation with her before kissing Lyon's head and walking out the door. A perfectly normal morning where he hadn't shot headlong into *The Twilight Zone* with host Rod Serling.

Hopefully this morning was a predictable trend for the future.

"Red and silver. It's who they are," Margaret was arguing.

He tuned in to the chatter around him.

Margaret moved her empty Starbucks cup to the side and flipped around an art board, featuring Windy City's current packaging, to show Brenda. "They've built a brand out of these colors." She gestured at the beauty shot of the bag next to a heaping bowl of thin, golden potato chips before tapping it twice with her fingernail. Once when she repeated "red" and tapped the red part of the bag, and again when she said "silver." Brenda leered at her from across the table.

Landon felt a migraine coming on.

"They've built a *not-so-well-known* brand," Brenda challenged. "For them to stand out, we have to think outside of the box, here. I say we start with tearing the brand down to the studs and rebuilding from scratch."

"Lay's has the color yellow cornered," someone piped up.

And then they went around again. Like they had for the majority of the morning. It became quickly apparent that the direction of this conversation, like the other earlier conversations, wasn't productive.

Landon drew in a solid breath and spoke for the first time in thirty minutes. Because he only spoke when he needed to, the room quieted when the first syllable exited his lips. "Margaret is right."

Margaret sat up straighter and batted eyelashes over round cheeks. "Thank you, Mr. Downey."

He resisted the urge to shake his head, and capped his frustration. His designers were like little puppies, desperately seeking pats on the head. Brenda sent Margaret a sneer. Margaret fluffed her dark hair in an arrogant manner.

Why they took their wins and losses personally, he had no idea. The *product* won or lost. A lesson for another day, perhaps. One for a day when he wasn't circling a hellacious headache at the hands of a group of corporate ladder-climbers. He scrubbed his face, aware his thinning patience was not their fault. Not technically. He had a lot riding on nailing Windy City's brand. Otto Williams had fired his last ad agency. Landon had seen the other agency's proposal Otto had called "crap on a stick." Even Landon could admit it hadn't been half-bad, though he'd kept that opinion to himself.

"The brand's colors aren't the issue," he announced, infusing his voice with authority. "It's their *image* that needs updating." A dozen wide-eyed stares greeted him. Waiting for him to solve this epic conundrum. He threw the problem back at them. "Suggestions?"

They exchanged glances. He rested his elbows on the table and folded his hands, waiting. No one commented. Okay. He pushed himself to standing and a few people shuffled, seemingly confused as to whether the meeting was over. Rather than walk out of the room, he paused at the coffee cart and grabbed a hardening Danish from a tray. He took a bite, chewed, and watched his team expectantly.

"Mr. Downey?" A skinny guy wearing a checkered shirt, his hair shaved into a short Mohawk, spoke up. "I have one."

Saved by the new hire. God bless him.

Landon licked the frosting from his lips. "Mr. Wilson."

Kirk Wilson hesitated and glanced nervously around at the older, seasoned—*jaded*, Landon mentally corrected—team members, as if weighing whether *this idea* was the right one to share with the table of cannibals.

"When you say image"—Kirk cleared his throat—"you mean like... as in who they are. As a company. Like... as a brand?"

He was going to have to muster more confidence than that to land an idea in this room. Landon tipped his chin in encouragement anyway. *Spit it out, kid.* He hoped it was good. For Kirk's sake. Margaret pursed her lips and narrowed her eyes, ready to draw blood.

Kirk swallowed hard, surveyed the room one final time, and addressed his colleagues. "Windy City has a reputation of being the chip that sits next to a sandwich. But what if consumers thought of the sandwich as something that sat next to the chips?"

Margaret's face pinched. Brenda craned her thin eyebrows. Stephen dropped his pen on his pad and blew out a breath, muttering, "Oh boy."

Contrarily, a smile slid across Landon's face. *Nailed it.* Kirk reminded him a bit of himself when he'd launched into the field of advertising.

Before Margaret opened her mouth, no doubt to chop Kirk's tender, sapling-like hopes into kindling, Landon cut her off. "Chips as the main course," he said. "I like it."

His statement garnered a look of flattered shock from Kirk and one of betrayal from Margaret and Brenda. *Look at that.* Finally. *Those two agree on something.*

Landon repressed a chuckle. "Order lunch." He dropped the petrified pastry into the wastebasket. "No one leaves this room until you're solid on a concept." He snatched up his pen and pad and walked to the door, pausing to tap the door frame. "Tomorrow, we'll reconvene and hammer out the details of the campaign. I want it built around Kirk's idea. Windy City. The main course."

He shut the door behind him, and his team's stone silence erupted into hushed chatter. Kirk was on his own now. Swimming with the sharks. It was the best way to learn.

Good luck, kid.

* * *

Kimber wanted to collapse on her bed and take a nap. She'd spent the morning chasing after Lyon, playing one game or another. First it was hide-and-seek, then tag, then a game he made up, which consisted of him hiding his Super-man figurine in the house and charging her with locating it. At least she'd been able to cheat via the video-outfitted baby monitor when Lyon hid the action-figure in his bedroom.

After lunch, when he'd finally wound down, she took the opportunity to clean the kitchen. That task complete, she walked into his room and found him on the floor, Legos scattered around him, his face pleated in concentration as he built Batman's dark domain, Gotham City.

"Some men like to watch the world burn," she said in her best Michael Caine voice.

Lyon smiled, a dimple punctuating his beautiful brown skin and lighting his blue-green eyes. He was going to be a real heartbreaker, this one.

"You like that movie?" he asked, attaching a Lego.

"A lot." *Especially the Christian Bale parts.* Her cell phone rang and she showed him the display before answer-ing. He smiled at the photo of his aunt.

She put the phone to her ear. "Hi, Aunt Angel."

"Hi, nanny Kimber. How is my adorable nephew?"

She smiled back at Lyon and answered Angel with a truthful, "He's great."

"Sucker. Felled by the Downey charm."

She thought of Landon last night: his disheveled hair, crooked tie, the accidentally sensual smile gracing his firm mouth. *You have no idea.*

"...wondering if you'd talked to him?"

Oops. She'd tuned out her friend while lusting after Landon. "Not much. He came in late last night and looked really tired. He wasn't all that conversational," Kimber answered. "I offered him spaghetti, but he declined. Does Landon like spaghetti?"

Angel was quiet for a beat. "Yes, he does. But I wasn't asking about Landon. I asked if you'd heard from Evan."

"Oh!" She let out a nervous laugh. "*Evan.* Of course. He, uh, he called this morning to talk to Lyon."

Angel fell quiet again. Kimber checked the screen of her iPhone to be sure the call hadn't dropped.

When she returned it to her ear, Angel said, "I am so dim!"

Her intuition prickled. Or maybe that was her pride. "What? No you're not." She snapped a Lego into place. Lyon pulled it off and put it on again, frowning in concentration. *Perfectionist.* She thought of his concise, intentional uncle and had no doubt who Lyon had inherited that quality from.

"It's Landon," Angel said.

"What's Landon?" Kimber offered the next piece to Lyon. He took it. She was glad. She couldn't take the rejection.

"Has it always been Landon?"

Uh-oh.

"I'm hungry." Lyon pouted and held his stomach.

"You're always hungry," she told him before returning to her call. "Angel, what are you—"

"I thought you had a crush on Evan all those years ago." She gasped and Kimber's skin erupted into goose bumps. "How could you keep this from me?"

Guilt pinged along her ribs like a pinball had been shot into her chest cavity. "I didn't mean to. I just...never corrected you when you assumed it was Evan."

Lyon frowned at the mention of his father's name. Right. She should watch what she said in front of the little playback machine.

Angel's good-natured laugh startled her. "Landon's a good choice," she said. "He's single, he's rich. He's not what I'd call romantic, so if you're suffering any chocolates-and-roses fantasies, I think you can hang those out to dry. But he is established. Stable. Lives close to you."

Only he did bring me chocolates. And potato chips are

better than roses. She shut her eyes. That *so* wasn't the point. "Angel, I'm not really looking for—"

"Can I have Teddy Grahams?" Lyon flopped to the floor, doing his best impression of a famished child.

"Yes," she answered him. "Do you need me to get them for you?" *And hang up with your prying aunt?* But he was already on the move, tapping into a store of energy that sent him bouncing out of the bedroom like Tigger hopped up on Red Bull. "It's not like that," she told Angel, raking her fingers through the pile of Legos. "I don't even know him."

But her friend wasn't about to be thwarted. "So *get* to know him. You live with him. How hard could it be?"

She thought of last night's conversation. Landon hadn't answered her when she prompted conversation about Windy City. Then he'd practically drawn a line in the sand when she'd offered him leftovers from dinner. *It's not your job to cook for me.*

"I don't...think he likes me."

"Pssh! Kimber. You're beautiful, you're stylish, and you're mothering his only nephew. He probably thinks you walk on water in your spare time. I know he seems like a fuddy-duddy, and I'll admit this whole Lissa situation was... weird."

Kimber frowned at the mention of Lissa. She wanted to ask, but refused to pry.

"Maybe he needs a real woman," Angel said. "A woman who knows who she is."

Whoa. Get ahead of herself much? "I'm here for Lyon," she reminded both of them. "And a paycheck so I can buy my ex-boyfriend out of my business. I'm not interested in Landon." She touched the tip of her nose to make sure it hadn't grown a few inches and sprouted leaves. Because there wasn't a bigger lie than the one she'd just told. She'd been interested in Landon since she'd laid eyes on him at age sixteen.

Angel sighed. "Fine. I just got all excited. You'd be good for him. Yin to his yang. Butter to his bread. He's a family man, you know. Underneath that ridiculous arrangement with Lissa, I believe he really wants to be in a stable relationship."

Ha! If he was looking for stable, he'd stumbled into the wrong nanny. Kimber had no idea where she'd be in five years, five months, or in five minutes. She was spontaneous and fell in love too quickly and made spur-of-the-moment decisions without much rational thought. *Like buying Hobo Chic with Mick.* Landon, with his details and lists and über-organized penthouse, would go crazy if someone like Kimber were his other half.

Now who's getting ahead of herself?

Angel covered the phone, muffling her voice. "I know. I'm not!" she called out, probably to Richie. "I'm back. My husband is berating me for playing Cupid. It's a pastime."

"Obsession," Richie said into the phone. Kimber had to laugh.

Angel whispered her next words. "Have a drink with him tonight. You owe yourself a break. Take it. And talk to him. Maybe you'll have more in common than you imagine."

She opened her mouth to tell Angel she didn't think it was a good idea, but then she heard the telltale beeping of the buttons on the microwave.

"I gotta go," she said, hoofing it down the hallway. No good could come of Lyon operating the microwave.

CHAPTER FIVE

Landon was reading through the e-mail he'd spent the last twenty minutes drafting when his desk phone rang. The button signifying his private line lit. His emergency line.

Lyon.

A myriad of horrific thoughts went through his mind in the nanosecond it took to punch the button and bring the handset to his ear. What if Lyon had broken his arm? Or his leg? *Or his neck?*

"This is Landon." The words didn't come out frantic, but they were stiff.

"This is Angel," came his sister's mocking voice.

His panic eased down a notch. If she was joking around, this must not be the emergency he'd feared. He uncurled his clenched fist. "Everything okay?"

"Of course everything's okay. Why? Is this number hooked to a red phone or something?"

He eased back and leaned an elbow on the arm of his chair. "I assume any call to my direct line is an emergency."

"Can't a sister call and talk to her oldest brother for no reason at all?"

"Sure she can. But she doesn't." He waited. He was right; he knew it.

An audible sigh confirmed his suspicions. "Fine," she said. "You got me. I wanted to call and tell you to have a drink with Kimber tonight."

He straightened his glasses. What was she up to? "A drink."

"Yeah. Make an effort to talk to her when you get home tonight."

Had Kimber...said something? He hadn't been in the greatest of moods last night when he'd come home. He'd been brusque, unintentionally. "Why?" he said, not letting Angel in on any of his thoughts. "She's a babysitter not an adult-sitter."

He nearly laughed when she blew out a frustrated grunt. "She's a *nanny*. And a professional."

"I know. Isn't it best for me to stay out of her way?" he asked, happily needling his only sister. "Let her do her thing?"

"You're so clueless." He heard murmuring followed by Angel answering, "Second drawer, Richie!" She addressed Landon again, her voice at normal pitch. "Kimber is marooned in your big, lonely house for the entirety of a week—"

"More like four days at this point," he interjected.

Angel ignored him. "—and her only company is a six-year-old with a fondness for fart noises. Did consider she might like to have a conversation that didn't involve apple-sauce or Superman?"

She was making her point passionately enough that he began wondering if she had talked to Kimber. Had Kimber filed a grievance with his emotionally unstable sister? "If she's unhappy with the job—" he started, about to issue an idle threat.

Angel didn't let him finish. "She likes you, Landon."

He blinked at his computer, which had gone into hibernation

mode. A Downey Design logo winked on and off in varying locations. So this wasn't a case of Kimber complaining to Angel. It was a case of his love-struck sister trying to set him up. "Listen, Cupid."

"Don't call me that."

"Okay. *Angel.* You have a Cupid complex. You see match-making everywhere you look."

"Kimber never had a crush on Evan," she blurted. "It was *you*. All those years ago when she hung around the basketball court, when she sat next to you at dinner, when she helped you with your English paper."

What? "Creative writing," he muttered, semi-stunned.

She huffed. "The point is Kimber liked you. *Still* likes you, if you ask me."

He sifted through a memory of her on the patio, winding a red curl around her finger and watching him play basketball with Aiden and Evan. No. No way had she been out there for him. "I was too old for her." Five years was a huge gap between a sixteen-year-old and a college kid.

"You're not now."

He wasn't. Kimber was thirty-two, her womanly curves as far from her gangly teenage years as possible, and as enticing as they came.

"Fine," Angel replied when he remained silent. "Don't believe me."

He blinked away the vision of Kimber's long legs wrapped around his waist, those retro shoes crossed at his back. "No worries. I don't." He cleared his throat, hoping the rasp in his voice conveyed disbelief rather than lust.

"Just...be nice to her instead of being your rigid, card-board self."

He opened his mouth to say he wasn't rigid and ask what she'd meant by "cardboard." Was she insisting he was bland? Dry? Stiff? Whatever she'd meant by it, it was unflattering.

She didn't give him a chance to argue further, forcing him into business mode with a question about a redesigned logo for a senior care facility due tomorrow.

He tried to tune out her previous comments and focus on work. He absolutely wouldn't consider Angel's claim that the gorgeous redhead currently occupying his penthouse—and his thoughts—*liked* him and had liked him for years.

Nope. He'd shut that out completely.

* * *

Kimber closed the door to Lyon's bedroom and stifled a yawn. It was after nine, but he'd finally gone down. Tomorrow, she needed to take them both out to do something. They'd been cooped up in the house for two solid days. She hadn't imagined an enormous penthouse with an entire wall of windows overlooking Lake Michigan was capable of causing cabin fever, but she'd been wrong.

Of course, that may not be the only cause of her anxiety. Ever since Angel had planted the seeds that Kimber should flirt with Landon, they'd grown into Jack's beanstalk. As much as she would like to lay blame at Angel's feet, she couldn't.

Kimber didn't need so much as a nudge to turn even a casual "hello" into picking out China patterns prematurely. Mick wasn't the only date she'd turned into a boyfriend too soon. She'd done that with those who'd come before him. Her secret superpower was the ability to morph a perfectly okay short-term relationship into a doomed one that zombie-dragged its decaying self to inevitable demise.

What she needed to learn was how to take things a moment at a time and stop worrying about the future so much.

In her bedroom, she toed off her shoes, smoothed her

patterned pants over her legs, and straightened the billowy jade-green top. *You could practice on Landon.*

She could.

She bit her lip and tightened the loose ponytail at the back of her head, winding the tendrils framing her face as she considered. Landon wasn't in the market for a relationship. And if he was, Kimber would be the last woman on the planet to garner his attention. She thought of Lissa Francine with a twist of her lips. Kimber was not a petite honeyblonde strutting her stuff and her bare midriff in magazines and runways.

But.

She was living in his house. Landon might even feel obligated to have a drink with her to be polite if she insisted. She could practice her small talk, her flirting techniques. It wouldn't be hard to flirt with him. Nowhere near a hardship.

After a few days of afterhours drinks and flirting, she could leave his penthouse, check in hand, and have proven to herself that she *could* walk away from a relationship. Yes. This plan was lame and had a loophole the size of Denver. But in a way ... it was brilliant. Satisfied with her newborn idea, she padded through the hallway and paused next to Landon's home office. The room was dark save for a strip of lights glowing over a small, barely stocked bar. She stepped into the room, past the wooden floor of the hallway to the deep brown rug. She followed with her other foot and stretched her toes over the piled carpet.

A few liquor bottles stood on the countertop, along with a row of gleaming crystal glasses. She imagined Landon in here, papers spread on the thick mahogany desk, brows lowered over his glasses in deep concentration. He'd lift a glass of amber liquid to his lips and sip, then rub that cleft in his chin with one hand ...

"Sexy," she whispered.

The clearing of a throat had her spinning around. Landon stood in the doorway, briefcase in hand, one eyebrow cocked over the rim of his glasses. Unlike the man in her mind's eye, this Landon was infinitely hotter. And real.

"Kimber."

She could listen to him say her name on a loop. The way his tongue kicked out the "K" sound, the way his lips pursed for the "b," the way his mouth held the "r" for a beat.

"Hi." She licked her lips, fervently trying to recall if she'd spoken her thoughts aloud while encroaching on his private space. Geez. What might she have said? "Sorry, I was just…" She gestured nervously at nothing in particular, unable to fill in the blank at the end of her incomplete sentence.

"Looking for a drink?"

Okay. She nodded.

"Me, too." He stepped past her and dropped his briefcase onto the desk, opened it, and unloaded a file. "Good news is there is plenty to drink." He closed the case with a pair of sharp *clicks* and lifted his face. "The bad news is I have scotch and scotch."

His voice penetrated the dim room, warming the space between them. He lifted a remote, and the lights over a white manteled fireplace flicked on, followed by flames inside. No heat came from it. *Must be for mood.* She kept herself from letting *that* thought turn rogue.

The heatless orange flames and lights warmed the space further, making the room look like the inside of a highly polished box of cigars.

"Scotch, then." She didn't know what to do with her hands, so she clutched on to the baby monitor. Since her pants had no pockets, she didn't have much of a choice but carry it wherever she went.

She gazed around the room at the rows of recessed

shelves packed with books—mostly industry-related reads. Marketing, design, and technical handbooks, on software she'd heard of but never used, lined the walls. At the back of the room stood a leather couch made to look worn. She wondered if Landon ever took the time to sit on it. If this was her house, she would only sit there, for the view behind it alone.

A bay window took up the entire width of the wall and overlooked several other tall buildings and the lake below. Twinkling, more from the buildings' windows than the stars, created a pleasant ambience perfect for a glass of scotch.

"Have a seat. I'm sure you're worn out from chasing Lyon around all day."

Landon was going to make this easy on her. Kimber decided to let him. Abandoning the monitor on the table in front of the couch, she sat.

* * *

Landon slid his gaze over Kimber's wild pants, and a smile tugged at his lips. The print was a loud, large pattern consisting of green leaves, bright orange flowers, and a tangle of fruit. Strawberries, limes, lemons . . . and what he thought may have been half an avocado on her ass. Not that he'd checked her out as she moved to the couch on the other side of the room . . .

But he had.

He rerouted his focus on the task of pouring two scotches, wondering if she had ever tasted scotch. Wondering if she'd surprise him by having a proclivity for it, or if she'd be like most women he'd encountered and turn her nose up after one sniff.

A test, then.

He dropped a few ice cubes into her glass, leaving his own glass at room temperature, and trayed up their drinks with a bottle of emergency water if she didn't like what she tasted.

He crossed the room and rested the drinks on the coffee table in front of Kimber, admiring the way her green top set off the red in her hair and made her eyes pop. So much so, that when she'd turned them up to him, he'd frozen solid for a second and nearly fell into their depths. She pushed a piece of hair behind her ear, then her eyebrows pinched before she brought it back to her face, twirling it just so. Almost like she was nervous.

Because she likes you?

Maybe. But he wasn't going to act on his suspicion, even if Angel was telling him the truth instead of concocting romance where there wasn't any. Still, Kimber's fidgeting was . . . interesting. He logged that thought for later.

He sat on the center cushion, testing the lack of distance between them. She straightened, pushing herself a bit farther into the corner. But not like she was uncomfortable in a bad way. Like she was uncomfortable in a *good* way. Palming their glasses, he used the forward motion as an excuse to scoot a few inches away from her. Careful not to touch his fingers, she focused on the glass as she took it from his hand.

Also interesting.

A soft, almost fruity fragrance wafted off her skin. But not like the cucumber body wash he'd purchased for her. Like something else . . .

"You smell like . . . grapes," he muttered. Ridiculous as it sounded, that's what he smelled.

"Oh." She inspected her hands and he silently swore at his sister. This was Angel's fault. Her suggestion Kimber *liked* him had him noticing her. Everything about her. The small swells of her breasts in the loose shirt she wore. Her bare toes, nails painted pale pink. Her neck and the tendrils of flame-red hair tickling skin he imagined sampling with his tongue.

Damn Angel.

He blinked Kimber into focus. She'd set aside her drink and licked one finger before licking the other and scrubbing vigorously with her free hand; bathing herself like a cat.

What the—

She paused when she noticed him watching and held out a palm. A smudge of purple decorated the crook of her first and middle fingers. "Scented markers."

He sipped his scotch and definitely did *not* think about lifting her hand to his lips to finish the job. Reclaiming her glass, she examined the liquid in the dim lighting of the office.

He leaned back against the sofa, laid an arm along the back—dangerously close to her—and opted for the road less traveled in his world: small talk. "So. Kimber Reynolds."

At the sound of his voice, her cheeks stained a pretty shade of pink. She sent him a confused smile. He smiled back. Couldn't help it. The look on her face was that of a woman who liked him. And he liked that. A lot more than he should.

"Tell me what you've been up to since you were sixteen years old." He leaned back on the sofa, content to let her talk while he watched her unabashedly.

Contrarily, she couldn't keep her eyes in one place. They jerked from the bookshelves behind his head to the window, to the glass in her hand. "Um. Wow. That's a lot of years to summarize." A breathy laugh escaped her lips. "I um, graduated high school." She tapped the bottom of her glass with her fingernails. "I did not go straight to college, but by the time I did, I moved so I could attend the Fashion Institute in New York."

He lifted his brows. She'd lived in New York.

She nodded. "Impressive, right?"

"Very." How unusual that she'd have an interest in a field

so similar to Lissa's. He wondered if they'd ever crossed paths. "So you wanted to be a big, famous designer with your own runway shows?"

She chewed the corner of her lip. "I did...until I worked for Karl Kingsley."

Lissa had done a show with Kingsley a few years back. She'd told him the nickname the models had for him. He wondered if that had been a universal moniker. "The Royal Shithead?" he asked.

Kimber laughed, a brief look of surprise crossing her face. Like she hadn't expected him to be crass. He liked that he'd surprised her. He liked her, period.

"That's him. Anyway, I got fired. From an unpaid internship. I was standing too close to a model who was spouting off at him and he fired her from the show, and me, and a seamstress who happened to be in the line of fire as well." She swirled her finger around the edge of her glass, the motion oddly erotic. "After that, I had...problems attaining another internship in New York. I spoke with the seamstress, who was my friend, and she'd had the same issues. We thought Kingsley had blacklisted us somehow. He has a lot of pull in the industry."

As most old guys who became relics did. Her story reminded him of the job he'd taken straight out of college. Brett Carmichael. The guy acted as if he'd owned the moon rather than RedAd, and when Landon had left to strike out on his own, Brett had attempted to smear Landon's reputation with his customers. Thankfully, he'd failed. Landon knew because many of those customers had come to him, leaving Brett's antiquated design where it belonged. In the past.

"I moved to Chicago with my friend Gloria," she continued. "Evan's agent"—she glanced at him to make sure he knew her by name. He nodded. "And then I worked in department stores on Michigan Avenue until about a year ago when I opened Hobo Chic."

"A vintage clothing store. Angel mentioned it."

"Did she also mention I made the tragic error of partnering with my ex-boyfriend to buy it?" She blinked, almost as if she was stunned that the words had come out of her mouth.

He was getting the idea she didn't do much planning… for anything. The words she spoke, her actions. He probably had that attribute to thank for her being here.

She waved a hand through the air, the subject along with it. "Anyway. Water. Bridge. What about you? What did you do after college?"

He pressed his lips together. He'd desperately tried to reconnect with Rachel the moment he'd set foot back on campus. She'd gone to live with her aunt in Texas. She'd never contacted him again. Ever. After they'd dated for a year and a half and made a baby she'd aborted.

"That's a long and boring story," he lied. Forcing a smile onto his face was like nailing Jell-O to a tree, but he managed. "I take it you're not a scotch drinker." He pointed to the glass and she stilled her circling finger.

"What gave me away?" She tilted the glass to examine it again. "What do I do? Swirl it, smell it?"

"Drink it." Lifting his glass, he demonstrated by pulling in a mouthful of the amber liquid. He swallowed, savoring the burn in his throat. Finally, he was starting to relax. He could feel himself sink into a slight buzz, in part thanks to his skipping dinner. He enjoyed the sensation of his shoulders dropping from beneath his ears for the first time in eleven hours.

She was studying her glass with apprehension. "Why does mine have ice and yours doesn't?"

"Smell yours," he said.

She sniffed. Shrugged. "Okay."

"Now mine." He tipped his glass in her direction and she

held his wrist to steady the glass. The simple connection had him subconsciously moving his body closer to hers, as if she'd dragged him there by an invisible thread. She inhaled, watching him from under a fan of ginger lashes, her eyes wide and watchful.

"Scotchy," she said.

"The ice tames the scent."

Every part of her, from her pink mouth to her darkening pupils, to the feather-light touch on his arm, said *Kiss me*. And, God, how he wanted to.

She moved her hand before he could act on the impulse, lifting her glass to the mouth he wanted to capture with his. She mumbled something like "Here goes nothing," her words echoing lightly off the cut crystal, before she took in a mouthful, held it for a second, then swallowed it down, a completely adorable scowl on her face.

She stuck her tongue out. "Really?"

A grin he couldn't contain covered his face. It pulled his cheeks and lifted his glasses. "Scotch is an acquired taste."

She stared into the glass as if it were filled with worms. "How do you acquire a taste for battery acid?"

His smile held. "Man. I was hoping you wouldn't be this predictable."

Her eyebrows tilted, making her look almost hurt. "I'm predictable?"

No. You're adorable.

"You knew I would make a face when I drank it?" Her voice was high and tight.

"I did."

"And you knew I'd need the water to wash the taste from my mouth." She lifted the bottle, uncapped it, and took a swig.

He dipped his chin. "I did."

"And"—she capped the bottle—"you knew I'd ask to taste yours next?"

He—what?

The side of her mouth curved, a feral little lift, and she gestured to his glass. "May I?"

He handed it over. "Sure."

"I want to see what scotch without ice tastes like." She took a drink, turning the glass to sip from the side he sipped from, her lips closing over the rim where his had a moment ago. This time she managed not to wince or frown. She did stick her tongue out, though. To lick a drop of Macallan from her bottom lip before covering it with her top lip and rubbing them together.

He shifted as subtly as he could manage with a two-by-four wedged against his zipper.

"Better." She offered his glass, her eyes turning up to his again.

He told himself to move away, give both of them some space. But he stayed where he was in spite of his mental orders. Her eyes traveled over his body, and the tingle in his balls moved up his spine and down both legs simultaneously. Her next question didn't help hedge his arousal.

"Do you ever take off that tie?" she asked.

He didn't miss the opportunity to flirt with her. "I don't wear it in the shower if that's what you're asking."

Kimber sucked in a deep breath, and he hoped it was because she was imagining him naked. It was only fair since he'd pictured her that way now, too. He was playing with fire, and it was far more fun than he remembered.

He slid a glance down her arms and up again, wanting badly to reach out and touch her. *Just a touch.*

"You look good in green," he said, sliding his fingers beneath the short sleeve nearest him and running the tip of his index finger along the satin-smooth skin on the inside of her upper arm.

She gasped, barely, but he'd heard it. He met her eyes, saw

the flash of interest, the war she was waging with propriety, or maybe she was simply reacting to the familiarity between them. He felt it, too. Felt the charge between the scant inch separating their legs, the electric current streaming through his fingers as he tickled her flesh.

"I'm thirsty."

He yanked his arm away from her at the sound of his nephew's voice. Lyon lingered in the doorway, rubbing his eyes and yawning and looking utterly uninterested that his uncle was hovering over his nanny.

"Hey, buddy." Landon had to clear his throat when the words came out as a croak.

Lyon shuffled over to the couch and climbed up and sat between them. Landon reluctantly made room. "I wanted to say good night but you were asleep," he told his nephew, smoothing his hair against his head.

Lyon yawned again, his eyelids as heavy as sandbags. "I can't sleep."

Sure he can't. He flicked a look over his nephew's head at Kimber, whose lips twitched in amusement.

She leaned down to eye level with Lyon. "How about I get you some water?" She smiled with a purity that squeezed Landon's chest. He loved Lyon like he would his own kid. He should have been here when he said he would. *Tomorrow*, he vowed. Tomorrow, he'd get home in time to tuck him in. Balancing business and family this week had proven to be a challenge he'd failed. Thank God for Kimber.

She moved to the door. "I'll put it by your bed, okay? Do you need me to read *Green Eggs and Ham* to you again?"

He shook his head, turning blue-green eyes up at Landon. "Will you read it, Uncle Landon?"

He smiled down at the boy swimming in what must have been one of Evan's T-shirts. Black Sabbath. Interesting choice for a six-year-old. "You bet."

"In that case, I'm going to go to bed." Kimber hesitated with one hand on the door frame. "Thanks for the drink," she told Landon. She flicked her gaze to Lyon, told him to sleep tight, and blew him a kiss.

When she pulled her palm away from her pursed lips and her gaze fettered to Landon's, he swore a whisper of wind brushed along his cheek a second before she disappeared down the hall.

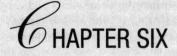

CHAPTER SIX

Kimber lifted her cell phone to her ear in time to hear it ring. She'd hung up on her employee, Neil, mid-conversation when she'd attempted to rest the cell on her shoulder while making Lyon a sandwich.

"You there?" she said when he answered.

"Here," Neil said. "I can't believe you were that close to a millionaire and didn't kiss him."

"I can. That would have been stupid." And fun. And terrifying. The mere *idea* of her lips against Landon Downey's had fear pooling in her stomach like an overfilling ditch. Only there wouldn't be anything *mere* if she were to kiss him. It would be epic. Massive.

Overwhelming.

"Hang on," she told Neil. Poking her head out of the kitchen, she found Lyon in the living room where she'd left him. "Lyon! Sandwich!"

He ignored her, as he'd done all morning, and continued swinging his plastic sword while wearing a Superman costume. Why the conflicting wardrobe and weaponry bothered her, she didn't know. Maybe she was a purist. She dipped her voice low. "*Lyon.*"

Her "mom" voice. Who knew she had one of those?

"Are you going to count to three, next, darling?" her employee-slash-smart-aleck friend asked merrily.

She walked into the living room and caught the sword with one hand. "Lunch," she said to the boy who was too cute for his own good. "Go eat and I'll let you watch *Man of Steel* before bed."

That worked. He ran into the kitchen and climbed dutifully into his chair, swinging his feet as he bit into a peanut butter sandwich.

"Color you Mary Poppins," Neil chimed.

"Have you ever heard of a kid who didn't like jelly?" she asked distractedly as she put the peanut butter back in the cabinet and brushed crumbs from the counter.

"Never."

"Right?" She wiped down the counter and tossed the dishcloth in the sink. "You have a question about the store," she prompted. Neil's first words to her when she'd answered had been "Mick said to call you" as if he was apologizing for interrupting. Little did Neil know his call was as welcome as the housekeeper that had arrived at eight a.m. today to clean the six bathrooms in Landon's penthouse. In a word, *very.*

Kimber missed Hobo Chic. Not just the store, but working—having a sense of purpose. She missed her morning habits she'd since abandoned to come and live in enviable luxury. Whether she was scheduled to work in the store or not, every morning she made her coffee and came down the stairs of her attached loft and into Hobo Chic. She'd sit on the for-decoration-only settee and turn on an elegant Tiffany lamp she refused to sell and take in her surroundings. She'd admire her handiwork: the clothing she'd procured at a recent estate sale or thrift shop, or a rescued piece she'd carefully mended the night before. Or sometimes she'd craft her homemade price tags, trimming squares of burlap, inserting gold eyelets, and threading pink silk ribbons to loop over the hangers.

Having something of her own made her feel proud. Proud in a way that living and going to school in New York, as lush as that had been, hadn't been able to match. Maybe because she'd gone on her parents' dime. They'd long since forgiven her for abandoning her major, and in her eyes, she was still very much in the fashion industry. Instead of forging ahead to the future, she was cleaning up remnants of the past, she thought with a smile. She wouldn't have it any other way.

"And then there is this rack of shirts and skirts off to the side without prices," Neil was saying.

Crap. She would bet she'd rushed off and left the pile of tags in her apartment.

"A beautiful career-esque woman, who would have probably gotten her promotion today if I sold her the shell tank top and vintage sage print skirt," he continued with a dramatic sigh, "was inquiring."

"Tell me you sold it to her," she pleaded. Why hadn't she remembered to price that rack? She was always forgetting some mundane, simple yet imperative detail.

"Can I have milk, Kimber?" Lyon asked, crumbs dotting his mouth.

"Chocolate or white?" she asked, moving to the fridge.

"Chocolate!"

Like she needed to ask. She pulled down two glasses with one hand and held the phone to her ear with the other, not repeating the mistake of face-ending the call with Neil.

"Of course I sold it to her," he said. "It brought out her cheekbones. What I need to know is how you want me to price the rest of these items; if you had something in mind."

"I did." But she'd forgotten. Had run off to her new gig and left her store in the hands of Neil; her near-useless ex,

Mick; and a twenty-year-old girl who was fresh off the farm-land of Indiana. "How is Ginny doing?"

"She keeps calling everything 'neat,'" he said with a laugh. "She's precious. And flirting with me."

Kimber nearly choked on the glass of milk she'd poured for herself. "You're kidding."

"No. She has no idea I like men."

"Speaking of, how's Mick doing?"

Neil grunted. He didn't like Mick. Had made his distaste for her ex-boyfriend no secret. "Yesterday he spent most of the evening perched on a stool playing the guitar."

Mick's talents extended to nearly every area of art. From decoration to design to music to painting. It was one of the things she'd fallen for when they'd been dating. If he'd managed to *hone* any of those skills into a career, she'd likely still be with him. But he quit everything. Like he'd quit her. And like he wanted to quit Hobo Chic.

"I'll be back on Monday," she said.

"We'll be fine. Hobo Chic is fine. You work your nanny gig for a rich hottie and enjoy it, missy," Neil teased.

She smiled. He had a way with words. "I get a come-to-Jesus talk, too?"

"No charge."

Lyon cast her a curious frown. "What's 'come to Jesus' mean?"

Great. With no graceful way to answer that question, she diverted his attention instead. "Use a napkin. You have pea-nut butter on your face." He swiped his face with the paper towel she gave him. "Finish your lunch and I'll give you a brownie." Once she baked some.

"So this is what you're doing this week? Bribing a six-year-old kid into doing what you need him to? Stuffing him full of brownies and ultra-violent movies?"

"Don't judge me. Get a notebook and go to the rack.

Describe each piece and we'll talk pricing. I bet you're going to know how to price them anyway."

As they worked, Neil paused to ask her questions she couldn't answer freely within earshot of Lyon. "I'm thinking forty-nine dollars," he would say, followed by, "What color are your millionaire's eyes?" Or, "There's a tear in the sleeve, toss or repair?" then, "What's his butt like? Big, small, firm, flat?"

"It's delicious," she said without thinking. Lyon had moved to his room a few minutes ago, his bath-towel cape flapping behind him. At least he didn't have the sword any longer. She cleaned off the kitchen table and loaded his plate and glass into the dishwasher.

"Describe," Neil said.

She lowered her voice. She didn't have to—Lyon was roaring in the back of the house, appeased with his own imagination for the moment. Closing the dishwasher door, she leaned a hip against the counter. "He wears these suit pants that sort of . . . cup each cheek, you know?"

"Oh, I know. Keep talking, honey."

She grinned. This was fun. She turned around and rested on her elbows, toying with a knife in a block with her free hand. Surely snuggled in a corner at the back of Landon's massive kitchen, with Lyon several rooms away, she could speak without being overheard. She glanced at the baby monitor on the counter behind her. Lyon had plopped onto the bed to play a handheld game. Yeah. He was in the zone. She was safe.

"Landon's tall, so he has these incredibly long legs. But even though he's lean, his body looks strong."

"More," Neil instructed. She pictured him perched on the ottoman at the back of the store, his legs crossed.

"I can tell because of the way he fills out his clothes—"

"Suits, you said. What brand?"

"Dolce."

"Yum."

"Right?"

"Continue," he said, likely with a flick of his arm.

Her smile returned as she pictured Landon the way he was last night. When describing him to Neil, she'd left out a few details. Details she wanted to keep for herself. Like the scratch of facial hair that had rimmed his lips, the way he looked rumpled and tired, but every hair had been in place on his head.

"His chest is broad," she continued. "And he has wide shoulders." Capable of handling a business, and the life he'd built with his own two beautiful hands. "But his *butt*"—she paused for dramatic effect—"Oh, Neil. His ass is a thing of glory."

He laughed, further encouraging her. She slid a knife in and out of the block, allowing herself to revel in the conversation. She hadn't had a grown-up conversation in days. She'd texted Gloria a few times, but it wasn't the same as their usual randy exchange.

She infused a little extra naughty into her voice. "And I got a great look at it this morning," she practically purred. "He'd bent over to retrieve a paper that had slipped from his briefcase and it was all I could do not to grab hold and—"

The clearing of a throat brought her out of her haze. She dropped the knife into the block with a *clunk* and straightened at the counter, but didn't turn around.

"And *what*?" Neil prodded after she trailed off.

"Um." She closed her eyes and tried to ratchet down her thundering pulse. Impossible. "I have to go," she whispered to Neil. *Because I'm going to have a heart attack.*

So long as it happened fast. She'd rather die on Landon's custom flooring than face him right now.

"Oh, my Turkish Delight!" Neil announced gleefully. "He's there, isn't he? He's behind you!"

She hung up on his laughter and turned, having planned a fake-startled expression. As it turned out she didn't have to fake it. "Oh!" She put a hand to her chest as her heart hammered against her palm. "*Evan*? What are you doing here?"

A sly, almost drunken-looking smile slid onto Landon's brother's face. His hair was a disheveled dark mess, his eyes a devastating aqua blue. Wow. He'd aged nicely.

"Hello, Kimber."

Oh, yeah, he'd heard her. Heard every last word.

"Just here to see my son," he said, holding his palms up as if to say, *Sorry to interrupt.* "I had a break midday and took the train back. Thought I'd take him for some ice cream."

She put her phone on the counter between them. Picked it up. Put it down again. "Yeah. He-he'd like that." Should she bring it up? Pretend it didn't happen? She mentally reviewed her conversation. She didn't think she'd mentioned Landon's name. Maybe Evan wouldn't know who she was talking about.

"I won't tell my brother you talk about his ass when he's not here."

Or he would. She wound her fingers around the hem of the long shirt she'd paired with black leggings. Evan's eyes flittered over her briefly while she grappled for an excuse... or an argument. Something. *Anything.*

No words came.

His face broke into an actual grin, more attractive than the smirk he'd worn a moment ago. "Angel was right," he said, a note of wonder mixed with teasing in his voice. "She told me you liked Landon that summer. I was so sure it was me."

Her face fell. Right onto the countertop. Angel *told* Evan she liked Landon? And for that matter had originally told Evan she liked him?

"Angel is officially the worst secret-keeper on the planet," she mumbled.

"Tell me about it," he said with a wry twist of his lips.

"Evan... if we could keep this to ourselves, I would—"

He held up a hand to stay her speech. "Relax. Your secret's safe with me." He winked and she simply stared, unsure if she believed him or not.

"Daddy!" Lyon scrambled into the room and leaped into his father's arms, talking ninety miles a minute about all the things they'd done over the last three days. Evan released his son and squatted in front of him, listening and responding with unadulterated pride and love. Her heart squeezed.

Again, she had the good fortune to be folded into the Downey family, albeit temporarily this time, too. At least she could hold on to these moments whenever she needed a reminder of what a rock-solid family looked like. Unlike hers and Mick's disjointed business ownership; unlike her parents' acrimony and cold shoulders. She watched, in awe and a smidge envious of the grand home life Lyon was blessed with. What would it have been like to have a receptive father? Evan had become an amazing parent. Probably not perfect, but then, who was?

"Kimber, would you like to join us for ice cream?" Evan asked.

No, thanks, I'll just be here. Reeling. She shook her head. "You go. Spend guy time together."

One of Evan's eyebrows jumped as he reached for the front door. She hoped he had been telling her the truth; that he wouldn't tell Landon what had happened. She pressed her hands to her overheated face. She hoped it a lot.

* * *

"She likes your ass."

Landon snapped the pencil lead on the legal pad where he'd been outlining his upcoming meeting for Windy City.

He lifted his chin and met eyes with his brother. Evan had dropped by his office unannounced, after he and Lyon spent the afternoon together, and was now talking gibberish while sitting on the arm of the couch on the opposite side of the room.

Landon lifted his brows. No way had he just heard that correctly. "Excuse me?"

"Kimber. She likes your ass. She was having a very colorful conversation about it when I stopped by your house today," Evan said with a wave of his hand.

"What are you talking about?"

Evan ignored his question. Landon was getting a lot of that lately. No wonder he came to work. Here, people respected him when he spoke.

"Everyone knows I have the best ass out of all of us. I guess there's no accounting for taste." Evan rested his hands on his knees. "Gloria got in touch with a small, Chicago-based children's book publisher interested in my work. She also thinks there is some potential to get a few of my pieces into an art gallery in Columbus."

"Close to home," he muttered noncommittally. In reality he couldn't concentrate on anything but the notion that Kimber talked about him when he wasn't there. Not just him, but... *his ass*? He knew they'd laid on the flirting pretty heavy last night, but he had assumed she'd been responding in kind.

"If I can't get picked up by a publisher," Ev said, "I need a backup plan."

Landon nodded and sat back in his chair, flipping his pencil end over end. But even though he was looking in his brother's direction, his mind was on Kimber's tropical pants. Specifically, her backside. From what he'd seen so far, that part of her anatomy held as much promise as the rest of her. The long legs, smooth, silken skin, pillow-like bottom lip...

"...I should be able to get Lyon Sunday morning." Evan stood, snapping Landon out of his fantasy about Lyon's nanny. "That's two more nights. And for the record, I think Kimber's great with Lyon. Despite her questionable taste in the Downey brothers' butts." He rolled his eyes.

Landon rounded the desk, rubbing his hands together. "Sunday is fine. Take all the time you need." He reached for the door handle to show Evan out.

"Hey, do you remember the guys I used to hang out with when we went to the lake every summer?"

The "hoodlums" as Mom called them. Landon lifted a shoulder. "Barely. By the time you were a teen, I was in college. I didn't go much after that."

"Oh. Right." Evan narrowed his eyes. "Do you ever miss going there?"

Landon pulled open his office door. "I practically live on Lake Michigan. So, not really."

"I know *that*. I mean do you miss *our* lake? It was like our own slice of paradise when we were kids. Where we all got to hang out as a family."

For Landon, family vacations had been about taking him away from his friends and the comfortable familiarity of home, then plopping him in a too-small house with three younger siblings who fought with each other nonstop. Though he did recall a few fun family game nights and dinners. "I haven't been there in years."

"Me neither." Evan crossed his arms and regarded his shoes. "You know how Rae hated the water. She had no interest in visiting a cabin by a lake."

At the mention of Evan's late wife, Landon's chest constricted. He'd have done anything to ease his brother's pain over losing his spouse. *Anything.* Rae's devastating and sudden loss had left Evan a widower far too soon. If it was natural between them, he'd pull Evan into a hug, but Aiden was the hugger. Landon was the stoic one. He stayed silent until the moment passed, waiting for Ev to say more. Predictably, Evan changed the subject.

"After I get these paintings done, I'm going to take Lyon. Show him what he's been missing all these years."

"That will be good for him." Landon stopped short of palming his brother's shoulder. He didn't need to. Evan smiled knowingly, okay with the dynamic between them.

Landon was glad Ev was starting to do the things he used to love doing. Pursuing his first passion, art, or visiting the lake they'd gone to every summer growing up. Whatever it took to help him move out of survival mode and begin to thrive. Maybe this meant he was healing. Or maybe he had healed. After losing Rae, their mother, Shane's mother—their aunt—in one tragedy after another, it was a wonder any of them were healed. So many amazing women, gone too soon.

"Oh, and Land, do me a favor?"

Caught up in his melancholy, Landon's voice came out a little wistful when he spoke. "Anything."

"Don't have sex with Kimber until I get my son out of the house. You know, as a courtesy."

"I wasn't—I didn't—"

A rogue grin broke across Evan's face. "Oh, brother, your colors are showing." He walked out the door and Landon started to shut it, stopping in time for Evan to poke his head back in and give him a wink. "See you Sunday."

"Not if I see you first," Landon said, then shoved him out the door and shut it.

CHAPTER SEVEN

$\mathcal{K}$imber's nerves had settled some since Evan's *unsettling* arrival earlier today. By the time he'd returned with a sugared-up Lyon, she'd managed to convince herself that Evan wouldn't tell on her and that Landon would never be the wiser.

Since Lyon was powered by ice cream for the rest of the afternoon, she'd had her hands full. His dinner had been spoiled as well, so he'd hardly touched the tuna casserole she'd whipped up stove-top. After a bite of it, she knew why. She'd certainly never snag a man with her cooking skills.

Landon hadn't come home early tonight, either, which disappointed her. Not for her sake, but for Lyon's. The boy had asked for his uncle Landon and insisted on waiting up. She let him, lying on his bed next to him and watching *Man of Steel* as promised. He had finally fallen asleep—miraculously during the loudest *crash-bang-boom* section of the movie—but Landon still wasn't home when she shut off the television and sneaked out of Lyon's room.

Back in her own bedroom, she left on her comfy leggings but slipped out of the bra pinching her breastbone. She debated lounging around without one, but thought the gray T-shirt with a beaded owl taking up the front would likely create enough camouflage to hide any nipple protrusion.

Figuring she'd more than earned a glass of wine, she went on a hunt, nearly crying with relief when she found an abandoned bottle in the back of a cabinet in the kitchen. She didn't think it was being saved for a special occasion. Moreover, she didn't *care*. Landon told her to help herself and that's exactly what she planned on doing.

She unlocked and opened the balcony door, swinging it closed behind her. Abandoning the monitor on a small table in front of the wicker patio furniture, she took to the railing overlooking the lake. Lake Michigan was calm in the warm night air, ripples on the water's surface reflecting the moonlight like a blanket of diamonds on its near placid surface.

The red wine trickled down her throat, leaving a pleasant trail of heat. She closed her eyes and took what felt like her first full breath of the day. How did parents do this every day, every week? Every *year*? Everything she'd needed had been at her fingertips, including a housekeeper scheduled for a three-times-a-week visit, and Kimber had needed this glass of wine as desperately as the air she breathed.

She opened her eyes and sipped again, her vision going blurry as she continued to appreciate the moment. This one silent moment where she wasn't cooking or cleaning or chasing around a little boy with energy to burn. If she had to work and care for a child, and satisfy a lover...how would she manage to do it all?

The thought of a lover shoved last night into her brain, front and center. The way Landon had slipped his fingers into her shirt, brushing a seemingly innocuous part of her body. But it hadn't been innocuous. As it turned out, the underside of her arm was as sensitive as if he'd touched her somewhere much, much more intimate.

Her neck flushed, her body flooding with desire as she remembered the look in his eyes. The mix of green and blue yesterday against his blue business shirt. He'd looked at her with a hunger that wasn't meant for nannies or friends of the family. Landon looked at her like she was a woman. Not like Mick had looked at her, like a friend or a fling. And not the way her parents looked at her, like she'd frozen in time at age sixteen and hadn't yet managed to rope her life in to some semblance of shape.

No, Landon looked at her like he knew she could hold her own. He didn't overpower her with sensuality or downplay her emotions when she spoke. He listened. Like what she said mattered.

But he hadn't offered much conversation of his own last night, had he? He'd been silent while she'd told him about her college life, even delving into the mess she'd made of buying Hobo Chic with Mick.

So? He doesn't spill his guts to virtual strangers. That only means he's normal.

But they weren't strangers. She'd spent the summer with Landon and his entire family. She'd celebrated Angel's birthday, gone with them to the lake for their annual vacation, had eaten dinner with them every evening...Maybe that familiarity was why she felt so attracted to him now. Because even though she didn't *feel* sixteen, parts of her body still reacted like she was. Her heart, for example, that fluttered at the thought of seeing Landon come home tonight. And the slight shake in her hand, rattling her wineglass, revealing her self-consciousness and frazzled nerves.

Ridiculous, those nerves.

He was a man and she was a woman. Flirting, attraction was a very real possibility. An acceptable side effect. Just because they'd shared some sly glances and comments laced with innuendo didn't put her at a disadvantage.

She bypassed a pair of Adirondack chairs on the sprawling balcony and sat on the wicker sofa. Weighed down by her thoughts as much as her vain attempt to unravel the mysteries of the universe, she leaned her head back and cleared her mind.

Many of the neighboring buildings' windows were lit, their occupants rummaging around the kitchens while televisions flashed in the living room. Turns out the rich lived much like everyone else did. Just with an infinitely better view.

She heard the balcony door open and turned her head. Landon stepped out, jacket off, sleeves cuffed, tie in place. Not exactly casual, but two out of three wasn't bad.

"There you are." His smooth voice poured over her like honey, sliding into her stomach and making her aware of that man-woman tension she'd been contemplating seconds ago. She ran her eyes over his forearms dusted with light brown hair, admired the elegant stride of his long body as he walked toward her.

Her next words exited on a soft sigh. "Here I am."

"I can join you," he said. "Unless you're having a moment of peace. If so, I'll leave this and go." He held up the wine bottle she'd opened.

"I hope you don't mind that I opened it."

"I was saving it for when I finished up with the Windy City account, but that's okay."

"What?" He tipped the bottle and she covered her glass with her palm. "You've got to be kidding me."

He raised an eyebrow. "I am."

Removing her hand, she pressed it to her chest to alleviate her pounding heart. "Don't do that."

He finished the pour and turned the bottle to catch a lingering purple drop. "Sorry." He didn't mean that. She could see the amused gleam in his eye.

"I didn't know you had a mean streak."

"Older brother curse." He was standing. He gestured to the couch, a question on his face. She nodded and he sat next to her. Not too close, but her chest tightened as if he'd sat down and pulled her onto his lap.

Mmm. She'd like that.

She gave her head a brief shake. Whenever he was near, her body went into some kind of high alert, her nipples thermometers registering his specific brand of body heat. She crossed her arms over her breasts, wishing she had left her bra on. *Of all the nights to go commando.*

He draped his arm along the edge of the sofa behind her head like he had last night. Casually. Calmly. Like he was content to sit on the balcony with her and savor his scotch. If it wasn't for the tightness around his eyes and the lines bracketing his unsmiling mouth, she would have believed he was both calm and content.

She wondered if he had anyone to talk to in his world.

"How was your day?" *Lame*, she chastised herself, but it was a start.

"T.G.I.F. Yours?"

That wasn't an answer. One of those wasn't even a word. He'd given her an acronym, then followed it with a question.

"I couldn't be more tired if I tried," she answered honestly. *Your turn, mister.* "Did you reimage the best potato chip in the world?"

He grunted. A definitive *no*.

"Probably too much to hope that you'd get it done in a week, right?" she guessed. She had no idea how long these sorts of things took, or how long it took for a brand switch to go from concept to completion.

He sipped his scotch. Licked his lips. Remained silent.

Okay. She'd go for the direct route. "You wanna talk about it?"

He slipped his finger and thumb under his glasses and rubbed the bridge of his nose. "You don't want to hear about it," he blew out on a sigh.

She should respect that he didn't want to talk about it. But she couldn't imagine who else he had to talk to. As the boss, he couldn't let his employees know he had doubts. And while she couldn't be sure, it was a safe bet that Lissa and Landon hadn't exactly lent their ears to one another.

That left... well... that left her.

"How do you know I don't want to hear about it?" She'd love to hear him talk about anything. Love to just sit here and listen to his deep voice interrupted every so often by a sip of scotch.

He dropped his hand and peered into his glass. He was silent for so long, she'd begun feeling guilty for backing him into a corner. He surprised her by speaking.

"You want to hear me rant about how I have a team of imbeciles assigned to the most important account of my career?" he said, eyes on his glass. "Tell you how, no matter which way I attempt to steer them, they mutiny and run us into the nearest iceberg? Or maybe you'd like to hear about how I stomped into the boardroom like a lunatic and demanded we reconvene tomorrow morning?"

"On a Saturday?"

He sent her a dry look.

She returned it with a weak smile. "Sorry."

He let out a sigh. "And I know you don't want to hear how I realized on my way home tonight that I'm placing blame where it doesn't belong. Railing on the best designers in the business because *I* am the one who's hit a creative block." His lips pressed together, then he spoke, almost talking to himself now. "Every direction I try to take the design, it runs me ashore."

"That's a lot of boat references," she quipped.

He squinted at the buildings in the distance, his lips tipping into more of a sneer than a smile. A light winked out, then another. "I can't believe I admitted that," he muttered quietly.

Kimber had given up on getting things one hundred percent right one hundred percent of the time. Hell, she was lucky to get things *half* right a *third* of the time. "You still suffer the delusion you're not allowed to make mistakes, don't you?"

He met her eyes and uttered a stern, "Yes."

She grinned. He was kidding. She was starting to pick up on his dry sense of humor. "When I find my brain in the way"—she paused to roll her eyes—"which doesn't happen all that often, I go with what feels right."

"What *feels* right." He repeated her words like she'd spoken them in a foreign tongue.

"Yes. You *do* have feelings, don't you?"

He answered with a bland blink. He wasn't Mr. Control all the time. Regardless of what he wanted people to think, she knew better. He wasn't who he pretended to be on the outside. The buttoned-up-and-down CEO who rarely let go. The rigid, disciplined man who checked his and Lissa's relationship off like a task on his to-do list. He could hide at work, even in public, but not in his home.

She'd seen him interact with Lyon enough to see the man practically melt in the presence of his only nephew. As if there'd been any doubt considering the piles of Lego sets and game boards he'd overstocked the boy's bedroom with. And, on a very personal level, she had seen the heat in Landon's eyes when he looked at her. Had felt the very real attraction between them last night. That hadn't been a mirage.

"Don't you ever go with your gut?" she pressed when he remained silent. She couldn't help herself. She wanted to talk to him. Especially after his out-of-character monologue. She was right. He did need someone to unload on.

One thick, dark blond brow rose. "My gut."

He'd gone back to echoing her every question rather than answer. Avoidance. Well, she was no longer in the mood to let him off the hook. "*Yes*. Don't you ever use something other than your big, thinky brain?"

The brow went higher, along with one corner of his mouth. "Did you just use the word 'thinky'?"

Stubble had pressed through his sharpened jaw, making him look a tad dangerous, even in half an Armani suit and designer tie. She had the overwhelming urge to reach out and touch his cleft chin, maybe run a fingertip along his lips. She'd longed to feel even the briefest brush of his mouth last night, only to be thwarted by a parched six-year-old. She wanted to shift her gaze to the monitor to see if Lyon still slept, but knew that Landon would read her as clearly if she said *All clear! Let's make out.*

"Which, by the way, is not a word," he added as she blinked out of her thoughts.

"You know what I mean." She leaned her shoulder against the back of the sofa, moving a smidge closer to him. "Do you ever follow your heart?"

She watched her hand lift of its own volition and feather the silken hair over his temple before resting her fingertips there and tapping lightly. "Instead of your brain."

* * *

Landon stilled when she touched him. It was the softest, barely there brush of her fingers, but it made his scalp tingle like a colony of ants skittered across his skull. And his head wasn't the only part of him tingling. So were parts in his southern hemisphere. Her head was cocked just so, her shimmering green eyes bare of any makeup. All he wanted to do was sift his hand into her fiery waves and taste that mouth.

Thinky brain be damned.

He settled for lifting a piece of her hair that'd been brushing his hand since she'd turned to face him. As he rubbed the thick strands between his fingers, he realized how intimate touching her like this was. They faced each other, her fingers pressing gently against his temple, his hand in her hair.

He swallowed thickly, remembering she'd spoken last. "No. I don't follow my heart," he said, talking about two things simultaneously.

She pulled her hand away and studied him, her pink mouth sliding into an adorable little pout. "Why not?" She looked like he'd just told her unicorns weren't real. Like the Easter Bunny was a sham.

"Because it's not smart," he said, his voice gruffer than he'd intended. "You cannot build a multimillion-dollar advertising business by 'going with your gut.'" And he sure as hell hadn't profited the one time in his personal life he'd followed his heart. He'd been willing to change his entire life for Rachel; had altered his future plans to support his girlfriend and their unborn baby. And what had she done? Thrown him away. Ridded herself of him, their future. *Our baby.*

He winced, pain slicing his heart. He *hated* reminders of that time in his life. Hated how utterly out of control he'd been back then. How powerless he was to stop an event Rachel had set in motion. Once he'd grieved, once he'd had some distance and looked back at them in a practical, pragmatic way, it was obvious how ill-fated he and Rachel had been. But up close, he hadn't seen their imminent demise. Not at all.

Yes, his heart had been his worst enemy back then. Not Rachel's though; she'd been thinking clearly. Had suffered no such qualms about walking away from him, from college, from being a mother.

That was the only time in his life he'd ever allowed his

heart to blind his brain. And since the brain's sole job was to process information, it seemed wise to use it instead of the organ that at best was unreliable, and at worst, put a majority of the nation into an early grave.

His lips pulled into a frown. Kimber's arrival back into his life had brought not only memories of first meeting her at his parents' house, but had also stirred up the settled dust of his past. Well he preferred to keep the past where it belonged. *In the past.* Not irritating his every nerve ending.

"I always go with my brain," he said solidly.

She had folded her arms over her chest, jostling her breasts beneath her top in a way that he noticed there was nothing harnessing them there. *No bra.* God help him. She shuffled her shoulders and sent the small mounds sliding along the material. He averted his eyes and took a drink of his scotch, wondering if she had any idea she was doing it.

"I follow my heart," she contested.

Of course she did. He could read her like a large-print book. Could see that she offered herself as a sacrifice when the situation called, could see her need to belong. To fit. To be loved. Her desire for a whole and complete family, likely because her parents had split up when she was young.

Ideals he'd let go of a long, long time ago. He had a loving family—his siblings, his father, his cousins, his nephew. They filled the empty space in his heart that had once been earmarked for a family of his own. They'd have to do. Because he wasn't going there. He couldn't.

"Are you where you want to be in life?" he asked.

Kimber frowned, a neat little pleat slicing between her amber brows. "What's that supposed to mean?"

"I didn't mean anything other than what I asked." He slipped his glasses off and dropped them on the table next to his drink. "You're listening with your heart, getting hurt by something I didn't say."

She placed her wineglass on the table and sat back again, quiet as if considering his words. And fidgeting. She pulled on her earlobe, stroked her hair behind her ear, brushed her finger over the tip of her nose. She was like a nervous squirrel. It drove him crazy, and not in a good way ... or in a *very* good way, depending on his perspective.

"I bet you couldn't hold still if you tried," he said, his voice a low warning.

She frowned at him, folding her hands into her lap. Her brows went up as she accepted his challenge, but a second later, she pulled the inside of her bottom lip between her teeth.

"Told you." He cupped her chin and pulled her lip free from her teeth with his thumb. The moment he touched her, his big "thinky" brain shorted out. He knew he shouldn't kiss her. Knew he was reacting to the stress from work, or Evan's and Angel's suggestions that Kimber liked him. Or maybe he was simply responding to the attraction that had lit between them last night in the brief, heated space separating their bodies. The same attraction that burned now. He knew all of those things. Intellectually.

But he leaned across the short distance and laid his lips against hers anyway.

A sigh drifted out of her mouth and her eyes fluttered closed. As if he was giving her the best gift in the world. His pants grew tight in an instant. A smart guy would pull back, excuse himself to bed, and apologize for being rash. He was a smart guy. So why was he still moving his mouth gently along hers?

Because she tastes too damn good, came the answer. He traced her bottom lip with his tongue; tasting the red wine on her mouth, savoring the notes of raspberry and dark cherries lingering there. *Delectable.*

Wrapping her arms around his neck, she leaned into him,

one knee digging into his leg, and pulled his head toward hers. She darted her tongue into his mouth while he fought to keep pace. He clasped her at the ribs, holding her against him, and matched her mouth blow for blow. It was erotic as hell to have this woman literally writhing against him, her soft braless breasts pressed into his chest, her mouth making his brain relay information in sluggish Morse code.

"Your knee," he said between her devouring his mouth. He cupped her knee in his palm to relieve the pressure—*the bruise* she was leaving on his leg—and slid her leg aside.

"Oh," she breathed into his mouth. Her glassy eyes cleared and she abruptly pulled away and sat back on her heels.

He sat in exactly the same position, his back to the couch, arms at his sides, erection throbbing loud enough for the neighbors to hear...

She grew restless, eyes darting around the porch, shoulders shifting. She reached for her Pinot Noir and took a drink. So fidgety.

He chuckled.

After she swallowed her wine, she frowned. "What?"

"Nothing."

The main difference between her and him was she had no clue what she was capable of; probably didn't know where she'd be in two years. He knew what he was capable of. Knew who he was, and who he wasn't. He'd plotted and planned his life out in incremental pieces for the last decade. Where he'd bet Kimber had been flying by the seat of her tantalizingly tight pants since adolescence.

"Where do you see yourself in five years?" he asked, curious if he was right. But he was. He knew it.

She let out a short laugh. "Back on the interview clock?"

"Just trying to prove a point."

Anger flared in her green eyes. "What point? Don't dance around it. Just say it."

Fair enough. "You're looking for who you are. You're tempting and sexy and I can see that you like me. But you also don't know what you want."

He'd offended her. A scowl bisected her forehead. "And you do?"

"Yes." He wanted predictability, a company that excelled, a glass of thirty-year-old scotch on the balcony of his penthouse.

"I've liked you for a long time, Landon."

Her honesty and the turn of the conversation took him by surprise. He broke his casual position by bending forward and taking a drink. When he leaned back, she was waiting for his reaction. Maybe for him to say he liked her, too. And he did. But telling her that would set high expectations.

Too high.

"I know you do." He hated to ruin her peaches-and-cream worldview, to point out the thorns in her rose-colored glasses, but he didn't want to lie to her, either. "I don't want to sully who you are," he said. "I don't want to see you jaded. Bitter." *Like me.*

She blinked a few times. "Wow. Cocky much?"

He sniffed. "Not cocky. Just honest."

She shifted in her seat, her shoulders going back, her chin lifting in defiance. Her nipples pressed against the beaded owl on the shirt she wore, a distracting view, but he forced his eyes back to her face. Eyes that flared with bottle-green anger. *Redhead.* He'd never dated a redhead before. Maybe the lore was true and she was every bit the hothead she appeared to be right now.

"Just because I follow my heart," she said adamantly, her face a confusion of strength and hurt. "Just because I'm transparent and not in control of my every body movement"—she gestured with her hands, sending her small breasts sliding against the shirt and turning him on even more—"doesn't mean I'm a doe-eyed innocent. I know what I'm doing. I think I can handle kissing you without losing all essence of who I am." Clutching the tie around his neck, she leaned in. "I am an independent, intelligent woman who does *not* need to be saved from anyone. Least of all *you*."

She was a woman all right. A seething, beautiful woman who was very close to him and smelling like the cucumber body wash stocked in her bathroom. He knew. He'd grown accustomed to the warm, sweet scent that eked its way into the hall every morning after her shower.

"I wasn't being insulting," he said, hiding his amusement.

"Yes you were," she challenged, tugging him closer. He went, the tension pulling the tie against the back of his neck, unable to keep from admiring how beautiful she was, even this close. Natural, naked skin, full lips…"But I forgive you."

The side of his mouth ticked. He was going to kiss her again. But he'd give her a chance to make the first move. She did, fisting his tie even tighter and laying her lips onto his, but she didn't stop there. With the swing of her leg over his lap, she settled on top of him. She sat right over his manhood, heat emanating from her core and through his slacks.

It wasn't often, if ever, he found himself turned on by being put in his place. Was rarely *ever* put in his place, come to think of it. He would concede he'd given Kimber less credit than she deserved. Either she knew what she wanted, or had opted to take the upper hand when she found herself at a disadvantage. He respected both tactics.

She deepened the kiss, running her hands through his hair and clutching his head. His hands went to her butt, cupping and kneading the soft globes in his palms, stopping short of grinding her against him and relieving the painful ache pounding his balls like a pair of bongos.

She stroked his tongue with hers, completely in control of this kiss and knowing where to take him. He fought to keep up, to figure out what she might do next, to catch the curveballs she was throwing. God, it was exciting. *Amazing.* The not-knowing... who knew that could be so enthralling?

Then she stopped. Abruptly. Just turned off like a switch, climbed from his lap, reclaimed her wine, and settled onto the cushion she'd been lounging on when he'd first walked out here.

He licked the side of his mouth, still tasting her there, his hands at his sides, chest heaving, hair probably a mess from her roaming fingers.

She wouldn't look at him, a study in casualness except for the one hand forced into a fist at her side. Trying to keep herself from fidgeting, no doubt. She was the sexiest thing he'd ever seen. And she'd more than proved her point. If he wanted a partner to spar with, in bed or out, she was a worthy opponent, not some delicate flower he had to handle with care.

Giving in and moving the hand she'd forcibly stilled, she pushed her hair over her shoulder and studied the skyline. The moon was an unimpressive half, not a fancy crescent or mournful full. His chin was elevated when she spoke next, her words stunning him so much, he snapped his head to face her.

"Hope no one saw that and is uploading it to YouTube." She blinked as if she'd stunned herself, too. "I'm so sorry. That was... wow. Rude. I'm sorry."

He found himself mildly amused. "It's fine, really." It was.

"It's not," she insisted. "It's mean."

"I know you didn't intend to be vicious. Trust me, Kimber, it's fine. Lissa and I weren't exactly head-over-heels-in-love there at the end." Or for most of the beginning. For six years, their relationship had been more controlled and organized than a lab experiment. Which had been fine by him. What *hadn't* been fine was the grainy video shown to him on someone's cell phone. There wasn't a good place to find out his fiancée was involved in some seriously heavy petting with another man, but a charity dinner for cystic fibrosis had to be one of the worst.

"That's sad," she said.

She had that heartbroken look in her eyes again. He didn't like that fragility. It made him want to...he didn't know what. Protect her, or something. Which was insane. Like he was in any position to be anyone's knight.

"It wasn't..." He didn't know how to go about explaining his and Lissa's relationship without sounding like a machine. "It didn't start out that way," he amended. "I cared about her."

Oh yes. Way to not sound like a machine.

But it was the truth. He'd cared about Lissa. He'd never loved her though. "By the time we were engaged, we were friends at best." They'd been over each other. He'd thought they'd been friends, had a kind of understanding most couples didn't have. They could travel, work, all without answering to each other. It'd been an ideal arrangement. Companionship, sex. A partner. But it hadn't been enough. Not for Lissa. He'd learned that the night he'd seen the footage of her and Carson Robbins. The prick.

"Then why did you get engaged?" Kimber asked, interrupting his thoughts.

"Are you a reporter?" he asked.

Her cheeks tinged with embarrassment. "I'm sorry."

He touched her knee, smiling for her benefit. "Kidding."

"Oh." He was rewarded by a small smile. He wanted to kiss her again; found himself wishing she would saddle him so he could once more grasp on to her cushiony, delicious body. Sounded like a better idea than them sitting here talking about his ex-fiancée.

"So... why did you?" she pressed.

She wasn't going to let that go. He would have to tell her the ugly truth. *Is there any other kind?*

"Because, like the YouTube video, Lissa thought an engagement would be good publicity."

Kimber's eyes widened. Naïve to the ways of the world. If only she knew how many things were staged, arranged, and pretended. He watched her. She watched him back.

Would she be strong enough to handle this about him? Or would she stand firmly on her moral high ground and use his revelation as an excuse to leave? There was a reason no one in his family knew he and Lissa were about as in love with one another as Democrats and Republicans. Because they would have lectured and browbeat him a long time ago.

Like Kimber was planning on lecturing him now?

He liked her. Too much, he realized a bit belatedly. But then, there was no danger of losing himself to her, was there? His head was efficiently separated from his heart. As they'd clearly just established.

But she didn't lecture him. She reached for his hand and squeezed. He wanted to turn his palm over and intertwine their fingers. Instead, he slipped his hand free and reached for his scotch.

"Don't be," he said after a thorough drink. "I am the Tin Man."

Her brows lowered. "You think you have no heart?" she asked with a hint of disgust.

He knew he didn't. At least, not in the way she was suggesting. "Lissa's nickname for me." He raised a shoulder dismissively.

"Well Lissa is a cheating, awful, horrible person who

took you for granted. If I were you, I wouldn't heed to her opinion."

He sat up taller, felt stronger. Kimber coming out swinging in his defense? He didn't need it, but he appreciated it. Other than his mother and sister—and *they* did *not* count—he hadn't had a woman in his corner in a long, long time. If ever. Kimber was so real. Authenticity radiated from her like steam from a kettle. So different from the women he'd shared his life with before.

Nice to know he could count on the truth for as long as she was around. She'd never use him up for her own needs, whether he was willing or not.

A spark of hope lit within him and he snuffed it out. Hoping for a future with Kimber was pointless. The lure of fake bait at the end of a fishing line. He knew who he was. And getting a glimpse of someone he could've been before he'd endured his unchangeable past didn't matter now. That man wasn't real.

"Heads up," she murmured, pulling him out of his darkening thoughts. He followed the direction of her gaze to the baby monitor. The screen showed Lyon's tangled bedding and abandoned Superman figurine, but his nephew was nowhere to be seen.

A moment later, Lyon appeared at the patio door. Kimber stood and Landon had the inconceivable urge to latch on to her wrist and pull her down next to him, despite their pint-sized company.

"Let me guess. Water?" she asked Lyon.

Lyon nodded.

"Come say good night to your uncle," she said sweetly. Landon's heart pinched as she turned those soft eyes on him before walking inside. Then pinched harder when he caught his nephew against his chest and managed to wrangle the boy into the seat next to him.

While his nephew recapped his adventurous day of Legos, Gotham City, and peanut butter sandwiches, Landon couldn't stop his eyes from going over Lyon's head to the swing of Kimber's bottom as she walked through the living room to the open kitchen.

Not going to happen, he reminded himself sternly.

For her sake. And for his.

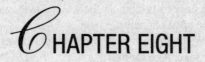

CHAPTER EIGHT

This is all your fault," Kimber teased after telling Gloria the gory details about what happened on the patio with Landon.

Glo choked out a laugh.

She'd sworn Glo to secrecy. Kimber didn't know what, if anything, Evan knew about Landon and Lissa's relationship, but she'd made it clear to Gloria not to repeat any of it.

"Well you, my friend, are welcome," Glo said, sounding satisfied.

"I'm 'welcome'?" She laid on the sarcasm pretty thick, but Glo didn't flinch.

"You shared a delicious lip lock with a powerful, wealthy man, sweetie. *You are welcome.*"

She made an excellent point. "Okay, well, maybe I'll blame Mick. If I didn't need the money to buy him out of Hobo Chic—"

"I warned you not to turn your boy toy into your business partner."

Kimber leaned on the bench, one eye on Lyon who waved before he slid down the slide in the playground. She smiled and waved back, then frowned at her best friend. "Do you really think now is the right time for an 'I told you so'?"

Glo took a sip from her extra-large Starbucks cup. "Maybe not."

"Anyway. If I hadn't needed the money, I could have said no."

"It's perfect, actually."

Kimber sipped her iced coffee and watched Lyon play on the slide. "What's perfect?"

"You always fall in love with every guy you date," Glo said. "Well, maybe not *with them* but with the idea of being in love."

Kimber didn't know what brought on that bit of psychobabble. Unfortunately, Glo was right. Mick. Joey. Stephen. All of them would have been perfectly suitable short-term relationships. It was Kimber who'd sunk her hooks in them and tried to drag it out. Tried to make it work.

"It's because of the divorce," Kimber said. "I'm trying to make up for the fact that I couldn't save my parents' marriage, so I try to make every relationship stand the test of time."

Glo's black eyebrows disappeared into her thick, ebony bangs.

"Dr. Phil," Kimber supplied.

"Huh."

"Kimber! Watch!"

"I'm watching!" she called to Lyon, applauding when he slid to the bottom and rolled to the ground. She laughed, then her laugh faded. If she had said no to Angel's offer to babysit, she never would have met Lyon. And he'd opened her heart in a way she couldn't describe. Like he'd knocked down a wall and let light in.

Yeah. And that light-filled, wall-less heart has nothing to do with Landon.

"You're so good with him," Gloria observed.

"I know. Weird."

"No. It's not the least bit surprising that you're good with children. You are a very self-sacrificing person. You love in a genuine, uncompromising way. Whereas I'm just...mean."

"You're not mean," Kimber said. Then frowned. Glo's description of Kimber reminded her of Landon's assessment last night. Was she really seen as a saint? She'd gone out of her way to prove to him she wasn't saintly last night. She'd risen with the worst feeling of dread this morning, and hoped she might not run into him.

She did run into him, of course. The house may be big, but the kitchen was the hub of all morning activity. There'd been no avoiding him. Lyon had been watching TV from the kitchen table while his Froot Loops went soggy while Kimber munched on an English muffin. Landon had stepped into the kitchen in a sexy charcoal suit and a pair of stylish silver-rimmed glasses she'd never seen before.

He made himself a cup of coffee, pausing to tell Lyon to eat his breakfast and to mention to her that he hoped he'd be home earlier than the last two nights. He'd also slid her a knowing look that made her nipples tighten before murmuring, "Red or white wine tonight? I'd like to prepare my palate."

She fanned her shirt now, her face growing warm as she remembered the way he'd licked his bottom lip and sent her a smile. Her palate was prepared for one thing for sure: more of his amazing mouth.

"Well. Whatever label you put on it, it's still perfect," Glo said.

Back to that? "Okay. I give. What, exactly, is perfect?"

"Your situation with Landon. A fun-night stand with him would be the perfect fix to your issue with thinking you're in love."

"I seriously doubt he has any interest in dating me." But her private parts tingled at the idea of taking his clothes off. Because *yowza*.

"Not dating. No dating. Sometimes I think your vintage lifestyle has seeped into your brain." Glo laughed at her own joke and elbowed Kimber good-naturedly. "Anyway, I'm not talking about dating or having a boyfriend. I'm talking about an affair. A clandestine one."

"Oh, I see. You're insane." Kimber sent her a wry smile.

"He kissed you. You kissed him. You're practically lovers already."

Kimber laughed but it sounded strange. And strained. And she was a little sweaty now that a visual of her sexing up Landon Downey had flashed onto the frontal lobe of her brain. She chewed on the inside of her lip while she stirred her iced cappuccino with the straw. Glo was right. He had kissed her. Heck, he'd made the first move. Well, if she didn't count stroking his temple with her fingernails. And the moonlit night had been romantic...

"You're thinking about it," Gloria sang.

"Yeah, I am. I've sort of been wandering in the desert since Mick and I split. I'm on a diet of no sex and arguing with my ex. And, you know...he's Mick." She gave Gloria a meaningful look. They'd dished about their sex lives before. Glo knew how unsatisfied she'd been.

Glo grunted. "Yeah, well Cameron was my last and that was over a month ago." She wrinkled her nose. "No good."

"Why do you insist on finding guys at the club if it never works out?"

"Because one day it might." Sad thing was, she knew Glo really believed that. That she'd find her Prince Charming in the midst of absinthe and Jäger bombs. "Too bad I don't like kids. Or my client might be a good option." She sent a meaningful glance over at Lyon.

"You don't mean..."

"Hey, Evan is *hot*. Hot with two Ts."

She couldn't argue. "He is. And he's a good dad."

Gloria sighed. Kimber said nothing. Gloria's home life hadn't been a pretty one. Compared to her druggie mother and various foster homes, Kimber's adolescence resembled *The Brady Bunch*. Glo probably thought she'd make a terrible mother. But what woman didn't worry about what kind of parent she'd be?

By comparison, Kimber couldn't fault her own parents. After she'd grown up, she realized they were disturbingly normal. Human. Accidentally pregnant with Kimber, her mother had married her father. The marriage lasted sixteen years before ending in divorce. It was the not-earth-shattering story of how two people who were once in love grew apart. Kimber planned on getting married one time, and one time only. But at this rate, even that was looking un-doable. She'd developed a bad pattern. A pattern of searching for longevity where there was none. Why she expected every next relationship to stand the test of time was easily deciphered: She wanted forever.

"Hey." Glo snapped her fingers. "Jack Handey. Having some Deep Thoughts over there?" She smiled at her own joke. "So what do you think of a fling?"

"A fling?"

"Do you prefer millionaire affair?"

"*Gloria,*" she reprimanded, appalled.

"Okay, okay," her friend said around a laugh. Fun-night stand."

"Mick was a one-night stand and that didn't work out." Or, at least, that had been the idea. It'd been Glo who'd suggested Kimber pick up Mick. He was supposed to help her get over an ex-boyfriend. It worked. A little too well.

"Not a *one*-night stand." Glo fell silent as a woman walked by with her toddler daughter in tow. When the mother was out of earshot, she continued. "A *fun*-night stand."

"And that is?"

She shrugged. "A fling that lasts until it stops being fun. Yours is pre-packaged to be just that. Landon doesn't do connection, obviously, if he was so willing to have an 'arrangement' with that supermodel."

Kimber wrinkled her nose. That arrangement didn't make sense. Not really. Landon was from a beautiful, giving, lovely family. He genuinely loved and cared for his siblings and nephew. She'd seen him around Lyon. He was great with him. And Angel told her how he hadn't wanted Lyon to stay at his business's day care. He'd hired Kimber so that Evan could take his art immersion classes. So that Lyon could have round-the-clock care. And Landon *wasn't* the Tin Man.

And now that she thought about Lyon... "It won't be easy. We sort of have a child in the house."

"A *big* house. Parents find a way. You"—Glo poked her arm—"will find a way."

She had to laugh. This was sounding more like a mission by the minute. "I'm not a sitcom character, you know. This isn't a romantic comedy where you can concoct a plot and a specific outcome."

"I know! This is your life." Glo opened her palms to the heavens, then shook Kimber's arm. "And your life doesn't have to be this much pressure! You've gone from long-term relationship to long-term relationship. Trust me on this. You need laid, not encumbered."

She could get behind that. The very last thing she wanted was to be encumbered. Again. "But Angel's my friend. Won't that be awkward?"

"Why? Do you go to her house for Christmas or something?"

Valid point. "What if Landon tells Evan and Evan talks to you about it?"

"They're men, sweetheart, they don't gossip like we do. If Landon did tell Evan, it'd never get back to me. Plus, I'd already know because you're going to tell me *everything*."

"Everything?" Kimber asked with a weak smile.

Glo waggled her brows. "*Everything*."

"A fun-night stand," Kimber murmured to herself. "It does have a nice ring to it."

Gloria grinned, satisfied. "Does, doesn't it?"

Lyon picked a dandelion and handed it to the very little girl who had walked by with her mother a moment ago. She was sitting in the sandbox, her chubby knees poking out of the sand. He offered again and the girl took the weed and rolled it between her tiny fingers. Then he patted her on the arm and smiled that charming Downey smile.

"God, he's cute," Glo said, something wistful and rare lining her happy-go-lucky voice.

"I know," Kimber replied softly.

You should see his uncle.

* * *

Landon hadn't wanted to go to work on Saturday, not when it was Lyon's last day here. He'd appeased himself by promising he'd come home early. He did; right around six, which wasn't half-bad.

And yeah, he'd been hard on his designers this week. Harder than necessary, truth be told. They weren't as dim or imbecilic as he'd accused them of being. He could be a tyrant when he was laser-focused. He'd gifted them with certificates to a local restaurant, enough for them to treat their spouses/significant others. They'd earned it. Windy City now had a solid visual concept everyone was behind. No slogan yet, but he breathed a sigh of relief at having made it this far.

When he'd overheard several people making plans to go out tonight, he'd found himself feeling the rare urge to be included in the celebration. Not that he'd intended on going—he never hung out with his employees in a casual environment. They didn't want him to, and he understood why. Who wanted to hang out with the boss? Watch everything they say? But he'd entertained the notion, picturing Kimber on his arm, her body decked out in a vintage dress showcasing the length of her legs, her hair a bright red twist at the back of her neck.

That's when he'd concluded the fantasy had nothing to do with going out with his co-workers. He wanted to go out with *her*. Especially after the kiss on the balcony last night. How many times had he caught his mind straying to the memory of her fingers on his neck, the press of her breasts against his chest, the erotic way she slid her tongue along his lips? Too many.

Or not enough.

The thought of Kimber at one of his work functions made him smile. Her presence would go over a lot smoother than Lissa's. Lissa saw herself as a work of art. As a result, she was constantly striking a pose or pulling her lips into a moue for whoever might be looking in her direction. She'd told him once her job was to be "consistently beautiful." At the time, he'd understood. His job was to be consistently professional; he could relate to the pressure of meeting expectations.

But Kimber wouldn't have to justify why she was doing what she did. And he'd bet she'd go a long way to bridging the gap between his employees and him. She wasn't just good with people. She was *real*. Real, and so darn likable. If they arrived arm in arm, he had no doubt everyone in the restaurant would wonder how he'd gotten the natural, fidgety, sexy redhead to accompany him. He wondered *if* she would go out with him. Odd that he wasn't sure what she'd say if he asked her.

Art board for Windy City under his arm, he stepped into his house planning on making a beeline for his office. Until the tantalizing smell of peppers and cheese stopped him cold. A pizza box stood on the countertop and he drifted to it like it was outfitted with a tractor beam. Or like those cartoon characters that lifted off the floor and floated toward the scent. He'd been so out of the habit of eating pizza—thanks to living with a raw-food-diet supermodel—he couldn't remember the last slice of Giordano's he'd had. Four years ago? No. *Five.*

A lifetime.

He abandoned the art board and his briefcase, chucking his jacket over a chair. Then he dove in to the box, eating one slice, and a second, pausing only long enough to scrub his mouth with a paper towel between big, greedy bites. He never would have found pizza in the house when he'd dated Lissa. "Cursed carbs" were strictly off her diet. He hadn't thought giving up pizza had been that big of a deal. After inhaling two slices, though...Lord have mercy.

He laid waste to a third piece, dug a bottle of water out of the fridge, and guzzled it down. Then he tracked through the house to find his nephew. What was with the lack of welcome home tonight? He was early and neither Lyon nor Kimber were anywhere to be seen. They wouldn't have gone somewhere without telling him, would they?

But then he heard them. His nephew's laughter punctuated by Kimber's mid-range *ha-ha-ha*. Landon followed the sound through the hallway, to the right...and straight to his own bedroom.

Lyon giggled, a sound of pure joy, and Landon felt the pressure from the week melt off him. Not wanting them to hear him coming, he toed his shoes off and stepped lightly on the hardwood floor.

"You look silly!" Lyon said, erupting again.

"Do I?" *Kimber.*

"Fix mine." *Lyon.*

What were they doing?

"Okay, here. Wait. Wow. I used to know how to do this. I used to be really good at it. If you don't use it you lose it, right?"

Landon crept to the door frame, not wanting to interrupt but too curious not to poke his head in on them.

"What's that mean?" Lyon asked. The kid was a master of questioning everything. Would make an excellent lawyer someday.

"It means if I don't practice tying ties, then I forget how to tie them. Even though you never forget how to ride a bike," she murmured to herself. "Or how to play Euchre."

Landon smiled at her logic. Illogical logic.

"What's Euchre?" Lyon asked. On second thought, the kid might make a better game show host.

"A card game."

"Can we play?"

"Let's finish this up first," she answered.

Landon gave himself up and peered around the door frame. Kimber and his nephew were seated on the floor, each of them wearing one of Landon's shirts. Lyon had on a blue oxford and she wore a dry-clean-only white. A slow, stupid smile spread across his face at the scene he'd just walked in on.

"Uncle Landon! Check it out." Lyon stood, then held his arms to his sides to show off his duds.

Kimber rose slower, looking a little chagrined...and gut-clenching sexy. A pair of black plastic glasses rested on her nose, and a tie around her neck was twisted into the most hopeless knot imaginable.

Lyon straightened his matching pair of glasses, too big for his face.

"Who are you dressed as?" Landon leaned on the door frame and crossed his arms, studying Lyon's glasses, shirt, and not-quite-right necktie. Had his nephew dressed like him? Something welcome unfurled in the center of his chest.

"We're Clark Kent!" Lyon pulled his shirt open to reveal his Superman pajamas.

Landon nodded his understanding. Kimber gave him a sheepish grin and pulled her shirt open, revealing a red "S" made of construction paper she'd pinned between her small, but amazing, breasts.

"Kimber says we're doing it right even though this didn't happen in *Man of Steel*," Lyon said.

"A purist," Landon said, keeping his eyes on her.

"Through and through," she mumbled, not quite meeting his gaze.

Lyon wrestled with his tie...which more resembled Jacob's ladder than a double Windsor. "Want me to fix it?"

"No. I'm done doing this." He pried the tie and shirt off and dropped them onto the floor before running down the hall, *faster than a speeding bullet*, to the living room. "I have to go watch *Man of Steel*!"

"Hey, you left—" Landon called after him. He stopped short at the feel of Kimber's fingers brushing his arm.

"It's okay, I'll get it." She bent to gather the discarded play clothes—his actual work clothes—from the floor. "Sorry about this." She gestured with the clothes in her hands. "Kind of invaded your space."

She was nervous. *Adorable.* She plucked the glasses off her nose and slid them into her hair. It was down today, in soft waves tickling her shoulders. When she screwed her eyes up at him, she looked small and guilty.

"You don't know how to tie a tie." He unfolded his arms

and pushed off the door frame where he'd been leaning. As he went to work unraveling it, his fingers brushed her neck every so often. Her skin was so soft. Memories of last night, of the taste of her lips, the way she'd ridden him fully clothed, tightened his next breath.

"I used to," she said quietly, pulling his shirt closed over her tank top and buttoning the buttons one by one.

"Don't they teach you that in fashion school?" He threw the wide end of the tie over the narrow end, then repeated the motion.

"Yes. I learned how when I was seven; used to love to tie my dad's ties."

The mention of her father reminded him of the summer her parents had divorced. She'd been upset. He'd seen the evidence in her defeated stature at his family's dinner table. His parents had been a unit, so in love that it'd nearly killed his father when Mom died. But Landon had a solid family, siblings. Kimber had no siblings, he remembered, and her parents' marriage had fractured when she was at a fragile age.

He didn't know what it would be like not to be able to count on his family. He'd probably taken for granted that his parents would be there for him when he came home from college that summer. And they had. They'd welcomed him back, no questions asked. Well, almost no questions. He'd been as vague as possible when his mother asked why he was home and not on campus. He'd told her that Rachel dumped him, that he was okay, but wanted to be home. She'd accepted his words at face value, never prying into his personal life. She'd died not knowing she almost had another grandchild. At least she'd gotten to know Lyon, he thought, suddenly sad.

He stuffed the bottom of the tie through the loop, shaking off his morose thoughts. "I never thanked you for helping me with my paper that summer you stayed with us." Creative writing. *Hell on earth.* One would think that as a marketing major, who was an excellent designer, he'd have a good grasp of writing a paper. He didn't. Slogans were a breeze compared to two-thousand-word fictional stories. Kimber had offered to look at his story—hell if he could remember now what it'd been about—and handed it back to him obliterated with red marks. She'd apologized profusely at the time.

"Oh, that," she said now, a smile tugging her mouth. "I was...overzealous back then."

"You were also right." The praise he'd gotten for that assignment was for the elements she had suggested adding. Advanced English Lit had treated her well. She was smart.

She finished buttoning the shirt. "Did you get an A?"

"I got a C." He tightened the knot of the tie, sparing her a glance. "Not your fault." The television blared from the other room, shocking the silence from the air and surprising him. He jerked, in the process knocking his hand against her chin. Her teeth clacked together audibly and she lifted a hand to cover her lips, scrunching her eyes shut.

"Oh my God, Kimber. Are you all right?" *Way to go, just punch her in the face, why don't you?* He cradled her jaw in his hands. Her damp eyes fluttered open. "I'll get you some ice."

Lightly touching his hand, she shook her head. "No. I'm okay." She blinked again, sniffing. "Natural reaction to being clocked in the jaw."

"I'm so sorry."

She smiled, though, holding no grudge. Rather than move his hand away, he trailed his fingers from her face to her neck. Her hair tickled the backs of his hands and her eyes darkened to forest green. His attention snapped to her lips and, in a rush, he remembered last night. The way she'd climbed on him, claimed him, stroked her eager tongue against his...

She thought about it, too. He could tell by the way she tipped her chin…And he was kissing her again. With no more invitation than that. He moved his lips slowly, gently over hers, his fingers resting on her neck, his thumbs under her chin. Then it was over and he was pulling his head back to train his eyes on hers.

"I want you." He brushed her lip with the pad of one thumb. "Badly."

She watched him, motionless and silent instead of fidgety and flabbergasted.

A good sign. "Say something."

"This is the part where I'm supposed to say this is a bad idea, right? That we should be responsible and think of Lyon and not get involved."

"Probably," he admitted.

Her eyes turned up to his. "I don't want to say that."

His hopes levitated. Hopes he had no reason to feel. Kimber wasn't like the women he'd dated before. She wasn't cold and calculating. Most of his girlfriends past were career-driven and would sooner dive into oncoming traffic than leave work for a week to do him a favor. Paid or not.

Despite his reasoning not to encourage her, he did. "Then say what you want."

"I want you," she whispered.

He wasn't the kind of guy led around by the silent partner in his pants. Did most of his thinking with the head on his shoulders. But he was having trouble processing— *recalibrating*—since those three words had tightened a cord of longing attaching his sternum to his balls.

"Honey," he rasped, tightening his hold on her arms. "You can have me." He went for her lips, but she spoke before he caught them.

"But it could only be temporary."

He hadn't expected her to say something along those

lines. Her face clouded with doubt, her words a question rather than a statement that she waited for him to confirm. Yet she'd spoken with authority. Certainty. Almost like she was letting him down easily.

He'd play along. For now. "Okay." She had assured him last night that he didn't have to handle her with kid gloves. "Tell me what you had in mind."

Because he had no clue what she was thinking. Lissa had been easy to figure out. She'd always been thinking of one of two things: herself or her career. Kimber, though ... the sky was the limit.

"We can make a list ... of things to do. Together ..." She flinched, just a little, making him fairly sure she didn't make a habit of creating sex lists with men. *Thank God.* "When we reach the end of the list," she said, "we can end things ... no harm, no foul."

Well, hell. He liked that. *A lot.* But he wasn't this much of a Cretan. "Honey, you don't have to talk yourself into this. If this is going to be a struggle—"

She surprised him by laughing. She clapped her hand over her mouth as if she'd surprised herself, too. Lifting her eyes, she met his gaze with that soft, green stare of hers. "It won't be a struggle for me. I've wanted you for as long as I can remember."

His chest expanded as he pulled all the oxygen he could hold into his lungs. He suddenly wanted to do right by this woman. This honest, sexy, amazing woman. Winding her hair around his fingers, he tested its softness. "Dorothy and the Tin Man," he murmured.

"You're not that heartless," she said. "And I'm not that innocent."

She tipped her lips and kissed him. His hands found the back of her neck as his eyes fell closed. Soon the kiss turned deeper, then borderline rough. His only thoughts were the taste of her, the feel of her against him, his ratcheting pulse rushing the blood to his crotch.

Until the television rattled from a digital explosion. Lyon cheered from the other room, and Landon pulled his lips from Kimber's and tried to catch his breath. Their privacy had yet to be breached. But it would be, and long before he'd gotten as far as he wanted.

"So?" she asked, licking her lips. "What do you think of my proposal?"

With a sly grin, he pulled her a fraction closer so that her body pressed up against his. He thought it was perfect. He wasn't in any position for a girlfriend—arranged or not—so her suggestion couldn't have fit into his life any better. They wanted one another and she, for whatever reason, didn't want to have a commitment. This was gift wrapped for him.

"What kind of list?" he asked.

"Top ten?" she suggested, a mischievous light in her eyes.

He loved how she kept surprising him. "As you wish."

"Then a clean break," she affirmed with a nod. This was an important part of the agreement, he was seeing. He wasn't sure why but wasn't foolish enough to ask.

"Ten locations?" He leaned in and breathed into her ear, loving how she shuddered. "Or ten positions?" He had no trouble thinking of twenty of each, maybe twenty-five, but he didn't want to send her fleeing.

"Both," she whispered when he kissed her neck. He lingered there a moment, tasting her skin before lifting his face to kiss her lips. She put her palm on his cheek to stop him. "What about Lyon?" she asked. "He rarely sleeps through the night."

So she wanted to do this tonight. He was flattered. And excited. He didn't want to wait, either. "Guess we'll have to be quiet." He smiled. "I'll add that to the list."

She chuckled, a decadent sound matching the rich

mahogany tones in her hair. "I feel like we're making battle plans."

"Not battle." No, making love to Kimber Reynolds wouldn't be a battle. It'd be nothing short of incredible; a perfect release of the tension he'd been stockpiling since he'd landed the Windy City account and his brother had appeared on his doorstep.

Locking his arms around her waist he kissed her again, tugging her against him. Like before, he eased into her, losing the pressure of the day in her mouth. His knotted shoulders lowered from his ears. But this kiss...this kiss was a promise of *more*. Tonight if they could swing it.

As much "more" as we can squeeze in after Lyon's bedtime.

CHAPTER NINE

*A*fter she escaped Landon's interlocking arms, Kimber retreated to her bedroom using the excuse of a shower. She'd been thorough, shaving every part of her body and following up with a sheen of moisturizer.

You can do this. You can do this.

She could. The hard part was over. The part where she'd suggested they use each other up. It was a tinge disconcerting how quickly he'd agreed. Purposefully, she threw her shoulders back. She was not over-thinking this. Fun-night stands, by definition, were supposed to be fun. And she intended to have some freaking *fun* for once. As she closed her eyes, she took a deep breath. A fun, sexy romp. A roll in the hay. Nothing more.

Don't make this into anything more.

With that mantra ringing in her ears, she opened a dresser drawer to search for passably sexy underwear. She hesitated over her underthings, laughing darkly when the closest thing she'd found to a set was a pair of black panties and a charcoal gray bra.

Landon's last girlfriend had been a Victoria's Secret

model, for goodness' sake, and Kimber couldn't find a matching set of lingerie. Her undergarments were far more function than form. Sturdy, not clingy or lacey or particularly sexy.

They would have to do. She wouldn't be wearing them long, anyway.

This is such a bad idea. Like seeing a train's headlight in the distance but refusing to step off the tracks.

Stop it. No more analyzing.

Glo may be a party girl, but she had her moments of pinpoint insight. And her friend's call on the situation with Landon was right on. Kimber and Landon wanted one another. Neither of them was in the space where they wanted more than something physical. This was the perfect solution.

Kimber, for one, was wildly attracted to him. She hadn't worked out yet if she was just convenient to him or if he really liked her, but she'd concluded it didn't really matter. *It isn't like we'll be making holiday plans together.*

After agonizing over what to wear, she settled on an off-the-shoulder striped T-shirt and short cotton shorts. She left her feet bare and navigated the hallway until she reached the living room. There she found Landon, in his suit pants, arm flung over the back of the couch with Lyon's head resting on his leg. It was so cute, her heart gave a little tug.

No tugging. This is your fun-night stand. No tugging allowed unless it's in the bedroom.

"Couldn't resist the lure of Henry Cavill, I see." Landon nodded at the screen.

"Who can?"

Lyon shushed them, eyes glued to the screen. Landon's lips twitched in amusement as he reprimanded him by ruffling his hair and saying, "Don't be rude. I am allowed to speak."

She sat on the couch at Lyon's feet, snuggling into the

fabric and calming her nerves with a deep breath. No matter what, she wouldn't sit here and fret over what might happen tonight. Over the agreement she'd made—the agreement she'd *needed* to make. An agreement that would allow her to have a clean slate, a do-over.

And the time of your adult life.

That, too. She wondered if Landon had taken her seriously. If he'd really made a list. She had started one. There were three things on it. And they weren't all that adventurous.

A flash of movement to her right caught her eye and she turned her head. Landon turned his palm up and watched her, head propped on his other arm, one eyebrow raised over the rim of his glasses.

She shifted and laid her arm over the couch before resting her palm in his. Holding her hand, he turned his attention to the screen and they sat that way the rest of the movie. Occasionally, he would rearrange their fingers or rub her thumb with his, but he never let go. Once, he looked over and she met his heated gaze, saw in it the promises of things to come. The heat transferred from his body to hers, causing her palm to grow damp.

The movie credits rolled and he lifted a snoozing Lyon off the couch and murmured he was going to tuck him in. "Meet you in your room," he'd whispered before vanishing into his nephew's bedroom, Lyon in his arms.

That left her to walk to her room alone, contemplating her "fun-night stand" along the way. Heated kisses, the slide of sheets against their nude bodies. She shuddered and closed her door. Then stared at it, chewing her lip. She hadn't taken this gig to get laid. Hadn't, in her wildest imaginings thought for one deluded second Landon would agree to sleep with her. If she'd known then what she knew now, would she still have said yes?

More than once, she thought wryly.

But sex with Landon was about more than sacking a hot guy. Being with him would be a dream come true, a fantasy sixteen years in the making, a night of—

Gloria's scolding face popped into Kimber's psyche, and her brain registered a warning.

Oh. Right.

The point was *not* to make this into more than what it was. The *point* was to prove to herself once and for all she could have a fling. She didn't have to turn every relationship into potential matrimony. She could love 'em and leave 'em with the best of them.

Kimber chewed on a fingernail. This was ridiculous. She was as skilled at not getting attached as she was at knife-throwing. In other words: *not at all.*

Time to turn that around then.

She'd never find a husband if she kept smothering the life out of her dates. If she kept caging them into her world and not letting them breathe. A small part of her started to argue that she wasn't quite the Black Widow she'd just accused herself of being, but she shut down her defenses. She had to get out of this rut. And it was a deep rut. One mired with mud, and desperation, and the bones of her past relationships.

Tired of staring at the door like a desperate dog waiting on its owner to return, she went to the bathroom and fussed with her hair. She brushed her teeth again, checked her toenail polish, swept powder over her nose. She sat on the bed. Then laid on it. Then got up and remade it so that there were no wrinkles on the duvet.

She frowned at the door, then at herself, for waiting around like a good little maiden. Either Lyon was awake and being a bear, or Landon was taking his sweet time coming to her. Either way, she needed to find out what was going on outside of her room.

At the end of the hallway, both Landon's and Lyon's bedroom doors stood open, Lyon's nightlight glowing in the darkness. She was headed that way when voices echoed down the bisecting corridor, coming from the direction of the kitchen. She recognized Landon's low murmur immediately, and a secondary voice. A man's voice. *Evan.*

She hesitated, her face heating as she remembered the compromised conversation Evan had caught her in the middle of not so long ago. But since she was being brave and bold—*ha!*—she took a deep breath and entered the kitchen anyway.

Evan sat next to his son holding a crayon. Lyon swung his feet back and forth under the kitchen chair, filling in the spaces on a fresh coloring book.

Lyon looked up when she walked in. "Look, Kimber!" he shouted, no evidence he'd been out cold minutes ago, "*Man of Steel* coloring book!" He lifted the picture he was working on and showed her.

"Wow, does your dad know you, or what?" She cast an approving glance at Evan.

Evan winked at her. But not in a flirty way. In an *I Know What You Did Last Summer* way. She licked her lips nervously and flicked her attention to the island where Landon was leaning on his forearms.

"Did we wake you?" he asked. Oh, that dirty devil. He didn't smile, didn't waggle his eyebrows, but she could see the heat in his eyes, the slight twitch of his lips.

"I wasn't asleep," she answered as evenly as she was able.

He gave in and smiled, sending her pulse into a hectic rhythm. She bit down on her lip, studying the dip in his chin, the way his capable hands were folded neatly on the counter where he leaned. He may be trying to look casual, but she could see the rigidity in his spine. No, he was coiled. Ready to pounce. Ready to get the hell out of this kitchen.

A shiver climbed her spine but heated as it licked its way down. She pressed her thighs together to keep flames from gathering between her legs and setting her alight. The man could level her with a look. While she stood next to his unassuming brother and nephew.

Good Lord, Kimber, pull it together.

She was about to make an excuse about needing a bottle of water when Evan spoke.

"I'll just crash in Lyon's room." He addressed Landon, obviously picking up the conversation they'd been having before she interrupted.

"Are you staying tomorrow, too?" Landon kept leaning, his eyes trained on his brother. Somehow, though, she felt him watching her from his peripheral; knew he had a plan he was working out this very moment.

Evan colored part of Superman's boot orange and Lyon argued he was doing it wrong. He relinquished the orange crayon and accepted the red one. "I want to take Lyon to Navy Pier, but yeah, we'll be out of your place by morning. We'll get breakfast out, too." He nudged his son. "Chocolate chip pancakes okay?"

The boy's wide smile showcased his toothless gap. "Yeah!"

Her attack of lust faded as her insides turned to mush. She was going to miss this exuberant kid. Much more than she'd anticipated.

"I showed my new paintings to Gloria," Evan told her. She recalled her friend's earlier claim about how Evan was "hot with two Ts" and wondered if Glo had flirted with him. *Probably.* Glo was never one to hold back, and he was obviously a complete flirt.

"How did they turn out?"

"She loved them." His eyes held a guarded sparkle. Because Gloria appreciated his hard work? Or . . . something more? The way he'd said her name made Kimber think he and Glo might have discussed more than business...without clothing.

She felt a displaced stab of jealousy. She'd lost the opportunity to make love to Landon tonight. They might be able to sneak past Lyon, but Evan was another problem entirely.

"Glo has good taste," she said noncommittally.

Evan narrowed his eyes, his thick, dark lashes almost obscuring the blue. "So." He smirked. "What are *you* doing tonight?" The tone of his voice suggested he knew full well her intentions.

"I'm turning in," she said, folding her arms over her chest. "Just...came in to say good night." *Yep. Just wandered down here to say good night to the Downey clan before returning to my lonely room. Alone. And by myself.*

Landon stood from his casual lean against the countertop. "Lyon, how would you like to sleep in the bedroom with the giant bathtub?"

"Can I take a bath in it?"

Evan and Landon exchanged glances. "Up to your dad," Landon said, eyeing his brother intently.

"You mean the bedroom on the opposite side of the house." Evan pointed to the room beyond the kitchen. The *only* bedroom on that side of the house. "Instead of over there." He pointed in the other direction. "Where yours and Kimber's bedrooms are."

Her face grew warm with embarrassment.

Landon didn't balk. "Right."

Evan looked over at her and she swore she flushed twelve shades of red. They were arranging the sleeping situation around the fact that Landon and she were going to...going to...

Lord. She had to get out of this room. "Good night," she blurted.

"'Night," Lyon said, not looking up from his coloring.

She knelt next to him before she went. "Don't forget to say good-bye to me in the morning, okay?" Lyon nodded and she kissed his cheek. He hugged her neck, and the feel of those small but strong arms made her chest tighten. She was going to miss this kid. Before her haphazard emotions got the better of her, she said a hurried good night to Evan, but didn't speak to Landon at all. He watched her silently, his face still and unreadable. Bravery gone, she ran for her bedroom and shut the door behind her.

The knock came fifteen minutes later.

She'd been lying on top of the covers, dressed, wondering if Landon would come to her. Her nervous heart was pummeling her ribs by the time she pulled open the door—just a crack—and found him leaning a shoulder on the jamb. He hadn't changed from his slacks and shirt he'd worn to work today, though he'd long since lost the tie he'd worn this morning. She allowed her eyes to trickle down his throat, to the top of his chest and back up again.

His lips quirked into a sharp, predatory grin. "Hi."

Her everything began to tingle. "Landon, I—"

He pushed on the panel and she let him in, holding the door open and waiting for him to enter. She flicked a quick look to the empty hallway, feeling stupidly guilty and nervous. Like they were doing something wrong.

But we're not. We're grown-ups. He was comfortable with this situation, why couldn't she be? *Because you're as adventurous as a thumbtack.*

He took off his glasses and dropped them on the dresser, then held up empty hands. "Look. No baby monitor."

"Yes. And you've conveniently reworked the sleeping arrangement for your brother and nephew so we can be alone."

He put one hand over hers and pushed the door closed,

palming her hip with his other hand. "Only fair. We watched Lyon while Evan got something going with Gloria." Both hands on her waist now, he pulled her toward him.

"Did he really?" she breathed, her pulse picking up on contact.

He shrugged. "Just a call." He considered her. "You look surprised."

"I'm not." She wasn't. Not really. Gloria said she'd wanted Evan, and... "Glo usually gets what she wants."

"Do you?" He was watching her intently. It was a slow pitch, that comment. Setting her up for a home run. She tilted her chin up. Shallow marks indented the sides of his nose where his glasses had rested all day. His dark eyes roamed her face, the color of them mirroring his charcoal shirt.

She let out a derisive sniff. "Not usually."

"Well, I always get what I want." His hands tightened at her waist. "What do I want, Kimber?" His minty toothpaste breath tickled her senses. If there was a protesting brain cell in the bunch, it didn't speak up.

She gulped when he tugged her nearer. The answer was as obvious as his hard length pressing against her middle. "Me?"

"You," he confirmed before taking her lips in an insistent, purposeful kiss. His fingers sailed along her waist and back. Hardly any space separated them. He smashed her against his hard male chest, wrapped her in his powerful, solid arms.

Savoring his lips, she ran her hands into his hair and ground against him, the nudge of his manhood growing harder. He let out a sound between a grunt and a growl and slid his tongue into her mouth, stroking her while his fingers played her spine like a harp.

This is happening. Finally. Truly.

If she could time-travel back to her sixteen-year-old self, that shy girl with the braces would laugh and call her a liar.

She'd never believed she'd get her hands—or her mouth—on Landon Downey. Back then, she hadn't had the mental capacity to come up with what this moment might feel like.

Even as an adult, he was blowing away her expectations, and they still had their clothes on.

His fingers brushed her stomach and ribs as he skimmed her shirt up, slowing when he got to her bra. He raised an approving eyebrow before lifting her shirt the rest of the way and tossing it aside.

When his lips landed on her neck, she pulled in a stuttered breath, alternately shivering and overheating as he tongued and kissed her, leaving damp spots on her skin.

He slowed when he reached her bra and tucked his tongue beneath the strap. He glided down to one cup, dipped the tip of his tongue inside, grazed the very edge of a nipple, then drew back. When he pulled away, he took her next breath with him, and she had to remind herself to inhale. He repeated the action—delving into the other cup and teasing her there, while she fought to regulate her breathing.

Her hands had wandered to the open triangle of his chest revealed by the undone buttons. She fisted his shirt, wanting to see him. All of him.

She'd seen him shirtless at the lake all those summers ago, and she'd been enamored by his long, lean torso, firm pecs, and rounded shoulders, the sheer male hardness of him. Longing to see how the body in her memory had changed, she undid one button. Then another.

The years had added width to his tall frame. Shoulders that had been rounded were broad, the chest that had been lean, full. Fumbling with the rest of the buttons, she managed to reveal his abdomen. What used to be an impressive flat, tanned stomach was a toned series of bumps beneath taut skin. She ran her fingers over his abs, stopping at the light brown trail of hair that vanished into his suit pants.

She traced her fingers up his torso as his muscles clenched under her touch. His skin was hot, and her hands shook as she splayed her palms over his pectorals and savored the feel of his skin. Goodness. He was beautiful.

While she explored his body, he explored hers. His fingers teased along her bra; the straps hooked over her shoulders, the tops of the cups, tickling her lightly as he went.

"Your skin is so soft," he murmured, running the tip of his finger between her breasts.

Emboldened by his appraisal, it was easy to shed her trepidations. If she was going to do this, she was going to do it right. Prove to him that he didn't have to handle her as if she were a fragile little thing. Trying on her dominant side, she yanked his shirt off his shoulders and trapped his arms at his sides.

"You're moving too slowly." Her voice came out all Jessica Rabbit–like, which made her want to laugh. She refused. Jessica Rabbit wouldn't laugh.

Really? That's who you're channeling for this scenario?

He dropped his hands from her body, allowing himself to be confined, letting her contain him. That effectively wiped the judgmental voices from her head. She knew she couldn't restrain all this masculinity if she wanted to. The only power she had over him was the power he granted. And that made her feel undeniably feminine. She wrestled with his shirt again.

"In a hurry?" he asked when her movements became jerky.

She licked her lips, her inner dominant flagging. "Nervous," she admitted.

"That's no fun."

She let out a weak laugh and hoped he wasn't as disappointed in her as she was in herself. "No kidding."

In a flash of movement, he shrugged off her closed fists,

lost the shirt, and dropped the balled material behind him on the floor. Then he hovered over her until she flattened against the door. The spark in his eyes wasn't one of concern. That was confidence. The kind a man got when he knew exactly what he was doing. A little thrill swirled low in her stomach. It'd been a long, *long* time since she'd been with a man who knew what he was doing.

He palmed the door on either side of her head and leaned in, choking the air with that spring-and-sunshine smell of his. "Would you feel better if you knew what was on the list?"

The list. She swallowed hard. Would that make her feel better? "Did you really make a list?" He was still leaning into her, but not crowding her, just . . . close. Too close for her to think.

"I did."

She sucked in a breath and he tilted his head to the side and ran his tongue along her top lip before kissing it softly. "Want to know the first thing on my list?" He licked a long, sensual line along her bottom lip and then kissed her damp mouth with his, sliding his tongue inside to tangle with hers in aching slow motion.

When he pulled away, she sighed, her bones the consistency of melted chocolate. "Was that the first thing?"

He licked his bottom lip. "Taste as good as you look," he said. "But no, we haven't started the list yet."

Her spine dissolved into the door, her legs barely holding her up. She managed a satisfied smile, though, both at his compliment and the fact he'd made a list after all. A list of all the things he wanted to do with her. Had he written it down? Would they check it off as they went? Not only had he taken her seriously, but he wanted her. Wanted her in the same way she wanted him.

She said a quick side prayer of thanks for Evan's showing

up tonight, grateful that Landon had rearranged the floor plan. For her?

For *them*, she decided. That seemed safer somehow.

No tugging heartstrings allowed.

She could appreciate that he'd set his sights on her with laser focus. That he'd approached this task with a single-mindedness she was learning was his usual MO. And she could do it without worrying about the future, about their relationship potential, whether or not her mother would like him.

A fling. Well and truly.

His fingers skated along her bra straps, effectively clearing away all those pesky thoughts. He slid the straps down, his fingertips tickling the sides of her arms, then her wrists, before he swept the bra away completely. He drew circles around her nipples, teasing but not touching them. The experience of being touched so patiently, being taken to the height of frustration was so erotic, she wanted to cry.

She was wrong a moment ago when she thought she hadn't been with a man this confident in a long time. She'd *never* been with a man this confident. Never had a man taken so much time to focus on her. Usually sex was a frantic rush. A race to finish. But Landon had made it clear he wasn't racing or rushing. His big hands circled her small breasts again, making her feel so feminine it hurt.

She decided then she would give herself over to him and his "list," regardless of what was on it.

How unexpectedly . . . *thrilling.*

His hands continued in an arc, but he didn't give in and touch her nipples. They peaked painfully and she arched against the door, straining toward him, begging with her body for his touch. His hands warming her body, he kissed his way down her jaw, to her neck, even ran his tongue between her breasts, but refused to touch the aching buds no matter how much she silently insisted.

Raising to his full height, he leaned in, stopping shy of touching his chest to hers. She closed her eyes and waited for the feel of his body on hers, but it didn't come.

"Just ask," he whispered.

Her eyes flew open. She panted, swallowed, and recalibrated her scurrying brain.

A sly smile crossed his lips. "There's something you want. I can see it." His breath feathered her ear when he spoke next. "I can *feel* it."

"Yes," she breathed. His body heat washed over her, causing her to shudder in anticipation.

He thumbed her lip and watched her, eyebrows raised, that sly—no, more like cocky—smile resting on his face like it had a right to be there. Only it did. Because his pattern of seduction was working on her. All too well.

Okay. He wanted to hear her say what she wanted? She could do that. She raised her chin and met his eyes. "I want you to touch me."

Without hesitating, he rubbed his chest against each of her aching breasts. She let out a stuttering sigh. Against her ear, he whispered. "You feel incredible."

Before she could reciprocate, or reset her addled brain, he lowered his head and pulled a nipple onto his tongue, sucking her deep into his mouth. A tight sound left her throat as she dropped her head against the door with a soft *thunk*. His mouth felt so good tears pricked the corners of her eyes. She squeezed them shut. He'd barely touched her and she was coming undone, her bones rattling hard enough to unhinge from her joints and collapse her to the floor.

And they hadn't even started yet.

He pulled his tongue from her flesh, and she met his gaze—the hot look in his eyes. "You need this," he stated.

She did. She hadn't had a release worthy of mentioning in…a while. "Am I that obvious?"

He thumbed a nipple and watched her expectantly. "Say it." A command.

Electric shocks radiated between her thighs. He thumbed her other nipple.

She squeezed her legs together and on a surrendering breath, said, "I need this."

* * *

Some part of Landon warned him to stop. Which was insane. He had Kimber naked, pressed against a door, her pert breasts heaving, her lips damp, her nipple between his thumb and forefinger.

Stopping now would be crazy.

But there was something in the way she'd said '*I need this*' that gave him pause. A sense of foreboding clouded over him.

Relax. She said she needs "this," not "you."

True. And isn't that what they'd discussed when they'd agreed to do the list in the first place? To indulge, then walk away unscathed? He felt the need to remind them both of that deal.

"Kimber."

She opened drowsy eyes and he moved his hands to neutral territory—her arms—so he'd have her full attention. He wanted her alert. It wasn't like she was the kind of girl who had lists and flings and short-term sexual relationships.

Hell, *he* wasn't that kind of guy. But he also wasn't willing to climb into the commitment boat again. Not after Lissa had thoroughly broken their agreement. Not after he had to start over at age thirty-seven. If he did make another arrangement with a woman, Kimber would not be on his list of options. She was transparent, fragile. Honest and giving. He didn't want giving. He needed a woman selfish enough to walk away if things didn't work out. He needed a woman who could compartmentalize their time in the bedroom and treat him like an acquaintance during the daylight.

Kimber was none of those things, he thought with a frown. *This is a mistake.*

"Don't say it," she warned. Vulnerability reflected in her eyes, even as she urged him on, palming the door and arching her back. He couldn't keep from sending a lingering, heated gaze down her supple body. He grew harder just seeing her there; offering herself up to him like some virgin sacrifice. No. Not a virgin.

Thank Christ. He for sure couldn't go *there*.

"You read my mind now?" he asked.

"You're going to ask me if I'm sure I can do this. If I'm cut out for a fling. If I can keep my heart out of it."

Good guess. "Can you?"

She grabbed the waistband of his pants, sliding her fingers into his boxer briefs and brushing the head of his penis. He let out a sharp, hot breath and he squeezed her arms, wedging his teeth together. His member throbbed. *You're not the only one who wants closer to her, buddy.*

But he had to clear this up, or he would refuse to go any further. Regardless of how badly he wanted her.

"I'll admit," she said, her voice holding a surety it hadn't possessed earlier, "this is not something I'm good at."

He had to disagree.

She frowned, then clarified, "I don't mean I'm not good at sex. I mean, I'm not bragging that I'm good, but—" She cut herself off, shook her head.

He couldn't help smiling. She was muddled and adorable and so damn different from any woman he'd known. She was…*Don't think it.* Kimber couldn't be some precious, special thing. He could like her. He could make love to her, but he wouldn't drag her into something long-term.

She wasn't cut out for it, not with a guy like him. No matter how sure she claimed to be.

"I have trouble with the walking away part," she blurted.

He wanted her to take it back. She was so transparent. *Too* transparent. Part of him didn't want to be trusted with any fragile piece of her.

"But I promise you this. I will walk away." The fierceness in her eyes made him believe her. It also made him question why this woman, who had so much love to give, who was irresistible and adorable, would settle for a short-term, meaningless fling.

"Why are you doing this?" He shouldn't ask. It shouldn't matter. But it did.

"Simple. I've wanted to kiss you since I was sixteen. I want to kiss you again. I don't want to stop kissing you until sunrise." Her hand slid lower into his pants, gripping him and breaking the dam of lust now flooding his body. "Why are *you* doing this?" she countered.

He blinked a few times, trying to pull enough words together to form a coherent sentence. She removed her hand from his pants and rested it against his chest and he regained his grasp of the English language. He'd also regained enough sagacity to know better than to answer her question.

"I'll make you a deal," he said. "You keep your promise to walk away when we reach the end of this list..."

She nodded. Cautiously.

"And I promise you can say or do anything in our time together and I won't take it the wrong way." He glided his hands down her arms, over her stomach, and to the undersides of her breasts. Her eyes had darkened. She was slipping into the hazy vicinity of lust. Just where he wanted her. But not until they were clear. He moved his hands to her back and pulled her against him, looking down into her depthless green eyes. "I don't want you worrying over the right way to approach or talk to me. I want you to react naturally." He leaned in and brushed her lips with his. "I want you to ask for what you want. Command me if you have to."

"A safe space," she concluded after he kissed her lightly.

"The safest. You are not in danger of hooking a husband, here." Landon forced a smile. He had to make certain this was what she wanted. That there was no doubt in her mind as to his intentions. There was no other way to be sure other than just saying it. He returned his fingers to her breasts. She closed her eyes. "You said you need this," he murmured, kissing her again. "What, specifically, do you need from me, Kimber?"

* * *

There was no need to weigh her words now. No reason to worry. He'd promised to take what she said at face value. He was a pragmatic thinker. He was reasonable, a man who led with his brain and not his heart. Completely capable of separating love from pleasure. Could she do the same? Well. She was sure going to try.

"I need to be cherished." She met his gaze firmly. Despite his promise that she could say anything she wanted, she expected him to recoil. He didn't. Instead, a veil of valiance slid over his face. The kind of determination worn by William Wallace before he charged into battle.

His chin dipped in a slight nod of agreement. "Then that," he said, "is what you'll have."

He kissed his way down her body, pausing at her breasts for a few long, lingering kisses that made her mind melt. He kissed her ribs, her stomach, her belly button, and down to the drawstring on her shorts. His tongue ran along one hip bone, then over to the other before tugging the string on her shorts and releasing the bow. She'd been holding her breath for so long she started seeing spots in her vision.

"Still with me?" he asked when she sucked in a breath. He bunched the edges of her shorts in his fists.

She managed a short puff of air she hoped sounded like "uh huh."

He must have taken her response for an affirmative because next he yanked the shorts down. Past her thighs, past her knees. His fingers grazed her body, his tongue and mouth following their path. One kiss here, another there.

Soft, barely there kisses meant to cherish.

She stepped out of her discarded shorts, and he caught her foot in his palm and rested it on his leg. Knelt in front of her, he kissed the inside of her knee, drew his tongue along the back of it, and tracked kisses up her inner thigh. All she could do was brace herself against the door and endure the prickling, shivering sensations echoing through her body as he continued his torturous ascension. At the edge of her panties, he abandoned her right leg and switched to the left. And, wow, the man was thorough. By the time his mouth reached her opposite thigh, she was panting, her breaths short and tight.

"Landon." She hadn't meant to wail his name so desperately. But she was safe, she remembered. Safe to ask for what she wanted. "Please."

He smiled, his cheek pressing against her inner thigh, and plucked her cotton underwear with his teeth. He let them go, and a sharp snap of elastic stung her skin. "That's what I was waiting for," he commented, his breath hot on her flesh.

Before she'd registered his thumbs hooking into the fabric, her panties were gone, swept down her legs and sailing over his head in the lamp-lit room.

Oh God. The *lamp*.

The light switch was on her left. She reached for it in an effort to extinguish the bulbs highlighting her exposed body parts in their unflattering glory. Her not-so-flat stomach, thighs more shapely than toned, her fair but lightly freckled skin...

So many imperfections. And being viewed by a man who'd last dated a woman who was the epitome of perfection.

Landon, on his knees before her, clamped on to her legs firmly and kissed her belly button. "Leave it, Kimber." It was a warning. He darted his tongue over the skin low on her stomach. Reminding her how utterly bared to him she was.

"I can't," she pleaded. She stretched for the switch, almost touching it with the tip of her finger.

He abandoned her stomach, draped one of her legs over his shoulder, and licked her center. One long, slow, deliberate lick that made her quiver. "I said leave it," he mumbled against her swollen flesh.

She considered the challenge in his voice, the fire in his eyes, as he watched her. Testing him one last time, she reached for the switch again. He slicked his tongue along the most intimate part of her, a little longer, a little slower, but with increased pressure. A breathy moan escaped her throat.

He pulled his mouth away, his gaze as sharp and as authoritative as his voice. "Do it again and I'll stop." Lines bracketed his lips as they spread into a smile. "And trust me. You do *not* want me to stop."

She knew better than to challenge him again. Doing her best to forget the lights, she dropped her arm. He grasped her hand and put it on top of his head. As she ran her fingers through the silken strands of his short hair, he nestled between her legs. She surrendered to his ministrations, the feel of his sweet, sensual mouth against her. When the pressure mounted, she stood on her tiptoes, her entire body coiling. He kissed and suckled her, adjusting his pace to her whimpers of pleasure. At the pinnacle of her release, she writhed against the door, attempting to disentangle her legs from his solid arms. To get away, to push closer . . . she didn't even know anymore.

But he didn't let her.

She pushed gently against his head, her voice coming out strained and watery. "Landon, I can't." She was on the edge of either something miraculous, or something that might kill her. Intense, forceful feelings washed through her body, tightening her muscles, igniting her nerve endings. He ignored her verbal pleas for him to stop, listening instead to the ones from her body begging him to continue.

Finally, she surrendered, losing herself in the myriad of sensations accosting her, to the bursts of light popping like flashbulbs on the screens of her eyelids. He had tapped into some deep, undeniably sexual part of her she'd never fully experienced before. Not like this. It exhilarated her to be taken so thoroughly, so confidently, the only goal on her partner's mind her complete and utter release. He released her elevated foot to the floor. She lost the urge to stop him and spread her legs wider instead.

Not stopping his careful work, he pulled her hands from his head. When he tucked them between her bottom and the door, she pressed the cushiony flesh against her fingers, trapping herself there. Boldly, she met his eyes and felt her face heat along with every other part of her body, as if her blood had turned to lava. She twisted her fingers together behind her back, obeying his unspoken command to hold herself there, and watched him. He wanted her to watch, to stop trying to stop him. His movements slowed, his tongue slicking over her. He kept his gaze glued to hers. She was so, so close. Her body jerked. He repeated the motion, pressing the tip of his tongue against her solidly. She moaned her approval.

"Kimber." His voice rumbled against her. "Come for me." He closed his eyes and laved her . . . *savored* her like he was tasting a fine wine. One more stroke and she obeyed, spinning out of control, her release taking every dab of tension from her body. All the insecurity and stress and worry washed away in one shuddering, insatiable orgasm.

He held fast to her legs, taking on her dead weight as she slid helplessly down the door, her hands skimming the polished wood behind her. When she would have reached the floor, he caught her on his lap and palmed her back.

His next kiss landed on her neck, the one after that beneath her ear. "Delicious," he breathed, causing her to tremble. Or maybe she'd never stopped. "Every inch of you." He sampled her earlobe and she shivered again, bringing up her shoulder to keep him from tickling her to death.

"Stop." She chuckled, the sound no more than a wheeze. A pathetically puny wheeze.

"Not a chance," he said. "Can you make it to the bed? I have nine and a half more things to do to you."

She laughed again, a weak, dry sound. "That was only *half* of item number one?" she managed.

"Yes."

Half. Good Lord, she might die by the time they got to the second thing. Whatever that was.

Kimber opened her eyes lazily, legs shaking as he helped her stand. She followed his backward steps to the bed, the gold and green flowered comforter rumpled where she'd lain and waited for him minutes ago. Or hours ago? She had no idea. It was like she'd fallen into some sort of lusty black hole. When he got her to the bed, she fell gracelessly onto a pillow.

"Is this how you're going to react after every orgasm?" he teased. He crawled over top of her, his pants brushing against her legs.

Wait. *Pants?* She was stark naked and he was still wearing pants. No fair.

"Because we won't get very far if you require lengthy recovery after each one," he continued.

After each one. Normally, she considered herself lucky to get one orgasm. And that last one was about five times better than any she'd had in the past. The way he talked, he had several planned. The tantalizing promise of more returned the strength to her fingers.

She unbuttoned his pants. "Guess I'd better buck up, then."

He grinned and she eyed the dent in his chin. He was so gorgeous it hurt her heart a little. *No hearts,* she reminded herself sternly. *No heartstrings. No fluffy, bouncy, rainbow poodles.*

Right. Just sex. Well, obviously not *just* sex. More like delicious, amazing, consensual, walk-away-without-regrets sex. She could handle that. She could handle a whole lot of that.

She slid his pants past his hips, over a pair of black boxer briefs and the same jutting bulge she'd brushed her fingers over earlier. He sucked in a breath between his teeth when she grazed the back of her hand over his erection.

There wasn't anything more fun than watching his control ebb. His nostrils flared, teeth bared in an almost grimace as she slipped her hand past the last barrier of cotton.

"What's next on your list?" She massaged the length of his shaft. "Tell me," she demanded.

His eyes had grown dark. He kept his gaze on her and wet his lips to answer. "Ladies choice," he said in a near growl.

She squeezed him. He grunted. She squeezed again and he slid up her body and kissed her hard, his tongue invading her mouth, his teeth scraping her lips. She drank him in but didn't stop her intimate massage. Not yet. He wasn't so in charge now, was he? He wasn't slow and intentional. Since he'd delighted in torturing her, it seemed only fair to return the favor.

"Losing some of your control, I see," she said. She toed

away his pants, slipping them down his legs. When they got tangled at his shins, he wrestled himself free with one hand, bracing his weight with his other arm. When the muscles lengthened and tightened there, she grasped his bicep with her free hand and pursed her lips. "Nice."

The nudge of his erection pressed against her core. Oh, no he didn't. She'd had about enough of him calling the shots. She pressed her palms into his chest. "On your back."

His eyes narrowed but she could see the flare of excitement there. He wanted to let go. To let her have her way with him.

"You said I could get whatever I wanted." She was paraphrasing, but whatever. He was in no position to argue. "Lie down."

He obeyed and she climbed on top of him. He caught her hips in his hands. "Like on the patio," he said. "You like this position."

"You're about to like it, too," she promised, moving one of his hands above his head and anchoring it to the pillow. She lifted his other hand, and his eyes darkened to almost black. "Don't move." Oh yeah. He liked this. He watched her under hooded lids, his muscular chest heaving as she pulled his briefs down his legs and freed his springing erection.

Wow. His penis was as beautiful as the rest of him. Long and hard, yet velvety soft. It bobbed. She met his eyes and he grinned. The site of an easy grin on Landon's face nearly undid her. He was so relaxed, so easy to be with right now. No shutters blocking out the light in his eyes. No proper rigidity protecting him like armor.

Tin Man, my ass.

Afraid her thoughts were straying outside of the confines of their agreement, she licked her lips seductively, thrilling when he tensed. She cupped his balls and his smile vanished. She was okay with that. He could smile later, when she was done with him. Lowering her head, she took him into her mouth. His body bucked the moment her tongue stroked him.

She pulled the most exquisite groan from his throat and mentally high-fived herself.

Oh, yes. This round would definitely go to her.

CHAPTER TEN

Landon had escaped Kimber's room before sunrise, showered, dressed, and reconvened in the kitchen. Lyon was in the living room, watching cartoons upside down, his head on the ground, feet propped on the couch.

"Good morning." Evan grinned. A shit-eating one. He abandoned the newspaper spread across the breakfast bar and studied Landon through narrowed eyes.

"How was your room?" Landon fired up the espresso maker and pulled a petite mug from the cabinet. Then traded it out for a larger size. *Better make it a double*. He was exhausted. In the best way humanly possible.

Flashes of what happened with Kimber lit his brain like a flickering movie reel. Her hot mouth wrapped around him, her caressing hands on his skin, her soft mewls of pleasure when he'd finally entered her. The way she'd laid against him after they'd made love: her hair sticking to her damp brow, how she'd been nearly incoherent as she praised his hard work. They'd finally stopped because they had to, collapsing in a heap of sweaty limbs and labored breathing. They'd managed a few hours of sleep before sunrise.

But he wasn't done with her. Not by a long shot. He planned on extending the list to ensure they didn't reach the end too soon.

"How was *yours*?" Evan hopped off the stool and rummaged through the refrigerator.

Landon shook his head, watching the espresso maker empty the black brew into his mug. He refused to grace his nosy brother with an answer.

"Oh man." Evan leaned against the counter and took a bite out of an apple. He chewed, pointing with the hand that held the Red Delicious. "*Her* room. Nicely played."

Yes, they'd played. They'd laughed and moaned one another's names and panted and *played*. It was cathartic and amazing, and not something he'd been used to. Over the years, sex had yielded a much-needed release, but he didn't remember it being particularly *fun*. Then again, he hadn't had sex in...a while. If he admitted how long, Evan would laugh him right off the balcony.

"When you taking off?" He collected his cup out from under the maker and spooned in a few granules of raw brown sugar.

"Okay, fine. I guess this isn't the time or the place to talk about your *sexcapades*." Evan took another bite out of his apple.

Landon sipped his coffee. Strong and sweet. *Like Kimber*. "Do you really expect me to talk about her with you? Lyon's in the other room and she is—"

Amazing. Honest and pure. Transparent.

Her words from last night crashed into him. *I need to be cherished.* How could he not grant *that* request? Her feminine tenderness was a call his masculine strength had to answer. He couldn't begin to describe the way she'd been so...*there* with him in that room last night. Present.

In the past, he'd wondered if Lissa had been reciting

her to-do list or mentally packing for her next trip for how little she'd been involved in the act. But Kimber... her eyes on his, their breathing in sync as he slid in and out of her body... she'd been fantastically different from what he'd grown accustomed to in the past.

Or what you settled for. There was an alarming idea.

His lips turned downward. He had to get a grip. She'd laid out the rules, and he'd promised to adhere to them. They knew what this was. He couldn't start thinking about how amazing she was, couldn't fold her close when she was supposed to keep him at arm's length. Enjoying himself was one thing, starting to think of her as anything else was forbidden. He didn't remember his emotions being a problem he'd had to contend with before now.

Except with Rachel. He scrunched his eyes to block that thought. Any thoughts of her, of the tragic summer sixteen years ago. *Don't freaking go* there.

Evan finished chewing and chucked the apple core into the trash can across the room.

"Good shot," Landon commented.

"So. You going to keep seeing her?" Evan asked.

Only as long as they had the list. Not like he would tell Evan about that, though. His brother would either accuse him of taking advantage of her, or accuse him of being a machine.

He took another drink of his coffee to buy himself time. Another thought hit him and he pulled the mug away and mumbled a curse. "I have to pay her," he said.

"Yes, you do. Cheapskate."

He sent his brother a bland look. "That's not what I mean."

"I know what you mean. Money exchanging hands is awkward at this point." Evan clucked his tongue. "Couldn't have waited one more day?"

"Right," he said, his brother's sarcasm apparently conta-gious. "Because *timing* could have cleared all this up."

Kimber picked that moment to step into the kitchen. She wore a white sleeveless shirt showcasing her toned, slender arms and a pair of cotton shorts revealing way more of her luscious legs than he wanted Evan seeing. She ran a hand through her damp, freshly showered hair and a memory lit his brain. *Kimber beneath him, arms pinned over her head, face flushed, mouth open in a sensual sigh.*

He'd have to see about adding to that list.

"You look refreshed," Evan told her.

After his boneheaded brother left.

She offered a light punch on Evan's arm as she passed by, eyeing Landon through her lashes. "Have one of those for me?"

"Sure." He reached for the cabinet, using the excuse to send Evan a telepathic message to give them a minute. But Evan was already backing out of the kitchen, palms raised as he mouthed the words *"Good luck."*

Landon got to work on Kimber's coffee while she leaned against the counter and studied her sneakers. "You don't have to feel strange about paying me."

He pressed his lips together. "You heard."

She shook her head. "I'm not going to be weird about it. It's fine. It's good."

The television in the other room was tuned to cartoons. Zany, silly sounds punctuated by Lyon's and Evan's laughter assured him they weren't being overheard. He stepped closer to Kimber, using whatever excuse he could to be close to her again. A voice in his head warned that wasn't advised. He ignored it.

"How are you feeling today?" He laid a kiss onto her tem-ple, hiding the smile he couldn't keep off his face.

She turned her head and spoke into his ear. "Amazing."

Gooseflesh erupted on his arms. Hands he didn't remember grasping her with tightened their hold on her body.

"Landon," she said on a soft giggle. "Not now," she whispered.

He looked into her eyes, lowered his lips to hers for a silent kiss, then forced himself to back away. He handed over her coffee. She sipped. What had she meant by *not now*? Because the second his brother was out of here, he wouldn't mind taking her straight back to bed.

He stifled a yawn. After another espresso.

"What are you doing tonight?" As soon as it was out, he had to fight to keep from retracting his question. He'd meant to play it cool, not ask her out within sixty seconds of laying eyes on her. *What the hell?*

"What do you mean?"

Her question did nothing to answer his, and put him at a disadvantage if he answered first. What if she didn't want him again so soon? In an attempt to be coy, he lowered his lips to her ear. "What do you think I mean?"

When he pulled away, she was smiling, looking shy and beautiful and damn, she smelled good. He made a mental note to keep her stocked in cucumber body products for as long as this thing between them lasted.

"I think I'd like that," she said.

She *thought*? "You think?" he repeated, feeling wounded. *What. The. Hell.*

"What do you think?" she parroted his words back to him, again giving him absolutely nothing to go on.

What did he think? He thought he'd like to see her out of those clothes within the hour. He thought he'd like to get her out of this penthouse and buy her a vintage or custom-made dress of her choosing. He thought he'd like to see her smiling at him over a candlelit table in the corner of an Italian restaurant.

"I think we should make some headway on the list," he said instead. "I hate unfinished business."

"What number did we do last?"

He blurted out the truth before he could stop himself. "Four."

Lips on the edge of her mug, she lifted an amber brow. "Is five what you had in mind tonight?"

And then some. "I thought I'd feed you first. How's dinner sound?"

"Far away," she murmured, sipping her coffee.

He couldn't read her expression. Did she not want to wait? Or was she simply responding to fill the air?

"And then, number five," he added, trying to keep things light. Suddenly he was worried she might turn him down, adding to the melee of confusion circling his brain this morning. He really should have gotten more sleep.

Her smile undid him, sparking his attraction for her into a full-blown forest fire. "I'm going to have to see this list."

"I'll e-mail it to you."

"It's typed?" She looked amused. And so gorgeous he ached to touch her again.

He shook his head and maintained his distance. "It's not typed." It was feverishly scrawled onto a Post-it and wedged into his wallet.

"Oh. You were teasing." She rolled her eyes. "I thought I was getting better at picking up on your sense of humor."

"Have you been trying to figure me out, Kimber?"

He leaned a palm on the counter behind her and hovered over her, flattered she'd thought about him in a way other than physical. The innocence in her eyes nearly floored him. And reminded him who he was. Who *she* was. Despite their promises not to make promises, he wondered if they were playing with fire.

He backed away abruptly. "That's a bad idea."

Ignoring her downturned lashes, he kissed her forehead and pushed away from her before giving in to temptation and taking back his last words. He trekked to the living room, putting some much-needed distance between himself and the gorgeous redhead muddying his brain.

* * *

Kimber knelt in front of the boy she'd mothered for almost a week and smiled at the Superman T-shirt stretched over his little chest. "Thank you for hanging out with me."

Lyon's face pinched slightly. "Are you going to come and see me at my house?"

"Um…" She wondered if he latched on to every woman he met, if he'd latched on to her. Or if, by telling him truthfully she would not be coming to see him—likely wouldn't see him anytime soon—he'd be hurt. Maybe not. Kids were more resilient than adults in most cases.

Who knew what was going on in that head of his?

"We live very far away, buddy," Evan said. "But you are welcome to invite her to your birthday party next month. Maybe Kimber can come if she doesn't have to go to work."

She shot Evan a smile, grateful he knew what to say.

"Yeah! You can come to my Superman birthday party!" Lyon smiled, appeased.

"Superman." She dropped her jaw in faux shock. "You're kidding."

"No. For real," he said so seriously, they all laughed.

She didn't want to promise and let him down so she said, "Send me an invitation and I'll do my best to make it." But even that sounded like a promise to her ears. And it hurt, lying to him. By next month, she and Landon would have long blown through the list, and their temporary relationship. She ignored the sadness trying to leak into her chest.

Lyon turned to embrace his uncle as Kimber stood. Seeing Landon smile at his nephew and give him gentle orders like "be good on the ride home" and "don't forget me" clenched her heart. He was wholly capable and loving with that boy. Another thought nudged the edge of her mind, but she refused to let it come forward. It was dangerous comparing herself to his flesh and blood; people he would love forever no matter what.

After Evan and Lyon made their way out the door, she excused herself to pack. Landon kissed her, promising to pick her up tonight at her place. "Wear a dress," he'd instructed as the elevator doors slid shut between them.

She paid the cab driver, sifting through her purse for another twenty as her fingers slipped over the check Landon had given her. It was a lot of money. A generous amount. And in a way, despite her protests, it did feel a bit like payment for what had happened between them last night.

But she couldn't think that way. She had a date with number five on his list...whatever that was. In truth, she'd been surprised that he'd asked her out on a date. Their parameters didn't exactly include social situations.

What did you expect? Just sex?

Maybe. Wouldn't just sex be easier? She was already having a hard time separating her emotions from the physical act they'd shared. Every other minute she had to remind herself not to feel anything for Landon. Or Lyon, for Pete's sake. Evan had also nudged his way into her heart. Like they had when she was sixteen, she found herself falling in love with the Downeys. All it'd take would be her showing up to Lyon's birthday party and being around the entire clan. Then she'd be a goner.

So. Maybe this fun-night stand business had been a tad ill-advised. In Gloria's defense, she hadn't known how close Kimber had grown to the Downeys that summer a hundred years ago. Too late to turn back now. Her feet were not only wet, they were encased in cinder blocks and she was sinking.

Stop being so melodramatic. You're not sinking. You're a loving person.

A loving person capable of walking away from Landon when they were through with the list. Or at least she hoped so. For both their sakes. She didn't want him to hate her when this was over. Ice pick to the heart, that thought. She shook it off as she climbed the stairs at the side of Hobo Chic leading to her apartment.

Keys hovering over the knob, she noticed the door open a crack. She froze solid in the doorway, her mind spinning. If someone had broken into her place, she had no weapon. Well, she had *one* weapon. Fingers at the ready to dial 9-1-1 on her iPhone, she pushed the door open with the tip of her house key.

The room was in its normal (not ransacked) state, and the usual cluttered mess of bills, reports, and fashion magazines was scattered across the breakfast bar. Mick sat on a backless stool, paper in hand. He lifted his head when she walked in.

Her shoulders dropped in relief. She pocketed her phone. "What are you doing here? I almost called the police because my door was unlocked."

"Relax. It's just me."

"You could have asked if you could come over and do whatever it is you're doing."

He put aside the sheet of paper he'd been reading and tipped a beer bottle to his lips. A beer he'd stolen from her fridge. She scanned his threadbare T-shirt, cargo shorts, and ratty Chuck Taylors resting on the rung of the stool. "I have a key," he said, cleanly transferring the blame to her. "I needed to check on a shipment. If you don't want me here—"

"It's fine." She held up a palm as she dragged her suitcase

past him and to her bedroom. Which, no thanks to this being a loft, was in the same room. There really was no escaping Mick Stringer as long as they co-owned Hobo Chic.

"Guess I could have called but I didn't want to interrupt your *millionaire affair.*"

She whipped around. How did he know about that?

He leaned an elbow on the counter and smiled. "Neil."

She should have known. Gloria wouldn't have told. "It isn't like that." *Only it is,* she thought, unpacking and tossing her dirty clothes into a hamper. It was exactly what it sounded like. She'd had sex with a millionaire while living at his place. Also, he'd given her some money. She mentally cringed.

"Is? Present tense? So you're seeing him again?"

She turned, bright, tropical-print pants in hand. "I don't see how that's any of your business."

"Wear the green dress," he said, unfazed. He returned his attention to his paperwork.

A clothing rack serving as her closet stood at the end of her bed. The new-to-her, safari-style green silk button-down dress he'd referred to hung in a primo spot at the end. She'd picked the dress out of her latest acquirements for the store the day she left to go to Landon's. Other than the one time she tried it on, she hadn't worn it.

Mick's mouth kicked into a half smile. "You look good in green."

She shoved the empty suitcase under her bed, not wanting to have this conversation with him. It was . . . weird. "Are you going to be here much longer? I have to get ready."

He spared her a glance. "*Tonight?* You're seeing him tonight?"

Frustrated, she held up her palms. "Yes. I'm seeing him tonight."

His face puckered, not liking that for whatever reason.

He slid off the stool and moseyed over to her and she tensed, unsure what he was going to do. He palmed her shoulders and she stood prone, wanting to swat him away but not wanting to hurt his feelings. They were in such a predicament. She didn't hate him. But she didn't really like him. And she'd never *really* loved him. More the idea of him. The idea that she could have forever with a man who enjoyed the same things she did. A man who had a vested interest in her future. Now they were co-workers and partners, no longer lovers or roommates, their relationship inconvenient and unpredictable in every way.

"You're not this girl, Kimber." As if consoling her, he rubbed her upper arms. She shrugged him off. Maybe because he had a point.

She'd never been the type of girl capable of an unattached fling, with a millionaire or otherwise. Look at her and Mick. She was supposed to take him home for one night of fun and had swathed him into her life instead.

"Maybe I am now," she said. She'd have to be. Because there was no way she and Landon were ending with her in retched heartache because she'd turned this into something it wasn't.

Mick sighed and turned away, taking the report he'd been reading with him. "Have it your way." He paused at the door. "But I'll hate gloating when this jerk ends up hurting you."

"No you won't," she said. Unfairly, probably. "But thanks. Your support is overwhelming."

Mick didn't argue and she was glad. He patted the door with one hand before shutting it behind him.

Kimber sat on the edge of her bed. She refused to *let* herself end up hurt. She could have an affair without getting super involved. Landon was in no position to get super involved, so in a way, he was as safe as they came.

She stood and lifted the green dress off the rack, holding

it against her body. The full-length mirror showed a woman with red hair, rosy cheeks, and the will and ability to have a fling if she damn well pleased. There wasn't time for any longer of a pep talk than that.

She had a date to get to.

CHAPTER ELEVEN

After dinner in the Hancock building's restaurant on the ninety-fifth floor—yeah, he'd been showing off—Landon held Kimber's hand as they walked down Navy Pier. He watched her lick an ice cream cone out of the corner of his eye. The sight of her tongue was enough to make him cut the date short and drag her home right then. If not for how fun she was to hang out with, he may have. She offered him the rest, and he ate it, keeping hold of her hand with his free one.

Even for August, the weather was cooler than usual, an almost refreshing breeze rolling off the lake and chilling his bare arms beneath the short sleeves of his polo shirt.

His eyes traveled over Kimber's dress again. Sitting across from her at the dimly lit restaurant had kept her body from view. Now, out in the open, he could look his fill. She looked... *God*. She looked incredible.

At first glance, the green dress was nothing remarkable: a simple, sleeveless number with pockets and a tie at the middle. But on her body... *Wow*. The dress skimmed over her supple thighs in a way that made his mouth water.

They'd stopped to admire the moonlight bouncing off the water, but he couldn't keep his eyes on the scenery. She'd worn her hair up in a ponytail, wavy strands framing her face. His gaze snapped to her thighs again, and he followed the length of her bare legs down to flat, strappy sandals and painted toenails. He remembered the feel of those legs wrapped around him, her heels digging into his butt as she'd pulled him closer. The sound of her high—

The weight of her gaze pulled him out of the memory. He was staring. Quite possibly drooling.

A small smirk sat on her mouth as if she knew what he'd been thinking. It was all he could do not to taste her lips. The only thing stopping him was the reminder that while this was technically a date, it wasn't a real one. This was the foreplay to what would come after. For both their sakes, he'd do well to remember that clause in their agreement.

He tugged her to a nearby bench. They sat quietly and listened to the sounds of the pier: musicians playing, children laughing, rides spinning. "We could get on the Ferris wheel, you know." He hadn't been on a Ferris wheel since he'd moved here straight out of college. Hadn't had the urge to get on one since, but with Kimber it sounded fun. With Kimber, everything sounded fun.

"And what, make out?" she asked.

He closed his arm around her waist, her silken dress beneath his fingers as smooth as her skin. "Yes." His voice came out a low growl.

She laughed and rested a hand on his thigh, her touch burning a hole through the light slacks he'd worn. Her fingers traced a circle over the material and he shifted, a certain part of him stirring. If she wasn't careful, she'd awaken the sleeping giant.

"I have to admit, I was surprised you asked me on a date."

"Why?" he asked. But he knew.

Her ponytail slid over her shoulder when she tilted her head to look at him. "Because it wasn't on the list."

Tensing, he gave a subtle shake of his head. "You really are all about the list, aren't you?" For some reason it frustrated him to have to plan for everything. Or maybe it frustrated him that she had to plan for everything. Which wasn't like him at all. He loved plans. Normally.

"I have to be," she muttered.

He tipped her chin, forcing her eyes to his. "What does that mean?"

She licked her bottom lip and clamped on to it with her teeth. A memory of the first kiss they'd shared, of the moment she'd climbed atop him and speared her fingers into his hair and kissed him for all she was worth echoed a sentiment stirring the giant to life. He was going to have to limp out of here if he didn't kill this line of thinking.

"I don't want to be your Lissa."

Her comment startled as much as angered him. She was nothing like Lissa. Kimber was warm and responsive and cared, probably too much, about everyone she came in contact with. It bothered him that she'd compare herself to the heartless supermodel who'd left him in the dust for no more than a publicity stunt. Further, it bothered him that Kimber could ever imagine he'd treat her like he had Lissa. He'd been more careful, more gentle, more open, with Kimber than he had with anyone in a long, long time.

The anger built the longer he considered her comment, which was probably why, when he did speak, the question came out surlier than he'd intended. "And what the hell does *that* mean?"

She placed a soft kiss on his mouth. "Nothing."

Something. But he'd better not push her. He'd already opened a can of thought best left sealed.

"You want to check off the list and walk away," he said,

reiterating her original request. He'd been all for that—still was all for it. But those two words "walk away" niggled at him. Why? *Because your list is ongoing and can't be completely checked off.*

"Exactly," she said, her expression stoic. She slid her hand higher on his thigh. "Back home?"

His heart gave the faintest clench. He knew she was referring to his home, not hers. For a short period of time it'd been her home as well. In her mind, maybe it still was her home. In the interim.

The realization warmed him. Even though it shouldn't.

* * *

Kimber pulled the sheet over her breasts as Landon held on to a corner to cover his bare butt. He arranged himself on the balcony sofa, head resting on the back of it, chest glistening with sweat in the moonlight.

"I can't believe we did that out here," she said, lifting a lock of hair from her forehead. She sent a furtive glance at the buildings surrounding them and prayed no one had equipped their window with a telescope. She'd seen a movie like that once.

"We had to," he said, his voice low and deep and damn sexy. "It was number five."

"And we have to go in order."

He turned his head and smiled at her, the sight of his straight, white teeth and faint, light brown stubble on his jaw nearly undoing her. And she was pretty well undone as it was. "Are you making fun of me?"

A little. She widened her eyes innocently. "Not at all."

"We stayed under the sheet." And the couch didn't face the surrounding buildings, which, hopefully, had thwarted any would-be voyeur neighbors. "Worried your ass is going to be on YouTube?" he asked.

A joke. At his expense. She'd pegged his sense of humor. Finally. *"Mine?* You were on top. I'm safe."

His throat bobbed when he laughed. He looked as sexy without his glasses as he had with them. She honestly had no idea which look she preferred. Suited up, bespectacled, fresh-home-from-work Landon or stripped-down, easy smile, relaxed Landon. Given that her heart ached as she watched him now, all disheveled and relaxed, she considered the buttoned-up version of him might offer safer passage out of this affair. Then again, he'd lost the ability to look foreboding and intimidating in that suit long ago. Because she knew him now. She knew what was under that no-nonsense powerhouse. A warm, smiling, laughing man whom she liked way too much.

He tugged the sheet, dragging it dangerously low and nearly exposing her breasts. Before she flashed the world— at least a section of Lake Shore Drive—her 34 Bs, she clutched the sheet to her chest.

"We should go in," he said. "Take care of six."

Anticipation thrummed low in her stomach. "I don't see how it could possibly be better than five," she lied. Everything had been pretty darn phenomenal, each experience better than the last. She took solace that there were five more items to tick off the list.

What happens when we reach ten?

Ignoring the voice in the back of her head busily proving Mick right—that she wasn't cut out for this—she allowed Landon to help her stand. He kept her wrapped in the sheet against them as they went inside. The heated press of their nude bodies had her sighing, anxious for more of him already.

"My room," he murmured.

They kissed their way through the house, stopping to untangle the sheet from their feet. At one point, she tripped and he caught her, bracing a hand against the wall to keep them both from crashing to the hardwood floor.

"That's it." He lifted her into his arms, yanking the sheet from her body.

"No! I'm too heavy!" She covered her face with her hands when he cradled her.

He adjusted his grip, his muscles bunching against her body. "Shut up." Showing annoyingly little exertion for his efforts, he carried her down the hallway and dropped her onto her feet on his bedroom floor. His gaze danced over her bare body. The light wasn't on, and the room, washed in darkness, made her bolder than usual. She straightened her spine, pushed her breasts out. Landon kissed her so softly, so slowly, and so thoroughly, she melted into him and forgot all about the list.

An hour or so later, she lay prone on the bedding, overly satisfied and overly warm. She kicked at the comforter, and it slid off the corner of the bed and onto the floor with a *shiff.*

"I'm thirsty," she said.

"I'm hungry." He kissed her forehead. "Be right back."

How he'd found the energy to bolt out of his bed and strut across the room, she had no idea. She also had no complaints, because watching his athletic backside cross the carpet could easily become her new favorite pastime.

A minute later, he padded back into the room, two bags of Windy City potato chips in one hand, a bottle of water and a can of Coke balanced in the other.

"Junk food." She smiled and stretched her overexerted limbs.

"You cannot refuel on health food after the night we've had." He traipsed his naked body across the room as she blatantly stared. He didn't mind, proudly wearing only his glasses and a smile. In bed, he opened both bags of chips.

She unscrewed the cap from the water bottle and took a drink. "Do you ever wear contacts?"

"Used to. Why?"

"I once knew a guy who needed glasses but refused to wear them."

"A guy, huh?" he fished. Wisely, she stayed silent. "Why didn't he wear them?"

"He thought they made him look weak."

Landon's brows scrunched. "Really? I always thought they made me look smart."

She grinned. That "guy" she'd referred to earlier had nothing on Landon. No one did. The thought made her grin fade. He offered her the BBQ chips from the bag in his hand, but she twisted her lips and went for the jalapeño ranch.

"You like the hot stuff."

"All evidence points to that fact," she said, laying the flavorful chip on her tongue. She poked his taut abs. "Hot stuff."

He ate a few chips. In bed. Never would she have guessed neat and tidy Landon Downey nommed potato chips *in bed*. "You're getting crumbs everywhere," she pointed out.

As if accepting a challenge, he crammed a handful of chips into his mouth. Crumbs tracked down his chest as he crunched. She brushed them out of his chest hair, off his abs, and stopped just short of palming the impressive length of manhood lying against his thigh.

"Stop staring."

When she opened her mouth to lie and say she wasn't, he put a chip onto her tongue. She ate the spicy morsel, losing her desire to argue. "These are good."

"*Good?*" He reached into one of the bags between them. Leaning on one elbow, he elevated a single, perfectly round chip, dusted to ranchy, jalapeño-y perfection between his finger and thumb. "These are not *good*," he said sternly. "These are the cornerstone of a sexy person's pantry. These," he let his eyes wander over the surface of the chip as if he was admiring a work of art, "are the Cadillac of chips."

He winked, then popped the "Cadillac of chips" onto his tongue, munching happily as he gave her a quick lift of his eyebrows.

She repressed a laugh, but couldn't help smiling. "That's a good slogan."

"Thanks. I came up with it myself."

This man was so much more layered than she'd known. In a way, it wasn't a surprise. Being a Downey, she inherently knew Landon couldn't have bypassed the charm so easily conveyed by his brothers. Even Angel was irresistible by her own right. Landon was irresistible, too. A shame. Since Kimber's sole job after their affair was to do just that. Resist him.

Four hours later, he opened the cab door and kissed her good-bye. A lingering, sweet, delicious kiss she was sure the cabbie gladly charged on his meter. No matter. She'd spend whatever it took to stand here in front of his building and kiss Landon like this.

The accusatory voice in her head whispered that she was being schlepped off like a lady of the night when she could be inside, snuggled deep in expensive bedding against Landon's naked body. She mentally silenced that voice. Even if he had invited her to stay, she would have had to say no. She had a business to run, and whatever was between them didn't include snuggling or overnight stays.

He finished the kiss and tucked a strand of hair behind her ear. "Good night, sweet girl."

"I'm not all that sweet," she murmured, inserting a sensual husk into her voice. May as well leave him wanting more. He'd done the same for her.

Leaning in, he brushed his lips along her ear. "Yes, you are. Like honey and port and melted caramel." He licked her ear, suckled, and Kimber forgot where she was . . . until she grappled the cab door for support.

Oh yeah. We're in public.

She pulled away from him and offered a farewell far more casual than her feelings at the moment. "See you around."

"You know where to find me." With that, he shut her in, leaned into the open front passenger side window, and palmed the driver a very large bill.

Just like that, her *Pretty Woman* complex was complete.

CHAPTER TWELVE

The A/C had been set so she wouldn't freeze, but Kimber's shoulders were still cold. She maintained her position on one of the stools at the breakfast bar, unwilling to move from her elegant pose.

She didn't quite have the guts to pull off the *Pretty Woman* nude-while-wearing-a-tie scene—not that she'd be able to tie the dang thing—so she settled for perching on a stool in the kitchen, legs crossed, wearing the dress Glo had dropped off for her this afternoon.

Between a black and deep blue, the neck scooped down to showcase her breasts and halted mid-thigh. Glo's boobs were too big and she claimed they kept busting out of the top (the poor dear), but Kimber chose to be grateful for the hand-me-down instead of jealous that her friend was better endowed than she. Since all of Kimber's dresses were vintage, she'd accepted the offer of the sexy cocktail number, deciding to surprise Landon with an attempt at elegance.

Legs crossed, she waggled one very tall heel and stole a glance at the clock. Seven thirty. He was supposed to be home an hour ago, and so she'd been sitting here, waiting, trying not to muss her updo or fiddle with the costume jewelry around her neck and dangling from her ears. Landon was right. She was a fidgety person. His every move always seemed so controlled.

Her shoulders slumped. Maybe she could wait on the couch, and then when he came in, dash over to her perch and resume her poise. She hopped off the stool, staggering in the stilettos she had no idea how Glo wore with any measure of success, and caught herself on the corner of the kitchen table with one palm.

"Stupid things." She cursed the shoes and reached for the right one, intending to take them off and toss them aside. That's when she heard the key in the door.

* * *

Landon stepped into his kitchen expecting to find Kimber. They'd planned to get together tonight, and he was woefully late. He'd debated over what kind of apology gift to buy, but flowers and candy were out of place in this . . . whatever they were doing, so he'd settled for something simpler.

But he nearly dropped the potato chips and wine when he found Kimber bent forward, one hand braced on the table, a spiked heel in her other hand. Wide, jade eyes regarded him, her red lips softly pursed.

My God. She's gorgeous.

She was gorgeous anyway, but tonight . . .

His eyes swept down to her breasts hanging free in the low-cut top of a patented "little black dress." She slipped the heel back on to her foot, teetered for a second, then adjusted the hem of her dress. A lock of crimson hair fell over her eye, the rest of it arranged into some kind of twist at the back of her head. The jewelry around her neck made him want to replace it with the real deal. Because she'd look amazing in real diamonds.

In only real diamonds.

He crossed the room, setting aside his apology gifts and briefcase. She gave him a smile that may have been slightly embarrassed, but he bent and captured her lips before she could say anything. While their mouths mated, he drew a line down her neck with the back of his fingers and slipped beneath the strap over her left shoulder.

He placed an openmouthed kiss on her neck and breathed her in. "You are exquisite."

There was no other word for her.

Her easy laugh tumbled around in his chest. "I was going for classy."

He raised his head but kept his fingers beneath the strap of her dress, stroking her skin with a light touch. "That, too." She was tall in those shoes. Tall enough that he barely had to lean down to kiss her lips a second time.

"I'm underdressed," he said. "I'll go change." He didn't want to take her out. He wanted to take her to bed. But a woman didn't get dressed up just to be stripped down, some logical part of his brain reminded him.

Her brow furrowed. "Change?" She reached for his tie. "I thought we'd"—she lifted one delicate shoulder—"you know."

Yes. He knew.

The demure smile on her face weakened his resolve. Sufficiently. "I know you didn't get dressed like this for me." He toyed with the strap again, enjoying the feel of her satiny skin.

"I did." She swept her hands up his torso and heat spread across his chest. "I thought you might like to see how well I clean up." She tugged on his tie. Little had he known he'd become such a fan of *that* move. Or maybe he was only a fan when Kimber was at the helm. She didn't have to tug hard to get him to lower his lips and kiss her again as she untied the length of silk and dropped it to the floor. "What's next on the list?" she said against his mouth.

At the mention of the list, he grew hard in an instant. The next item might be his favorite, a fantasy he'd never played out.

"The desk," he growled. He didn't mean to growl. But the idea of making love to her in his office tightened his vocal cords, turned his muscles to steel. He'd been saving the desk for later...for now, apparently.

"Oh, the desk," she purred, smiling against his lips. "Yes, that's better than a night on the town."

He grinned. "I must be in heaven."

"Not yet." she said, her low, sultry voice making him even harder. She tugged his glasses off his face and set them on the counter behind her, then slid her hands over his shoulders, pushing his suit jacket off his arms.

He mirrored her movement, slipping one strap of her dress off her shoulder. The dress fell dangerously low, exposing the pale flush of one areola. His other hand fell to her hip and he squeezed, an attempt to hold on to his dwindling willpower long enough to get her to the desk and not throw her down on the kitchen table. Then again..."How about here instead?"

She laughed off his suggestion and he felt a wave of relief. He hadn't meant to say that out loud.

"Come with me." Weaving her fingers in his, she led him down the seemingly mile-long corridor to his office. Not that he could complain about the view—he kept his eyes on her derriere the entire time, loving how she moved, the way her dress hugged her hips. He couldn't wait to get it off her. To have her under him.

In his office, she dropped his hand and flicked on the fireplace with the remote. The fake flames licked to life, softening the room in an orange glow. She crooked a finger and he went to her, his body practically vibrating. How is it he'd had her repeatedly and still wanted more?

She unbuttoned his shirt, parting the material and sweeping her fingers over his chest. He sucked in a breath, loving the feel of her hands on his body. The way she reverently touched him. He molded his hands over her shoulders, warming her with his palms before pushing the straps aside and exposing her breasts. Such perfect breasts. He cupped them in his hands and thumbed her nipples as her eyes closed. How was it they both enjoyed touching one another in equal measure? He shouldn't question it. And then he couldn't, because next she reached for his belt.

When his pants slid to his knees, he unzipped her dress, letting it fall to her hips. He stomped on his pants and left them inside out on the floor while she wiggled out of the dress, her lithe movements causing his erection to throb painfully.

She hadn't been wearing a bra, he'd known that. But now he saw she hadn't been wearing underwear, either. Eyes on the *V* between her thighs, he shucked his boxer briefs and reached her in one step, his lips hitting hers hard, suddenly unable—or unwilling—to slow down.

Kimber was no longer smiling or teasing, but she was responding. Kissing him as hard as he kissed her, her tongue in his mouth, her hands roving over his chest. He palmed her ass at the same time she grabbed his cock. With a low grunt of satisfaction, he backed them through the room toward the desk, sucking in greedy gulps of air between kisses. His leg hit the corner of his mahogany desk, rattling the pen cup sitting there.

The disruption made her pull her lips from his. He watched as she took in the blotter, the stapler, the wooden inbox, then lifted her eyes to his, a question simmering there.

"Do it," he told her, half a smile creeping onto his face.

With wide eyes, she glanced at the surface again. "I don't think I can. It's all so...neat."

He moved her aside and, much as he hated to, let go of her hips. Arm on one side of the desk, he lifted an eyebrow. *Dare me?*

She bit her lip, something irreverent and fiery in her expression. That was all it took. Starting at one side, he swiped his arm across the desk, knocking everything off. Various office implements clattered to the floor.

When he faced her, she had her hand to her throat as if in shock. She was a vision, completely nude save for those tall, tall shoes, her nipples peaked, her hair coming down, her mouth forming a perfect *O*. "I can't believe you did that."

He didn't speak, but crushed his mouth into hers. She tasted like peppermint, smelled like cucumber, and the scent curled around his brain and stalled his every thought. Kicking his chair out of the way, he lifted and sat her onto the shining desk, then took hold of her ankles. "Worth it," he said. He spread her legs and she let him, a foxy little smile on her face.

He draped her knees over his shoulders, kissing first one breast and then the other. A breathy moan sounded in her throat as the heels of her shoes scraped his back. She arched toward him and he purposefully made his way to her thighs.

"Landon." Her fingers tangled in his hair as he traced the tip of his tongue along the inside of her legs. She pushed his head away, then pulled him closer, like she didn't know what she wanted. But he knew what she wanted. He knew because she'd told him, because he'd paid close attention to her body's needs over and over again.

Dipping his head, he took his time tasting every square inch of her until she squirmed. Until her soft mewls of pleasure swirled around him, and the spicy scent of her was imprinted on his brain. Only when she yanked his hair did he come up for air.

"Now." Her cheeks were flushed, her hair a disaster.

He smiled. He loved what he did to her. "But I'm not finished yet."

"Oh, yes you are."

Well. How could he argue with that? He opened a desk drawer and fished out a row of condoms.

"Planner," she teased with a puckish smile.

"Hey, you bought these. I just put them in here." Because he *was* a planner.

Condom in place, he took a mental photograph of this moment. He'd never be able to write another proposal at this desk without picturing Kimber sprawled across it. Pink, pert nipples, heavy-lidded eyes, her red hair spread around her head like a deviant halo.

"What's funny?"

"Absolutely nothing." If he was grinning it was because he was happy. Go figure. He gripped her hips with both hands and slid into her in one long, slow, smooth motion, encasing himself in her warmth. Back arched, eyes scrunched, she held tightly to the sides of the desk. And he vowed to give her a reason to hold on. He drove into her, slowly, deeply, basking in each keening sound that echoed in the room as she thrashed and called his name loud enough for the entire building to hear.

She was on the edge. He could feel her tightening around him. Palms on the desk on either side of her head, he switched his angle and she cried out. But when he would have sent her over, she crossed her ankles behind his thighs and held him in place. Her eyes were fierce, her lips full and wet when she spoke. "On the chair."

He damn near came right then.

"That's not on the list." He flexed his hips and broke her hold.

The high heels dug into his ass. "Sit down," she commanded, her voice a breathy, throaty whisper.

"Sounds like a threat." He slid out halfway, clinging to his control while making her lose hers.

"Or else." She gasped, a weak one at that.

He thrust forward, taking his time with each inch, nearly losing it right then. "Or else what?" he managed despite the slight tremor in his voice.

"Why don't you sit down and find out?"

* * *

Landon stood over her, the look on his face a mix of determination and lust.

All she wanted was for her legs to cooperate so she could make good on her promise. Since he had laid her onto his desk, she'd been coming apart at the seams, her mind dancing, her thoughts muddled. But she didn't want to be sated and as boneless as a jellyfish while he continued to exert himself. Well…she did want that, but more than that, she wanted the position of power.

And right now, she had his full attention. So she was going to take advantage of it.

"On. The. Chair." It was more a sigh than a command, but he obeyed, sliding from her body on an expelled breath and making her almost regret her request. He shot her a heated look that said *this better be worth it* before pulling the cushy, dark red chair over and sitting down.

This would be worth it; he had nothing to worry about.

Willing her muscles to work, she sat up. The hard surface of the desk wasn't all that comfortable. Her spine protested, her butt bone, too, as she pushed to standing. Landon's hands gripped the arms of his executive chair and a mini boss/secretary fantasy she didn't even know she had popped into her brain. She eyed the wide seat before arranging her knees over his thighs, lining up and, without a word of warning, sliding home.

His head dropped back as his hands clutched her bottom, his fingers grazing the inside of each cheek. She rocked against him, delighting when he closed his eyes and gave himself over to her. Low sounds of pleasure eked from his throat as he lost himself in the rhythm she set.

Using the high back of the chair as an anchor, she picked up the pace. His hands tightened around her ass, and she rode him until his entire body went rigid, his muscles turned to steel, and a drop of sweat formed on his brow. He was trying to hold out, but she wasn't about to let him. One last pump and he came on a shout, her name bursting from his lips, his teeth grinding, his eyes squeezed tightly shut.

Her orgasm followed; her high cries of ecstasy mingling with his in the warm air of his office. She'd been trying to make this about him, but her body greedily took its own release. Unable to support her own weight, she dropped her arms from the back of the chair and fell against him.

He turned his head, his heavy exhalations fanning her hair. With a soft kiss against her temple, he breathed her name again.

* * *

The sexiest woman he'd ever seen draped over him like a wet towel. Only Kimber didn't feel like a wet towel. She felt like a warm, sated woman. Her limbs and soft scent wrapped around him, rendering him useless.

When he'd followed her in here, the goal had been to make her come twice...maybe three times, but she hadn't allowed him to get that far before she'd demanded he sit down and she gave him the ride of his life.

He had no regrets.

Tonight had been a fantasy come to life.

Number eight. Check.

What were there? Two left? Maybe once they reached the end of the list, they could start over at one again. Against the door...

He smiled. He could go for another round against the door.

Her teeth closed over the tendon running from his shoulder to jaw, and she bit him lightly. "You're tense here," she said against his heated flesh. She pursed her lips and kissed him gently, soothing the phantom sting of the bite.

"I don't know how." He was still inside her, his arms lying limply at his sides. He wanted to wrap them around her, lift her off his lap, and carry her to the nearest shower. Or to bed. But he couldn't find the energy.

"Me, either," she mumbled. "This is the least stressful week of my life."

Her delivery was so dry, he laughed, the sound tumbling through his chest, loosening him more. Being with her was so easy. He didn't remember ever having been with a woman and it being easy at the same time. Lissa hadn't been cuddly, and he hadn't, either...until now, apparently. All he wanted to do was sit here and continue breathing in the faint sweetness of Kimber's hair. And he was in absolutely no hurry to remove her from his lap.

She had more willpower than he had, pushing off him. He groaned when the cold air hit his skin, his eyes still closed, his brain on vacation.

"Oh," he heard her say.

"Oh?" he repeated. A tap on his shoulder forced him to open his eyes. She stood at the front of his chair, gestured to his lap, and bit her lip.

He dipped his chin and looked down at the condom. *Oh?* More like *Oh shit.*

The latex had broken. Wide open. And he'd stayed inside her long enough to...

Shit. Long enough.

"I'm...um..." She shook her head instead of finishing her thought, then pointed to the door and shuffled out of his office. He heard her footsteps retreat down the hall, toward one of their bedrooms, he guessed.

He surveyed the mess on his lap again. *No good.*

Potentially *very bad,* if he were being honest.

After a brief stop in the bathroom bisecting the hallway to clean himself up, he checked his room. Empty. He walked the corridor to the opposite end and entered Kimber's old room. She was in there; he could hear the shower running in the attached bath.

He let himself into the steam-filled room and refused to panic. Or maybe he refused to accept the possibility that they'd just made a baby on his leather office chair. Wasn't like there was a whole hell of a lot they could do about it now, anyway. The shower in here was smaller than the one in his room, the air infused with cucumber body wash his housekeeper must not have thrown out. It smelled like Kimber in here. Cool, refreshing, sexy Kimber.

"It's me," he announced like a moron. Who else would it be? He parted the dark blue curtain and found a soapy and very distraught redhead inside. "Wash your back?"

She smoothed her wet hair and nodded, rivulets of water running down her face. He stepped beneath the hot, hot spray to stand next to her. "I hope you're not trying to scald me off of you." He thought he was kidding, but the words were a lance to his chest.

She shook her head. "I'm not." She braced her arms over her breasts, looking...well, terrified.

He planted his hands on her arms and rubbed, bending to meet her eyes. Green eyes filled with doubt. With fear.

"What are the odds?" he asked her, a smile plastered to his face. Because the truth was, the odds were pretty slim with him and Rachel but she'd wound up pregnant, too. He swallowed a wave of nausea.

This is not that. It wasn't the same at all.

"Slim," she admitted, closing her eyes.

"Take a deep breath for me."

She lowered her arms and sucked in a lungful of air. He shouldn't, but couldn't keep from admiring her pert pink nipples and the water streaming off of them. It took everything in him not to put his tongue on one for a taste.

A bottle of body wash stood on a shelf over her head. He poured some on his hands and rubbed them together. "One more breath." She inhaled again, and he put his hands on her shoulders and turned her around, rubbing the stress from her back and from her arms, kneading the tension from the muscles in her lower back. Her shoulders fell and she relaxed into his slow, gentle massage, his touch meant to soothe and pull her out of her panic.

Caught up in his task, he didn't register at first that she'd spun around until he was palming her breasts. His hands stilled. She tilted her chin, asking for a kiss. So he kissed her, stroking her tongue with his as they stood under the pounding water. Then he slid his hands from her breasts to her bottom and massaged there, too.

When the kiss ended, she sent him a smile. "I don't think even that accident made me want to stop having sex with you."

"That's a relief." He wasn't done having sex with her, either.

"Is it?" The worry returned, a line forming between her frowning brows. Rather than answer, he made quick work of rinsing her off. They toweled dry and he steered her from bathroom to bedroom.

The sheets were fresh and cool against his overheated body as he slid in next to her. She scooted closer, draping a leg over his. "What's number nine?"

He'd created a monster. Which made him kind of proud. But more sex wasn't what she needed right now, and they both knew it. He pushed a wet strand of hair off her forehead. "Nine is talking in bed after a hot shower."

Her gaze clouded. "I don't want to talk."

"Sure you do." He trailed his fingers down her face and thumbed her bottom lip. "You're a woman and women love to talk. Let's have it. What's on your mind?"

The clouds cleared from her vision. She watched him with her crystal-clear gaze. "What if we just made a baby?"

A jolt of anxiety lit his bloodstream. He caged it. If he let the beast free, he'd stumble down the pained and brambly trail of *what-if*s and *yeah-but*s. That was the last thing either of them needed.

"We'll deal with that if it happens." The intentional calm in his voice even reassured him. He forced the next question out of his lips, unsure how he'd managed to ask it without bursting into hives. "Have you ever been pregnant before?"

She shook her head, her hair brushing against the pillowcase. He lifted his eyebrows. "There you go."

Sure. Like that is the end of this discussion.

She didn't buy it, either. As evidenced when she asked the question he should've seen coming. The last question he wanted to answer. "Have you ever gotten anyone pregnant?"

The query busted him open like a piñata. And he wasn't sure if he should spill the truth to her or keep his secrets to himself.

* * *

The answer was *yes*.

She could see it on his face, the way his mouth tightened at the corners, the bob of his Adam's apple as he swallowed, the subtle tensing of his shoulder muscles.

Then his expression eased into a controlled mask, and he forced a calmer-than-you smile onto his face. "You have nothing to worry about, Kimber. Either way." He leaned in and kissed her and she let him. But it bothered her that he hadn't told her the truth she so clearly read in his eyes. Against the white pillowcase, his eyes appeared their natural green-mixed-with-gold hazel. They had no color to blend with or fade into. He was naked before her. In every sense of the word. It occurred to her that his eyes were a representation of who he truly was. Hiding, blending in to his environment, and rarely showing his true self.

Only, she thought he'd shown her his true self. Had she been wrong? The urge to point that out, to call him on his lie, was strong. She resisted. She didn't want to lay skin to skin on potentially their last evening together, and lob accusations in his direction. She didn't want to fight with him.

It didn't stop her imagination from concocting scenarios of what the truth might be. Was it Lissa who'd been pregnant? Did she miscarry? Terminate? Was a secret baby the real reason behind their relationship's demise? Kimber shut her eyes.

Don't jump to conclusions. Don't make yourself crazy.

Landon's low voice cut into her thoughts. "My girlfriend from college."

Her eyes flew open. His lips were pressed together as if conflicted about how much more to say. Or like he'd regretted saying anything at all.

She should tell him he didn't have to talk about it... but

curiosity forced a question from her lips. The two words were a whisper of sound in the dark, quiet room. "What happened?"

"She...she...didn't have it," he said with a frown.

Kimber stroked her fingers up his arm, up the length of sinew and long, lean muscle to his solid biceps. "She lost it?"

Silence permeated the room, and his eyes lingered, unfocused on something over her shoulder. "She had an abortion."

Those four words begged more questions. Was it at his request? Did they go to the clinic together? Had he persuaded her to get it, or had she made that decision on her own? Guilt radiated off him, so much of it, her stomach tossed. She glided a palm onto his chest and rested it over his heart. Beneath the impressive muscles, golden skin, and fair hair, beat his heart.

His broken heart. Broken for a baby that never saw this world. Her heart pinged in sympathy, even as she warned herself not to feel his pain like her own. "I'm sorry," she said.

He clutched her hand and squeezed, his eyes boring into hers. Eyes filled not with tears, but regret. She didn't push, couldn't bear to make him hurt any more than he hurt now.

The initial panic over the broken condom had passed. She was relaxed and warm, had Landon's full attention, and an entire house to themselves without interruption. They also had time. As much time as they needed.

The chances of her getting pregnant were slim. She'd never had a condom blowout before, and reason suggested using one form of birth control was more risky than two. But she'd never gotten pregnant before, and the incident that happened to Landon had happened years ago.

Sixteen years ago, to be exact. She remembered when he'd returned home that summer, sadness hanging over him like a dark cloud. The sound of defeat in his voice when he'd told his mother he and his girlfriend had split.

She'd lost the baby by then.

And Landon had been mourning. Over more than just a girlfriend.

She palmed his face, and his brows lowered, maybe in confusion. There was no way he could know the direction her thoughts had taken. That she ached for him. Ached for the loss he'd suffered back then. Ached for the loss he still suffered.

"I love you," she whispered.

His eyes widened, his cheeks darkened, and his mouth pressed into a hard, unforgiving line.

She hadn't meant to say it. She'd meant to say something about that summer, or let him know she'd witnessed his sadness back then. But her stupid heart, that always fell too hard, too fast, had wired a message to her mouth. The very last thing she should have said aloud. Or to herself. At all, really.

So dumb.

He recovered quickly and tweaked her chin, bringing a halt to her panicky thoughts. "Safe space, remember? That was part of our agreement."

She shook her head against the pillow, tears welling in her eyes. Tears of anger, tears of fear that what she said might really be true. What if she did love him? She felt like she meant what she'd said, but didn't she always?

"I'm sure when you suggested a safe space you didn't mean for me to say..." she trailed off, her voice wobbly. "I'm—this is something I do. I feel too much." A tear escaped her eye and rolled down her cheek. She wasn't sure if she felt embarrassed...or...or *doomed.* But something. Something not good.

A soft kiss landed on her lips, and he scooted close

enough to touch her nose with his. "You're walking away, remember? This is your fling. This is yours to savor."

She blinked several times, weighing his words. What could have been an awkward ending to an already awkward evening felt almost...normal. He was giving her an out. An out she'd be stupid not to take. "It's...I'm not sure why I said that."

"So say something else," he said simply. "Then we'll move on to the last item on the list."

The last item on the list. And then she could walk away and leave her awkward pronouncement behind. A shimmer of pain spread across her chest. Was he really so unaffected by her words? *It doesn't matter.* She decided not to think about it any longer, to take the reprieve he'd offered.

Earlier she'd wondered if Landon, man of many talents with his lips and tongue and body, had started going warm and gooey on her. He'd soaped her up and hadn't taken advantage of her even when she'd put her breasts in his hands. And she'd been desperate to get them focused on the physical, out of the emotional cage she'd been trapped in since she'd stepped into the shower to wash the remnants of him from her inner thighs.

Flings were supposed to be fun. Flings were supposed to be string-less. Pregnancy sounded downright *stringy.*

He stroked her thigh now, but not in a sexual way, just with the tips of his fingers. Just to let her know he was here while she worked through her meandering thoughts. His touch felt so good, she wanted to curl into him and purr. Except that he wanted her to talk. And she wanted to talk about something other than pregnant girlfriends and her haphazard emotions. There was one foolproof way to douse that fire.

"Tell me about yours and Lissa's relationship," she blurted.

His fingers stilled halfway up her leg before starting back down again. "You want to talk about Lissa?"

She didn't answer.

Taking a breath, he spoke. "Lissa and I didn't have a romantic relationship."

He'd told her about their "arrangement," but their relationship hadn't been a romantic one at all? The thought hit her like a dead fish to the face. A slimy slap that made her want to scrub her skin with both hands. At least when she'd been with Mick she'd convinced herself she loved him at the time.

Is that what you're doing with Landon?

She refused to answer that question.

Trailing his fingers back down her leg, he let a few seconds pass, even though she was sure he saw her unfavorable reaction to his admission. "I met Lissa at a party for RedAd," he continued. "I was employed there right out of college. Stayed ten years. They still want my head for branching out on my own." He smirked, proud of that achievement, she could see. "Anyway, the cocktail party celebrated some account we'd landed and they'd hired pretty girls to hand out drinks at the event. She was one of them."

"I'd ask what drew you to her, but I think that's fairly evident," she said, picturing Lissa's long, honey-colored hair, slender, tanned body, perfectly proportioned breasts, and an ass that defied gravity.

"She's very beautiful."

Why it hurt to hear him confirm the obvious, she had no idea.

"In a commercial way," he added.

He was downplaying her. For Kimber's sake. That was nice of him, but she didn't need coddling. "Is this the part where you tell me I'm beautiful, too, so I don't get jealous? Because I don't need you to."

He didn't have to move much to reach her lips since they were nose to nose on the pillow. He kissed her, a soft brush of his mouth over hers. "Sure you do. I'll make you a promise. When we're done in here, I'll take you to my bed and kiss all the parts of your body I like better than hers." He watched her, gaze steady. "Will that convince you?"

"Will it be more than my nose and my earlobes?"

The twitch of his lips told her he was about to smile, but he reeled it back in and had her on her back a second later. Startled laughter tittered from her throat. He tucked her beneath him and spread her thighs with one knee. Eyes on hers, he nudged her. She wasn't surprised to feel him half-hard already. She wanted him again, too. To show it, she rubbed against him like a shameless hussy.

But he backed away, laying a harmless kiss on her forehead as he did. "Don't break the rules. This is the talking bed."

She pouted. "I hate this bed."

He rolled off her but stayed close. "And to answer your question, I'm planning on kissing you everywhere *but* your nose and earlobes."

Flattered, she smiled.

"Since we're massacring the rule of discussing exes in bed, tell me about yours." Back on his side of the bed, he shoved an arm under his pillow.

"My ex..."

Where to start? Not with the truth. She couldn't very well tell him that she'd gone out after a particularly bad breakup with a guy she thought she'd loved with frightening intensity only to find out he'd cheated on her. At Gloria's suggestion, Kimber had sought out a one-night stand to scrub Joey from her mind. She couldn't tell Landon that she'd spotted shaggy, disheveled Mick Stringer across the room and decided *yes, that will be who I turn and burn.* Or that she'd failed on every level with Mick. She'd been attempting a fling with him, too, and had blurted out an I-love-you not in a dissimilar fashion as she'd done with Landon. And she sure as heck couldn't tell him *that*.

But she'd been wrong when she'd made that declaration to Mick. She'd fallen into lust and had mistaken it for love. Had been trying to make him permanent since he'd moved in to her place and bought a business with her. Because without a commitment, all of that had seemed... wrong.

"Must be some story." Landon's expression was sullen.

She poked his chest. "Now who's jealous?"

He smoothed his features. "Impossible. I am the Tin Man, remember? And you love me, so who would I have to be jealous of?" Before her face stoked enough heat to catch fire, he said, "Spill it. Or I'll cut your kisses down to half as many."

The threat, though an empty one, coaxed her into talking. "Because of a lapse in judgment, or debatable temporary sanity"—she paused to admire his quirked lips—"Mick owns half of Hobo Chic. Truth is I didn't really think things through. We'd only been dating a year when we bought it. We broke up shortly after and now we're stuck." She shrugged. "Unless I agree to sell it."

"Is it sellable?"

"Probably. But I don't want to sell my shop. I want to keep it."

"Is it profitable?" Whoa. Landon had snapped into business mode. His brows were drawn in concentration. He watched her like an eagle might watch a prairie dog. Intently.

"It does okay. Hobo Chic is a solid business; it's in the black. But it's not one Mick and I want to run together. He can't afford to walk away, and I can't afford to buy him out. Yet."

She held up a finger to make her point, stopping short of saying, *But I will soon, thanks in part to your monetary contribution.* She knew it was silly to feel badly about having accepted money from him, but she couldn't help it. Sure, she'd done a job and he'd paid for her nanny services, but the line had blurred between babysitting for Lyon and flirting with Landon. She couldn't help struggling with separation.

"I can help you with traffic," he said. "One visit to the store and I can assess several attributes, look at your numbers, find a way for you to advertise to your potential customers. Do you—"

She pressed her finger to his lips to shut him up. Landon at Hobo Chic, helping her advertise, giving her business advice... that all sounded very un-fling-like. Kimber didn't need another man entrenched in the business she should be running by herself. She didn't want him to be anything more than he was right now.

Unless he ends up being the father of your child.

The thought crashed into her brain like a runaway shopping cart into a minivan. She shoved it away. And ignored the dent.

Putting on her "Everything's Okay" mask, she threw back the covers and climbed out of bed. "Race you to your room. You owe me a few hundred kisses."

As she rounded the bed, he lashed one strong arm around her waist and pulled her back in. Laughing, she bounced on the mattress as he arranged himself on top of her and kissed the underside of her chin. "There's one."

Her laughter ebbed as relief rushed through her. The intensity from earlier fading. If he was willing to overlook her verbal grenade, and the gaffe of failing birth control, so was she.

"This is the talking bed," she teased as he licked a path to her collarbone.

"So, talk." He kissed her arm. "Start with something like *Oh, Landon*"—he tongued her shoulder—"then *yes,*

Landon." He smiled, his teeth lightly nipping her flesh. "Maybe throw in a *please* and a *don't stop*."

As he slid down her body, she found herself murmuring those words in order, then out of order. Until there was nothing left but incoherent syllables.

CHAPTER THIRTEEN

This is how a fling works." Gloria snatched the ringing phone out of Kimber's hands and pressed Ignore. "You have to let it end. That's the point."

Glo had insisted that now was the best breaking-off point since Kimber and Landon had parted without promises or plans to see each other again. Just a kiss good night after they'd fulfilled the list, then her cab ride home.

"It feels immature not to answer," Kimber said as her voice mail chimed, alerting her about a new message. "Even if it is to tell him it's over." She swiped her finger to unlock the screen.

Glo took the phone.

Kimber fiddled with her thumb ring. "Fine! I won't check it!"

Her best friend handed over the phone and moved to a jewelry display on the other end of the counter. She lifted a pair of feather earrings to her ears and admired them in the small, round mirror by the display. "Is it over for you?"

Not unless she started her period, she thought with a tremble. Until they knew for sure she wasn't pregnant, she and Landon were intertwined.

On a sigh, Kimber looked around. The store was empty.
Neil was at lunch. She and Gloria were alone in the space.
Kimber desperately needed someone to confide in. Despite
the fact there was no one around to overhear, she whispered.
"We had a condom break."

Gloria's ink-black eyebrows lifted. "Whoopsie."

"Yeah. Had a little size issue."

"Condom too big?" She asked with a smirk.

"*Too small*. I bought a box but didn't know there were...
sizes."

Glo held her palm up for a high five.

Kimber groused at her.

"Don't leave me hanging."

"I can't high-five you over his pen—"

The bell over the door rang, cutting her sentiment short.
An advertising executive dressed in a three-piece suit and
red tie strolled in, adjusting his glasses on his nose. Kimber swallowed, studying the buttoned vest with unabashed
approval, which basically meant she struggled not to drool
on the countertop. The man was a sexy beast.

"Holy Hot Pockets," Glo muttered under her breath. She
ran a hand through her sheet of silken black hair and pushed
her breasts up in her low-cut top. Kimber had to bite back a
smile. Because Landon had come here to see *her*, and that
made Kimber feel sexy just the way she was.

He spotted Kimber and crossed the room casually,
his long legs eating up the space between them. When he
reached the counter, he sent Glo a perfunctory, polite smile
and Kimber a full body graze that made her stomach tighten.
She loved it when he looked at her that way.

"Welcome to Hobo Chic," Kimber said. "Everything we
have is on the floor." She tamped back the smile pulling her
lips as he sent a sharp, inquisitive gaze around her shop.

He gave an approving nod. "Nice place."

"She's the owner," Gloria interjected, stepping behind the counter to stand next to Kimber. "This is her baby."

She kicked her best friend, who no doubt had carefully selected the word "baby." Unless she was mistaken, Kimber didn't think Glo had figured out who he was yet.

A secret smile tickled his lips. "You don't say."

Kimber had to bite her lip to keep from grinning.

"I can't help but wonder," he told her, his eyes locked onto hers, "if more people knew about your location you'd be busier."

Fun as this was, it was about time to let Glo in on the joke. Kimber opened her mouth to introduce her best friend to her "fling," but Gloria cut her off. "I agree. She's tucked back here away from the main drag, but there is an excellent café across the street, and a jewelry maker, too. If more people knew about this neighborhood, Hobo Chic would be swamped."

He focused his attention on Glo and offered a hand. "You must be her agent."

So, he'd figured out who Gloria was right away. That sly devil. Evan must have done a good job describing her.

Gloria blushed, actually blushed, and took his hand. "I'm not *her* agent. But I am a literary one. Children's books."

He shrugged with his lips as if impressed and glanced at Kimber.

She rolled her eyes. *Stop playing and tell her who you are.* He ignored her silent suggestion.

"That's impressive," he said to Gloria. "I know a children's book artist."

"Do you?" She was still shaking his hand. "Does this artist have representation?"

A smile. "Yes. He does."

"May I ask his name?"

"Sure. My brother, Evan. Downey."

Gloria's smile slid off her face like suds from a freshly washed car. She pulled her hand away. "Jesus."

"Landon," he corrected. "You must be Gloria."

"You don't look like your brother," she commented.

He didn't. Landon was taller by a few inches, his hair lighter, his refined way of dress and speak a far cry from Evan's laid-back swagger.

"The shape of their noses, and their eyes, are the same," Kimber said.

He flicked those eyes over to her—gray today. "I called."

"I ignored it."

He pressed a hand to his chest like he was hurt. "Ignored."

"I told her to," Glo said. "I was trying to tell her a story and didn't want the interruption. I'm selfish that way. Well, I have to get back to my clients. She's all yours now." She gathered her purse from behind the counter, mouthing the words *Call me* on her way out of the store.

Once she'd gone, Landon faced Kimber. "Is that true?"

She smiled sheepishly. "Which part?"

"You don't want to see me any longer." It wasn't a question, but he waited for a reply all the same.

"The idea was to walk away." A clean break before she turned a spontaneous profession into a relationship doomed to fail.

"I know." He plunged his hands into his pockets and studied the battered floor. "Okay, I'll go." She thought he meant he was leaving, but then he spoke. "I like spending time with you. I'd like to take you out again." A mischievous twinkle sparked in his dark eyes. "I'd like to have you over again."

"I'd like that, too," she admitted. She'd like to laugh with him over dinner, to kiss him in the shower, to lie in bed and eat potato chips. *But at what cost?* "I thought, you know... we shouldn't press our luck."

"You mean because of what happened."

He meant Condompocolypse. She didn't exactly mean that, but he'd brought up a valid point. "Yes."

He walked behind the counter and invaded her space, breeching her boundaries like he belonged there. Funny thing was, he sort of felt like he did. She knew Landon on a different level now. A level where no clothes were required and hectic breathing ensued.

"What if we're extra careful?" he asked.

The *in bed* was implied. Like with a fortune cookie. But she was determined not to lay waste to another relationship—not to take what they'd had to its inevitable demise. No matter how she thought she felt about him.

"Maybe we should quit while we're ahead," she said.

He tipped her chin and watched her. The tingle from his touch shot all the way down to her toes. "Maybe you're right." She saw the sadness in his polite smile a second before he dropped a soft kiss on her lips. A good-bye kiss.

Then he turned and walked out of her store, leaving her to wonder if she'd cut her losses or made the biggest mistake of her life.

* * *

Landon digitally signed the approval sheet for the billboard and e-mailed it back to the designer. He smiled at the image, proud of the work. Work he'd pulled off with only Kirk and Janie assisting him.

In the weeks since he'd last seen Kimber, he'd been looking for a way to help her with Hobo Chic whether she'd asked for it or not. And he'd known she wouldn't. She was probably avoiding him—regretting her unplanned three-word admission... but he'd taken her words with a grain of salt. She'd been sated and happy followed by terrified and worried. That situation could make anyone blurt out something they didn't mean.

After that night, after he'd covered her body with kisses and they'd made love, she'd left. And she'd left him literally aching to see her again. He missed her. Not just the sex—amazing as it was—he missed talking to her, sharing a drink or a laugh. He missed her presence in his cavern-like penthouse.

Going home had become an exercise in frustration. When he and Lissa had split, he'd felt the opposite. He used to love returning to his empty, quiet home, his only mistress a glass of Macallan. He'd enjoyed his drink and the view on the balcony before turning in for a restful night's sleep.

But now . . . now his place was a tomb. Devoid of his nephew's laughter and clutter. Bare of Kimber's warm presence. The scotch in his glass each evening only served to remind him of the drinks he'd shared with her; the night on the balcony they'd made love under the stars.

In a word, it *sucked*.

But it didn't have to keep sucking. He had a plan to get her attention, to get her to come to him. The billboard he'd just signed off on ought to do it, or at least lure her into calling him.

In the hall, his secretary scuttled by with an armload of large, yellow envelopes.

"Cindy, I'm heading to lunch. Be back in an hour," he told her.

The owner of Windy City potato chips, Otto Williams, was waiting for him at Grand Pine Café. Landon agreed to meet him, despite the fact that having lunch together was a pointless waste of time. Otto had approved Windy City's designs a week ago. He'd signed off on the ads and had purchased a marketing package big enough to pad Landon's retirement. But Otto, well into his eighties, had a way of doing things. When a deal was done, he liked to drink an Old Fashioned and bond over chewy steak at Grand Pine.

So, Landon set out to accompany him in both endeavors.

He paid the cab driver and strode to the door, nodding at a few passersby weaving along the busy walkway. The sun was hot and making him sweat—late August in Chicago—and he slipped his jacket off before he went inside.

A teenager nearly mowed him over as Landon reached for the door. The boy mumbled a rushed *sorry* and brushed by wordlessly, earbuds in, head down. Landon sent him an irritated glare before moving aside to let the woman following—his mother, he assumed—chase after him.

"Gregory," she called, then turned to Landon, he presumed to apologize or thank him. She did neither, instead froze in place, her mouth opened in a stunned gape.

Chicago was a big city. Because of that undeniable fact, the odds of running into someone he knew were slim. Slim, but not *none*. Apparently, considering he now stood eye to eye with his girlfriend from college.

Rachel.

Dressed in what could only be described as a power suit, Rachel Hannigan looked every bit the cutthroat lawyer she'd aspired to become when they'd dated. Her dark hair was cut into a sharp bob, her mouth—now that she'd closed it—a flat red line. The tightness around her eyes made him wonder if she ever smiled.

Only then, she did.

"Landon." A professional smile.

Stunned, he continued to hold the door as a patron exited the restaurant. She stepped aside to let the other man pass.

"How are you?" he asked automatically. Numbly. Fucking *Rachel.* Unbelievable.

She nodded, a typical non-answer to the throwaway greeting. "This is my son, Gregory." She palmed the boy's shoulder and the kid lifted his head, hair sweeping his forehead and falling over his sunglasses.

He studied the teen's sandy-colored hair, rangy build,

and slouchy skater-wear. He couldn't see his eyes and found himself wondering if they were hazel. Like his own. Landon swallowed, his gut churning, mind reeling.

"He turned fourteen today." Rachel gave him a meaningful eyebrow raise. In other words: *He's not yours.*

Landon's lips twitched. It was a bitter smile. And the wrong time and place to resurrect that demon. He flicked his eyes back to Gregory who tapped on the screen of his phone, utterly undeterred. Another diner exited between them, giving a surly *"Excuse me"* as she passed by, clearly annoyed that they were clogging the entrance.

"Good to see you," Rachel lied. He could see the untruth in every rigid muscle in her face.

He refused to echo it. "Happy birthday, Gregory."

The kid tossed his hair out of his eyes and muttered "Thanks" as Rachel slid her sunglasses onto her nose and waved for a cab.

Landon turned and walked inside, his legs shaky. He felt like he'd taken a two-by-four to the gut. For one scant, surreal moment, he'd thought Rachel had lied to him sixteen years ago. That instead of terminating her pregnancy, she'd kept the child they'd created. Had moved to her aunt's house, not because she wanted to finish school at a different college like she'd claimed when she left him, but to have the baby. Their baby. For a split second, he'd thought *I'm a father.*

Then Rachel had set him straight. *He turned fourteen today.*

Definitely not his.

Otto waved a gnarled hand from a corner booth in the crowded, dim steakhouse. Landon strode over and sat across from the man. He wondered if Otto had children. Grandchildren. The waitress brought two Old Fashioneds while Otto complained about the heat, and Landon lifted the disgusting drink and downed half of it in one putrid swallow.

The older man watched, his untamed, wiry eyebrows shooting in all directions. "Easy, son, we have to make a toast," he said, cheeks red from the last Old Fashioned he'd drank.

Son. Landon nearly laughed.

"To Windy City and Downey Design." Otto raised his glass. As their glasses clinked, he added, "And leaving a legacy."

He was talking, of course, about the legacy of his potato chip business. The mark on a town his family had inhabited for at least the last century. None of which would have been possible if there were no future or past generations to start and finish it.

Otto continued to jabber on about his various body aches and how his doctor recommended he stop drinking. "The drink is the only thing I look forward to," he said gruffly as he studied the menu.

Landon stabbed the cherry at the bottom of his glass with the plastic straw, and there, in the last place he'd expected to find himself, in the oddest company for such a poignant moment, he had an epiphany.

It was a thought he'd never imagined entertaining again. But it was there, and as real and solid as the glass in his hand.

CHAPTER FOURTEEN

It was unfair to show up like this. Just barge into Landon's office unannounced. He was a busy man. A man who—

"May I help you?"

Kimber turned to the smiling secretary, a woman in her fifties with dyed orange hair and a flowery blouse.

Too late to run now.

"I'm here to see Landon Downey. I wasn't sure if I needed an appointment. I guess I could call him." She should have called him. Only she hadn't known she was coming to see him until she stepped into his building. She'd gone out shopping today and then found herself wandering. *Like a moth to the flame . . .*

"Kimber?"

She turned to see Landon stepping out of the elevator, one hand casually in his pants pocket, his sharp navy suit making his body appear powerful, solid. Like a good place to cast her worries. And her worries were ample. They walked toward each other, both stopping short of inappropriate distance.

"How are you?" she said.

His eyebrows were drawn together. He had to know what she was doing here after not seeing him for almost a month. There was only one reason for her to be here. Only, she was here for more than the obvious reason. She missed him.

Her life had been empty, strange, since they'd parted that day in Hobo Chic. Even though she knew she had no claim to him, she'd begun bargaining with herself. Asking questions like, *why couldn't she date him a while longer?* And finding no suitable answer.

Her loft apartment above her store used to be her sanctuary. Over the last two weeks it'd felt less homey than before. She couldn't explain why. Nothing had changed. Except for her. She felt like she hadn't taken a full breath since she'd left Landon's penthouse for the last time.

And now she wasn't sure if she'd take a full breath ever again. Not until she talked to him.

His eyes flitted around the lobby before drilling into hers. "I'm late for a meeting across town." He pulled his hand from his pocket and grimaced at the oversized watch on his wrist. "I can't miss it, but I don't want to leave you like this."

Like this. He thought she was pregnant. "It can wait," she insisted.

He breached the space between them and palmed her shoulder. "It can't, but I have to go." Anguish clouded his eyes. "Do me a favor."

Anything to get the look of hurt off his face. She nodded.

"Go to my house. Order some lunch. Make yourself comfortable. I'll be home in two hours, three tops. But don't…" He shook his head like he was at a loss for words. "Don't *do* anything until we talk."

Don't do anything. Like have an abortion? Her thoughts went back to his confession about his college girlfriend. The pain and regret clouding his eyes when he'd confessed.

"Okay," she promised.

He closed his eyes as he pulled in a breath, and she could swear he looked relieved. Then he shocked her by leaning in and kissing her. Nothing alarming about a chaste, feather-soft touch of their lips, other than the fact he'd done it in front of a sea of people he worked with; who worked for him.

"Wait for me," he whispered. Then he strode out of his building and into the bustling street.

* * *

If he was at the business end of a loaded gun, Landon wouldn't be able to recite a single topic covered of the two-hour meeting he'd just attended. Concentration had been a pipe dream; his thoughts trained only on Kimber, and how beautiful she'd looked standing in the lobby of Downey Design. The way she'd worn her hair, in smooth copper waves around her face. The oversize shirt and leggings coasting along those deliciously curved calves.

He had no idea if she was pregnant, or if she'd come to tell him she wasn't, but whatever the news he wouldn't ask her to blurt it out in the twelve seconds before he'd had to rush out the door.

He also had no idea what he was hoping for—positive results or negative. Yes, seeing Rachel last week had thrown him for a loop. Had cemented the decision that he'd like to have a child. *In the future.* He wasn't sure when the best time was to start a family, but he knew now wasn't ideal.

What about college? Was college ideal?

Impatiently, he pressed the button for the penthouse floor twice. One of his co-workers had quipped once that there was no perfect time to have kids, only bad timing and worse timing.

He chuffed a bone-dry laugh.

During the short elevator ride up to his house, he allowed himself to think *what if.* What if she was pregnant? He was a radically different man than he'd been in college. Income was no longer an issue. He owned a stable, thriving company that was relevant and sought after in a respectably big city. And he was older now, and hopefully wiser. He knew what it took to provide for a child.

On paper, anyway.

He wondered how Kimber felt about all of this. If she'd continue to run her clothing store if she was pregnant. He winced as he walked to the door and pulled his keys out of the lock. All those hours on her feet wouldn't be good for her or the baby. And he'd have to see about moving the store to a safer neighborhood, somewhere closer to his place...near a good private school. Maybe a charter...

Not that he was getting ahead of himself or anything.

He put his hand on the knob, then paused. Best to prepare for the other likelihood. That she had started her period and was here to set his mind at ease. Or the other, *other* option. That she was pregnant but didn't want to keep their baby. His stomach twisted to the point of nausea. Surely, God wouldn't let that happen to him twice. If she didn't want to have this baby, he'd have to convince her. He wouldn't lose the opportunity of fatherhood. Not again.

If there was a baby.

He walked in to find Kimber at his kitchen table, waiting for him like he'd asked. A can of Sprite with a straw sticking out of it stood in front of her. Late-day morning sickness? Avoiding caffeine for the baby?

Could you jump to any more conclusions?

He dropped his things on the kitchen table and pulled up a chair. "Hey," he said much more casually than he felt.

She sent him a small smile. "I'd ask you about your meeting but you probably don't want to talk about it."

He shook his head. Tried to read her expression. Failed. He wanted to lean forward and touch her somehow. Put his hands in her hair, wind his fingers around hers, tug her chair closer. But he didn't.

"Not unless you want to. Pretty boring stuff." He relaxed his back against the chair while his insides churned.

She surprised him by standing. "I want to show you something." He took her outstretched hand, longing flooding his body on contact. He'd really missed her. The kiss he gave her at his office had left him wanting more. Of all of her.

She led him through the hallway, around the corner, and into her old bedroom. Then into the bathroom.

Pregnancy tests were scattered from one end of the sink to the other. His heart collided with his rib cage and his knees actually weakened. He held on to the door frame and stared.

Unopened. The boxes were unopened. He shot her a questioning look. *What's going on?*

"I'm late. A week or so. But I didn't want to get the results until you were here. I didn't want to steal this moment from you. I wanted you to have the same amount of time to process once we find out. Together."

She didn't know if she was pregnant or not. And he didn't know if that made him feel better or not. He nodded, dazed. "Okay."

"You look sick."

Because he had no idea what she was thinking. He barely knew what *he* was thinking.

"I've been downing water and soda since I got here. So I have to pee." She laughed lightly. *Lightly,* during one of the heaviest moments of his life. "I'm going to take as many of them as I can so we'll know for sure. And then we can talk."

He braced one foot against the door to keep from passing out.

Kimber came to him, feathering her fingers into his hair. "I won't do anything without you. No matter what the tests say."

Her words cracked him open, split him in two like a dividing continent. The offer meant more than she knew. Rachel had robbed him of the opportunity to decide with her the best thing for all of them. She hadn't waited for him to offer any alternatives. She'd taken the option from him like he hadn't had a vested interest in their baby.

Kimber may not know how deeply her offer affected him, but he meant to show her. Straightening, he speared his hands into her hair and kissed her. A deep, intimate kiss, thanking her, drinking her in, and letting her know he'd be here for her as well.

She ended the kiss with a wiggle. "Gotta go." Reluctantly, he released her and stepped aside, allowing her to shut him out of the bathroom.

At the edge of the bed, he sat, elbows on his thighs, thumbs pressing against his closed eyelids. *Dear heavenly Father*, came the automatic thought. It was the way his mother had always started her prayers. Only he didn't know what to say next. He didn't know whether to pray for positive or negative results on those tests. And he didn't know if Kimber was behind the bathroom door hoping for the opposite of whatever he prayed for.

Mind a confused canvas of colors and shapes, Landon blew out a breath, lifted his chin to take in the ceiling above him, and, on a sigh, uttered a simple, "Help me do the right thing."

* * *

Kimber lined up the three tests she'd managed to saturate. She'd recapped the lids and washed her hands, leaving them to rest. She checked her teeth, straightened her clothes, and fluffed her hair.

The stalling wasn't necessary. Every package said to allow two to five minutes for results, but her results had appeared instantly. She ran a finger along the bottoms of the sticks. Two lines, two lines, and this one actually read *Pregnant*, in case she'd misinterpreted the whole double-line thing.

Now all she had to do was open the door and tell the father of her unborn baby the good news. Or the horrific news. *The happy-slash-terrifying news.* How would he take it? When she'd left him in the doorway, he'd been the color of pea soup. She had no idea if she should open the door and just announce her findings, or bring him in here and show him the evidence. How would he need to process? How did *she* need to process?

Right now her mind was an utter blank. Other than getting through the next sixty seconds, when she was forced to face Landon. Her fling. Her *fun*-night stand. She shook her head. She was such an idiot. There was a lesson to be learned here. Sex was anything but string-less. They'd knowingly played with fire…several, *several* times. What had they expected? But. She wouldn't turn this relationship with Landon into something it wasn't just because there was a Baby on Board.

She'd made the mistake of lashing Mick to Hobo Chic; had tied the ropes into double knots. And now they were stuck with a business one of them wanted and one of them didn't. They were trapped. Much like her mother had felt in the marriage to Kimber's father. She had given up everything when she'd learned she'd had Kimber in her belly. She'd shelved her dreams for duty. Then her parents had gone from happy people separately to miserable people together.

Kimber wouldn't repeat her mother's mistake. She wouldn't allow a baby to mandate her and Landon's combined future. Her focus was on becoming the best mother she could. Kimber knew she'd be an amazing, caring mother. And she'd share custody—assuming he wanted it—with the incredibly capable man outside of this door. But she refused to force herself into a familial unit destined to fail. She wouldn't lead Landon down the aisle only to watch his resentment for her deepen over the years.

What they'd had together was beautiful. What they'd made even more so. No sense in ruining it. She thought of the *I love you* she'd thrown out a few weeks ago with a wave of sorrow.

She couldn't allow herself to love Landon. Love was messy. A tangle of emotions he obviously didn't return. And she wasn't going to allow her soft heart to feel that way. For her baby's sake. For her sake. She was going to have to be stronger, grow up...all at once, it would seem.

Kimber tried to smile at the bathroom mirror as she smoothed her shirt over her flat stomach. She managed... until she thought about all the things that could go wrong. So many things could happen. To the baby. To her. To Landon. The best course of action was to take things as they came—a day at a time. She could plan for this day. For this moment. And she could decide not to get overly emotional and sentimental about what Landon and she had shared in the past.

She found him sitting on the bed, elbows on his legs, chin in his palms. He'd lost the jacket, loosened the tie, and cuffed his sleeves. If this little bud growing in her tummy made it, the kid would be absolutely gorgeous. Her tummy fluttered as she pictured a boy with color-changing hazel eyes and a sandy mess of hair, then later as a lean, lanky teenager with freckles like hers. Tears sprang to her eyes.

Swiping her eyes, she blinked them back. Landon stood and scraped both hands through his hair and paced over to her as she fought to compose herself, to deliver the news in the best way possible. He reached for her hands, his expression grave.

She waited until his eyes had locked on to hers, then she told him. "I'm pregnant."

Of all the reactions she'd anticipated, not a single one was a silent nod. He licked his bottom lip and swallowed. The slightest tremor shook his hands in hers. "Will you keep it?" he mumbled, his voice barely audible.

She didn't hesitate. "Of course." Was there ever a doubt she would? There wasn't in her mind. Had there been in his?

His composure cracked, and he pulled her into arms that had no softness to them at all. Caged against him, she smoothed her hands along his taut back muscles. She rested her face against his chest as they held each other. "Are you okay?"

"Am now," he said into her hair. He hadn't let go. She didn't think she wanted him to.

"I wasn't sure what you were hoping to hear."

"Neither was I." His voice shook the slightest bit.

That was when realization struck. Like a flash of lightning revealing what once was dark.

His girlfriend in college who'd had the abortion... All the hurt and regret in his eyes made perfect sense. "You didn't know," she said, holding him tighter. He rubbed a palm up and down her back without answering. But he didn't need to answer. She knew the truth. She *felt* the truth in every thud of his heart.

Landon hadn't been a part of the decision to terminate the pregnancy. He hadn't learned until it was too late.

CHAPTER FIFTEEN

*L*andon released Kimber from his clutches and lowered his head. He had to kiss her. Had to connect with her in the same way that had gotten them into this mess. Only it wasn't a mess. He felt almost . . . free.

When she turned her soft green eyes up at him, he put his lips on hers before she could speak. He didn't want to talk. Especially about the pieces of his past she'd mentally slid together. The kiss started tentative but turned rough when she tangled her arms around his neck and went at him with all she had. He caught her copper hair in one palm and held her, just held her to him with one hand on her head, the other against her lower back. When he moved to palm her breast, she grunted. He eased off.

"They're really sore."

"Sorry. If you don't want to—"

Her mouth was on his before he could make the offer he really, *really* didn't want to make. Every cell in his body, every last part of him from brain to groin, wanted to lay her out beneath him and make slow, sweet love to her until she cried.

She was *pregnant*. With his child. They'd formed an unbreakable, unfathomable bond. Had created a life together. One she wasn't going to take away from him. He was so grateful he could hardly catch his breath.

He lifted the billowing shirt over her head and gingerly freed her breasts from the bra. He touched her ever so softly, slipping his fingertips over her nipples and cradling her breasts in his palms while he sipped her lips with butterfly-winged kisses.

She moaned into his mouth, hands clasping his shirt. He laid her out on the bedspread and removed her clothes, dropping each piece to the floor. Then all he could do was stare. Stare at her smooth, pale skin. The line of fiery auburn hair between her legs, the purple nail polish tipping her delicate toes.

Beautiful, incredible. And, for this moment, all his.

He undressed, watching as her eyes flared beneath heavy lids. Standing over her, he admired her small breasts, rising and falling with each quickening breath as her pulse fluttered against her neck.

"You're so hot," she said.

Her compliment wasn't poetic, but that didn't mean it wasn't appreciated. He laughed as he fell on top of her, careful to keep from crushing her into the mattress.

"You're the hot one, sweetheart." He kissed the protestation he saw forming on her lips, allowing his hands to roam to her bottom and the back of her thigh. He trailed his fingers along her center and found her slick, ready.

Keeping her leg elevated slightly, he flexed his hips and slid in to the hilt, encasing himself in her body. He shuddered and an echoing gasp stuttered from her lips. She was heaven. An answer to a prayer he hadn't known how to say.

He dropped his forehead and laved her breasts as he continued to move inside her, the sensation of being wrapped in her tight warmth almost too much. Holding on to his orgasm at this point would be like stationing a train with a length of dental floss, but he'd try. For her, he'd try. She lifted her other leg and braced both feet at his lower back, pulling him closer. *Deeper.*

She ran her fingertips along his jaw and stared at him with depthless eyes. He held her gaze as they moved together, rhythm perfected, no reason now to interrupt and put on a condom.

"You feel so good." Her breaths had shortened, her body coiled, ready for release. Slipping an elbow under her knee, he lifted her leg and deepened their connection. The intake of breath told him she liked this. So he eased into her again, drawing another high-pitched gasp from her throat. A few more thrusts and she'd come undone. He could see it on her gorgeous face. From her parted mouth, to the slender amber brows pressed together over her nose. But her eyes were closed. That wouldn't do.

"Look at me." He stopped moving and she opened them. "Good," he told her. "Keep them open." He slid out slowly, then just as slowly, back in.

Her lids fluttered closed. "Can't."

"You can." He drew out of her.

She blinked, her eyes training on his.

This time when he pressed into her, he drew another gasp from her lips, but she kept her eyes open. *Good girl.* He wanted her to see him, wanted her to know it was him who was driving her out of her mind.

But she wasn't the only one out of her mind. Another forward movement and he'd be incapable of keeping the promise he'd made to himself to hold out for her release. Thankfully, right then she let go, pulsing around him with such force that he followed, spilling inside her with a groan of ecstasy mixed with relief.

She caught his face in her hands when his forehead dropped to hers. He took another stuttering breath before he was able to open his eyes. Then he drank in the sight of her. Of her tipped smile, hooded eyes, her hair aflame on the white pillowcase behind her head.

Your baby growing in her belly.

Time froze. What he wanted—what he thought he didn't want—solidified in that moment. He didn't want to compartmentalize Kimber as he had every other woman in his life. Didn't want to fit her into his schedule here and there or when it suited him. He wanted to fold her in so seamlessly that she couldn't tell where he began and she ended.

They were supposed to talk when she exited that bathroom. Talk about the baby. About the future. About *them*. But now that he'd made love to her, now that his very foundation had splintered, he was afraid to say a word.

Or three words.

That would be extra bad.

He kissed her lips, holding them between his. As if he could keep the conversation from happening. He pulled away, knowing the words that came next weren't likely what she wanted to hear.

"I have to get back to work," he blurted. Desperately.

So fucking desperately.

He couldn't stay. Not while she looked at him with that open vulnerability in her eyes. Not while his brain cells were writing sonnets and lifting boom boxes into the air. He kissed her again, hoping she didn't hate him for running out on her.

"Feel free to stay," he added as a caveat. Like that would be enough. He considered making a promise that he wouldn't be long, that he'd bring dinner when he got home. But he could tell by the look on her face as she pulled the sheet over her breasts that she wouldn't be here when he came back.

And he didn't know what to say about that, either.

He climbed out of bed, gathered his clothes, and turned back for one last kiss. She stroked his cheek with her fingertips and gave him the smallest smile, saying nothing. There was nothing to say. Their bodies had said it all in the minutes they were entwined together.

Naked, he walked to his bedroom. They could pick this up later. Later, after he'd been at work for a few hours and could figure out what to say. The right thing to say, not the unhinged emotional vomit working its way up his esophagus.

As he saw it, they'd already sorted out the two most important things. Kimber was pregnant and she was keeping the baby.

The rest would work itself out.

* * *

The road trip to Ohio had started first thing the next morning. Kimber had made excellent time, pulling into the driveway of her mother's immaculate condominium around two thirty.

Not too shabby.

She closed the creaky door on her charcoal gray Cavalier, kissed her fingers, and pressed them to the hood. Thank God the car made another road trip. Bless all of its two hundred thousand miles.

"There she is!" Her mom was dressed in a striped top and black capris, her toenails and fingernails matching blood red, her hair a coppery chin-length coif. Kimber had rarely, if ever, seen Grace Reynolds looking anything less than put together.

"Hi, Mom."

"To what do I owe the honor of you visiting me on a workday?"

"You don't owe me anything. I, however, owe Neil and Mick raises and Ginny a one-hundred-dollar shopping spree for Hobo Chic."

Grace wrinkled her nose. "You had to bribe them?"

"It's worth it."

"Come in, tell me why you're here." She held the front door open. Kimber had sent her a text to let her know she was going to visit, but hadn't told her any more than that.

She followed her mother inside. "Just wanted to see you." *And make you a grandmother.* The kitchen was a sophisticated black and white with red rugs and curtains to accent. Understated was another thing her mother had never been.

Grace waved a hand. "Yeah, right. You drove here from Chicago 'just to see' me." She retrieved the coffee canister from a cabinet and spared her a Mom-knows-better glance. "You may as well tell me what's on your mind sooner than later."

"After coffee," Kimber promised. She ran to the bathroom, dumped her bag in her mother's spare room—purple walls, white curtains, and a black wrought iron bed frame piled high with purple and white bedding. She faced herself in the mirror on the vanity in the corner and took a steeling breath. Here went nothing.

In the kitchen, her mom poured a cup of coffee for each of them. "Oh," Kimber muttered. "I don't think I should have caffeine."

"Anxiety?"

She choked out a laugh. "You could say that. You could also say pregnancy."

Grace froze, both mugs in her hands, eyes wide for a few seconds. Then her made-up face melted into a mask of happiness, her eyes brimming with tears, her voice a high squeak when she spoke. "I get a grandbaby?"

Abandoning the mugs on the kitchen table, she hugged

Kimber hard enough to crush ribs. Well. She'd taken that much better than Kimber had expected.

"Sit, sit." Grace shoved the coffee in front of her. "It's half-caff. And anyway, doctors say you can safely have a cup a day. Don't fret."

Kimber warmed her palms on the mug. Her mother's house was a chilly, air-conditioned tomb. Menopause.

"Who is he?"

Just a guy I worked down a list of sex acts with.

"Um…well…funny story. Remember Angel Downey? My best friend from high school? I spent a summer at her house the year you and Dad divorced."

Her mother's mouth tightened. Amazing how the mention of the divorce hurt her after all these years. More reason to make sure Kimber married only once. "Of course. Lovely family."

"I'm glad you said that." Kimber gave her a sheepish smile. "It's her older brother, Landon."

"The one who's engaged to a supermodel?"

"Was," Kimber corrected. "They weren't really…engaged. They had an arrangement of sorts." Ugh. Did that sound horrible? "Anyway, I babysat for his nephew recently and we…well…we hit it off."

"I'll say," her mother quipped, sipping her coffee. "Congratulations. You'll be a remarkable mother. Especially since you'll insist on keeping your identity, your job, your independence." Grace speared her with a look, her brows angling.

Kimber gave her mom a tight smile. It was a speech she'd heard before. How Grace had given up her dreams, goals, and life to be a mother. As much as Kimber loved and appreciated her, there was always a part of her that felt responsible for her mother missing out on the part of her life Kimber had essentially taken.

Grace's voice went hard, her eyes focused on the table as she lifted her mug. "Whatever you do, Kimber, do not marry this man."

"His name is Landon," Kimber said, frustrated her mother had called him *this man* instead of by his name. "We're not really at the marriage stage…" Which made her sound like a bit of a trollop, but it was the truth.

"Good." Her mother's no-nonsense tone had replaced the gushy grandmotherly one. "You don't want to lash yourself to him forever because you made a baby together."

Like I did, her tone implied.

"I see no reason why two parents can't raise a child apart," she continued. "You will need breaks. And if the father is sidebar, available to babysit, you'll have more time to date."

Kimber winced. That painted a… not fairy-tale-like picture. But she supposed fairy tales didn't start and end with lists. Arrangements.

Last night wasn't an arrangement.

Didn't she know it. Landon had made the sweetest, softest love to her, watching her closely, the most frightening clarity in his eyes. He'd been gentle and perfect and…*loving.* So loving. Or had she been projecting her love onto him?

Maybe it's not love. Maybe it's the idea of love. The romanticism of carrying his child.

"I don't want to date anyone, Mom," she grumbled through her confusion. *Unless I date Landon.* So much for keeping emotional distance. Already, her thoughts were a jumbled, unsorted mass, like the unorganized boxes in her storeroom. She closed her eyes. Maybe there were more to these pregnancy hormones than she'd first thought.

"I want you to understand why it's important that you don't tie yourself to him." Her mother, the jaded wonder, said. "Marriages like these start out with the best of intentions. You do it for the baby. You think you're in love. You try and hold things together...then one day...you can't stand looking at the man you vowed to stay with forever. Forever is a very long time."

Her mother's eyes were focused on a spot across the room, fuzzy with a memory Kimber was pretty sure she didn't want to hear about. Grace refocused on her daughter, a diamond-hard glint in her dark eyes. "Don't waste your best years, sweetheart. You have an amazing career. You can have everything."

Was her mother really that unhappy with how her life had turned out? *Yes*, Kimber decided. Under her highly polished veneer, Grace was bitter and sad, and angry. *And still in love with Dad.* Kimber could only hope the subject of his new wife didn't come up. She didn't know if she could take a "Jill the Pill" rant today.

Is this what would become of Kimber if she gave into the feelings of love filling her chest right now? If she made the mistake of believing she and Landon were "forever" material? Would she be here, in her mother's position thirty-two years later, casting shadows of doubt over her own daughter's future?

God. She hoped not.

"You will keep your business, right?" her mother asked worriedly.

"Yes, of course." In every imagined scenario of her future Kimber hadn't dreamed of giving up Hobo Chic. The store was her lifeblood. Her mother knew about Mick, knew they'd dated and split, but she didn't tell her how Mick owned half of Hobo Chic. Heaven forbid Grace find out her only daughter had attached herself to a man who was now partly responsible for keeping her business afloat. She would totally freak.

"You don't have anything to worry about, Mom. I'm going to raise my child, and Landon is...very well-off.

Child support will not be an issue," she added for her mother's benefit.

"They say that in the beginning, but you know your father complained about the two years he had to pay yours."

TMI. But this wasn't her argument. She rested her hand over her mother's. "Let's focus on now. What's the first thing I need to do to prepare for this baby?"

The next afternoon, Kimber kissed and hugged her mother after loading up her car with purchases from the local Babies 'R' Us. Grace had gone a little shopping-happy, but as she was a future grandmother, Kimber figured that was her prerogative. Plus, unless Kimber dipped into the money she had squirreled away to buy Mick out of Hobo Chic, she really couldn't afford expensive items like strollers and breast pumps. Grace's doting, in this case, was much appreciated. Planning very, *very* far into the future, but appreciated all the same.

"You won't miscarry," her mother had told her as she climbed in the car. "Unplanned pregnancies never miscarry."

She'd tried not to take her mother's remark too personally.

Since hauling her purchases up the steep stairs to her apartment was not advised, Kimber had no choice but to ask for help when she returned home. She thought about calling Landon. He'd called yesterday but she ignored it, unsure what she'd say if she answered, or if she wanted him to know she'd driven to Ohio by herself.

For some reason, she was afraid if he knew she'd left town without telling him, he might feel hurt. Or worse, offer to show up. Then ask her to go to his father's house and share the news with him, too. The idea of telling his family scared her. Probably because she felt as if she and Landon were in a waiting period. Only, waiting for what, she had no idea.

Inside Hobo Chic, Neil was busy with customers and Mick was in the storeroom. She debated for a moment before approaching him. Did she really want Mick to know so soon?

He's going to find out eventually. Like when you're the size of a parade float.

With no way to argue her own logic, she cleared her throat to get Mick's attention. He'd pulled back the front of his hair with a clip so it wouldn't fall into his face when he bent over. The urge to resurrect an old argument—he always procrastinated getting his hair cut—sat unspoken in her throat. *This is not why you're here.*

"Can you do me a favor?" she asked with a smile.

He skimmed her body with eager eyes and waggled his eyebrows. His lips lifted into an almost charming curve, making her remember his rakish appeal the night they'd met. Too bad they got along as well as a pair of cats in a potato sack.

"I am at your service, Red."

"You are a pain in the butt," she told him, an errant smirk on her face. "But Neil's busy. Come on." She led him outside to the alley and popped the trunk. The stroller was in there, price tag still hanging, along with several bags.

His eyes flitted over the store name on the bags, leaving no doubt as to what she was stockpiling *for*, then back to the stroller, then to Kimber. "Say it ain't so."

She sniffed. "Thanks a lot. Can you take the heavy stuff up?" She reached for one of the lighter bags.

He stopped her hand. "I'll take it all up. You rest."

"I'm pregnant, not sick." Fortunately, that was true. The dreaded morning sickness hadn't come. Yet, anyway. Maybe she'd be lucky enough to avoid it altogether.

Mick had the supplies in her house in three trips. With the last haul, he collapsed on the sofa to catch his breath. "Where are you going to put a baby in this place?"

She followed his eyes around her tiny loft. If only her

apartment had been the size of the store downstairs. It wasn't. Over three-quarters of the building's upstairs was being leased out for use as storage, Kimber's apartment making up the diminutive difference.

"He'll fit."

"It's a boy?" Mick's eyes twinkled.

She shook her head, perplexed by everyone's über-happy reaction to her unplanned surprise. She expected to argue and explain herself. Could be her age helping with the free pass. She was thirty-two, not sixteen. "Too early to tell."

He nodded. "Need help putting anything away?"

"No thanks. I kind of want to nest." She glanced around her apartment, her mind rearranging the room. "Or something."

Mick surprised her by standing and cupping her jaw in one hand. He tipped her chin. "This guy. Is he going to be around?"

She shrugged. She assumed Landon would be around, but in actuality had no idea. After the intense sex the other night, he'd run away like he'd been late for dinner with the president of the United States. They were supposed to talk that night, but she hadn't wanted to wait around for him to pull himself together. And he'd been obviously frazzled. She'd left a note telling him she'd be busy the next few days, and that they'd talk soon. She hadn't expected to go to see her mother until she'd woken the next morning needing to talk to someone. Someone who wasn't her baby's father.

"I'll be here," Mick murmured, stunning her further. "I won't let you be alone in this, Kimber."

"I'll be fine." Mick had never wanted the responsibility of . . . well . . . anything. What was he talking about?

His eyes flickered over her face, brows arched at a sympathetic bend. "You've always been so independent."

She took a breath and, desperate for a subject change, reached up and plucked the clip from his hair. The strands flopped down in every direction, and she rearranged them on his head. "There. Now you look—"

Before she could pull her hand away, he lowered his lips and placed a feather-light kiss on her mouth. When he backed away, Kimber registered a man standing in her open doorway.

Landon.

In that single second in time, he'd walked in to find her hands in Mick's hair and Mick's mouth on hers, making one thing certain.

Landon had the worst timing imaginable.

* * *

What. The fuck.

Landon gripped the shopping bag, his fingers numb, his vision blurred by a sea of red at the sight of the guy kissing Kimber. Had to be her ex. He'd heard enough about him to know this guy had no problem eschewing basic decency.

And kissing Kimber, after Landon had made love to her days ago, was definitely *indecent*.

She plucked her hand from the guy's hair and pushed him aside. But the sight of Mick's frown didn't make Landon feel marginally better.

"Landon," she said. "What a surprise." Her smile was fake. As fake as the photos in Lissa's portfolio.

"I should have called." *Apparently.*

"Yeah, you should've," her ex said, taking a step toward the door.

"No." She stayed his next step with a hand around his arm. Landon would like it if she stopped touching the tattooed, pierced dickweed altogether. "I'm glad you're here," she told Landon. It sounded like the truth. "Mick, why don't you go help Neil in the store?"

"Yeah, Mick. Get to work." He shouldn't have, but he couldn't help himself.

Mick met him at the door, a few paces from where Kimber was standing, and stopped short of scuffing Landon's shoes. "Peddle your prissy ass elsewhere, *millionaire*. Let us common folk handle our business."

After mentally determining he wouldn't injure the mobile and stuffed dog inside, Landon dropped the shopping bag. He leaned in, marginally, but enough for Mick to move his chin back a fraction. "This *is* our business, Mick. She's carrying my baby. You're just a guy she used to date."

He raised a finger, Landon presumed to poke him in the chest with it. If he did, Landon would break it. So help him, he'd snap the digit in two.

"You—"

"Enough!" Kimber shouted. Mick's finger halted midair, centimeters from needing a splint.

Mick lowered his arm but kept his eyes trained on Landon. Landon reclaimed his bag, sidestepped Mick, and walked in. He thought about planting a deep, slow kiss on Kimber's mouth, then remembered that Mick had just kissed her and thought better of it. His stomach pooled with disgust.

"Mick. Out." She pointed, authority ringing in her voice. In spite of the situation, or maybe because of it, she sounded sexy. "Close the door behind you. Please and thank you."

Mick wasn't happy about it, but he went. Landon started to put Kimber's gift on the couch, but the cushions were already littered with Babies 'R' Us bags.

What the hell?

Had they gone baby shopping together? Landon suddenly felt like he'd been missing some major component. Was it possible the baby she carried wasn't his? Possible that she'd been pregnant before they'd slept together? Or worse. Maybe she'd always wanted a child and had rigged the condom to—

"Would you stop jumping to a hundred different conclusions and let me explain?" she asked.

He turned to find her arms crossed over her chest. Miffed that she'd read his mind, he mirrored her posture. Fine. He'd let her explain.

She pointed at the bag in his hand. "Is that for me?"

"Yes." He held fast.

A slightly bemused smile lit her lips like this wasn't a big deal. But it was a huge deal. Enormous. He took in her simple, patterned dress, weathered leather bracelets, and sandals. She looked pretty today, inviting and familiar. And like that, his heart softened to room temperature butter. Wait. No. He was angry.

"My mother bought this stuff for me," she explained. "I drove to Osborn yesterday morning to tell her in person. She's excited, by the way."

Very angry, he reminded himself, keeping his expression stony.

"I got home a few minutes ago and I couldn't carry all this stuff up the back stairs so I asked for Mick's help."

Some of his anger dissipated. That sounded...reasonable. "And the kiss?" He hated to ask, for fear of the answer. But he deserved an explanation.

She shook her head. "I don't know. He kissed me. I was taking a clip out of his hair." She still held it. She opened and closed the plastic jaws before resting the clip on the kitchen counter. "I think he has some sort of misguided, innate male protectiveness. He didn't want to be a part of my life when it was just him and me. And, more importantly, I don't want him."

Her words hovered in the air, and he waited for her to say *I want you* or some other proclamation that would make him feel like less of a cuckold. That he felt this way at all made him want to hit something, and he wasn't a violent guy. Though wrapping his hands around Mick's skinny neck would make him feel better.

With a gentle touch, she loosened his fingers around the handle and took the bag out of his hand. He let her, watching silently as she set it aside. Before he could remind himself he was still upset with her, she wrapped her arms around his neck, and her scent looped his brain. Not the cucumber fragrance he'd grown accustomed to, but something tangy and sweet, and one hundred percent Kimber. "Thank you for the present."

"You haven't opened it yet," he said rigidly. He was still sulking, but he *really* hadn't liked the way Mick had touched her. The way he'd *kissed* her. Like he was staking a claim on her. *Or because Mick had kissed her before?* Yes. That pissed him off most of all.

"I don't care what it is. It's from you," Kimber said sweetly. "I'm sorry about Mick."

The slide of her silky dress beneath his palms did wonders to lower his blood pressure. He'd missed her over the past few days, but had resisted calling more than the one time. He wanted to give her some space to think. Give *himself* some space to think. What he'd figured out during his alone time was that he wanted her and this baby in his life more often than not. Like all the time.

She was lucky he hadn't slipped an engagement ring in with her gift. But even he wasn't that stupid.

"I wish you'd kiss me," she murmured, closing in on him and wrapping her arms tighter around his neck. "I miss you."

Predictably, he caved at her request. But first…Palm cupping her jaw, he swiped his thumb across her lips. Knowing what he was doing, and why, she scrubbed her mouth with the back of her hand before smiling up at him.

Landon took her lips captive, the kiss starting sweet and edging into wet, wild territory in a manner of seconds. All of their kisses had been like this one. Hot. Ferocious. Combustible. His jealousy melted into the need to claim her. He spied a bed on the other side of the room and backed her toward it, careful to sidestep the stroller—*a stroller, too?*—and other bags littered around the room.

At the bed, she sat, then fell back. "I'm exhausted."

He followed her down, knee between her legs, arms on each side of her face. "I'll do all the work," he promised, kissing her neck. She tasted so good. As good as he remembered.

"And I'm starving," she said.

Concern outweighing his physical need to bury himself in her skin, he lifted his head. She was making a human being. That had to be tiring. "Then you need to eat." Lovemaking forgotten—well, not forgotten, but definitely on hold—he backed off the bed and tracked the short distance to the kitchen. Behind the cabinet doors, he spied meager offerings, but he could cobble something together... He shuffled around a few cans and boxes. "Tuna salad?"

"Mercury," she called from the bed.

He turned his head. "Excuse me?"

"In the fish. It's bad for the baby."

"Okay. Well. The only other thing you have in here is a box of macaroni and cheese. And"—he pulled open the freezer—"a bag of peas." He squeezed the bag, hearing the telltale crunch of freezer burn. "How long have these been in here?"

"Who knows."

He abandoned the peas to her empty freezer and came to the bed. "Let's go. I'm taking you out."

"I don't want to go out." She was whining, which he wasn't accustomed to hearing from her. It was sort of cute.

Offering his hands, he helped haul her to her feet, bending to kiss her when she stood. "Sure you do. Pack a quick overnight bag and get in my car."

She raised an eyebrow. "Overnight bag?"

"Yes. You're staying with me tonight." *And as far away from Mick as possible.* "No arguments."

The sweet curve of her lips undid him. She definitely belonged at home with him. Not here. Forlornly, she looked at the bags on the sofa. "I'm supposed to prepare my apartment for a baby."

"You have months to prepare," he said. But he didn't want her to waste her time. If he had his way—and most likely he would—Kimber and his child would live with him. He wanted his family under his roof. He wanted her out of this crowded loft, away from her eager ex-boyfriend, and living in the lap of luxury.

Close enough to Landon's lap that he could haul her into it each and every night and kiss her senseless.

* * *

Kimber awoke thinking about her parents. How wrong she'd been to lump her and Landon into the same category as her parents' failed marriage. She wouldn't lose her identity if she stayed with Landon. And yeah, maybe she wasn't sure *exactly* what they were to one another, but she knew he cared for her. Otherwise he'd never have whisked her away from her apartment last night. And she'd needed to get out of her house. The more she thought about the way Mick had lifted his leg to mark his territory, the more upset she became. She wasn't a prize to be won, especially by Mick, who hadn't bothered fighting for her before now.

A low, male sigh came from the other side of the bed, sending a tingle of awareness down her spine. She turned and laid her cheek on her folded arms and studied Landon Downey asleep. He was a sight. Stubble surrounding his firm lips, the strong line of his nose leading up to a fan of light eyelashes, sandy-colored brows, and mussed, golden-brown hair.

Not only was he beautiful this morning, she could add to that how gentle and loving he'd been last night, completing her transformation into "swooning mess." He'd treated her to dinner as promised, indulging her voracious appetite by allowing her to order way too much food. By the time they returned to his house, she was too full to think and nodding off. He'd tucked her into bed next to him. They hadn't had sex. Yet she felt closer to him than ever.

Which was . . . bad? *Gah!* She was so confused. Gloria and her mother believed it best for her to distance herself from him before their relationship became too much. Or, at this point, too much *more*. Mick had obviously been in agreement. Hell, *Kimber and Landon* had both been in agreement until junior, here, turned two pregnancy sticks blue and one into a two-syllable, eighteen-year-to-life sentence.

She flicked her eyes to the digital clock on the nightstand on Landon's side of the bed. She needed to get up and get going. A full shift awaited her today—ten hours on her feet, *ugh*—and she needed to check the storeroom for repairable garments. Since she'd neglected her sewing machine for a month, the "Mend" box had piled up.

"What's wrong?" Landon opened his eyes. They looked hazel with flashes of gold in the filtering sunlight.

"Nothing. I'm great."

He blinked. "You have to work."

"Don't you?"

"Yes. But you don't want to."

"Of course I do." Mending wouldn't be so bad. The hard part would be maintaining enough energy to move from sewing machine to sales floor to ring up customers as well as crunching this month's numbers and paying bills. Little did she know pregnancy consumed brain cells. Last night at dinner, she'd forgotten the word "paisley" and described her new dress as "covered in teardroppy things."

Landon reached over and touched her face. "No. You don't. You want to lie here for another two hours. Eat breakfast in bed." He rolled over and smiled softly. "And I want you to."

Sigh. That sounded lovely.

A serious expression crossed his features. "I've thought a lot about you. About the baby." His voice dropped to a low husk. "About us."

She wound her fingertips in the hair on his chest, unable to stop touching him now that he'd mentioned the word "us." Like she was afraid if she pulled her hand away, he'd say the best move was to end what they had. She wasn't sure she could. Or maybe hormones were to blame for her worst-case-scenario thinking.

Although, her hormone theory had holes. She trailed her hands over his strong torso, down to the white sheet draped over the lower half of his body. The sheet jerked and she sent him a sneer.

"He likes you," Landon quipped, making her laugh. He cupped her cheek and kissed her, and she thought about how nice it'd be to meld into him and hide in bed for the day.

But there were things to do. Things to discuss. "You were going to say..." Something she probably didn't want to hear. Then again she didn't know what she wanted to hear. It wasn't like she wanted him to propose—*heaven forbid.* She didn't want him to offer her a Cinderella story. Take her out of poverty and gift her with a new-and-improved, struggle-free life. She hoped he didn't see her life as inferior to his. It'd taken her years, but she'd built a life with her own two hands, her own ideas, and yes, her own mistakes. That's what made her life special. Because of those things, it was hers and no one else's.

"I want you to move in."

The comment was so far from what she'd expected him to say, she simply blinked at him. He hadn't asked. More like made a decree.

"The baby can have the room down the hall." He hitched an eyebrow. "We already have a baby monitor."

She had no idea how to respond. What to say. "Move in?" she repeated, then grabbed on to the first objection she thought of. "I'd be so far from work."

And her apartment. Her neighborhood.

"Yes. About that." He was far too serious for her taste. A trickle of uncertainty flowed through her. Like when she hit her funny bone too hard...only her heart was the part of her tingling with pins and needles. She took her hand from his chest and sat up.

He leaned on an elbow and continued. "I found a building two blocks from here for lease. It's bigger than Hobo Chic and has an office. Or, if you prefer, you could use the space to expand your storeroom and set up your office here."

He'd found a building? For her store? "Were you planning on talking to me about this?"

"We are talking about it."

"Mick owns half of Hobo Chic. I can't just—"

"We'll buy him out."

"We?"

Landon rolled onto his back, an impatient sigh exiting his mouth. He slid on his glasses, sat up against the headboard, and pulled his hands through his hair. "Yes. We."

Did he have any idea how loaded that two-letter word was? How she didn't know if they *were* together? If they were a "we," no one had told her.

"Neil and Ginny don't live anywhere near here. Even with what I pay them, I doubt they could afford to commute—"

"That's what the L is for. And if they can't commute, we can hire a new staff. Probably best to replace Mick before you reopen."

Reopen? She couldn't keep up with the plans he was spouting off like they were no big deal. The move would be time consuming. She'd have to announce or she'd lose business. "We. There it is again," she mumbled.

"I'll cancel the billboard I ordered since the address will change," he said, talking to himself now.

She blanched. "Billboard?"

His lips tipped into a smile. "I was going to surprise you. It's going to be visible from the highway, but I can change the design for a fee. If we get the new location and info to them by—"

"This is my business, Landon." And evidently she needed to remind both of them of that fact. "My store. My *life*."

His mouth twitched. "I know that."

"Do you? Because this is the first I've heard about moving my residence and store, advertising, and letting my employees go. How many decisions were you planning to make without talking to me first?"

He sighed again, and for some reason the sound made her angry. "Kimber, I'm not allowing you to live in a questionable neighborhood, at the top of a very tall flight of stairs."

" 'Allowing' me to?"

He ignored her. "How are you going to carry heavy groceries into your house? What about when you go into labor? Are you going to walk down forty steps and drive your rusted old car to the hospital by yourself?" His jaw clicked and then he added, "Or are you planning on having Mick help you with all of that?"

Her mouth dropped open. Mick? This was about Mick? Wonderful. Jealous *and* overbearing. "Mick has nothing to do with any of this. And—and I like my car. I like my apartment. I like my store where it is."

Stunned, she couldn't think of anything more to say. Just because she was pregnant didn't give him the right to take over. He wanted her living in his house, running Hobo Chic the way he wanted, with the employees he wanted. "How can you even be sure a vintage store would do well in this affluent of a neighborhood?" *So* not her biggest concern, but she was desperate to find solid ground for this argument.

He shrugged. "If not, we, I mean *you*," he amended, "can change what you're selling. Purses or jewelry or something." He waved a hand like the subject was closed.

Like her life, her *passion*, was a trivial thing that could be altered on a whim. "Jewelry *or something*?"

He gave her a small smile. "Whatever you want."

She threw back the blankets and climbed out of bed. Geez. She was starving. She braced a hand on the nightstand when her head swam. Landon reached for her and she stayed him with an outstretched palm. "I'm fine."

He probably wanted to fix her. He liked to fix things. Clearly. Since he'd tried to fix her entire life around his.

"I can't believe you did all this without talking to me," she said, lowering her arm.

"I didn't *do* anything." His tone ratcheted up to peeved.

"You did plenty." She slipped her dress over her head, a simple sheath that coasted down to her toes, and shuffled into her sandals. "This is my life. My call." She unplugged her cell phone from the charger and shoved it into her purse.

"That may be true, but the life you have growing inside of you," he said, "is ours."

Indignant, she spun on him. Had their child become a bargaining chip already? "You did not just say that."

Rather than answer…or apologize…he pushed out of bed and stalked naked to the bathroom. "I'm going to get a shower." He shut the door behind him.

Well. She could walk out, too. Leave. *For good*, she told herself.

Or until Landon quit acting like a horse's ass.

*C*HAPTER SIXTEEN

*L*andon drummed his fingers against a yellow pad on his desk as he stared down his office phone. Kimber had vanished by the time he'd climbed out of the shower. But he'd purposely stayed in the bathroom long enough to give her the opportunity to leave.

What he didn't get was why his suggestions had upset her so much. What expecting woman *wouldn't* want the father of her child thinking of her well-being first and foremost? What woman didn't want to be taken care of?

She had a monkey on her back, two if he counted Mick, he thought with a juvenile curl of his lip. Landon's offer to move her and her business to a nicer part of town, buy out her moronic ex, and further financially support her would reduce her worries by half. Probably more. Couldn't she see that?

Frustrated, he had the irrational desire to talk to someone.

Not about Kimber and the stupid fight they'd had. Arguments happened. He understood that. He planned on tracking her down after work. After she calmed down... after *he* calmed down. But he wanted to talk to someone about the whole situation first. Just to run it by another set of ears and make sure he wasn't overlooking some major component.

Outside his office windows, his employees gathered in front of the boardroom across the hall. He wasn't close with anyone at work, but if he was, he couldn't imagine pulling someone into his office and spilling his guts. Keeping them at arm's length had been a strategy when he started his business. In case he had to let someone go, demote or choose someone for a promotion. He couldn't afford to play favorites. It benefited his business to remain impartial. The unfortunate side effect of that rationale was that he'd created an island and marooned himself on it.

Steepling his hands, he debated calling Evan. But Landon wasn't sure if Kimber had told Gloria about the pregnancy yet. If he told his brother and Evan told Gloria...well, Landon didn't need *another* reason for Kimber to be pissed at him. Breaking the news to her best friend would do just that. There was always his sister, Angel, but again, her connection with Kimber was reason enough not to call her. His cousin Shane was an automatic out. August sucked at this relationship stuff—or used to, anyway, before he'd gotten married. And there was the probability August would want to talk business and Landon didn't want to get sidetracked.

That left Aiden.

Landon's blissfully happy, walking-on-sunshine, recently married younger brother picked up on the third ring. "Yeah."

"It's Landon."

"I know."

"You have a minute?"

"I have many minutes. Sadie's shoe shopping and I'm holding up a pillar in the center of Osborn Mall."

"You're not at work?"

"You do know it's rounding eight o'clock, right?"

Was it? No wonder his stomach was rumbling. "Forgot."

"You are a machine."

The Tin Man, to be precise, he thought wryly.

"Evan said you hit it off with Angel's friend, Kimber," Aiden said. "That you guys were dating or something."

Or something. "Did he?" Landon said flatly. So much for being incognito.

"Yes," Aiden said, dragging the word out and sounding bemused. "Is that why you called me?"

"What are you talking about?"

"To get relationship advice. Not like you can call Evan or Angel since they're only one degree removed from your new girlfriend. And Shane isn't much of a talker when it comes to feelings."

Mind reader. "She's not my girlfriend."

"Now we're getting somewhere." Landon could hear the smile in Aiden's voice. "What is she?"

Just tell him. "She's … going to be. It's probably too soon to make plans but, ah … Kimber is …"

"Is … ?" Aiden prompted. "Come on, man. What *is* she?"

"She's pregnant." He blew the words out on a dizzying breath. "And I am not sure what to do next," he admitted with a wince.

A string of swear words floated through the phone … followed by a predictable whoop of laughter. "Congratulations, man! That's … that's effing *awesome* is what it is! I get another niece or nephew? Sweet! Man, I hate that you beat Sadie and me out of the gate, but I am so happy for you guys!"

Landon found himself smiling at his keyboard, trying on Aiden's reaction for size. It *was* pretty exciting. He had a lot of reasons to be happy when he thought about it. A baby was something to celebrate. A baby with a woman he liked a whole heck of a lot. A woman his family knew and approved of.

"Thanks, man," Landon said, adding, "We're really excited."

He didn't know if "excited" was the right word to describe Kimber, but they'd both been in a state of shock since they found out. They'd still been trying to figure out how to deal with the whole thing this morning. How to deal with one another.

It took him a moment to digest that last thought. He and Kimber were in a relationship. A real one. One where they wouldn't see eye to eye on everything. A period of adjustment and some arguing could be expected. What they had was disturbingly...normal.

After fervently avoiding this kind of connection with another person for over a decade and a half, Landon had stumbled into a girlfriend...*a family*...by mistake.

"So, what do you need to know?" Aiden asked. "If we'll babysit? Because we totally will. I don't know how the commute will work, but if you two ever need a weekend alone, we're all over the kid. Man! A baby! Do you want a daughter or a son?"

Landon nearly blacked out at the question, then realized it was because he hadn't taken a breath in several long seconds. "Either," he managed, his throat tight, tears barely barricaded behind his eyelids. He'd underestimated how much the news of a child would mean to his family. He thought of the stroller, all the bags of baby things. To Kimber's mother. To *everyone*. This wasn't a project he could craft a to-do list around; this was a baby, a life that would make his father a grandfather for the second time, would make his brothers uncles again, and his sister Angel...God. Angel. What would he tell her? After her issues with fertility, how could he call and tell her he and Kimber had made an *Oops Baby*?

"Sadie's waving at me. Holy crap, how many pairs did she buy?" Aiden muttered.

"Listen, I'm not sure how to tell everyone yet, so keep this to yourself, okay, Aid?"

"Yeah. I mean, I'll tell Sadie, but she's Fort Knox."

"What am I Fort Knox about?" he heard Sadie ask.

"I'll let you go. Thanks," Landon said in a hurry. He hung up the phone, more confused than he was before. He'd called Aiden because he'd needed someone to talk to, and instead had reached a conclusion he hadn't expected.

This whole thing with Kimber wasn't nearly as casual and easy to organize as he'd thought. He was navigating through relationship territory and that was dicey. He had no idea what he was doing.

He swept his eyes down the legal pad under his hand. Everything a baby needed in a tidy, neat list. Crib, blankets, onesies, pacifier, diapers, rocking chair, and about a hundred other things he'd found online. He'd checked off each item after he purchased it. The page was full of checkmarks from top to bottom and would have run his American Express card up to the limit if it had one.

He'd gone on an Internet shopping spree in a blaze of jealousy over Mick and Kimber's mother...and to prove to Kimber that she needed him. Because, quite frankly, he was afraid that she didn't.

In his hustling to make himself look important, he'd neglected to consider what Kimber needed. What their child might really need. He'd handled this situation the way he handled everything else. Going through the motions. *Arranging*. Because that's what he did.

No wonder she's pissed.

What he should've done was let her know how he felt. All he had to do was figure out what he was thinking first.

No, you don't.

No. He didn't. He knew. He may not have relationship experience, but he'd had enough non-relationship experience to recognize what he and Kimber had was different from anything in his past. He hadn't had this with anyone—not even Rachel, and that had been the deepest relationship he'd had.

Until Kimber. She'd raised the bar so high, it was in orbit.

He chucked the list into the trash. He'd tell her tonight. Make her understand how he felt...how much she meant to him. How much he...

A lump formed in his throat.

How much I love her.

* * *

"Well?" Gloria asked when Kimber exited the doctor's office.

Kimber looped her arm in her friend's as they walked to the door. "It's official. I'm pregnant." As if there'd been any doubt. Her rogue craving for olives and bone-draining fatigue was proof enough. She cast a glance around the waiting room. Several women eyed them with interest. "And I'm pretty sure everyone here thinks we're a couple," she mumbled to Glo.

They left the doctor's office and headed to the mall to eat junk food and buy things they didn't need. She filled Glo in on her mother's concerns, on Mick and Landon's pissing contest, on Landon's corporate takeover of her life.

Glo handed over one of two Häagan-Dazs bars she'd just purchased at a stall in the food court and directed her to a small table with two chairs.

"Mmm. Nothing could be better than this," Kimber said, chocolate melting on her tongue. Sun streamed in through the glass ceiling overhead, and water splashed onto tall, tropical plants arranged around the decorative fountain next to them.

"Want to know what I think?"

She wasn't sure she did want to know what Glo thought.

Actually, she was pretty sure she already knew what Glo thought. "About the ice cream?" she hedged.

Gloria slow-blinked.

"I'm kidding. Of course I want to know what you think."

"I love you. I just want you to know the truth. The way I see it, anyway. You are capable of making decisions without my jaded input, you know."

Kimber smiled wholeheartedly. "I respect your opinion, Glo. No need to warn me. Come on, I count on you for zero sugar coating." Especially now when she didn't want to hear the one thing she needed to hear most.

Glo lowered her ice cream bar and met Kimber's eyes. "You and Landon are going to have a hard enough time raising a child together."

Kimber quirked her lips. Tell her something she didn't know.

"You're from two different worlds," Glo continued. "He can't expect you to live in his worry-free world any more than you can expect him to be happy amongst boxes of frayed clothing and retro furniture."

Hmm. Her rust-colored couch would look odd in his elegant space. And what about her clutter of papers and bills for Hobo Chic? His office was pristine, everything in neat stacks and labeled ... or at least it had been until he'd cleared the desk and threw her on top of it, she thought with a satisfied smirk. A smirk she wiped off her face before Glo caught her daydreaming about amazing sex with the father of her unborn baby.

"Could you imagine sharing a closet with him?" Glo said, taking another bite of her ice cream.

Kimber pictured her beat-up wardrobe next to Landon's multi-thousand-dollar suits and shoes so shiny they could signal a plane. It was kind of ridiculous. Kind of like them.

He was a streamlined, sleek, suave businessman with a

million-dollar company and a zillion employees. She was lucky to hold on to the three co-workers she had and tallied her inventory on a thirty-five-dollar program she'd downloaded off the Internet. She was scrappy. He was refined. She was mac-and-cheese-from-a-box. He was Tuna Tartare.

Glo cleaned the remainder of her ice cream from the stick. "What if he wants to send junior to a private or charter school and you want public or home school? What if he doesn't share your views on religion? Vaccinations? Politics?"

Kimber's ice cream dripped on the napkin she'd spread on the table in front of her. She hadn't considered any of those things. Shouldn't she at least know his political affiliation or if he believed in God before they raised a child together?

"The best thing for both of you"—Glo pointed at her with the bare popsicle stick—"is to talk through the major issues now. Before the baby is born and your judgment is completely clouded."

Well. That sounded reasonable.

"Work it out ahead of time." Kimber nodded, seeing the first glimmer of hope since Glo had turned into Debbie Downer. Landon was in his element in planning mode. If they sat down to have a conversation outlining the basics of bringing up their child, he'd handle it perfectly. She stared into the splashing water of the fountain next to her table, her worries beginning to dissipate. He was pragmatic, organized, and thorough. Everything she wasn't.

"Honey." Glo reached across the table to grasp her hand. "There's only one way you'll be able to make unbiased decisions with this man."

She pegged Glo with a look that asked *And that is?*

"Break it off," Glo answered firmly.

She felt the side-to-side motion of her head shaking.

"I mean it, Kimber," her best friend insisted, concern

coloring her blue eyes. "As long as you keep having sex with him, you'll let him talk you into anything."

"Ha!" She pointed her melting ice cream bar at Glo before making a face and dropping the mess onto her napkin. "That's not true," she said, cleaning off her fingers. "He didn't talk me into anything this morning."

"You didn't have sex with him last night."

Damn. She was right. Was the sex clouding her judgment? *It is and you know it.*

"*No más,*" Glo said with a wag of her finger. "It's the only way."

The terrifying part was that she suspected Glo was right.

* * *

At dark, Kimber parked her clanking car in the alleyway behind Hobo Chic and took the back stairs up to her apartment. As she slid the key in the lock, a scuffling sound came from the bottom of the steps. The safety light behind the man at ground level cast his face in shadow, but she easily made out his long, lean build and spiked, stylish hair.

"Landon." Saying his name hurt, especially considering what she had to do.

"One and only." He climbed the long flight, and she waited, pushing the door open and gesturing for him to go in ahead of her. He swept his arms around her, she assumed to pull her close for a long, wet kiss. Since that had been recently determined as ill-advised, she palmed his chest and pushed, just a gentle shove.

He blew out a sigh of frustration, and she walked into her apartment, rested her shopping bag on the kitchen counter, and tossed her keys beside it.

"I didn't think that would work," he said as he shut the door.

"What?"

He came to her. "Kissing you so you'd forget you're mad at me."

Wow. Gloria was a genius. Because right about now she thought a kiss could make her forget anything. Her own name, even.

"I'm not mad at you," she said. He leaned against the counter over her, and her eyes traced the shape of his biceps beneath his sleeves, the strong line of his confident posture. She blinked and forced herself to stay on task. "I think we need to sort out where we are in this...whatever this is we have. We haven't been very responsible about stating our positions."

He nodded, barely. A sign for her to speak.

She didn't know where to start... "We're going to have a baby." There. Start with the basics. "I'm not interested in moving in with you. Or taking your money to buy Hobo Chic from Mick," she added. "That's something I'm saving for on my own. Something I will do on my own." His eyebrows pinched but he remained silent, so she said the next thing on her mind. "We can share custody. We can share parenting. And I think we should make as many major decisions as we can before we have a slobbery, pink, adorable baby distracting our focus." Bringing up their baby tightened her chest, but she swallowed down her feelings. This was for the best.

Meanwhile, his face had fallen during her mini monologue. She didn't know if his reaction was due to her saying she wasn't moving in with him, or more because she'd taken control of the conversation. She liked that control. Liked creating her future instead of him creating it for her. Glo was right. This was easier without lust sullying her brain.

"As far as us..." This was the hardest part. Suggesting the one thing she didn't want to suggest. But she had to. For their child's sake. They couldn't raise a kid together who didn't know where his or her parents stood. They couldn't just keep doing what felt good and lay waste to anyone in the path between. "We can be partners in raising our child. But as far as us…" She shook her head, the words refusing to come. "We can't…" She closed her eyes. *Say it.* But she didn't have to. Landon said it for her.

"We can't be lovers," he said, his voice barely a whisper.

* * *

Oh, the irony.

If he wasn't mistaken, Kimber had just suggested an arrangement. *An arrangement with the Tin Man.*

He'd spent his life making lists, drawing up agreements, arranging his relationships to prevent them from eking into territory beyond his control. For the first time in his life, someone was doing the same thing to him. And, for the first time in a long time, he had no control.

She wanted to categorize him, maintain an emotionless, neutral position where he was concerned. He'd be angry if he didn't see her point of view so clearly. It'd been his view as well, at least until the redhead before him turned his world upside down. Still, he couldn't work up the anger to storm out.

He didn't want what she offered. He didn't want her living here, keeping her distance from him, working with Mick. But, he amended, he could get over that part if forced. And he didn't mind discussing and debating topics regarding their child. He wanted to talk about what would be best for their bundle of joy from birth to college—if he or she decided to go. What he *did* mind, what was tearing his heart in two, was her suggestion to stop seeing each other.

He wondered what she would say if she learned that for him, what they had superseded sex. That he wanted affection more than her body. Hell, he wanted both. For the second time in his lonely, miserable life, he wanted it all and couldn't have it.

He raked a hand through his hair, closed his eyes, and tried to think of a way out of this. A way around it. He was a smart guy...normally.

If he argued, he doubted she'd welcome the disagreement. He could tell it hadn't been easy for her to lay out how she's feeling, and he respected her for telling him so bluntly. He supposed he could go along with what she offered for a little while, then seduce her into seeing things his way. While that would be fun, for both of them, he knew they'd wind up right back here again, at her kitchen counter or his, discussing this same topic. Only then she'd be ten times angrier. He didn't want her to hate him.

I want her to love me.

At one point, she'd claimed to. Should he remind her of the day she laid across from him in bed? The day her eyes softened as she touched his cheek and told him under no uncertain terms "I love you"? Or had she simply been on the emotional roller coaster of did-we-or-didn't-we-make-a-baby? And now that they had, she what...decided she didn't love him after all?

Pain speared him. His own indecisiveness pissed him off. He used to be in control. He knew his limits, was capable of checking his emotions at the door. Now he was all over the place. And not just over a baby—*A baby*. Would that ever sink in?—but also over Kimber. He opened his mouth to remind her of the day she'd made that promise, that vow he'd been so sure he hadn't wanted to hear.

But the words "I agree" came out of his mouth instead.

It was the first time he'd ever lied to her. It wouldn't be the last. Each and every time he saw her over the next eighteen years, whenever he met her new significant other, whenever they exchanged their child, he'd have to pretend he didn't love her. Hide how hurt he was that they weren't together, that he couldn't touch her.

Something told him eighteen years wouldn't do it. That he might love her forever. And how much worse would it be to see the living, breathing evidence of how compatible they'd been once upon a time? Having a human being, half him, half her, around reminding him what he could have had if their relationship hadn't started and ended with a list?

"Oh. Okay. Good." She sounded surprised by his reaction. She'd probably had a speech in queue, probably expected him to stand his ground. Start with talking her into moving in with him again, or argue that moving her store to the Magnificent Mile was the best course of action. He wanted to do all of those things. But to what end? Her decision was made. Even if he could coerce her into one or two things, what would be the point? She'd made up her mind. And he'd make it as easy on her as possible.

"Want to start today?" His voice was neutral, his shoulders pulled down in defeat. Getting through this part was paramount for him, a stage of grief he wanted to get through as soon as possible so he could move on to the next. Her casual response kicked him while he was down.

"Yes. That would be best." She opened the fridge and pulled out a container of orange juice. "Look, I went to the grocery store." She smiled proudly. She was taking this better than he was. That hurt.

She couldn't be more beautiful. With her natural, wavy hair draped over her shoulders and the casual V-necked shirt coasting over her narrow shoulders. His eyes veered to her stomach even though it was too soon for her to have a "baby bump." Would he be around to see that happen? The thought made his heart sink because he wasn't sure. She poured a glass of juice and took a drink, and all he wanted to do was taste her lips. Breathe her in for a minute and pretend she hadn't completely marginalized him or his unspoken feelings.

But he couldn't. He wasn't *allowed*.

"Um, okay." She licked her lips, her eyes bright. Unaffected. "Let me think. We should probably start with—"

"Legal pad?" He had no tone, lacked the energy to fake one. Reaching into his jacket, he extracted a pen and glanced around the room for something to write on. "Lists are what I'm good at," he added dryly.

Kimber didn't smile or laugh or offer any acknowledgement of a list before this one. *The list*. Whatever they had—or had started to have—was over. His gut twisted.

"I have printer paper."

"Fine." He accepted the sheets she pulled out of the printer on the kitchen counter. *A printer on the kitchen counter*.

Why wouldn't she let him move her into his larger, roomier penthouse? Then she could decorate the office to her preference, buy whatever she needed. Like a desk. For her printer.

But this wasn't about her having an office or about him providing what she needed. The issue, the real one, is she didn't want *him*. He wanted her so badly he thought he might throw up at any moment.

Why won't she love me?

Whatever. That conversation wasn't happening. Pressing his lips together, he vowed to compartmentalize. He laid out the paper and jotted down a header. *Communication*.

He wrote a second header: *Custody*.

The word made him so sad he wanted to die.

A third column he titled *Privacy*.

This is how arrangements were done. He knew because he'd set the terms for an arrangement with Lissa. With Megan. With Natalie. The three girlfriends he'd had since

Rachel had ruined his heart. Although, now, the title of "Heart Ruiner" could be awarded to Kimber. She'd not only destroyed his heart—hey, he had one, go figure—but she would continue to destroy it for years to come. He traced the line of her delicate neck to the arms that had once held on to him like he was her port in a storm.

You deserve this.

He did. He deserved this hurt. For attempting to marginalize her. For ignoring his true feelings each and every time he sank into her body. For lying to her right now instead of admitting how unfair this was. For both of them.

For the three of us.

But he couldn't change who he was this late in the game, could he? If he was Evan, he could swear and yell, and slam doors, showing his feelings through overzealous behavior. If he was Aiden, he'd have the right words, be brave enough to tell Kimber the truth, and bare his heart.

But Landon wasn't his brothers. He was stuck with his own personality. An air of control, a penchant for order and organization, and a past that had primed him to expertly execute the arrangement Kimber had asked for.

And that's what he'd do.

Because he loved her.

$\mathcal{C}$HAPTER SEVENTEEN

$\mathcal{K}$imber didn't know what sucked worse. That Landon hadn't argued with her or that he'd made a plan with so much efficiency it masqueraded as relief.

Only he hadn't been relieved...she didn't think. He'd been almost cold. His usually bright eyes had been shuttered; flat and dark. *Emotionless.* Now that she thought about it, he'd avoided her eyes the entire time they talked, despite her attempt to lighten the conversation with a gentle joke here and there. He'd simply kept his eyes on the sheet of paper in front of him and filled in the blanks.

Did I do the right thing?

She studied the agreement now, sliding her fingers over his neat penmanship. In one part he'd requested copies of the doctor's bills and prior knowledge of any special visits or emergencies. He'd been very amicable. They'd agreed on most things, to her surprise. And the items they hadn't agreed on weren't deal-breakers.

Which made her think they really would have been good together. But maybe she misread him. Maybe his amicability, his distance, had everything to do with his concern for their baby, not her. If he cared for her at all, would he have allowed her to make this list in the first place?

Something *felt* wrong. Then again, every time she'd trusted her feelings, she'd made a mistake. She thought of Glo, her mother, Mick. Everyone around her agreed single motherhood was better than staying with Landon. And since she couldn't trust her own feelings, she had defaulted to the people closest to her. Her hand strayed to her stomach. She had more to think about than herself.

Her heart ached as she pictured Landon at the door before he left. His face wasn't set in stone like it had been earlier, but his eyes were as expressionless as before. "If your insurance doesn't cover something, will you let me help?" he'd asked. *Asked* instead of demanded. Which was likely why she'd agreed.

At least we have guidelines, she thought the next day while spacing the hangers on a rack in Hobo Chic. Their new list wasn't as fun as the original list they'd worked their way through. The list of ten ways to curl her toes and make her feel like a woman. *Cherished*. She'd asked him to cherish her that first night, and oh, he had. He had every day. Until yesterday.

"Whoa, sweetheart." Neil stepped in her range of vision, and she blinked at his overly gelled hair. "You've been zoning out at this rack of peasant dresses for a while now. Either you're about to get your *Little House on the Prairie* on, or your mind is on someone tall, hot, and wealthy." He lifted a manicured eyebrow.

"I'm pregnant," she blurted.

Neil's expression clearly revealed his thoughts, but he spoke them, too. "*Whaaaaat*?"

"May as well tell everyone. It'll be obvious soon, anyway." If not by her expanding belly, then by the way she'd been inhaling rocky-road brownies from the bakery across the street. If she wasn't careful, that could become a seriously bad habit.

That evening, over *another* of Jilly's SinSational brownies, Kimber worked a pencil down the sketchpad on her lap. One of her favorite hobbies before she'd opened her store had been designing her own clothing. She used to create her own patterns, too, though she'd never worn any of her creations. They'd been more for fun than function. *Yet another dream that hadn't come true.*

She took another bite of her brownie, brushing crumbs from the page, watching as the dress appeared almost magically. Whenever a vision was in her head, getting it from her brain to paper happened seamlessly, in a flurry of motion. Drawing complete, she finished the rest of her brownie and admired her work, adding in a line here or a shadow there to finish it off.

One of my better ones, she thought without an ounce of bragging. She used to believe at one point she'd be designing dresses like these for the Lissa Francines of the fashion world. She'd pictured her creations prancing across the catwalk while she watched from behind the curtain.

Man plans and God laughs. *Ain't it the truth?*

After the snafu with fashion royalty Karl Kingsley, and her eventual shunning from the fashion world, Kimber had slunk away, beaten and bruised. None of it mattered now. Even if she would entertain the outrageous possibility of reclaiming her passion for design, she was in no position to act on it. Not now. Not with a baby on the way. She'd be lucky to maintain her current schedule and care for an infant full-time. Although Landon would have partial custody. She'd never take that from him. He'd make an amazing father.

What would that be like? she thought with a dart of pain to the chest. She pictured him cradling their child, murmuring softly to him in the dark and shushing him to sleep. Just envisioning Landon in a rocking chair, their tiny child in his large, capable hands, had a lump forming in her throat.

She wouldn't get to witness those nights. She'd miss the moments where he learned to be an amazing dad. And he would be. She'd seen the evidence when he was with Lyon. He loved his nephew, had spoiled him rotten. He'd do the same or more for their baby.

With a sad smile, she imagined what would have happened if she'd said yes to his offer. Yes to the idea to moving her store, moving in with him. To having a partner at her side when she became a mother, the most difficult job on the planet.

But she hadn't said yes. She'd refused. She'd opted to work and struggle and keep up with her apartment, the business, and the schedule, and be a full-time mom. Because if their story didn't have a fairy-tale ending, she couldn't bear tearing her child away from him. Leaving angry, fighting for custody, being embittered like her mom or fading away like her dad.

Landon had been right about one thing—probably many things—but at the moment she'd grant him the one. Kimber needed help. She'd have to hire someone else to work at Hobo Chic in her place. She'd have to lessen her hours. That would cost money, time. Sacrifice.

She would sacrifice. Because she knew what waited at the end of the road if she stayed with Landon. She knew what became of a relationship that started and ended for the sake of a child. With her emotions and hormones wreaking havoc in her body, how could she trust her heart? How could she believe that she and Landon could have—against all odds—formed an unbreakable, forever bond in such a short span of time?

She couldn't.

And because she couldn't trust herself, she would have

to trust the people around her who loved her. Her mother, Gloria. Neither of them had a thing to gain by steering her in the wrong direction.

She glanced at her drawing again—at the smooth lines of the skirt, the arching ruffles over the neckline, the marks meant to emulate winking rhinestones—tore the page from the sketchbook, and crumbled it in one fist.

A tear slid down her face, but she wasn't crying about the lost opportunities of her youth or about the life of motherhood she'd chosen with open eyes. No, the regret swimming in her stomach had nothing to do with her and everything to do with Landon.

And how much she would miss him. Her heart said she loved him... and more than anything she wished she could allow herself to believe it.

* * *

"I'm leaving in an hour," Landon told Evan over the phone. He closed the boardroom door behind him, leaving his capable team in charge while he was away. He wouldn't miss Lyon turning seven for anything. Not even a Cheez-Bitts account.

He ended the call and allowed himself to feel a modicum of pride at successfully breaking into the food industry. Windy City had helped Downey Design have a reputation for being capable of selling the common man's brands.

The memory of landing the Windy City account brought with it memories he'd prefer to forget. Like the moment he and Kimber had eaten potato chips in his bed. The way he'd shoved a handful into his mouth and she'd laughed as she brushed crumbs off his body. The cute way she wrinkled her nose and smiled whenever he did something she didn't expect.

Way to go, bonehead. You've tied a painfully present memory to something you can't escape for the rest of your days. Windy City's brand was *everywhere*. Every local sandwich shop, grocery store, the framed ads adorning the walls of his office building. He studied the ad for the jalapeño ranch flavor hanging outside his office, his thoughts on Kimber.

He hadn't spoken to her since he left her apartment that night. She'd e-mailed him about a doctor's appointment she had coming up. He'd entered it in his calendar, unsure if she wanted him there, but he planned on showing up anyway. If for no other reason than to catch a glimpse of her when she walked outside. If something went wrong, even if it didn't, he wouldn't let her go through her pregnancy alone. He was here for her. And if that didn't matter to her, it mattered to him.

After an uneventful flight to Osborn, Ohio, he drove to his father's house with the radio loud. But like during the plane ride, he couldn't keep his mind off Kimber. He turned the rental car onto his father's street, when his phone rang.

Lissa? *What the hell?*

He pulled the car over at the end of the street, a few houses away. No way did he want Dad overhearing this conversation... whatever it was about.

He cleared his throat and answered with a curt, "This is Landon."

"Hi. It's Lissa. Francine."

"I don't think a last name is necessary."

"I know. I just." A sob. "I need to talk to you."

Despite all he'd been through with her, despite the fact that she'd left him, despite that she'd made him a publicity stunt, he felt for her. He may not have been in love with her, but he'd cared about her. Caring wasn't something one could simply turn off. Not even him.

"Carson left me, Landon. He went back to his fat ex-girlfriend." She sobbed again, the sound muffled by sniffling.

"I'm sorry." He meant that. Which surprised him. Whatever bitterness he'd harbored while watching the amateur video of Lissa sliding lips with Carson had vanished. No, not vanished. Had been *absorbed*. Kimber had taken it from him. Soaked in his ambivalence, the hardness that had made him a terrible partner in the past. She'd infected him with her softness, her vulnerability.

"...come back?" Lissa was saying. "Maybe we could try one more time."

He snapped back to present, her comment as sobering as a slap to the face. "You want me back." So that's what this phone call was about. Lissa was lonely.

"Please, Landon. I never stopped caring about you. I never stopped wanting you." That wasn't hope in her voice. It was desperation.

"Yes, you did," he stated. "When you left. You stopped wanting me on a dime, Lissa."

Her sobbing stopped abruptly. "You're the same as you always were, do you know that?"

But he wasn't. "How would you know?"

She didn't answer him, only continued her self-indulgent speech. "You're the same pompous jackhole you've always been. You shut down your feelings when things get hard. Did you ever think if you'd actually shown me how you feel you could've held on to me? If you'd let me see who you really were, maybe I wouldn't have left your stuffy ass for Carson Robbins."

Her tirade didn't upset him. If he'd have told her how he "actually" felt, she would've left him sooner. "If that's true, then why do you want me back? Why would you want to be with a man who shut you out and pushed you away? Wouldn't you rather have a man who told you, no matter the cost, how much he loves you?"

Like you should have done with Kimber. Idiot.

Lissa was railing, volume escalating, her vocabulary becoming less refined and beginning to smack of the trailer park she'd prided herself on escaping. She ended the call with name-calling, which she knew he hated. Then she hung up on him. Which he also hated.

Shaking his head, he threw his car into drive and peeled into his father's driveway. Scotch was calling his name.

CHAPTER EIGHTEEN

Red and blue balloons tied with silver ribbons were strung throughout Aiden's house. Aiden stood on a chair tying another pair of balloons to the curtain rod.

"We're here," their father, Mike, announced as he and Landon walked through the open front door.

"Hey, Pop. Landon, you made it. Nice!" Aiden climbed down and met them at the door. Mike hugged him, then wandered into the kitchen and struck up a conversation with Sadie.

Landon took his first look around at Sadie and Aiden's house. "Good-looking place, bro."

"Yeah." Aiden hugged him, then stepped back to admire their home. "It's modest, but we manage."

"Nothing wrong with modest." Nothing wrong with modest or vintage or simple. *Or women who wear your work shirt and play dress-up with your nephew.*

Aiden's eyes went to his empty entryway. "Where's Kimber? Lyon said he invited her. Hasn't shut up about her, Evan says."

Great. So Landon had ruined more than his own heart by

letting Kimber go. He thought back to what he'd told Lissa last night. Wished that he was the kind of man who could say what he thought, what he felt. Wished he could convince Kimber to come back to him. But she'd made her decision, and he would abide by it.

"She's in Chicago."

Aiden grunted. Landon waited for him to reprimand him, but instead Aiden handed over a roll of tape. "Help me with the rest of these streamers."

He obliged, happy to have something to do with his hands. Evan and Lyon arrived soon after, and Angel an hour after them. She'd left Richie at home, blaming a work assignment and teasingly accusing Landon for forcing weekend labor. Three more kids and their parents filed into the house, friends Lyon played with when he was in town, Landon guessed. Sadie and Angel corralled them into the yard, where tables covered in confetti and games waited.

Landon was about to head out to help with the piñata when Crickitt walked in, her bright blue eyes shadowed by dark circles, her curls in disarray. Shane walked in behind her...carrying the reason for her dishevelment.

"There's my cheeseburger!" Aiden rushed to the carrier before Shane could put it down and extracted the baby girl from the cushioning. She was gorgeous. Dark hair, dark eyes, chubby cheeks. Landon pushed away every thought in his head revolving around Kimber and his child—which was basically all of them.

"Cheeseburger?" Landon tickled the baby under the chin. Wide blue eyes found his and held. The edge of her lips pushed pudgy cheeks aside in an attempt at a smile, nearly breaking him in two. Landon's head flooded with thoughts of Kimber, of their baby, despite doing his best to avoid them.

He took hold of the baby's hand, her fingers clutching his.

His eyes started to burn. This was what he'd walked away from. Like Shane's and Crickitt's child was half of each of them, Kimber carried a baby in her womb one part her, one part Landon. He imagined their son or daughter with flame-red hair and bright emerald eyes. Or dark blond hair and hazel eyes like his own. The thought had pain crushing his chest with two thousand pounds of pressure.

"Yeah, Blair Kathleen. BK, as in Burger King." Aiden's voice plucked him out of his morose thoughts. His brother sent Crickitt an approving nod as she shook her head at the silly nickname. Shane and Crickitt had named their daughter after Shane's mother and Landon's mother. Blair August. Kathleen Downey. It was an endearing tribute.

Crickitt shrugged. "My mom didn't want her granddaughter named after her, anyway. She said one Chandra was plenty."

"No kidding," Shane grumbled, and she gave him a playful slap. He grabbed her up and kissed her. Landon's heart gave another envious squeeze.

Aiden handed over their precious bundle, and the family of three wandered into the kitchen.

Over dinner—pizza for the kids and, since Sadie had admittedly ruined Mom's recipe for lasagna, pizza for the adults, too—Landon stayed close to Shane and talked business.

Lifting a bottle of water to his lips, he chugged down half its contents, wetting his parched throat after the salt-laden dinner. The local pizza place was no Giordano's, but pretty good. "So, Aid," he said to his brother who sipped a bottle of beer, "how's the Axle's thing coming along?"

Aiden had made plans to buy five motorcycle shops last year from Axle Zoller, the former owner.

"Right on schedule," Aiden said, keeping his eyes on the kids' table. Sadie looked up from the cake, sparing a smile for her husband, and Landon could have sworn he saw Aiden blush. "'Scuse me," he said, zooming over to his wife as if he'd been called.

"That went well," Landon muttered to himself.

Shane lifted his own beer bottle and chuckled.

"What's the best way to slip him some cash?" he asked his billionaire cousin.

Shane shook his head. "If there'd been a way to do that, I'd have done it already. You know that."

He did. Aiden and Shane were close, and there was nothing his cousin wouldn't do for any of them. "What about Sadie?"

"Not a prayer, man." He pointed at the couple with his bottle. "Those two are a unit. And you don't want a piece of that feisty blonde." He'd meant it as a compliment, Landon could tell. Aiden, far from the henpecked husband, strolled over to where they were standing, Sadie wrapped around his waist.

"Sorry for the pizza." She wrinkled her nose. "I'll get Mrs. Downey's lasagna recipe right one of these years."

Aiden mouthed the words *No she won't.* Sadie caught him and tagged him in the arm. "It's okay, beautiful," he said, pulling her close and kissing her forehead. "I didn't marry you for your culinary abilities."

"Yeah, he married me for my rad tree house skills." She winked at Crickitt, who joined them, BK cradled against her chest asleep.

Aiden flushed—actually flushed—and smashed a kiss onto Sadie's mouth, preventing her from saying more. Landon raised a brow. Shane looked equally confused, while Crickitt looked suspiciously in the know. Landon was pretty sure he didn't want to know.

Lyon's friends left and Dad took Evan and Lyon back home where they were staying the night. Landon had planned on sleeping here tonight. Angel, too, who was now helping Sadie clean up the remnants of the party.

Landon pulled down the last of the balloons and shoved them into a trash bag. "Want to get plowed?"

Aiden sent him a sideways glance. "Hell, yes. But I don't have any scotch."

"Brought my own." Sadly, Landon had planned on getting tanked tonight. After the stress of losing Kimber and worrying about the baby—and the irritating call from Lissa—he had made a beeline for the liquor store. Macallan Limited Release was costly, and usually reserved for celebration, but what the hell?

He was celebrating being a dumbass. So there.

Shane wandered back into the living room, keys in hand, little BK in her car seat, snoozing away. "What are you guys doing tonight?"

"Getting hammered," Aiden said with a smile.

"Nice." Shane raised an approving brow. "Any reason why?"

"Other than Landon getting his girlfriend pregnant? Nope." Landon coiled his hand into a fist, but Aiden's smile only widened. "They had to find out sooner or later, man." He slapped Landon's shoulder.

"Who's your girlfriend?" Crickitt asked, brightening for the first time tonight.

"Kimber," Sadie chimed in, stepping into the living room from the kitchen. "Angel's friend who spent a summer with their family when they were kids. She had a crush on Landon."

Crickitt melted. "Aww."

Angel came into the living room, drying her hands on a dish towel. "I heard my name."

"We were talking about Kimber," Aiden filled in. "And how she and Landon have been knockin' boots."

Landon shot his brother a look. *Really?*

"I knew it!" Angel said, waving the dish towel at Landon. "I guess that drink went well."

"And she's pregnant, in case you didn't overhear that part." Aiden took a step away from Landon. Smart move. Landon was already coiled to throw a sucker punch in his direction.

Angel's eyes grew wide. "Kimber is pregnant?"

"Yes." Landon's eyes sank close. *Defeated.* "Kimber is pregnant."

"Well, where is she?" Angel looked left, then right, as if Kimber had been hiding in a nearby closet the entire party.

Landon tried to say something to the effect of, *In Chicago. Avoiding me,* but the words wouldn't come. He shook his head instead.

"Oh," Crickitt muttered after no one spoke. "Oh no." She put a palm against Landon's chest and gazed up at him with earnest concern. The warmth of her hand over his heart caused his cheeks to heat. The confusing emotions simmering under the surface this evening suddenly clawing to get out.

Crickitt, the human tuning fork, picked up on it. Sympathy filled her eyes. "Things will work out for the best," she murmured, patting him. "Look at Aiden and Sadie. Look at Shane and me." Tears shimmered in her eyes. "Keep the faith."

She pulled her hand away and turned to Shane. "Do you want to stay here and have too many drinks with your cousins?"

Lucky bastard.

"I can drive him home," Sadie offered. "I'm not drinking since we're trying to get into the same situation you've gotten Kimber into," she told Landon.

Aiden wasn't doing half-bad in the wife department, either.

"No, I'm going to go home." Shane tugged his wife against him. "Try and let Crickitt get some sleep for a change."

Landon didn't know if that was a baby joke or a sex joke—or if couples had sex after having babies, but Crickitt smiled up at her husband, pleased with his answer. Shane probably thought that by leaving, he'd be dodging the relationship-talk bullet, but he'd be wrong. Landon wasn't going to talk about Kimber. The plan was to drink so he *didn't* have to talk about—or think about—Kimber.

No way was he bringing her up.

* * *

"She doesn't want a relationship. She wants an *arrangement*."

Except instead of "arrangement" Landon had muttered a garbled version of "*harranguement*," which most assuredly was *not* a word.

Aiden regarded him with a raised brow.

"This is why people butcher the English language," Landon said, doing a decent job of butchering it now. He lifted his glass again. "It's fun." He took another drink. Relinquishing the glass, he sat back and focused on the dark outline of the fruit trees at the back of the moonlit yard.

They were quiet for a while, until Aiden spoke. "Hell of a pickle you've gotten yourself into."

"It was supposed to be a fling," Landon grumbled, keeping his eyes trained at a distance.

"A fling that turned into a baby."

He slid a gaze over at his brother. Aiden leaned an arm on the edge of the patio table between them. Landon remained silent. Mainly because he was having a hard time speaking without slurring.

Aiden's blond brows lifted into his too-long hair. "Did you

literally draw up a contract with her? Like with signatures and a notary public stamp? Because that's effing nuts."

Landon opened his mouth to ream him, but Aiden wasn't serious. His brother offered a crooked smile and sipped his beer. Content to bust Landon's balls, evidently.

"Do you want her back?" Aiden asked after another permeating silence.

Landon's face pulled into a grimace. He rubbed a hand over his jawline, the hint of growth scratching his palm. Had he been this miserable in his entire life? He didn't think so.

"Thing is…" He didn't know how much more he should say. He scrubbed his jaw again while he thought. A woman's voice coming from behind him read his mind.

"You love her." Aiden's smart-as-a-whip-crack wife came around to sit on Aiden's lap. His brother pulled Sadie close and buried his nose in her long, fair hair. She wrapped her arms around his neck, but her attention was focused squarely on Landon. "You love her or you wouldn't be out here drowning your feelings in scotch."

Landon thrust out his bottom lip and regarded his glass silently.

"Should I yell for Angel, or are you going to talk to me?" she demanded. For a petite thing, she was a pistol. Shane had warned him. Aiden shot Landon a smile, one that said he'd be glad to watch Landon go a round or two with his other half.

Landon flicked a look from her to Aiden and attempted to look wounded by her words. "Sadie, *et tu*?"

She only smiled. Aiden squeezed one of her thighs just below a short pair of shorts, making Landon feel like a third wheel. An incredibly inebriated third wheel, but still.

Sensing her husband's growing impatience, or maybe Landon's growing discomfort, she slipped from Aiden's lap and settled onto the empty chair between him and Landon instead.

But Sadie didn't know who she was dealing with. He was the Tin Man. Impervious to emotion. She stared him down. He stared back. Or tried to. His vision blurred in and out. Maybe she'd forget what she said if he remained silent for long enough. Landon took turns grousing at her and his half-empty glass before realizing the standoff could last until the End of Days.

"Fine," he growled. "I love her."

Aiden sat up in his chair, a confused-slash-concerned look on his face. Was it so unbelievable that Landon could be in love? Then he thought of how often his family had seen him with a woman. How distant he and Lissa had been when she had been around his family. He hadn't brought another woman around before or since.

On a surrendering sigh, Landon went for broke. "I don't want to be a part-time dad," he said. "I want to be a father full-time. I want to be with Kimber full-time. I want…" He lifted a hand, dropped it into his lap. "I want all of her, you know?"

He tried to focus on Sadie, but she kept going out of focus. At one point there were three of her. That wasn't good. He shoved his glass aside. He wasn't quite pass-out-in-the-yard drunk, but he was close.

"You should tell her that, Landon." She rested her hand over his and, for the second time tonight, tears dammed his throat.

Lovely. The drunk cry. He'd experienced that once before—the night he found out Rachel had the abortion. Ah, shit, here came the feelings from back then, too. Great.

Pile it on, Life.

"Aiden, we should go in. Let Landon have a few minutes,"

Sadie said. Then to Landon, "We'll check on you later, but you take all the time you need, okay?"

He clenched his jaw and nodded. A tear tumbled out of one eye as Aiden and Sadie turned to go inside. He heard Sadie mumble something and Angel mumble something in return. Landon sniffed, sucked it up. Sitting here and blubbering like a baby wasn't going to solve anything. Truth was, he'd fucked up and he needed to fix it. He'd tried being compliant and look where it'd gotten him. He'd agreed his way into a corner.

He pulled the phone out of his pocket. On the third try, he successfully dialed Kimber's number. He'd have to apologize to Kenneth Winger and Kim Schantz when he got back to the office for the drunk-dials at two a.m. Ohio time.

Predictably, Kimber's voice mail picked up. He thought about hanging up. There was at least one sober brain cell shouting about how this wasn't the best time to leave a message, but he ignored it.

"Kimber," he started, his tongue tripping over her name. "Hi. It's Landon." He let out a mirthless laugh. Yeah. This was going well already. "I called because... well, I shouldn't be calling. I know that. But I've been drinking and scotch makes me brave. Or stupid. Or a combination of brave and stupid. Anyway." He scrubbed his eyes under his glasses. "I don't want an arrang...a harrang...a *contract* with you. I want a life with you. And yes, I've had too much to drink, but the reason I drank is because of you. Not that it's your fault, but I love you. That probably is your fault. You're lovable." He stumbled over that word, too. He licked his dry mouth and drank down another mouthful of scotch.

"I love you and it's killing me to stay away from you," he admitted. "I didn't want Rachel to have the abortion. It was finals week and I was focused on school, and she was upset and ignoring me. I went to her, Kimber, with a fucking baby name book and a bouquet of the ugliest flowers in the world. I was going to make it work, become a family. She took it away from me. She took that future away from me. I was too late."

Hearing that his mother had been diagnosed with stage four cancer was the only time he'd come close to feeling that helpless again. In Rachel's dorm room that long ago night, he'd shaken his head over and over, as if he could will away what she had told him; keep it from being real. But the abortion had been real. She'd dug out the clinic bill when he'd demanded proof. He'd cried all over that sheet of paper.

"Before you think that I'm trying to make up for what I lost, let me assure you, I'm not. I have been avoiding—rather successfully, I might add—relationships since that night. Until you. When I met you, Kimber, everything changed. My heart changed. Because of you. Working down that list—"

The voice mail beeped, signifying the end.

"Shit." His finger was hovering over the Call button when Angel appeared in his peripheral. He turned and saw her saddened expression. She took the phone from him and sank into the plastic lawn chair next to his.

"I didn't know about Rachel," she said.

He nodded. "It sucked."

"You never told any of us."

Aiden and Sadie crept out behind her. Landon wasn't sure how much they'd heard, but he waved at the empty chairs, gesturing for them to sit.

"You were high school kids," he said to Angel and Aiden. "And it wasn't the type of story I wanted to worry Mom and Dad with. I was trying to make them proud." He shook his head.

"This explains so much," Angel said.

He pointed at his phone. "I think you came out here about

two minutes too late." What had he done? He ran his hands through his hair and propped them on the back of his head, looking up at the star-pocked sky, then back at his family. "She's going to hate me for that."

Sadie was the only one who spoke.

"I wouldn't if I was her," she said. "I'd love you for it."

CHAPTER NINETEEN

*K*imber dropped the box into the chute next to the serve-yourself shipping center. She'd neglected getting the package in the mail over the weekend, which was what had brought her here on Monday morning before she headed in to work.

She'd hated missing Lyon's birthday party Saturday, but she wouldn't miss the opportunity to send him a gift. In this case, a "real" Superman costume complete with cape, and a replacement copy of *Man of Steel*. No doubt he'd wear his DVD out soon enough.

Much as she'd wanted to be there for the party, the implications of seeing Landon, his entire family, and discussing their awkward situation were too great. Besides, she and Landon were supposed to be practicing distance.

And she missed Lyon. She would have loved to see his face light up as he opened his gifts, would have loved to watch him blow out the candles on his Superman birthday cake. And she would have loved to see Landon standing behind him, arms crossed over his impressive chest, a proud smile on his face.

Picturing him made her mouth water. She could see him

in a T-shirt snuggled around his biceps, in shorts that cupped his rear end.

Wait. She wasn't supposed to be fantasizing about Landon.

Stupid pregnancy hormones. Yes, she was back to blaming them for her every impulse. Speaking of, she was starving. She glanced at the clock on her phone. Ten a.m. She'd eaten breakfast at eight. At this rate, she'd gain a hundred pounds growing a seven-pound baby.

Not that she was eating her feelings or anything, she thought miserably, walking a block to a café. An array of pastries: Bagels, scones, muffins, and donuts were lined up beneath the glass case. Sinful, tempting.

And buy-one-get-one-free. *Bonus.*

She ordered a donut and a muffin and told herself the latter would cancel out the former. *Liar.* But then she'd gotten good at lying to herself, hadn't she? She had almost convinced herself she was happy with the arrangement she and Landon had made. And she was on her way to believing she didn't miss laughing with him, talking to him, waking up next to him, or making love to him on every piece of furniture in his house. A few more months of delusion and she might also con herself into believing she could survive natural childbirth.

She picked a table by the window and dunked the teabag into a mug of hot water. Not the same as coffee. Not by a long shot. But even if it was "okay" according to some websites (and her mother) for pregnant women to have a cup of coffee a day, she didn't want to risk it. The life growing inside of her had become real over the last several weeks.

Maybe because her apartment was now filled with baby furniture. Cramped, but it had all fit. She'd expected to feel an overwhelming sense of accomplishment after she'd stuffed her tiny space. She didn't. What she felt mostly was bone-tired. Fatigue was the houseguest who wouldn't leave, settling in and joining her at the least convenient times. She'd fallen asleep in the *storeroom* yesterday, for Pete's sake. Ridiculous.

Kimber had never been the kind of girl to dream of being pregnant, but she'd assumed that when and if she was, the father of the child would be in her life. Landon had tried to be in her life, in the most demanding way. At the time that'd upset her, but now...now that she was dealing with things alone...

If she had overreacted, it was too late to take back now. This wasn't the kind of situation where she could conk herself on the head and say, "Oops, my bad." Not that anyone said "my bad" anymore anyway.

The ugly truth was her apartment *was* too small. And he'd been right. The stairs were inconvenient—had been since she'd moved in. Exhausted at the end of a long day, the trek was like scaling the side of a mountain. And Hobo Chic, the store she'd fought to keep on Meringue Avenue, the store that had started out as her passion, her living, breathing dream, had turned into something else. She enjoyed working there, but the place wasn't the end-all-be-all it used to be.

The baby had taken the store's place...along with the sketches she drew on the nights she was unable to sleep. She'd been creating new clothing designs and dreaming up a new venture in the process. Her own clothing line. A store on Michigan Avenue.

It'd have to be a slow-build. Like, really slow. Maybe after she bought Mick out she could increase her clientele at Hobo Chic, sell the store at a profit...

Sure and then I'll win the lottery, and ride a unicorn into the sunset, she thought grimly. The fantasy of moving her store, having her own clothing line, *and* raising a child was...well, a fantasy.

Babies were expensive. Even babies of millionaires. And she refused to ask Landon for more than his fair share. She was no gold-digger. She wouldn't ask him to provide her with a lifestyle she hadn't earned. Didn't deserve.

I never should have pushed him away.

The thought was so out of left field, she choked on her tea. She waved at a neighboring table when they looked on with concern. "I'm fine," she croaked.

But she wasn't fine. She was an idiot. She'd ignored her heart, ignored her feelings. All because...because she was trying to be someone she wasn't. Because she'd allowed her past to predict her future. She'd ignored every instinct she had about Landon. And why? Because she'd failed in the past? But this situation was unlike anything she'd ever experienced. She'd never been pregnant, and she'd never known anyone—never loved anyone—the way she loved Landon.

He'd been a recurring thought, looping her brain every day. Maybe because half of him grew inside of her. Of course she'd think of him. If she hadn't been pregnant, she wondered if they would have stayed together? Yes. They would. There was too much connection, too much desire, too much joy between them to walk away.

So why did she insist on walking away when they shared something as epically life-changing as a child? Because she'd screwed up, that's why.

Picking a corner off the muffin, she chewed forlornly, no longer hungry. When he'd come to her house, she'd shoved him away. Demanded an agreement. An *arrangement*, she thought with a wince. And he'd been there...why? Why had he come to her apartment?

She sipped her tea and thought back to the night he'd climbed her stairs and tried to kiss her. After she'd refused him, she'd steered the conversation and, like the captain on the *Titanic*, had gone down with the ship. Landon may have taken charge when it came to drafting their agreement, but only because she'd asked. He'd looked downright resigned while doing it, she recalled with a stab of certainty.

What if...she shouldn't think it...but she did anyway. *What if he came there that night to say he loved me?*

She loved him. No doubt about it. All the pragmatic and practical arguments she'd been making were forced. That had been her, trying to be someone she wasn't. She wasn't practical or pragmatic. Why hadn't she trusted her heart? Just one more time?

She'd denied her feelings, denied the man she loved. And why? Because she was a modern-day woman who had a baby in her belly? A baby that *wouldn't be there* if not for Landon. A baby that was as much his as hers. A baby he'd been so terrified of losing that he'd agreed to a rigid, black-and-white arrangement at her behest.

What have I done?

And what would that arrangement look like to their child? She'd been concerned over becoming an embittered housewife, but now what would she look like? A woman going robotically through the motions each time she talked to Landon? Denying their emotional connection—her love for him? Did she really want her child seeing her as some emotionless robot?

And what if she wanted a second child? What if she wanted a brother or sister for the baby growing in her womb? Could she really date again? While the man she loved was in the same town, sharing custody, and making her long for his touch each and every time she saw him? No way.

Kimber shoved her food away and stared into her cooling, flavorless tea. She'd made a horrible mistake, and all she could hope for was that Landon would be magnanimous enough to hear her out. Would he consider giving her another chance to make things right between them? She hoped so.

Her phone chimed: e-mail. She tapped the screen and read the message, confused for a handful of seconds.

To: kimberr@email.com
From: shaneaugust@augustindustries.com
Subject: Voice mail

Dear Ms. Reynolds:
    Please read this before you open the attachment.
    You may recognize my name, you may not. I'm Landon's cousin/business partner who lives in Ohio. Last night, he seems to have gotten incredibly inebriated and called my secretary Keena by mistake. The voice mail was meant for you. I debated sending it, and I'm still not entirely sure you want to hear a slurring speech of undying love from my eldest cousin, but in the end, I can't not forward it on. It's here, in the attachment. Sounds like he got cut off at the end, but I'll leave it up to you to call him and hear the rest.
    For what it's worth, Landon is a good guy. He's about as hardheaded as I am when it comes to women, but his heart's in the right place. I was lucky enough to find the woman who was willing to wait out my stupidity. On the chance you might be that woman for Landon, I didn't want to deny you the same opportunity.
    We're a thick bunch sometimes.

Sincerely,
Shane August, CEO August Industries

Kimber's thumb hovered over the attachment as she digested Shane's e-mail. She reread it, stopping to think about what "a slurring speech of undying love" might sound like.
    She was about to find out. There was no way she wouldn't

open it now. She wanted to hear what Landon had to say. Drunk or not. She clicked the attachment and brought the phone to her ear.

"Kimber. Hi, it's Landon…"

* * *

His head pounded harder this morning than it had Sunday morning. And Sunday's hangover had been a whopper. Probably wasn't a good idea to drink last night, too, but he figured why not? He'd made a grievous error—not letting Kimber know how he felt—followed by another grievous error. The phone call where he had. Maybe if he kept drinking, he'd kill off enough brain cells that one day he wouldn't be able to remember doing either.

He'd held out hope she might hear his message and call him, but his phone stayed silent all day Sunday. No messages. No calls. Just a silence that spoke louder than anything she could have said to him. She may not hate him, but she didn't love him. And she hadn't appreciated his profession being soaked in thirty-year scotch.

Imagine that.

He remembered the gist of what he'd said in that voice mail: *I love you, I miss you.* Even though he'd spoken it through a throat burning from Macallan Limited Release, the sentiment had demanded a reply. But she hadn't replied.

Which he took to mean she didn't care. That was the only reason not to call back. If the opposite of love was apathy, it wasn't hard to reason that Kimber felt nothing but indifference toward him. Maybe he was better off spending his nights drunk and alone in his enormous and lonely penthouse. Maybe he should get a dog.

"Mr. Downey?" his secretary's voice came over the speakerphone in his office.

"Yeah, Cindy." He grabbed his head with his hands to stop the throbbing in his skull. Speaking made his brain ache like he'd shouted instead.

"I have a Ms. Reynolds here to see you. She doesn't have an appointment but—"

"Send her in." He stood from his desk, knocking his chair with the backs of his legs and rolling it several feet from his desk. He raced across the room to his private bathroom, shocked by the man staring back at him from the mirror. He looked like hell. If hell had been subjected to freezer burn, then microwaved. He dampened his fingers and ran them through his hair, swishing mouthwash around his teeth at the same time. By the time he'd stepped into his office and slid his glasses back onto his nose, Cindy opened the door.

She ushered Kimber inside, and he nearly buckled at the sight of her. Seeing her was like walking into the bright sunshine after a long day under fluorescent lighting. She practically burst with light... the pregnancy glow.

He wanted to drop to his knees, bury his head into the folds of her green dress, and beg them both—Kimber and the baby—for a second chance. Melodramatic? Maybe. But he'd do anything—*anything*—to get her back. He'd give up his business and his penthouse. Move into her teeny little apartment and become a stockroom boy for Hobo Chic if he had to.

Because nothing else mattered. Not his career. Not his top-floor penthouse. He'd worked hard to craft a perfect façade of a life. Then Kimber had come into it, and left, proving the life he'd worked so hard to build as flimsy as a matchbook house. One that had gone up in flames the second she walked out of it.

Cindy shut the office door and Kimber gestured to the couch. "Mind if I sit? I'm exhausted."

"Please," he said, holding the crumbling walls of his

heart together with both hands. Maintaining as usual. Mr. Control. Sometimes he hated that about himself.

She patted the cushion next to her and he sat, obediently. Tired of not saying what was on his mind he blurted, "I want to touch you so badly."

She smiled, her eyes shining. There was something in them that was real and warm, and not the least bit indifferent. A spark of hope lit within him. Tentatively, he reached for her face.

She leaned into his palm and floored him with her next four words. "I love you, too."

He simply stared at her, mouth ajar for several seconds. When he finally got his tongue to cooperate, he said, "You heard my message."

"I didn't get it until this morning. I came straight here."

What? He blinked, digesting that bit of information. "I thought you heard it and were ignoring me."

She shook her head. "I heard it and cried in the middle of a café over a half-eaten muffin."

He pulled her close, and relief washed through him when her arms locked around his neck. "The one time I didn't listen to my heart," she whispered against his ear, "and it was right."

He held her tighter, not a hundred percent certain he wasn't having a very vivid, alcohol-induced dream.

"I may have apologized for saying 'I love you' that first time, but it was the truth. Crazy as it sounds, part of me just...knew."

He loosened his hold on her just enough to focus on her bright green eyes. "I don't care if you keep your store where it is." He wanted to make sure she understood he was not trying to cage her. This was her life, *their* life. "I don't care if you stay in your apartment. I mean, I do care, but only because I don't want you away from me for another second."

He gave her a watery smile. It was true, he didn't. And telling her felt undeniably right. Throat choked with emotion, he managed to hold back the tears when he said, "Please don't shut me out. We can move in together later. Or I could move in with you."

A bemused twinkle lit her eyes. "You'd move into my five-hundred-square-foot loft?"

"It has everything I need." He kissed her, savoring the feel of her lips for what felt like the first time in forever. "You." He palmed her tummy. "Our baby."

She grinned, and he thought it might be the most beautiful sight in the world. "But I love your place. The bedroom, the shower," she said, ticking off rooms on her fingers. "Your desk." She lifted one eyebrow and gave him a saucy smile.

"You're teasing me at a time like this?" But he couldn't help smiling back at her. He had a vivid memory of those rooms. They'd made love in each of them during the week when he'd been too blind to see what was right in front of him.

"I remember." He palmed her hair and rubbed the silken strands between his fingers, kissing her when she tipped her chin. "I remember every breath," he said. "Every sound." He kissed her again.

"Do you remember the balcony?" she whispered against his lips.

"I remember you."

She caught his face in her hands, keeping her soft, pink lips just out of reach. "I remember you," she repeated. "We could make a few new memories at my place. You know, before I move in with you."

He was trying really, really hard not to simultaneously laugh and cry. "You're moving in with me," he said as she nestled the tip of her finger in the cleft in his chin.

She raised her eyes to his. "I am."

He grinned, a big, dopey grin that made his cheeks hurt.

"I'm going to marry you, too," she said, draping her arms around his neck. "I'm going to design and sew my own wedding dress, though, so it might be a while."

His chest tightened, his eyes burned. He was so grateful, so blessed for this second chance, that he scrunched his eyes closed and thanked God before he realized he was doing it. Thanked Him for answering the prayer of a drunken moron who had no idea how to talk to the Almighty. Then he thanked his mom. Because he knew she was up in heaven putting a good word in for him. It was the only way that prayer had a chance of making it through.

And when he opened his eyes, he focused on Kimber: his love, his future wife, the mother of his unborn child. She was smiling, *glowing*, and probably had no idea she'd just pulled him out of the deepest depression he'd ever suffered.

"Take as long as you want," he said, his voice tight with emotion. "Take whatever you want."

She stroked the stubble on his face. "I want you."

Pressing her close, he dropped his forehead on hers and uttered the same words he had the night she'd been playing dress-up in his clothes. Only now, they meant more. Now, they meant forever.

"Honey," he said, kissing her softly before speaking the rest in a low, husky baritone. "You can have me."

EPILOGUE

"Push! Push!"

If Angel said "push" one more time, Kimber was going to punch her in her perfect nose. "It's fine," she growled under her breath. Wait...growling? On her wedding day? That wasn't right.

Her soon-to-be sister-in-law gave up on trying to shut the stubborn door to the chapel's small bridal room—more of a glorified closet—and regarded her, an indignant frown tilting her mouth.

"Your brother and I have a baby together, you know. There's nothing he hasn't seen." Especially after the birth of their son, Caleb Henry.

Somehow, Kimber had prepped and planned and sewn, and managed to throw together a respectable wedding while pregnant. At the same time, she had hired additional staff for Hobo Chic, as well as opening a new, upscale store on Michigan Avenue. Of course, she'd had help. Without Landon and Shane on marketing and advertising, and Angel on logo design, Cheeky Chic wouldn't exist.

Kimber had help getting into her wedding dress, too, thanks

to a pit-bull personal trainer she'd hired. After the "I dos" she planned on eating her weight in wedding cake. She'd earned it.

"Well, he hasn't seen you in a wedding dress," Gloria argued from the other side of the room. Her ink-black hair swept along her shoulders, her lips painted in shiny red gloss. Not to mention the healthy rack bursting from the bodice of her purple gown. Kimber's son happily dropped his head into Glo's cleavage and fell asleep whenever he had the chance. Boys and boobs. The fascination started at birth.

Kimber adjusted her top, her own swollen breasts a new challenge.

"She's right," Angel agreed, looping her arm in Gloria's. Her long brown hair was up, revealing gorgeous shoulders.

"You two are so beautiful," Kimber said. "I have to take a picture. Where's my phone?"

A camera on a strap appeared through the gap in the door. "I have one. If it's safe to come in."

"It's safe, Evan, come in." Kimber flicked a look at Gloria, who flashed him a warm smile. But she didn't smile at him like she used to—like she wanted to strip him bare and do torrid things to him. No, the only heat between Glo and Evan now was the blazing trail of his illustration career.

As he slipped through the door, Kimber heard her baby's coo. She clutched her chest and sent a look of longing toward the hallway.

"Oh no, you don't!" Angel ran for the door to block it, but Caleb's soft clucks outside the door effectively broke his aunt's will.

"Come on, Angel." Kimber smiled at her friend as Landon's deep, soothing words spoken to their son lifted on the air. "Please let them in?"

Reluctantly, Angel opened the door. Landon smiled at his sister. "I was about to hand him off to Dad, but he and Lyon are ushering the final guests..." His words faded as his eyes strayed to Kimber. Angel hefted Caleb into her arms as Landon's face pulled into a wide grin.

She stood, brushing out the skirts of her white dress while she studied the man she would marry minutes from now. Landon wore a trim, black tuxedo, black bow tie, and a crisp, white shirt. Classic. Handsome. Sexy as sin.

A *snap* sounded from behind her. Evan, looking fetching in his own rented tux, lowered the camera until it rested on his chest. "You should see your face, man. Priceless."

But Landon ignored his brother, not taking his eyes from Kimber. She felt the tears begin to pool behind her lids. There was too much joy to contain. Too many blessings to count.

He took her hands and looked down at her, his eyes their true color. "Not having second thoughts, I hope."

She shook her head from side to side, the veil on her crown swishing.

Feeling the weight of their audience, he tilted an eyebrow at the crowd in the room, and Angel and Caleb, Gloria, then Evan exited through the door that wouldn't quite close.

Landon's brow raised above the rims of his black glasses. "We have a few minutes." A wicked grin crossed his face. He pulled her close. "Whatever shall we do?"

"You wouldn't," she said with mock alarm. "Not in a church, it's like...illegal or something."

The look in his eyes went from predatory to reverent. "I wouldn't. Next time I make love to you, I'll be your husband."

Husband. The word sent chills over her entire body.

"You look beautiful, by the way."

"Thank you."

"Thank *you*," he said with a twitch of his lips.

"For?"

"Suggesting the list that brought us together. Which reminds me..." He dropped her hands and pulled a folded yellow note from his pocket. A Post-it note.

"It's not," she breathed. She'd never seen it. Had begun to question if it existed outside of her imagination.

"It is." He offered, the note held between two outstretched fingers.

She carefully unfolded the paper, revealing a list written in Landon's neat, block handwriting. Her eyes flitted over the words, a smile finding her face. *The balcony. The desk. The shower.* Then she gasped as she noticed a new number—an eleven, written with a different colored pen.

"The Louvre?" She blinked. Yep, that's what it said.

"Surprise."

No. He couldn't mean... "But we don't have time for a honeymoon," she murmured. "The new store just opened. And Caleb is so young..."

"Ginny can handle the store. And Angel's already begged to take Caleb. If you aren't comfortable leaving him, he can come along. He might make sneaking sex in the Louvre more complicated, but—"

She threw her arms around his neck and crushed her dress into his chest. She didn't care. It was worth it. *He* was worth it. "A honeymoon in Paris," she said, hardly able to believe her good fortune.

Landon huffed a laugh into her ear, straightening her veil as she lowered to her heels. "I'm glad you like my surprise."

"I love it."

"I love you."

She'd never tire of hearing him say it. Never. "I love you. But the Louvre?" She made a face.

"It's a big museum," he said with a rogue lift of one brow. Before his lips caught hers, Angel burst into the room.

"Oh my lord! They're making out!"

Gloria was next. "Don't either of you have any respect for tradition?"

"Don't either of you have any respect for privacy?" Landon asked, his tone bland but teasing.

"It's time." Landon's dad, Mike, poked his head in the room.

Angel's expression morphed into one of comical panic. "Did you ever find your something blue?"

Kimber fisted the folded note in her hand. Plenty of blue ink on this sheet of paper. "I have it." She and Landon shared a secret smile.

Mike and Landon hustled to the front of the church as the music started playing. Angel darted out the door, gesturing to Lyon, who sneaked a wave to Kimber before preceding Angel down the aisle.

Glo positioned herself in front of Kimber, peeking over her shoulder before she went, "What is your something blue, anyway?"

Kimber had tucked the Post-it into her bouquet. "A love letter from Landon," she said. That's what the note was. A list of all the ways he'd sworn to cherish, adore, and love her. And it had brought about the most amazing gift of all. Caleb Henry Downey.

At the front of the church, Kimber released her father's arm and took Landon's. Her future husband smiled down at her, sending her a wink as the preacher started to speak.

During the ceremony, Landon's eyes locked onto the note nestled between the bouquet of carnival roses, and she watched as he bit back a smile.

They were announced husband and wife, and when Landon kissed her, Kimber sank into the warmth of his mouth, realizing in the midst of applause and cheers that their happily ever after may never have begun if she hadn't suggested the list. A list starting with *one* and, as long as she had anything to say about it, not ending any time soon.

Business or pleasure?

Please turn this page for
an excerpt from the first book
in Jessica Lemmon's
Love in the Balance series,

Tempting the Billionaire.

CHAPTER ONE

Oscillating red, green, and blue lights sliced through the smoke-filled club. Men and women cluttered the floor, their arms pumping in time with the throbbing speakers as an unseen fog machine muddied the air.

Shane August resisted the urge to press his fingertips into his eyelids and stave off the headache that'd begun forming there an hour ago.

Tonight marked the end of a grueling six-day workweek, one he would have preferred to end in his home gym, or in the company of a glass of red wine. He frowned at the bottle of light beer in his hand. Six dollars. That was fifty cents an ounce.

The sound of laughter pulled his attention from the overpriced brew, and he found a pair of girls sidling by his table. They offered twin grins and waved in tandem, hips swaying as they strode by.

"Damn," Aiden muttered over his shoulder. "I should have worn a suit."

Shane angled a glance at his cousin's T-shirt and jeans. "Do you even *own* a suit?"

"Shut up."

Shane suppressed a budding smile and tipped his beer bottle to his lips. It was Aiden who'd dragged him here tonight. Shane could give him a hard time, but Aiden was here to forget about his ex-wife, and she'd given him a hard enough time for both of them.

"This is where you're making your foray into the dating world?" Shane asked, glancing around the room at the bevy of flesh peeking out from beneath skintight skirts and shorts.

"Seemed like a good place to pick up chicks," Aiden answered with a roll of one shoulder.

Shane tamped down another smile. Aiden was recently divorced, though *finally* might be a better term. Two years of wedded bliss had been anything but, thanks to Harmony's wandering eye. Shane couldn't blame Aiden for exercising a bit of freedom. God knows, if Shane were in his shoes, he'd have bailed a long time ago. This time when Harmony left, she'd followed her sucker-punch with a TKO: The man she left Aiden for was his—now *former*—best friend. At first Aiden had been withdrawn, then angry. Tonight he appeared to be masking his emotions beneath a cloak of overconfidence.

"Right," Shane muttered. "Chicks."

"Well, excuse me, Mr. Moneybags." Aiden leaned one arm on the high-top table and faced him. "Women may throw themselves at you like live grenades, but the rest of us commoners have to come out to the trenches and hunt."

Shane gave him a dubious look, in part for the sloppily mixed metaphor, but mostly because dodging incoming women didn't exactly describe his lackluster love life. If he'd learned anything from his last girlfriend, it was how to spot a girl who wanted to take a dip in his cash pool.

He only had himself to blame, he supposed. He was accustomed to solving problems with money. Problem-free living just happened to be at the top of his priority list. Unfortunately, relationships didn't file away neatly into manila folders, weren't able to be delegated in afternoon conference meetings. Relationships were complicated, messy. Time-consuming.

No, thanks.

"I can pick up a girl in a club," Shane found himself arguing. It'd been a while, but he never was one to shy away from a challenge. Self-made men didn't shrink in the face of adversity.

Aiden laughed and clapped him on the shoulder. "Don't embarrass yourself."

Shane straightened and pushed the beer bottle aside. "Wanna bet?"

"With you?" Aiden lifted a thick blond eyebrow. "Forget it! You wipe your ass with fifties."

"Hundreds," Shane corrected, earning a hearty chuckle.

"Then again," Aiden said after finishing off his bottle, "I wouldn't mind seeing you in action, learn what not to do now that I'm single again. Find a cute girl and I'll be your wingman." Before Shane could respond, Aiden elbowed him. "Except for her."

Shane followed his cousin's pointing finger to the bar, where a woman dabbed at her eyes with a napkin. She looked so delicate sitting there, folded over in her chair, an array of brown curls concealing part of her face.

"Crying chicks either have too much baggage, or they're wasted."

Says Aiden Downey, dating guru.

"Drunk can be good," he continued, "but by the time you get close enough to find out, it's too late."

Shane frowned. He didn't like being told what to do. Or what not to. He wasn't sure if that's what made him decide to approach her, or if he'd decided the second Aiden pointed her out. He felt his lips pull into a deeper frown. He shouldn't be considering it at all.

A cocktail waitress stopped at their table. Shane waved off the offer of another, his eyes rooted on the crying girl at the bar. She looked as out of place in this crowd as he felt, dressed unassumingly in jeans and a black top, her brown hair a curly crown that stopped at her jawline. In the flashy crowd, she could have been dismissed as plain...but she wasn't plain. She was pretty.

He watched as she brushed a lock from her damp face as her shoulders rose and fell. The pile of crumpled napkins next to her paired with the far-off look in her eyes suggested she was barely keeping it together. Grief radiated off of her in waves Shane swore he could feel from where he sat. Witnessing her pain made his gut clench. Probably because somewhere deep inside, he could relate.

Aiden said something about a girl on the dance floor, and Shane flicked him an irritated glance before his eyes tracked back to the girl at the bar. She sipped her drink and offered the bartender a tight nod of thanks as he placed a stack of fresh napkins in front of her.

Shane felt an inexplicable, almost gravitational pull toward her, his feet urging him forward even as his brain raised one argument after another. Part of him wanted to help, though if she wanted to have a heart-to-heart, she'd be better off talking to Aiden. But if she needed advice or a solution to a tangible problem, well, that he could handle.

He glanced around the room at the predatory males lurking in every corner and wondered again why she was here. If he did approach her, an idea becoming more compelling by the moment, she'd likely shoot him down before he said a single word. So why was he mentally mapping a path to her chair? He pressed his lips together in thought. Because there was a good chance he could erase the despair from her face, a prospect he found more appealing than anything else.

"Okay, her friend is hot, I'll give you that," Aiden piped up.

Shane blinked before snapping his eyes to the brunette's left. Her "hot friend," as Aiden so eloquently put it, showcased her assets in a scandalously short skirt and backless silver top. He'd admit she was hard to miss. Yet Shane hadn't noticed her until Aiden pointed her out. His eyes trailed back to the brunette.

"Okay," Aiden said on a sigh of resignation. "Because I so desperately want to see this, I'm going to take a bullet for you. I'll distract the crier. You hit on the blonde." That said, he stood up and headed toward the bar...to flirt with the *wrong girl*.

The platitude of only having one chance to make a first impression flitted through Shane's head. He called Aiden's name, but his shout was lost under the music blasting at near-ear-bleeding decibels. Aiden may be younger and less experienced, but he also had an undeniable charm girls didn't often turn down. If the brunette spotted his cousin first, she wouldn't so much as look at Shane. He abandoned his beer, doing a neat jog across the room and reaching Aiden just as he was moving in to tap the brunette's shoulder.

"My cousin thought he recognized you," Shane blurted to the blonde, grabbing Aiden by the arm and spinning him in her direction.

The blonde surveyed Aiden with lazy disinterest. "I don't think so."

Aiden lifted his eyebrows to ask, *What the hell are you doing?*

Rather than explain, Shane clapped both palms on Aiden's shoulders and shoved him closer to the blonde. "His sister's in the art business." It was a terrible segue if the expression on Aiden's face was anything to go by, but it was the first thing that popped into Shane's head.

The music changed abruptly, slowing into a rhythmic techno-pop remix that had dancers slowing down and pairing up. Aiden slipped into an easy, confident smile. "Wanna dance?" he asked the blonde.

The moment the question was out of his mouth, the scratches and hissing of snare drums shifted into the melodic chimes of the tired and all-too-familiar line dance, "The Electric Slide."

Aiden winced.

Shane coughed to cover a laugh. "He's a great dancer," he said to the blonde.

Aiden shot his elbow into Shane's ribs but recovered his smile a second later. Turning to the blonde, he said, "He's right, I am," then offered his hand.

The blonde glanced at his palm, then leaned past Shane to talk to her friend. "You gonna be okay here?" she called over the music.

The brunette flicked a look from her friend to Shane. The moment he locked on to her bright blue eyes, his heart galloped to life, picking up speed as if running for an invisible finish line. Her eyes left his as she addressed her friend. "Fine."

It wasn't the most wholehearted endorsement, but at least she'd agreed to stay.

Aiden and the blonde made their way to the dance floor, and Shane gave his collar a sharp tug and straightened his suit jacket before turning toward the brunette. She examined him, almost warily, her lids heavy over earnest blue eyes. He'd seen that kind of soul-rendering sadness before, a long time ago. Staring back at him from his bathroom mirror.

"That was my cousin, Aiden." He bumbled to fill the dead air between them. "He wanted to meet your friend."

"Figures," the brunette said, barely audible over the music.

He ignored the whistling sound of their conversation plummeting to its imminent death. "She seems nice. Aiden can be kind of an ass around nice girls," he added, leaning in so she could hear him.

She rewarded him with a tentative upward curve of her lips, the top capping a plumper bottom lip that looked good enough to eat. He offered a small smile of his own, perplexed by the direction of his thoughts. When was the last time he'd been thrown this off-kilter by a woman? Let alone one he'd just met? She shifted in her seat to face him, and a warm scent lifted off her skin—vanilla and nutmeg, if he wasn't mistaken. He gripped the back of the chair in front of him and swallowed instinctively. Damn. She *smelled* good enough to eat.

She dipped her head, fiddled with the strap of her handbag, and Shane realized he was staring.

"Shane," he said, offering his hand.

She looked at it a beat before taking it. "Crickitt."

"Like the bug?" He flinched. *Smooth.*

"Thanks for that." She offered a mordant smile.

Evidently he was rustier at this than he'd thought. "Sorry." Best get to the point. "Is there something you need? Something I can get you?"

Her eyes went to the full drink in front of her. "I've had plenty, but thanks. Anyway, I'm about to leave."

"I'm on my way out. Can I drop you somewhere?"

She eyed him cautiously.

Okay. Perhaps offering her a ride was a bit forward and, from her perspective, dangerous.

"No, thank you," she said, turning her body away from his as she reached for her drink.

Great. He was creepy club guy.

He leaned on the bar between the blonde's abandoned chair and Crickitt. Lowering his voice, he said, "I think I'm doing this all wrong. To tell the truth, I saw you crying and I wondered if I could do anything to help. I'd...like to help. If you'll let me."

She turned to him, her eyes softening into what might have been gratitude, before a harder glint returned. Tossing her head, she met his eye. "Help? Sure. Know anyone who'd like to hire a previously self-employed person for a position for which she has little to no experience?"

He had to smile at her pluck...and his good fortune. Crickitt's problem may be one he could help with after all. "Depends," he answered, watching her eyebrows give the slightest lift. He leaned an elbow on the bar. "In what salary range?"

* * *

Crickitt scanned the well-dressed man in front of her. He wore a streamlined charcoal suit and crisp, white dress shirt. No tie, but she'd bet one had been looped around his neck earlier. She allowed her gaze to trickle to his open collar, lingering over the column of his tanned neck before averting her eyes. What would he say if she blurted out the figure dancing around her head?

Two hundred fifty thousand a year? Oh, sure, I know lots of people who pay out six figures for a new hire.

Well, he asked.

"Six figures," she said.

He laughed.

That's what she thought. If this Shane guy were in a position to offer that kind of income, would he really be in a club named Lace and hitting on a girl like her? Why hadn't he hit on someone else? Someone without a runny nose and red-rimmed eyes. Someone like Sadie. But he'd rerouted his friend to talk to Sadie. Why had he done that? She smoothed her hair, considering.

Maybe you're an easy target.

He saw her crying and wanted to help? It wasn't the worst pickup line in the world, but it was close.

Crickitt instinctively slid her pinky against her ring finger to straighten her wedding band but only felt the rub of skin on skin. For nine years it had sat at home on her left hand. She used to think of it as a comforting weight, but since Ronald had left, it'd become a reminder of the now obvious warning signs she'd overlooked. The way he'd pulled away from her both physically and emotionally. The humiliation of scurrying after him, attempting to win his affections even after it was too late. She lifted her shoulders under her ears, wishing she could hide from the recurring memory, the embarrassment. Fresh tears burned the backs of her eyes before she remembered she had a captive audience. She squeezed her eyes closed, willing the helter-skelter emotions to go away.

When she opened them, she saw Shane had backed away some, either to give the semblance of privacy or because he feared she would burst into tears and blow her nose on his expensive jacket. She could choke Sadie for bringing her out tonight.

Come to the club, Sadie had said. *It'll get your mind off of things*, she'd insisted. But it hadn't. Even when faced with a very good-looking, potentially helpful man, she was wallowing in self-doubt and recrimination. She could've done that at home.

"What experience do you have, Crickitt?" Shane asked, interrupting her thoughts.

She tipped her chin up at him. Was he serious? His half smile was either sarcastic or genuinely curious. Hard to tell. The temptation was there to dismiss him as just another jerk in a club, but she couldn't. There was an undeniable warmth in his dark eyes, a certain kindness in the way he leaned toward her when he talked, like he didn't want to intimidate her.

Maybe that's why she told him the truth.

"I'm great with people," she answered.

"And scheduling?"

She considered telling him about the twenty in-home shows she'd held each and every month for the last seven years, but wasn't sure he wouldn't get the wrong idea about exactly what kind of *in-home shows* she'd be referring to.

"Absolutely."

"Prioritizing?"

Crickitt almost laughed. Prioritizing was a necessity in her business. She'd been responsible for mentoring and training others, as well as maintaining her personal sales and team. It'd taken her a while to master the art of putting her personal business first, but she'd done it. If she focused too much on others, her numbers soon started circling the drain, and that wasn't good for any of them.

"Definitely," she answered, pausing to consider the fire burning in her belly. How long had it been since she'd talked about her career with confidence? Too long, she realized. By now, her ex-husband would have cut her off midsentence to change the subject.

But Shane's posture was open, receptive, and he faced her, his eyebrows raised as if anticipating what she might say next. So she continued. "I, um, I was responsible for a team of twenty-five salespeople while overseeing ten managers with teams of their own," she finished.

She almost cringed at the calloused description. Those *teams* and *managers* were more like family than co-workers. They'd slap her silly if they ever heard her referring to them with corporate lingo. But if she had to guess, Shane was a corporate man and Crickitt doubted he'd know the first thing about direct sales.

"You sound overqualified," he said.

"That's what I...wait, did you just say *over*qualified?"

Crickitt stammered. She blinked up at him, shocked. She'd fully expected him to tell her to peddle her questionable work background elsewhere.

Shane reached into his pocket and offered a business card between two outstretched fingers. "Even so, I'd like to talk to you in more detail. Are you available for an interview on Monday?"

Crickitt stared at the card like it was a trick buzzer.

"I'm serious." He dropped the card on the bar. "This isn't typically how I find employees, but"—he shrugged—"I need a personal assistant. And someone with your background and experience is hard to come by."

She blinked at him again. This had to be some elaborate scheme to get her to bed, right? Isn't that what Sadie told her to expect from the men in these places?

"How about one o'clock, Monday afternoon? I have meetings in the morning, but I should be done by then. If the job's not a good fit, at least you looked into it."

Well. The only interview she'd managed to arrange since her self-inflicted unemployment was for a thirty-thousand-dollar salary and involved her working in a government office. And she'd lost that job to a kid ten years her junior. She'd be stupid to pass up the opportunity for an interview with this man. Even though part of her couldn't imagine working for someone as put together as Shane. But he didn't seem demanding, or overly confident, just...nice.

Which brought about another niggling thought. This was too easy. And if she'd learned a lesson from recent events, wasn't it to be cautious when things were going suspiciously well? And this, she thought, glancing in his direction again, was going a little *too* well.

"What do you say?" he asked.

Then again, as her dwindling savings account constantly reminded her, she needed to find some sort of viable income.

And soon. If the interview turned out to be a sham, the experience would still be worthwhile, she thought with knee-jerk optimism.

"One o'clock," she heard herself say.

Shane extended his hand and she shook it, ignoring how seamlessly her palm fit against his and the warmth radiating up her arm even after he'd pulled away. He excused himself and made his way to the door. Crickitt watched his every long-legged step, musing how he was taller than Ronald and walked with infinitely more confidence.

A tall, confident man had approached *her*. And, okay, it may have been because she looked needy, but she couldn't keep from being flattered that Shane had taken it upon himself to talk to her.

Lifting the business card between her thumb and fingers, she studied the front. The top read, AUGUST INDUSTRIES, LEADER IN BUSINESS STRATEGIES. No name on the card, just an address and a phone number. She flipped it over. Blank.

Sadie returned as Crickitt hopped off her bar stool.

"Where're you going?" Sadie asked with a breathless smile. Shane's cousin stood at Sadie's side, a matching grin on his tanned face. Crickitt regarded his surfer-dude style skeptically. Cute. A departure from Sadie's usual type, but cute.

Of course, there was a good chance Sadie would never see Aiden again given her first-date-only rule. Crickitt looked down at the business card again, chewing her lip. Maybe it wasn't a good idea to see Shane again, either. She already felt as if she'd revealed too much about herself in their short conversation. Wasn't it too soon for her to trust a man after the one she'd trusted implicitly had left her behind?

"What's with the card? Did you get a date?" Sadie asked.

"No." She laughed, her temporarily reclaimed confidence ebbing. She considered crumpling the card in her hand, dropping it onto the bar. The message would get back to Shane via his cousin, she was sure. Then she wouldn't have to worry about standing him up or canceling the interview.

Chicken.

Despite the very tempting option to stay in her comfort zone, Crickitt decided maybe it was time to take a risk. Even a small one.

"Better," she told Sadie, snapping up her purse. "A job."

Sadie Howard never dates a guy
more than once—but fate has other
plans for her when it comes to Aiden
Downey, the one who got away...

Please turn this page for an excerpt
from book 2 in the Love in the
Balance series,

Hard to Handle.

CHAPTER ONE

Aiden Downey spun his beer by its neck, the now warm contents sloshing against the sides of the bottle. He'd been watching Sadie from his chair at the back of the reception tent for the better part of thirty minutes, unable to shake the guilt swamping him.

Shane and Crickitt, God bless them, had been so careful when they asked Aiden and Sadie to be the only two members of the wedding party. But if there was one thing he and Sadie could agree on, it was doing right by their friends. They'd put aside their differences for the big day and had managed to be cordial, though not sociable, until the start of the reception.

That's when Aiden had bumbled his way through a long-overdue apology. While he'd never apologize for prioritizing his mother during her fight with cancer, he realized too late it was a mistake to allow his ex-wife back into his life. He meant well when he decided to keep the divorce quiet, but Aiden should have told his mother before she died. Now she'd never know the truth, never get to meet Sadie. A regret he'd have to live with.

Sadie's buoyant giggle, a fake one if Aiden had to guess, lifted onto the air. He turned to see her toss her head back, blonde curls cascading down her bare back as she gripped Crickitt's younger brother's arm. Garrett, who had been Krazy-Glued to Sadie's side the entire reception, grinned down at her, clearly smitten. Aiden dragged his gaze from her mane of soft golden waves to her dress, a pink confection hugging her every amazing, petite curve. He couldn't blame the kid for staring at her intently. Sadie was beautiful.

"Rough," he heard Shane say as he pulled out the chair next to him and sat, beer bottle in hand.

His cousin looked relaxed with his white tuxedo shirt unbuttoned and the sleeves cuffed at the elbows. He'd taken off the tie he'd worn earlier, a sight that almost made Aiden laugh. Before Shane met Crickitt, Aiden would've bet Shane slept wearing a tie. Crickitt had vanquished Shane's inner workaholic and in return, Shane had stepped up to become the man Crickitt needed.

Aiden had had a similar opportunity with Sadie. It was a test he'd failed spectacularly. "She has a right to be mad," he said, tilting his beer bottle again.

"You were in a difficult situation," Shane said magnanimously.

Maybe so, but after his mother succumbed to the cancer riddling her body, after he'd grieved and moaned and helped his father plan the funeral, Aiden had seen things more clearly. Remembering the way he'd shut Sadie out of his life, rejected her in the worst possible way, stung like alcohol to a fresh cut. He should have brought her in, no matter how bad the circumstances. His mother would have accepted her.

His mother would have loved her.

"If I could go back, I'd tell Mom the truth." He swallowed thickly. "She deserved the truth."

"Don't do that, man." Shane clapped him on the shoulder.

"You did what you believed was best. It was never going to be an easy situation."

True, but he'd taken an already hard situation and complicated the hell out of it. At his mother's diagnosis, Aiden went into Responsibility Mode. With his sister in Tennessee, a brother in Chicago, his other brother in Columbus, and his father simultaneously grieving and working, everything had fallen on Aiden.

When his mother said she wanted to move to Oregon to seek alternative treatments, Aiden rearranged his entire life and helped her do just that. Later, his siblings had argued with him that they would have helped if they'd known about any of it. Aiden had known in his gut there wasn't enough time to pull everyone together for a powwow.

"I appreciate you being here," Shane said.

Aiden snapped out of his reverie. "Oh man, I'm sorry. I'm being a jerk on your big day." He straightened in his chair, ashamed to have let melancholy overshadow his happiness for Shane and Crickitt.

Speaking of, here she came, poured into a slim white wedding dress, fabric flowers sewn into the flowing train. She grinned at Shane, her face full of love, her blue eyes shining. When she flicked a look over to Aiden, he promptly slapped a smile onto his face.

"You look amazing, C," he told her.

Crickitt's grin widened. "Thank you."

"And this reception"—he blew out a breath for effect—"the lights"—he gestured to the hundreds of strands draped inside the tent—"the flowers, the band." The three-piece band included a formerly famous singer a decade past his heyday, but the guy still had it.

Crickitt rested a hand on her husband's shoulder. "Shane insisted on all this. I wanted something simple. When he suggested getting married in a tent in Tennessee...I didn't expect *this*." She waved a hand around the interior of the tent: the shining wooden dance floor, the thick swaths of mosquito netting covering every entrance, the tall, narrow air conditioners positioned at each corner to keep the guests cool and comfortable during the warm June evening.

She smiled down at Shane. "But it is pretty great."

"*You're* pretty great," Shane said, tugging her into his lap and kissing her bare shoulder. The wedding photographer swooped in, capturing the picture for posterity, a good one by the looks of it.

Aiden picked the moment to excuse himself for a refill.

Or maybe two.

* * *

Sadie caught movement out of the corner of her eye and swept her attention away from Crickitt's attentive brother to see Aiden tracking his way across the tent in that easygoing lope of his.

She'd never seen him in a suit until she preceded Crickitt down the aisle. He didn't wear the tie he'd worn earlier, picked to match her bridesmaid's dress. She knew the intricate design by heart. She'd traced the tiny pink and silver paisley design, all the while trying not to allow the sorrow in his voice to crack through her defenses. He'd not only broken her heart last summer with a phone call, he'd broken her will, demolished her sense of true north. She couldn't forgive him—or herself—for allowing it to happen.

She'd cut the conversation short tonight, recalling the promise she'd made to never show her vulnerability to this man again, and stalked away from him as fast as her sparkly pink heels would carry her.

Garrett turned his attention to someone else standing in their little circle, and Sadie took the opportunity to watch

Aiden. Tailored black pants hugged his impressive thighs and led up to a tucked white shirt, open at the collar and showing enough of his tanned neck to be distracting.

I made a mistake last summer, Sadie. One I'll regret always.

A pang of guilt stabbed her. She hadn't expected the flood of emotion that crashed into her when she saw him for the first time in nearly a year. She'd planned to tell him she was sorry he lost his mother. And she was. She may have never met the woman, but she saw her once. And she saw the connection between mother and son as clearly as she saw Aiden now.

Sadie kept up with Aiden's mother's illness via updates from Crickitt. The decision not to go to the funeral went without saying, but Sadie hadn't been able to stop herself from sending an anonymous bouquet to the funeral home. Losing a parent was one of the worst things in the world, she knew.

Sadie straightened her spine, wiggled her heel into the floor, and reminded herself *again* not to dwell on her own heartbreak. Her best friend's wedding wasn't the place to dig up the past. Even so, she'd spent most of the day desperately trying to tamp down one emotion after the other. Thank goodness girls were supposed to cry at weddings.

Which is why she'd been avoiding him. Aiden had a knack for seeing right through her. That was the clincher. He *knew* her. Picked her apart with those clairvoyant sea green eyes of his, and left her defenseless. And being called out by Aiden Downey was at the tippy-top of her "To Don't" list.

Aiden pulled a hand through his thick hair, the length of it landing between his shoulder blades. Sadie recalled the texture of it as if she'd run her fingers through it yesterday. She hated that.

Damn muscle memory.

Crickitt's mother, Chandra, approached the bar and gave Aiden a plump hug. Aiden smiled down at her, but Sadie saw the sadness behind it, and for a split second, it made her heart hurt. She'd gotten good at reading him, too. Knowing that reminded her of just how close she'd been to losing her heart to him...until a phone call annihilated everything between them.

Whether it was the invisible cord of awareness strung between them or coincidence, Sadie wasn't sure, but Aiden chose that moment to look in her direction. His smile faltered, the dimple on his left cheek fading before he flicked his eyes away.

Sadie used to love the way he shook her up. From across a room. With nothing more than a look. But now her heart raced for a far different reason. One she refused to name. She frowned down at her empty champagne flute. She was going to need more alcohol if she hoped to toughen her hide. This exposed vulnerability simply wasn't going to cut it.

"Refill?" Garrett asked, gesturing to her empty glass.

"Yes," she said, grateful for his doting. She handed it over. "Keep 'em coming."

* * *

Aiden bid the last lingering guests farewell, watching as a sophisticated older couple by the name of Townsend walked out to the driveway.

Shane and Crickitt August had made their exit hours ago, amidst cheers and handfuls of heart-shaped biodegradable confetti. Since he was staying at Shane and Crickitt's cabin for the weekend, Aiden was left in charge of supervising the caterer, breaking down the tent, and clearing away the remains of the celebration.

"Do you need me to get you to a hotel, Sadie?"

Aiden turned in the direction of the slightly exasperated voice to find Garrett gesturing with his hands. Sadie was the picture of stubbornness, her arms folded over her ample breasts, her bottom lip jutting out. Aiden allowed himself a small, private smile.

"You're in no condition to drive," Garrett said. He reached out to palm her arm and Sadie expertly swung out of reach.

Aiden felt kind of bad for the kid. Twenty-two-year-old Garrett Day was far too inexperienced to handle a woman of Sadie's magnitude on his best day, and even then...

"There a problem?" Aiden approached with his hands in his pockets, trying to broadcast that he didn't care if Garrett was trying to take Sadie with him when he left. He supposed he *shouldn't* care. Aiden had no interest in getting into a pissing match with him, but if Garrett tried to take Sadie when she didn't want to go, he'd have hell to pay. C's little brother or not.

Garrett gave Aiden an assessing glance before answering. "Just making sure Sadie has a ride tonight."

"I don't need a ride. I'm staying here," she practically spat.

Aiden rocked back on his heels. She was staying at the cabin? Hell's bells. What were Crickitt and Shane up to?

"I'll make sure she gets inside okay," Aiden said.

"I'll get *myself* inside, thank you very much." Sadie tipped her head and propped her hands on her nipped waist. Aiden knew he shouldn't allow his eyes to chase the line of her slender neck to the bodice of her dress. And he shouldn't linger at the point where her breasts met in shadowed cleavage, but he did it anyway. Good thing he was watching her. A moment later, she took a step toward the cabin and wobbled in her dangerously tall heels.

Both men rushed forward to steady her. Aiden got there first. A victory. He gripped her waist and Sadie's hand came up to clutch the front of his shirt. He desperately tried to ignore the warmth spreading across his chest, the feel of her against him. Even though the circumstances were all wrong, the timing completely off, there was no denying this gorgeous woman belonged in his arms. Sadie didn't let go, and Aiden didn't think he could unless someone physically pried his hands off her.

He turned his attention to Garrett. "You can head out. I have her." Aiden held his eye. Dared him to argue. Garrett frowned, and for a second Aiden thought he might, but then Crickitt's mother, queen of impeccable timing, intruded.

"Garrett, we have the car. Is Sadie... Oh! Aiden, perfect." She sent him an approving smile. "Do you need my help?"

"No, Mrs. D, I'll make sure she's all right."

She made a *tsk*ing sound. "Poor dear had an entire magnum of champagne."

Garrett didn't look as if he wanted to leave but did anyway, walking his mother out of the tent. Maybe he'd come to the conclusion Sadie was more than he could handle after all.

Aiden guided Sadie to the house as she teetered on those pink stilts she called shoes. He had fond memories of her shoes. Fond because the added inches brought her within kissable reach. His heart gave an echoing ache. "You should take those off," he said, stopping short of offering to carry her. He'd lifted her in his arms once before. One year ago. Felt more like a dozen.

"I'm fine," she said, tipping again. Her argument was garbled but genuine.

"I assume your things are already in your room?" He tucked her against him as they stepped inside the cabin, then shut the door behind them. He also assumed their matchmaking friends had put them both upstairs. Since there were only two bedrooms on this floor, and since he was staying in the master on the right, he assumed Sadie's was to the left.

She mumbled something and he moved to settle her into the recliner.

"No," she protested, locking her arms around his neck. "I have to get out of this stupid dress." She gazed up at him, her brown eyes slightly glassy.

Aiden swallowed thickly, taking in all that blonde hair falling in waves around her heart-shaped face. She always was beautiful. And those lips. She licked her bottom one and he was half-tempted to lean in for a taste.

She's drunk, you idiot.

She started toward his room and he caught her hips and steered her away. "Not in there."

She spun on him, narrowing her eyes. "Why not?"

Lie. But he couldn't lie to Sadie. He never could. Even when it would have benefited him the most. "Because my stuff's in there," he mumbled.

She blinked at him and he readied for a fight. It didn't come. "Fine. I'm too tired to argue. And I have to get this off." She moved one hand to the bodice of her dress and wiggled it back and forth, sending her breasts jiggling inside the fitted top.

Aiden stared. Actually *stared.* Like when he'd found his older brother's stash of *Playboys* for the first time. No one filled out their clothes like Sadie.

She cleared her throat and he jerked his eyes north. "Help me?"

Crap.

He was being tested, here, in the cruelest way. She was asking him to undress her? Exposing herself to him, and Aiden to her naked body? He couldn't do it while sporting a woody or she'd cut him off at the knees. Drunk or not.

Aiden mentally tied a noose around his mojo. And pulled. "Sure thing."

He followed her into the room and she dropped on the

bed, falling back with an *oomph!* She toed at her shoes until they hit the floor. Aiden retrieved them, dangerous-looking spikes covered with winking rhinestones. How women walked in these things, he'd never know. Sadie told him once that because of her diminutive size she preferred the tallest shoes. He'd concurred at the time. Without them, Sadie only came to the middle of his chest. He was in favor of any contraption if it meant bringing her lips closer to his.

And now he was thinking of kissing her. Again.

He shook his head to wipe away the memories of the intense kisses they'd shared in the past: the sound of her truncated breaths against his ear, the feel of her fingernails spearing into his hair. He tracked back to the bed, jaw set, brain focused squarely on the Stay Puft Marshmallow Man. He pulled back the covers intending to bury the tempting vision of her breasts bursting from the top of her dress, but she rolled onto her side before he could.

"Unzip," Sadie demanded, her manicured nails fumbling at the back of her dress. When he hesitated, Sadie shot him a displeased look over her shoulder, crinkling her heavily made-up eyes at him.

Even sexier when she's angry, he thought with a groan.

Aiden reached for the zipper, ignoring his impulse to go slowly, listen to every snick as he examined all of her smooth, porcelain flesh beneath the bridesmaid's dress. It'd been too long since he'd been allowed to touch this woman. Too. Effing. Long. The zipper parted to reveal what appeared to be a sleeveless white straitjacket with about a hundred hooks.

"Now this." She did a backward point.

Aiden paused. The thing looked as penetrable as Fort Knox. "Can't you sleep in it?"

"Just do it. Nothing you haven't seen before." She turned her head at an awkward angle so she could look at him. A little pleat formed on her brow as if she was reconsidering. "I mean, not me, but other girls." She flopped her head onto the pillow with a *whump*.

Thanks for the reminder, Aiden thought tersely.

He and Sadie hadn't had a chance to get that far. Okay, that wasn't true. They'd had plenty of chances. Each time they saw one another, the dates had lasted at least six or seven hours. Or overnight. They couldn't seem to escape one another, or stop talking, or stop *touching*. She'd seen him stripped down to his briefs, and he'd seen her bare legs poking out of one of his T-shirts, but they'd always stopped short of going further. Both of them had been hurt before and neither of them was anxious to repeat their painful pasts.

So, yes, Sadie was right. He hadn't technically *seen* her naked, but he had felt enough of her bare flesh under his palms to give his imagination a hell of a show.

He scooted the bedside lamp closer to investigate the contraption she'd bound herself in. He could dismantle a car; surely he could handle this. Turns out he had to make the thing tighter before the hooks would release. Each time, Sadie grunted, until he got halfway down her back and she blew out a *whooshing* breath. He made quick work of the rest.

"Thank God." She sat up, one hand covering the sagging top of her gown, withdrew the corset, and dropped it unceremoniously to the floor. "I owe you, Downey. Now help me out of this dress and go away."

He swallowed thickly, recognizing the painful familiarity of the moment. The night she was on his couch and slipped her bra out from underneath her tank top. He'd clutched her to him, and she'd panted against his neck as her nipples abraded his bare chest. It was then she'd hesitated. Wordlessly, but he'd felt the slightest bit of tension creep into her shoulders. He backed off, but didn't let her go, tucking her into bed against him and sleeping next to her through the night.

That was his Sadie. Minx on the outside, lamb on the inside. Seeing this side of her again, being reminded of what they'd had—what he'd thrown away...

Man. It hurt.

"I'm too tipsy to do it myself," she growled. Despite her efforts to keep it out, vulnerability leaked into her voice. Aiden's weakness was her trust in him; her showing who she really was. He gripped her elbows and helped her to her feet, stopping short of crushing her lips with his and admitting he was wrong a hundred ways from Sunday.

He steadied her elbows as she wiggled out of the dress with a perfunctory "No looking." He obeyed, keeping his eyes focused out the bedroom window. But with the bedside lamp on, he couldn't see out the window, only himself reflected in the pane, and Sadie's thong panties as she stepped out of the dress. He shut his eyes and reminded his johnson to remain *at ease*.

"Aiden."

"Yes."

"I need you to get my pajamas for me."

"Okay."

"No peeking while I crawl into bed."

This was the side of Sadie people *didn't* see. Her modest side. Everyone assumed they knew her—with her litany of first dates and explosive personality, Sadie was mistaken as confident and outgoing. Which she was, both of those things. She was also modest, careful. Fragile. And despite the increasing pressure in his pants, Aiden vowed to honor her request.

"Okay," he muttered.

"Promise," she commanded, brushing against his arm as she turned. Something very soft grazed his skin and he tried to convince himself it wasn't what he thought it was.

"Promise," he said through clenched teeth.

When he heard the wisp of sheets he opened his eyes. Sadie wore the comforter over her breasts and pointed with one arm. "The big suitcase," she said around a yawn.

The big suitcase also had a big lock. The key, he assumed, was in her purse. He approached The Purse, which was about the size of a small country, and stopped short. Going through a woman's purse was a lot like sticking a hand in the garbage disposal. While he was pretty sure he'd be able to get what he needed out of it, there was the risk of losing a digit while rooting around in there.

He glanced back at Sadie, who had lain back and shut her eyes. Her breathing was already steady and deep. Making a snap decision, he walked to his room and dug a T-shirt out of his duffel bag. When he returned, he wondered if it was even worth it to wake her. But then he thought of her waking in only her panties—a thought that had him swallowing a lump of lust—and worried she might think something had happened tonight. He regarded the gray shirt in his hand. Not that she'd be thrilled about waking in one of his tees. Again.

Was that night on auto-repeat?

Ignoring the overwhelming sense of déjà vu, he stretched the neck and slipped the shirt over her sprayed hair, feeding first one arm into a sleeve followed by the other. Now the tricky part. Looking up at the ceiling, he palmed her back and pulled her toward him. But as he started to tug the shirt down, Sadie's arms clamped around his neck, her breasts smashing against his cardboard dress shirt.

A sound emitted from his throat he was pretty sure was a growl.

"I loved you," Sadie said, her eyes wide and earnest. "And you blew it." That said, she tugged the shirt to her waist, flopped onto one side, and pulled the covers over her head.

Aiden's shoulders slumped, heavy from the weight of her admission. She loved him. Or at least she used to. He'd had his suspicions but had never known. Would it have changed how he ended things between them? Would he have confessed the same?

Of course he would've.

And you blew it.

He had. Completely effing stepped in it.

And now it was too late. Sadie probably never would have told him what she just had if she hadn't been marinating in champagne tonight. As much as he'd love to deny hearing her say it, there was a part of him glad to know the truth. The masochistic part of him, apparently. He'd earned the pain fair and square, but Sadie... Sadie had come out the other side. She was okay now, or would be after a couple of Advil in the morning. Her journey with him in it had reached an end. Now he was a bystander and couldn't allow himself to be anything more. Asking her to take another chance on him was wrong. Maybe more wrong than the way he'd ended things with her last year.

After several seconds, he finally stood from the edge of the bed, as heavy as if he'd strapped a pair of anvils onto his back. At the door, he hesitated over the switch, watching her take a few deep breaths. One night, a long, long time ago, he'd been right next to her, feeling as hopeful about their future as he felt devastated now.

If only time were reversible. If only he knew then what he knew now.

If only.

Most useless two words ever.

* * *

Stupid champagne.

Sadie downed the last sip of her coffee and dragged her suitcase to the car. She hauled it ungracefully into her trunk and vowed to call Crickitt and give her what-for for pulling the Aiden-and-Sadie-slumber-party bit.

Only she couldn't. Because Crickitt and Shane were on their honeymoon having the blissful, married time of their lives. She stalked back into the house, doing a once-over to make sure she hadn't left anything behind. That's when she spotted Aiden's T-shirt.

When she'd woken up wearing it, she'd tossed it aside and run around packing with the one single goal: get the hell out of the cabin before he woke up and offered breakfast. The morning was already beginning to smack of the morning they'd spent together a year ago—a morning she wouldn't dare repeat.

She held the soft cotton between her fingers, recalling the night he'd tenderly dressed her and curled up next to her to sleep. That morning she'd woken to his shirtless back, traced the length of the scar with her fingers, and come to the terrifying realization that if he'd died in that motorcycle accident before she met him, she'd have missed out on knowing Aiden Downey.

Yeah. Well. He's fine, she reminded herself. *And so are you.*

Yippee-skippy. Everyone was fine.

She tromped to the room he'd slept in. Empty. Turned out Aiden was an early riser nowadays. She threw the wadded-up shirt onto the rumpled bedding, shutting out the memory of what the length of his seminude body looked like taking up half a bed.

Time to go.

Outside, she shut the trunk and reached for the driver's side door handle. Aiden's motorcycle, Sheila, stood on the driveway, her orange glittery paint job sparkling in the sun. She shook her head. Just seeing it there reminded her that Aiden had wrecked once before. *Damn death machine. Why did he ride it all the way down here? Wasn't there a safer mode of transportation for a six-hour trip?*

She reminded herself she didn't care. *Couldn't* care. Not after what had gone down between them. Not after the phone call that tore her heart out, left her weeping and curled into the fetal position.

But then you got up.

Hell yeah, she did.

Aiden appeared from the woods wearing a white shirt with the sleeves cut off. She could see the entire length of his torso as he jogged to her and a flash of something...a tattoo? *Doesn't matter.* His steps slowed, and he palmed his side, puffing and watching her as if he was afraid to come any closer.

That's when the memory of what she'd said to him last night hit her like a freight train. She'd looked into his ethereal green eyes and confessed she loved him. Wow. Stupid.

By the hurt-slash-reproachful look on his face, it was the moment he was recalling now, too. He started walking toward her, but before he got any closer, Sadie clambered into the car, started it, and drove down the lane. She stopped short of turning onto the steep mountain road and allowed herself a final glance back. In the rearview mirror, she saw Aiden pace over to his bike, run a hand through his long hair, and then, noticing her hesitation, raise a hand and wave good-bye.

Sadie didn't wave back, turning down the tree-lined road and driving as fast as she dared. Good-bye between her and Aiden had happened a long time ago.

And that was something else she wasn't willing to repeat.

THE DISH

Where Authors Give You the Inside Scoop

♥ ♥ ♥ ♥ ♥ ♥ ♥ ♥ ♥ ♥ ♥ ♥ ♥ ♥ ♥

From the desk of Debbie Mason

Dear Reader,

While reading CHRISTMAS IN JULY one last time before sending it off to my editor, I had an "oops, I did it again" moment. In the first book in the series, *The Trouble with Christmas*, there's a scene where Madison, the heroine, senses her late mother's presence. In this book, our heroine, Grace, receives a message from her sister through her son. Grace has spent years blaming herself for her sister's death, and while there's an incident in the book that alleviates her guilt, I felt she needed the opportunity to tell her sister she loved her. Maybe if I didn't believe our departed loved ones could communicate with us in some way, I would have done this another way. But I do, and here's why.

My dad was movie-star handsome and had this amazing dimple in his chin. He was everything a little girl could wish for in a father. But he wasn't my biological father; he was the father of my heart. He came into my life when I was nine years old. That first year, I dreamed about him a lot. The dreams were very real, and all the same. I'd be outside and see a man from behind and call out to him. He'd turn around, and it would be my dad.

I always said the same thing: "You're here. I knew you weren't gone." Almost a year to the day of his passing, my dad appeared in my dream surrounded by shadowy figures who he introduced to me by name. He told me that he was okay, that he was happy. It was his way, I think, of helping me let him go.

I didn't dream of him again until sixteen months ago when we were awaiting the birth of our first grandchild. I "woke up" to see him sitting at the end of my bed. I told him how happy I was that he'd be there for the arrival of his great grandchild. He said of course he would be. He wouldn't be anywhere else.

A week later, my daughter gave birth to a beautiful baby girl. When I saw my granddaughter for the first time, I started to cry. She had my dad's dimple. No one on my son-in-law's side, or ours, has a dimple in their chin. He used to tell us the angels gave it to him, and we like to think he gave our granddaughter hers as proof that he's still with us.

So now you know why including that scene was important not only to Grace, but to me. Life really is full of small miracles and magic. And I hope you experience some of that magic as you follow Grace and Jack on their journey to happy-ever-after.

Debbie Macomber

♥ ♥ ♥ ♥ ♥ ♥ ♥ ♥ ♥ ♥ ♥ ♥ ♥ ♥ ♥

From the desk of Kristen Ashley

Dear Reader,

Usually, inspiration for books comes to me in a variety of ways. It could be a man I see (anywhere), a movie, a song, the unusual workers in a bookstore.

With SWEET DREAMS, it was an idea.

And that idea was, I wanted to take a hero who is, on the whole, totally unlikable, and make him lovable.

Enter Tatum Jackson, and when I say that, I mean *enter Tatum Jackson*. He came to me completely with a *kapow!* I could conjure him in my head, hear him talk, see the way he moved and how his clothes hung on him, feel his frustration with his life. I also knew his messed-up history.

And I could *not* wait to get stuck into this man.

I mean, here's a guy who is gorgeous, but he's got a foul temper, says nasty things when he's angry, and he's not exactly father of the year.

He had something terrible happen to him to derail his life and he didn't handle that very well, making mistake after mistake in a vicious cycle he pretty much had no intention of ending. He had a woman in his life he knew was a liar, a cheat, and no good for anyone and he was so stuck in the muck of his life that he didn't get shot of her.

Enter Lauren Grahame, who also came to me like a shot. As with Tate, everything about Lauren slammed into my head, perhaps most especially her feelings, the disillusionment she has with life, how she feels lost and really has no intention of getting found.

In fact, I don't think with any of my books I've ever had two characters who I knew so thoroughly before I started to tell their story.

And thus, I got lost in it.

I tend to be obsessive about my storytelling but this was an extreme. Once Lauren and Tate came to me, everything about Carnal, Colorado, filled my head just like the hero and heroine did. I can see Main Street, Bubba's Bar, Tate's house. I know the secondary characters as absolutely as I know the main characters. The entirety of the town, the people, and the story became a strange kind of real in my head, even if I didn't know how the story was going to play out. Indeed, I had no idea if I could pull it off, making an unlikable man lovable.

But I fell in love with Tate very quickly. The attraction he has for Lauren growing into devotion. The actions that speak much louder than words. I so enjoyed watching Lauren pull Tate out of the muck of his life, even if nothing changes except the fact that he has a woman in it that he loves, who is good to him, who feeds the muscle, the bone, the soul. Just as I enjoyed watching Tate guide Lauren out of her disillusionment and offer her something special.

I hope it happens to me again someday that characters like this inhabit my head so completely, and I hope it happens time and again.

But Tate and Lauren being the first, they'll always hold a special place in my heart, and live on in my head.

Happily,

Kristen Ashley

♥ ♥ ♥ ♥ ♥ ♥ ♥ ♥ ♥ ♥ ♥ ♥ ♥ ♥ ♥

From the desk of Rebecca Zanetti

Dear Reader,

I'm the oldest of three girls, and my husband is the oldest of three boys, so we grew up watching out for our siblings. Now that we're all adults, they look out for us, too. While my sisters and I may have argued with one another as kids, we instantly banded together if anybody tried to mess with one of us. My youngest sister topped out at an even five feet tall, yet she's the fiercest of us all, and she loses her impressive temper quite quickly if someone isn't nice to me.

I think one of the reasons I enjoyed writing Matt's story in SWEET REVENGE is because he's the eldest of the Dean brothers, and as such, he feels responsible for them. Add in a dangerous military organization trying to harm them, and his duties go far beyond that of a normal sibling. It was fun to watch Matt try to order his brothers around and keep them safe, while all they want to do is provide backup for him and ensure his safety.

There's something about being the oldest kid that forces us to push ourselves when we shouldn't. When our siblings would step back and relax, we often push forward just out of sheer stubbornness. I don't know why, and it's sometimes a mistake. Trust me.

SWEET REVENGE was written in several locations, most notably in the hospital and on airplanes. Sometimes

I take on a bit too much, so when I discovered I needed a couple of surgeries (nothing major), I figured I'd just do them on the same day. Why not? So I had two surgeries in one day and had to spend a few days in the hospital recuperating.

With my laptop, of course.

There's not a lot to do in the hospital but drink milkshakes and write, so it was quite effective. Then, instead of going home and taking it easy, I flew across the country to a conference and big book signing. Of course, I was still in pain, but I ignored it.

Bad idea.

Two weeks after that, I once again flew across the country for a book signing and conference. Yes, I was still tired, but I kept on going.

Yet another bad idea.

Then I returned home and immediately headed back to work as a college professor at the beginning of the semester.

Not a great idea.

Are you seeing a trend here? I pushed myself too hard, and all of a sudden, my body said…*you're done.* Completely done. I became sick, and after a bunch of tests, it appeared I'd just taken on too much. So at the end of the semester, I resigned as a professor and took up writing full time. And yoga. And eating healthy and relaxing.

Life is great, and it's meant to be savored and not rushed through—even for us oldest siblings. I learned a very valuable life lesson while writing SWEET REVENGE, and I'll always have fond memories of this book.

I truly hope you enjoy Matt and Laney's story, and

don't forget to take a deep breath and enjoy the moment. It's definitely worth it!

Happy reading!

Rebecca Zanetti

RebeccaZanetti.com
Twitter @RebeccaZanetti
Facebook.com

♥ ♥ ♥ ♥ ♥ ♥ ♥ ♥ ♥ ♥ ♥ ♥ ♥ ♥ ♥ ♥

From the desk of Shannon Richard

Dear Reader,

When it comes to the little town of Mirabelle, Florida, Grace King was actually the first character who revealed herself to me, which I find odd as she's the heroine in the second book. I knew from the beginning she was going to be a tiny little thing with blond hair and blue eyes; I knew she'd lost her mother at a young age and that she was never going to have known her father; and I knew she was going to be feisty and strong.

Jaxson Anderson was a different story. He didn't reveal himself to me until he literally walked onto the page in *Undone*. I also didn't know about Jax and Grace's future relationship until they got into an argument at the beach. As soon as I figured out they were going to end up together, my mind took off and I started plotting everything out, which was a little inconvenient as I wasn't even a third of the way through writing the first book.

Jax is a complicated fella. He's had to deal with a lot in his life, and because of his past he doesn't think he's good enough for Grace. Jax has most definitely put her on a pedestal, which is made pretty evident by his nickname for her. He calls her Princess, but not in a derogatory way. He doesn't find her to be spoiled or bratty. Far from it. He thinks that she should be cherished and that she's worth *everything*, especially to him. I try to capture this in the prologue, which takes place a good eighteen years before UNDENIABLE starts. Grace is this little six-year-old who is being bullied on the playground, and Jax is her white knight in scuffed-up sneakers.

Jax has been in Grace's life from the day she was brought home from the hospital over twenty-four years ago. He's watched her grow up into the beautiful and brave woman that she is, and though he's always loved her (even if he's chosen not to accept it), it's hard for him think that he can be with her. Jax's struggles were heartbreaking for me to write, and it was especially heartbreaking to put Grace through it, but this was their story and I had to stay true to them. Readers shouldn't fear with UNDENIABLE, though, because I like my happily-ever-after endings and Grace and Jax definitely get theirs. I hope readers enjoy the journey.

Cheers,

♥ ♥ ♥ ♥ ♥ ♥ ♥ ♥ ♥ ♥ ♥ ♥ ♥ ♥ ♥ ♥ ♥

From the desk of Stacy Henrie

Dear Reader,

I remember the moment HOPE AT DAWN, Book 1 in my Of Love and War series (on sale now), was born into existence. I was sitting in a quiet, empty hallway at a writers' conference contemplating how to turn my single World War I story idea, about Livy Campbell's brother, into more than one book. Then, in typical fashion, Livy marched forward in my mind, eager to have her story told first.

As I pondered Livy and the backdrop of the story— America's involvement in WWI—I knew having her fall in love with a German-American would provide inherent conflict. What I didn't know then was the intense prejudice and persecution she and Friedrick Wagner would face to be together, in a country ripe with suspicion toward anyone with German ties. The more I researched the German-American experience during WWI, the more I discovered their private war here on American soil—not against soldiers, but neighbors against neighbors, citizens against citizens.

A young woman with aspirations of being a teacher, Livy Campbell knows little of the persecution being heaped upon the German-Americans across the country, let alone in the county north of hers. More than anything, she feels the effects of the war overseas through the absence of her older brothers in France, the alcohol troubles of her wounded soldier boyfriend, and the disruption of her studies at college. When she applies for a teaching job in hopes of escaping the war, Livy doesn't realize she's simply traded one set of troubles for another, especially when she finds herself attracted to the school's handsome handyman, German-American Friedrick Wagner.

Born in America to German immigrant parents, Friedrick Wagner believes himself to be as American as anyone else in his small town of Hilden, Iowa. But the war with Germany changes all that. Suddenly viewed as a potential enemy, Friedrick seeks to protect his family from the rising tide of injustice aimed at his fellow German-Americans. Protecting the beautiful new teacher, Livy Campbell, comes as second nature to Friedrick. But when he finds himself falling in love with her, he fears the war, both at home and abroad, will never allow them to be together.

I thoroughly enjoyed writing Livy and Friedrick's love story and the odds they must overcome for each other. This is truly a tale of "love conquers all" and the power of hope and courage during a dark time in history. My hope is you will fall in love with the Campbell family through this series, as I have, as you experience their triumphs and struggles during the Great War.

Happy reading!

Stacy Henrie

♥ ♥ ♥ ♥ ♥ ♥ ♥ ♥ ♥ ♥ ♥ ♥ ♥ ♥ ♥ ♥ ♥ ♥

From the desk of Adrianne Lee

Dear Reader,

Conflict, conflict, conflict. Every good story needs it. It heightens sexual tension and keeps you guessing whether a couple will actually be able to work through those serious—and even not so serious—issues and obstacles to find that happily-ever-after ending.

I admit to a little vanity when one of my daughters once said, "Mom, in other romances I always know the couple will get together early in the book, but I'm never sure in yours until the very end." High praise and higher expectations for any writer to live up to. It is, at least, what I strive for with every love story I write.

Story plotting starts with conflict. I already knew that Jane Wilson, Big Sky Pie's new pastry chef, was going to fall in love with Nick Taziano, the sexy guy doing the promotion for the pie shop, but when I first conceived the idea that these two would be lovers in DELICIOUS, I didn't realize they were a reunion couple.

A reunion couple is a pair who was involved in the past and broke up due to unresolved conflicts. This is what I call a "built-in" conflict. It's one of my favorites to write. When the story opens, something has happened that involves this couple on a personal level, causing them to come face-to-face to deal with it. This is when they finally admit to themselves that they still have feelings for each other, feelings neither wants to feel or act on, no matter how compelling. The more they try to suppress the attraction, the stronger it becomes.

In DELICIOUS, Jane and Nick haven't seen each other since they were kids, since his father and her mother married. Jane blames Nick's dad for breaking up her parents' marriage. Nick resents Jane's mom for coming between his father and him. Jane called Nick the Tazmanian Devil. Nick called her Jane the Pain. They were thrilled when the marriage fell apart after a year.

Now many years later, their parents are reuniting, something Jane and Nick view as a bigger mistake than the first marriage. Their decision to try and stop the wedding, however, leads to one accidental, delicious kiss, and a sizzling attraction that is as irresistible as Jane's blueberry pies.

I hope you'll enjoy DELICIOUS, the second book in my Big Sky Pie series. All of the stories are set in northwest Montana near Glacier Park, an area where I vacationed every summer for over thirty years. Each of the books is about someone connected with the pie shop in one way or another and contains a different delicious pie recipe. So come join the folks of Kalispell at the little pie shop on Center Street, right across from the mall, for some of the best pie you'll ever taste, and a healthy helping of romance.

Adrianne Lee

♥ ♥ ♥ ♥ ♥ ♥ ♥ ♥ ♥ ♥ ♥ ♥ ♥ ♥ ♥

From the desk of Jessica Lemmon

Dear Reader,

A *quiz:* What do you get when you put a millionaire who avoids romantic relationships in the same house with a determined-to-stay-single woman who crushed on him sixteen years ago?

If you answered *unstoppable attraction,* you'd be right.

In THE MILLIONAIRE AFFAIR, I paired a hero who cages and controls his emotions with a heroine who feels way too much, way too soon. Kimber Reynolds is determined to have a fling—to love and leave Landon Downey, if for only two reasons: (1) She's wanted to kiss the eldest Downey brother since she was a teen, and (2) to prove to herself that she can have a shallow relationship that ends amicably instead of one that's long, drawn-out, and destined to end badly.

When Landon's six-year-old nephew, Lyon, and a huge account for his advertising agency come crashing into his life, Landon needs help. Lucky for him (and us!) his sister offers the perfect solution: her friend, Kimber, can be his live-in nanny for the week.

The most difficult part about writing Landon was letting him deal with his past on *his terms* and watching him falter. Here is a guy who makes rules, follows them, and remains stoic…to his own detriment. Despite those qualities, Landon, from a loving, close family, can't help caring for Kimber. Even when they're working down a

list of "extracurricular activities" in the bedroom, Landon
puts Kimber's needs before his own.

These two may have stumbled into an arrangement,
but when Fate tosses them a wild card, they both step
up—and step closer—to the one thing they were sure
they didn't want...*forever*.

I *love* this book. Maybe because of how much I
wrestled with Landon and Kimber's story before getting
it right. The three of us had growing pains, but I finally
found their truth, and I'm *so* excited to share their story
with you. If Landon and Kimber win your heart like
they won mine, be sure to let me know. You can email
me at jessica@jessicalemmon.com, tweet me @lemmony,
and "like" my Facebook page at www.facebook.com/
authorjessicalemmon.

Happy reading!

Jessica Lemmon

www.jessicalemmon.com

Find out more about Forever Romance!

Visit us at
www.hachettebookgroup.com/publishing_forever.aspx

Find us on Facebook
http://www.facebook.com/ForeverRomance

Follow us on Twitter
http://twitter.com/ForeverRomance

NEW AND UPCOMING TITLES

Each month we feature our new titles
and reader favorites.

CONTESTS AND GIVEAWAYS

We give away galleys, autographed copies,
and all kinds of exclusive items.

AUTHOR INFO

You'll find bios, articles, and links to personal websites
for all your favorite authors—and so much more.

GET SOCIAL

Connect with your favorite authors, editors, and
other Forever fans, and share what's important to you.

THE BUZZ

Sign up for our monthly romance newsletter,
and be the first to read all about it.

VISIT US ONLINE AT

WWW.HACHETTEBOOKGROUP.COM

FEATURES:

OPENBOOK BROWSE AND
SEARCH EXCERPTS
•
AUDIOBOOK EXCERPTS AND PODCASTS
•
AUTHOR ARTICLES AND INTERVIEWS
•
BESTSELLER AND PUBLISHING
GROUP NEWS
•
SIGN UP FOR E-NEWSLETTERS
•
AUTHOR APPEARANCES AND TOUR
INFORMATION
•
SOCIAL MEDIA FEEDS AND WIDGETS
•
DOWNLOAD FREE APPS

BOOKMARK HACHETTE BOOK GROUP
@ WWW.HACHETTEBOOKGROUP.COM